OUR MISTAKEN IDENTITY

Printed in the United States of America
Cover design by: MiblArt

First Printing, 2019

ISBN-13: 978-1-966238-01-0

Our Mistaken Identity

ARIANA TOSADO

© Covenaan Press | 2024

Contents

"You understand that because of *that*," Momma told me from her desk, pointing at the window that exposed the school's gym just outside her door, "you can never use magic in here even if it seems like we're alone, right?"

I sighed in frustration, leaning against the whiteboard and looking up at the fluorescent lights overhead. This had been the everyday lecture for the past *week*. I didn't need any more reminders that my school used to train the secret agents who hunted down people like me.

I crossed my arms against the air conditioning. "Yes, Mother, I'm not eight anymore."

She scoffed, folding her hands on the desk. "You sure still

like to show off like you did back then. You don't remember how you wanted to show people the books on the coffee table rising into the air, the front door unlocking on its own, or your hot chocolate turning frozen?"

I deadpanned. That was almost eight years ago! I'd been *well* aware of the consequences of someone finding me out for the better half of my (apparently short) life.

"Look." Momma softly sighed. "As long as you don't use magic, you're safe here since the school only specializes in self-defense now. That's what matters. We can't ever be too careful."

A plea weighed down her honey-colored eyes. Right then, I almost wished I'd inherited them instead of the Atera's signature blue. Sometimes it feels like Momma's chestnut hair is all I got from her; she isn't like me, but she still acts like she knows what it's like to be a magician.

"I'm sorry I kept you hidden for this long," she said next, "but you know there was no room for risk, and you couldn't afford not to practice. Sure, you missed out on your first year of high school, but at least you get to explore your second with your best friends."

"My friends who can never know the truth."

"Emma..." Momma's eyes asked for sympathy again.

I kicked at an invisible pebble on the tile floor. "Fine, sorry... I know none of it's your fault. And you can trust me here."

Her waves perfectly framed her narrow face as she nodded. "Remember that I placed you here for a reason. You should know how to defend yourself in *all* forms."

"I know: no magic unless necessary."

"Exactly." She stood from her desk and strolled over to me. "Okay, I need to get ready for a meeting starting soon. I'll see you tomorrow for the *first day of school.*" With an excited grin, she cupped my face and kissed my forehead. "I love you, honey."

"Love you, too."

I left her classroom and made my way back to the Grand Foyer, passing and waving at other girls settling in. I recognized some of them from orientation last week, and the rest, I'd depend on tomorrow to reintroduce me.

Either way, I was facing two hundred other girls to keep who I really was from. Some year this would be.

Every step up the Main Staircase was a surreal reminder of whose stairs, whose carpet, I was walking on—of why Momma and I were here in the first place. Even though the Callistro Academy was dedicated to just self-defense now, President Caldwell swears that the whole country is out for the "evil" blood of magic. America's greatest Hunters have been killing us off by the dozen since he was elected—four terms ago. (He's the first president since FDR to manage that, and if I think about it for too long, I'll get mad enough to start ripping out these pages.) And yet, somehow, my people are still out there. Probably because they're doing something as crazy as I am to survive. Every single one isn't dead. It's impossible to completely eradicate magic, it has to be.

Dad, I couldn't help but think, arriving at the top floor with my legs burning. *I'll meet you someday. Hopefully.*

Frankly, it was a miracle that Callistro still hadn't reopened its Hunter classes, considering it was the first Hunter school ever established. With that history, naturally, despite being an ex-Master herself, my mother thought that enrolling her *sorceress* daughter here was the wisest course of action. I get it, she wanted to make sure that, in case anyone did find out about me and ended up attacking me in a dark alley, I could defend myself past the basics. After all, Callistro was for providing young ladies advanced self-defense—and, scarily enough, the higher-level education Hunters usually got anyway during training.

Far down the left hallway of the top floor, I found and opened the door to my dorm. Sarah and Breanne were mischievously swift as they unpacked their clothes, taking turns between the drawers and walk-in closet on the right side of the room. A white dresser stood next to me, and a white desk stood in the corner, now decorated with Breanne's excessive notebooks, textbooks, and stationary materials. A large purple circle rug now lay in the middle of the room, in front of Sarah's bed that was sandwiched between mine and Breanne's.

I couldn't help but smile to myself a bit. *At least we get to explore our first year here together.*

Breanne threw a pair of denim shorts at me before I could open my mouth. "Those are yours," she said in front of her bed, tossing her straight blond hair out of her face. "You left them at my house last week. Come on, hurry!"

"For... what?" I asked, tossing the shorts onto my bed.

Sarah walked out of the closet as if at my words, her bright-green eyes, enhanced by a perfect eyeshadow job, hopelessly ecstatic. "The school is thinking about reopening the Hunter's Room!"

Just like that, my cover had one less brick to stand on.

Only authorized staff are legally allowed to use the gadgets and weapons on display down in the Hunter's Room. It was closed when magic was legalized in 1900, but even after the law was repealed fifty years later, it had remained closed since. As long as the Hunter's Room was closed, our disguise as a prestigious school specializing in self-defense was actually the truth.

"That means they're gonna continue the Hunter classes!" Sarah exclaimed, hands jubilantly expressing her words. (Her trip to the Bahamas earlier that summer had definitely added a nice glow to her copper skin.) "We could graduate as Hunters and then become *Masters* together, can you imagine that?"

Nope—considering I'd probably be dead if that ever became the case.

Breanne spared her a skeptical brow on her fair face, subtly decorated with sparse freckles. "Even *if* they do, it's not going to open for a long while. Sarah wants to get a sneak peek before security comes back from a staff meeting happening right now."

"Come *on*," Sarah urged before I could speak, tossing her hair over her shoulder. "Are you done yet?"

Breanne lugged a half-empty cardboard box onto her bed. "Okay, fine, I'll finish later."

There was cause for concern for more than the obvious reasons. The last time Breanne Shaw had broken the rules was in seventh grade, when Sarah had convinced her to hack into their school's roster to see where the new foreign exchange student was from so they could learn his native tongue to "get a head start". My *life* would have to be on the line before that girl risks her permanent record, so where was the willingness to venture into forbidden territory coming from—and how was I supposed to stop it?

Instead of the stairs, we ducked into the elevator right by them. It's only meant for students and staff with physical disabilities, but it's also the only way to get to the Hunter's Room. According to Breanne, we had about fifteen minutes to be in and out without getting caught by either other rebellious Callistro Girls or staff able to suspend us.

The silver doors closed behind us as we stepped inside. Nerves burned in my stomach like acidic starvation as Breanne leaned toward the round buttons on the wall. "There's a button for the basement," she said, "but that's just for maintenance supplies and the boiler room... Maybe this keypad unlocks the one for the Hunter's Room."

Under the small array, said keypad was installed on a metal panel—like a door.

"That feels too easy." Sarah tossed her black hair over her shoulder and then crossed her arms, leaning against the crimson wallpaper of the elevator. "You can't have a whole room dedicated to government purposes and *not* keep its entrance hidden from the common public."

Good point.

Based on the yellow keys and worn-out numbers, the keypad was at least a couple of decades old. Breanne stepped aside as I walked to it and kneeled, citing my options in my head.

My brows knit together. *No way. Seriously?*

"1", "5", "8", and "9" had the least amount of black paint remaining. September 5, 1827 was too easy to guess, but only because most don't care to memorize Callistro's birthday—and it's only easy for me because, go figure, Callistro's birthday is the same as mine.

It's like Caralyn Callistro built this place knowing I'd be here two centuries later and just wanted to taunt me.

I entered the date, ending with the first two digits of the year the school was established. A green light flashed under the zero, and my friends gasped in excitement behind me. I opened the panel, revealing a red button with the white initials "HR".

"Emma!" Sarah exclaimed. "How did you do that?"

I scoffed. "I kid you not, it's literally the school's birthday."

"They really should change that," Breanne remarked dully in the corner of my vision.

My chuckle died down to a quiet, shaky breath. Was I really about to do this? Going into the enemy's lair had to be betrayal of some kind! Everything I could find down there, the reminder of what its gadgets had already done to too many to count, to people like me—

"Press it!" Sarah chirped. "Let's go!"

I obeyed, half of me seeming to rip itself from the other and shouting betrayal and warnings. Curiosity has always been a silent killer.

The elevator lightly jerked down, paranoia dropping into my stomach with it. What if one of the devices was built to sense magic and suddenly went off on its own once I walked through the doors? What if we tripped some kind of silent alarm? What kind of security was in place?

Okay. *Those* two questions, I could ask.

"Security is temporarily deactivated since the staff is coming and going so often," Breanne effortlessly answered, picking at the light hair on her pale arms. That relaxed me somewhat: she was nervous, too. Her blue-hazel eyes shifted to Sarah. "There's *no* way I'd do this otherwise, I can't even believe I let you talk me into it to begin with. This is a pipe dream, you know!"

"Exactly," Sarah said, holding up a perfectly manicured finger. "All the more reason to check it out while we can. The other stuff is cool, but the main thing I'm after is the Hall of Generations in the back. The family trees of the greatest Hunters who've ever lived are hung down a hall on the left, and on the right—"

"The most powerful magicians!" Breanne finished with an astonished breath, round eyes wide. "I forgot about that! Isn't the Atera family tree there, too?"

And there it is.

To be completely honest, I can't stand using "magician" for the people of magic (seeing as we're not a Vegas act or an entertainer for kids' parties), but the Atera name is one I *wish* I could hear more often. Momma changed her surname to "Marie", in honor of one of the Atera family middle names, shortly after she married to protect us. I'm not Emmalynn Atera to my best friends, but it's still my name; every time they say it, it's like dangling a chocolate bar that'll call the government if I grab it.

"They *should* be there," Sarah said, "considering they're the most powerful family of sorcerers. That's literally the whole reason the school's thinking about—"

The metal doors slid open, introducing us to the most opulent room any of us (well, Breanne and I) had had the privilege of laying our eyes on. Fleur-de-lises stamped the crimson wallpaper plastered on the twenty-foot-high walls encasing us, golden baseboards and crown molding accenting them. A dark-oak floor supported us, a crimson rug covering most of it. Dark shelves lined the walls, surrounding a total of eight classroom doors. Display pillars made of white polished quartz stood throughout the middle of the room like regal chess pieces. In the back, a towering archway beckoned us to the Hall of Generations.

My friends and I walked in silent awe, our minds separating

us and pulling us to the most interesting toys our eyes caught.

"Okay, remember, we have to be quick," Breanne said next to what looked like a black hand-sized speaker. I could bet my magic that it did a lot more than play music. She faced Sarah at the pillar behind her. "What were you saying about the Ateras?"

"Whoa," I said before I knew the word was in my mouth. Curiosity was stronger than gossip down here, pulling me to the display pillar ahead of Breanne. What looked like a small, open laptop installed on a flat printer-like base sat on the quartz. My fingers were careful not to touch the wooden plaque mounted on the front of the pillar. "An—'electromagnetic cardiograph'. What's that?"

"A magician has a stronger reaction to electromagnetic waves than a mortal does on the molecular level," Breanne replied effortlessly. "The readings probably flew off the charts when these were tested on a person with magic. I've heard that some have tried to control what they read to try to avoid getting caught."

Sarah's pear-green eyes jumped from display to display. "I wish the plaques said what these things actually do."

I turned to the pillar on my other side, where a polygraph-like device sat on top, and slightly bent down to the plaque.

"Cerebral Polygraph".

I actually knew about this one because of the time Momma used it on a caught magician. It's a lot more accurate in detecting lies because it also measures brain activity, which a lie naturally stimulates more of. If a magician is caught and debriefed under one of these, it's practically a death sentence.

I suppressed the shiver wrapping around my spine. *I hope I never see you again.*

"*Come on*, let's get to the Hall!" Sarah urged, meandering to the other side of the room. "I wanna tell you about the Atera rumor I heard recently..."

I immediately straightened. "The what?"

She smiled slyly, turned her back to us, and skipped to the Hall of Generations. Breanne and I weaved our way through the pillars and followed after.

The Callistro crest of a sword through a rose proudly boasted itself above the entry arch. Passing through, I stuck my gaze to the small chandeliers hanging down the hall like ducks in a row. Their yellow glow lent a familiar aura, like I was enjoying an evening back home with Momma. Simple archways stood on both sides, leading to the halls that the family trees were mounted on. I glanced at the top of them: golden plaques nailed to dark-oak boards dated the time period. We were standing at the beginning of time, as close to it as records could recall.

Sarah sighed wistfully, peeking into each entrance on both sides before taking another step. "All these people have made history. Imagine getting our families' names up here because we're that good at hunting."

The standards to get a name up in the Hall of Generations are higher than Breanne's IQ. It may have families from multiple millennia recorded, but not many individuals are actually listed. We ended up walking past dozens of world-changing eras, from the Roman Empire period to the Cold War, until reaching Postmodernity.

Breanne ran into the Hunter's side of the Hall with no more than a gasp. Sarah and I caught her scrutinizing one of the most recent family trees mounted on the wall.

"Before we get to the Ateras," she said in her most speculative voice, "I've been really curious about the Bleus lately. They made a name for themselves recently because they've caught more people with magic than almost any other Hunter in the past two decades. And they're really loyal to the president, which means they're still out there looking for the last few magicians alive."

"Few". I really hope you're wrong about that.

Momma always says to never judge someone for what they are, but what they do. Until you meet someone, you have no true first impression. Until you know someone, you have no true judgment. But I was pretty sure that hating anyone who'd *chosen* to stay in the Hunter career for so long was fair game, wasn't it?

"William Bleu," Breanne added, pointing at the last name on the tree, "isn't even an on-field Hunter. He works behind the scenes for almost every mission. But then..."—her excitement swelled as she skipped far back down the hall from where we'd come, almost at the beginning—"he married Alexa Delphine!"

"I remember that!" Sarah lit up, her posture bouncing to perfection. "It's insane, the Delphines are literally the masters of their profession."

"Yep." Breanne's thin lips stretched so wide with mischief that it even touched the faded freckles on her cheeks. "They've captured more magicians than anyone in the past *six* decades, and they've been hunting for centuries. It just makes me curious—I mean, you have to wonder, would Alexa and William ever have kids? Do they already? What do those kids' lives look like?"

I was more or less perfectly all right with not knowing—and, if said kids already existed, avoiding them at all costs.

Sarah smirked, tossing her hair behind her shoulder. "Their

stories make mine even more interesting."

She hurried back out to the main hall and entered the start of the magician side—starting with the Atera family tree, the first one listed.

My true awe surrendered behind Sarah as she stepped up to it, my eyes soaking up my history. Momma had never been able to say much about my father's side of the family. She could only tell me about the people she'd actually known and everyone she remembered from my dad's and aunt's stories. Seeing my family in front of me for the first time, Momma's words became reality: grandparents, aunts, uncles, siblings, and cousins were stitched together on this one large sheet of aging paper. A sense of pride that had been forced to hide all my life finally poked its head out. This was my family. And most of them were already gone.

Well, we still have Grandpa Atera, even though Nevada is a five-hour flight from North Carolina. That only leaves Aunt Becca, which I wouldn't complain about; she was the only person I knew on a deeper level than friendship who understood what I felt and how I felt it. Actually, she was the only other magician I knew. Plus, at least she'd moved into my childhood home while Momma and I were here, so she was close by instead of an hour away in Charlotte.

"The line ended at Tristan and Rebecca Melicent-Marie Atera," Sarah began, pointing loosely at their names as if the paper would disintegrate if she did so too firmly. "Still 'missing'."

"What a name," Breanne said, cocking her thin brows. "How did they end up with something so elegant?"

"I don't know, but the only thing anyone *knows* about Tristan is that he was chased out of the country almost twenty years ago,"

Sarah replied. "He actually managed to leave without getting caught! Like, how?"

I thought back to the story I'd heard from Momma my entire childhood: how my dad had to kiss his wife goodbye and reluctantly begin his escape, left to the mercy of the hope that he'd see her again someday. A month later, Momma found out she was pregnant and had no way to contact her husband. She spent the next eight months shaping and creating a life she and her baby could survive.

Of course... that meant my father didn't even know that he had a daughter. And that was if he was even alive.

"Okay, but," I began, hoping my gossip could match their eagerness as I took Sarah's attention, "what about the *rumor?*"

Sarah laughed, crossing her arms. "I can't believe you haven't heard it yet! *They're* the whole reason the school's thinking about opening the Hunter's Room last minute. The government suspects that the Ateras are still alive, and apparently they're also—"

No sooner than she spoke did the elevator doors slide open on the other side of the Hunter's Room. We froze, the mechanical whir echoing straight down the Hall and into my very being.

Breanne's pale hands flew to her mouth in terror, blue-hazel eyes wide. "The staff is back!"

Sarah pulled us to the empty wall adjacent to the Atera family tree. We tightly pressed our backs against it. Hiding would only buy us a few seconds at maximum, but at least they were a few seconds.

"We've barely been here for five minutes!" Sarah whispered-screamed. "How are we supposed to sneak past them?"

The stranger's footsteps were muted on the rug in the Hunter's Room, but they'd be loud and clear once they reached the wooden floor of the Hall's foyer. The question was, how much time did we have before they reached us?

"It—it's okay," Breanne stammered, viciously picking at the

hair on her arms. "If we come clean, they should let us off with a warning. It's the day before school starts, teenagers do stupid things all the time—"

"We practically broke into a top-secret room we're not even supposed to know how to *get* to," Sarah snapped. "You seriously think they're gonna 'let us off with a warning'?"

"Calm down," I whispered, "before they *actually* catch us!"

I wasn't even kidding myself. Sarah was anything but exaggerating, and my heart beat like it was trying to break the cage protecting it. Rationality was telling me that the school would have no reason to test me with a gadget that would expose my magic, but Momma's wrath was nothing to be grateful for as an alternative if I was suspended.

A classroom door clicked shut far down the Hunter's Room. My shoulders dropped in relief against the wall.

"They're searching the classrooms first," I whispered. "It sounds like just one person. We can sneak past them and get to the elevator."

"We have to check if it's clear to run," Sarah said.

I scoffed. "Be my guest, since *you* wanted to come down here."

Breanne perked up, eyes still wide. "I second that."

Sarah pressed her mauve lips together before begrudgingly stepping toward the first archway. It only took her a second to peer around the edge and then turn back to us. "I don't see anyone."

I couldn't really blame her for the superficial check, but anger was bubbling in my throat: with every second, Breanne's suggestion of turning ourselves in inched closer and closer to becoming our only option—our only option that involved free will. But at least then I'd be caught with my friends. Maybe that would earn us a lighter punishment and stop a chain reaction of events leading to them and the school finding out—

"What are you doing here?" a woman snapped, appearing behind Sarah and startling us.

Relief poured into my chest, and I sank against the wall. "You scared us!"

"Probably because you shouldn't be down here," Momma hissed, jabbing her index finger down the main hall. "Get upstairs. Now."

I glimpsed at Breanne next to me: only when I met her still wide-eyed stare did she detach from the wall, Sarah already scampering ahead of us.

"You're not, um..." Breanne began hesitantly as we passed Momma, "part of security, too, are you?"

"No," Momma stated, amber eyes hardening with her narrow jaw. "And I hope you realize how much trouble you would've been in if I were."

She followed us like a police officer as we reentered the Hunter's Room. There are a number of reasons that I love my mother, but her ability to make my friends just as afraid of her as I am is in the top five.

Neither girl beside me said a word as we walked the side of the room to avoid the display pillars in the middle. All we managed were glances between each other, stifling laughter from embarrassment and adrenaline. Momma was right about one thing: I didn't want to explore my first year of real school with anyone else but these two.

It was only after I turned eight that Momma was convinced that I treated our secret with the same respect she did. Then she finally let me meet the girls I'd always spy on from our living room window as they biked, drew with chalk on the sidewalk, or played some form of soccer in the street. We set up our first playdate at the white gazebo in Capperson Park, what's now "our spot". That was also where we swore that from that day forward, we'd have "an everlasting bond of best friendship".

Sarah gasped next to me, gawking at the corner of the high ceiling. "You guys!"

Breanne and I followed her gaze: security cameras. Mounted in all four corners of the room.

I mentally facepalmed. *Thank God I didn't use magic down here.*

Sarah leaned forward to better look at Breanne on my other side. "When can you erase it?"

Breanne went rigid, a furrow scrunching her thin brows. "You want me to *hack* the feed and erase the footage? I'm not doing that!"

"I'm concerned that you know *how* to do that," Momma remarked behind us. I'm not sure why—she knew that the girl had already taught herself HTML *and* JavaScript before most kids learned the basics of algebra.

Well, good news for my mother: I knew how to tamper with footage, too.

I met our eyes, which was enough confirmation: she had the same idea.

"I mean," Breanne stammered, staring shyly at the crimson rug, "I don't do it *often*, but—"

"Don't worry about it. Just get back upstairs." Momma nudged them both, nodding at me with her permission as they passed. I looked up at the camera above us.

"*Obliviscor hodie*," I whispered, repeating the process three times before rushing to the elevator.

Breanne may know how to hack and erase, but I can give someone permanent amnesia with nothing but my mind. I'm just not *allowed* to unless my life literally depends on it (or Momma's feeling rebellious and wants to defy the one-coupon-per-customer rule). Most of the time, though, magic is just easier.

The steel doors closed in front of us, and I turned to Momma. "Can you do anything about the cameras?"

"Don't worry about it," she said again, gently emphasizing each word. "Nobody watches the footage unless security is given a reason to, like if someone commits a crime. You're fine."

If nobody ever watched it, why had she told me to erase it?!

"But," she added, "you're still not allowed down there until further notice. And if you accidentally commit a crime next time, I'm not bailing you out. So promise me that there won't be a next time."

The three of us nodded.

No next time. But if the school reopens that place...

I discreetly bit the inside of my lip. "Is the school gonna reopen the Hunter's Room?"

"They're considering it,"—Momma nodded once—"but nothing's definite and won't be for a long time. The only thing the three of you need to worry about is the year already ahead of you."

"I'm hoping they do," Sarah said as the doors opened, revealing the Grand Foyer. We followed her out and onto the crimson rug. "I was saying before, the government suspects Tristan and Rebecca Atera are still alive—and *in* the country. That's why Callistro wants to reopen the Room."

"What?" Breanne and I exclaimed in unison, the shock in her tone overriding the panic in mine. "Where did you hear that from?" I asked.

"Opal Dubois," Sarah replied, like it was obvious. "Her mom's the chief editor of *Magic Magazine*."

I suppressed an eye roll. *Magic* exclusively touches on the mortal-versus-magic war, known for getting the most accurate and closest leads on any scandal the writers can find. Whatever Opal Dubois was telling people, it was most likely about to be printed in the latest issue. But based on *Magic*'s (admittedly) almost flawless reputation for accuracy... could that rumor actually be true?

But Aunt Becca's staying at our old house. She never had to leave the country. Dad, though... It was a miracle he'd even left to begin with. Canada and Mexico were just as dangerous, planes were impossible to sneak onto unless someone was willing to risk their life, and stowing away on a ship was hard enough for mortals to accomplish, let alone magicians.

"So they *are* alive," I said flatly, barring hope from my tone.

Sarah shrugged. "That's where the latest intel's coming from, but it's just another rumor."

"Latest"—how recent was that?

One glance at Momma and her slightly arched brow all but screamed her message: stop asking questions. Intense curiosity would do me no favors in maintaining our cover.

I looked out at the Grand Foyer. A few Callistro Girls were enjoying the last day of free dress as they roamed, some walking into the Dining Hall on the left side and others carrying packed boxes up the Main Staircase. My eyes landed on the tall, wide double doors of the manor's entrance. Tonight was our last night of freedom before we'd need to start signing out with the headmaster to go off campus.

I doubt Mr. Dawson would make exceptions for me just because I'm his goddaughter.

In other words, it'd be my last opportunity for a *long* while to be alone and wrap my head around things...

I turned back to Momma. "I'm gonna head into town."

She tilted her head, twisting the golden wedding band on her finger. "Okay. But make sure you'll have enough time to finish unpacking. They want everyone in bed by 9 tonight."

"Oh, we'll take care of that for you," Sarah said, offering me a runway-worthy smile and understanding my tacit request to be alone. "It'll be our 'welcome to your first real school' gift."

"Thanks," I chimed, touching Breanne's shoulder in a good-bye as I walked past her.

After verifying with the headmaster, students would then need to verify with the security guards at the entrance of the black metal gates that encircle the manor. Our ID cards opened them. Just for today, my card was all I needed.

I pulled out my phone as the gate shut with a metal clang, and started my trek into the Callistro Forest:

> **E:** How did you know where we were?? What about your meeting?

Momma probably has some sort of built-in GPS that sets off an alarm any time I'm remotely near anywhere I shouldn't be. Or she chipped me. She definitely chipped me. That would explain a lot of things...

M: I went to drop off one of your boxes I accidentally took to my room. Nobody was in your dorm, and with Sarah in your group, there's only one other place you'd all be the night before school starts. So did we have the same idea back there?

E: Yeah, the cameras shouldn't have anything from today. But if nobody watches the footage, why delete it?

M: Because I'd rather have security thinking the cameras glitched and didn't record anything from today instead of knowing you three broke in somewhere. So please, don't go back.

Just barely got to the meeting in time, have to go. Be safe.

No wonder she's scared I'm gonna accidentally blow it... Even I was scared that I'd accidentally blow it, especially because I didn't have nearly that level of caution or wisdom yet.

Then again, she was the fully trained Hunter—but with the school year I had ahead of me, my biggest fear was that I'd never have the chance to get to where I needed to be before those four walls turned on me nonetheless. Just like they almost had today.

THREE

Strolling out of the forest and onto the sidewalk along Main Street, I was just in time to catch Capperson's late-summer sunset. A gentle, cool wind breezed by, relieving the warm air as I passed under the streetlights. I reminded myself to savor every second of my last few moments of alone time; not only were they now rare, but they were also the one thing left that gave me complete freedom. There was no pretending to side with the enemy's belief, no standard of how to react around those who spoke against me. And if I chose to think about what made me different and about my hope of my father coming back, I could. These moments were my only real getaways now.

The lampposts' comforting yellow glow infused the early evening's air. All around the square, couples enjoyed an evening walk while singles shopped and made phone calls. I took one last glimpse at my old reality, soaking up the details of the town square I'd grown up in.

Reaching the center, I paused on the sidewalk. *Why isn't the fountain on tonight?*

Okay, this was probably going to be the only fun I'd have in a while. And the timing made this all the more perfect—there was a technician somewhere that turned the fountain on, or it was set to a schedule, right? This would look completely natural. Nobody would know.

Mindful of the magic that would flash in my eyes, I bent my head down. "*Interfluo.*"

Water flowed to life from the spouts in slow motion, trickling down the top two stone tiers. Just as I'd thought, nobody spared more than a glance before minding their own business again.

I smiled: I'd successfully snagged an opportunity for magic. From the moment Momma and I moved to Callistro, I knew that that would never be guaranteed again. I didn't know how, but she knew a lot about magic despite being mortal. We still had to figure out a whole new schedule for our mentoring sessions.

A wooden bench sat against each side of the fountain. I walked to the other side and sat down on the bench facing the strip of stores, turning my back to Main Street. Shivering in the cool breeze, I exhaled the last remaining tension of what had happened in the Hunter's Room. I knew it had been real, but I hated that it *felt* real. Too close to the reality that magicians actually suffer every day at the hands of those devices I'd just marveled at with my best friends. And we'd been caught. By my mother, but caught nonetheless—

This isn't helping. My eyes closed, and I forced my mind to shake away magic altogether. Maybe I *didn't* have my moments of freedom anymore; maybe I was going to have to trap my thoughts in the habit of normalcy. Practice makes permanent, and if I practiced mortality, I'd more permanently execute it...

I shivered again, goosebumps prickling my bare arms and legs. An icy bite lingered in the breeze now, slithering around my limbs like the truth: I was in a different arena now whether I thought I liked it or not, and magic was forbidden. No more until—

Is that... cologne?

Something black flash in my peripheral, warmth encasing my arms. I sprang up and turned around. A jacket just as quickly invaded my previous spot on the bench. My eyes snapped up.

Oh no.

Brown eyes—the first thing I noticed were the boy's round brown eyes that radiated more warmth than his jacket. He stood behind the bench with his lips slightly parted and light-brown hands frozen in the air. Mahogany hair went down to his ears and swept upward at the tips. He stared back at me for just a second before his lips broke into a grin.

"I'm sorry," he quickly said, "I swear, I was gonna introduce myself before you stood up, you just looked cold so I figured—"

"Oh, it's okay." I smiled back, subconsciously flinging my hair out from behind my ear to cover it. "I forgot my jacket at home, but—um, I appreciate the thought."

"Well, I'm glad *that's* your initial reaction."

I bit my lip to subdue the laugh. To be honest, I had no idea whether to feel creeped out or flattered that a boy *this* cute had been concerned about if I was warm enough and tried to sneak his jacket onto me. Something was off, but... well, what harm could a smile like that do?

"Nice eyes."

I froze, words stuck in my throat like a fly to honey. It wasn't the first time someone had complimented the icy Atera blue of my eyes—but he was a handsome stranger complimenting *my* eyes.

"Thanks," I said, barely stopping myself from mentioning the Atera part. "You, too."

I mentally facepalmed. *I did not just say that.*

But he chuckled, held out his hand, and said, "I'm Jak."

The foolproof method to keep a stranger trapped in conversation. The worst part? Part of me was glad.

And despite everything Momma's ever told me about strangers, I accepted his handshake and locked myself in. "Emmalynn—Emma, sorry. Um, people usually call me 'Emma'."

Jak walked around the bench to stand in front of me, fully exposing his height: four inches taller than me? Five? "I promise, I really was planning on actually sitting down, if that makes you feel less—creeped out. Um..." He paused, as if saying the words out loud had held up a large mirror in front of him. "Okay, clearly I don't get out much."

My teeth lost their grip on my lip as I grinned, my laugh set free. How had he done that?

"Neither do I, believe it or not," I told him, scratching a non-itchy spot on my forehead. "I get that."

"In that case, I also usually grab coffee to warm up, if you're still cold."

What a suave way of asking someone out.

Wait. A guy was actually *asking me out*! For the first time ever!

In full honesty, I didn't know the response to that. I'd only trusted so many strangers growing up, but I'd always had Momma's help to gauge the boundaries of the relationship. That was just how it had always worked out, but I was going to be sixteen in a week. I definitely wouldn't have her help forever...

I'll let him decide how much he wants to do this.

"I would, but I didn't bring my purse," I said.

Jak shrugged. "My treat."

Okay. This was definitely a date.

"Really?" I hugged myself against the breeze, shifting my weight to one foot. "That's really nice of you... You're pretty bold for a stranger."

"And you're still cold." He nodded to my stance with a soft smile. Then, he turned around, grabbed his jacket from the bench, and held it out to me. "Plus, how do you know we're not friends just because we hadn't met till now?"

He was good. He was all the more dangerous because he was so good.

I ran through each of Momma's rules regarding strangers in my head: 1.) Never tell them a thing about either of your parents. 2.) Never reveal which part of town you live in. 3.) Never take anything from them, especially if they offer it to you for free. 4.) Always assume your conversation will last for thirty seconds, because then it will. 5.) If they ask for your number, give them the number to the pizza place two blocks away from home. 6.) If they try to follow you, go to the bathroom and make them forget about you (or, if a bathroom isn't nearby, scream).

But a teenage boy? This was a new game with different rules.

"Funny you say that," I said, my resolve softening under the anxiety. "I don't think I've seen you before, are you from here?"

"No," Jak answered submissively. "I'm from Topa."

My head jerked back. "Isn't that an hour away? What're you doing here?"

He seemed to think about his answer for a second, glancing off to the side. "Interest, I guess. Getting something out of my system before school starts."

I did understand *that*; I was doing the same thing.

"I did *not* have the best start to this conversation to begin with," he said next, holding up a hand, "so believe me, if you're not comfortable, I will gladly see myself somewhere else—"

"No, it's—" I caught myself saying, my own realization cutting me off. Apparently I *didn't* want him to leave, and I didn't need Sarah's help to know what that meant.

I glimpsed the red cement underneath us, unable to look Jak in the eye when I asked, "Do you have to be back soon?"

"No. You?"

I pressed my lips together to bar the giddy, idiotic grin. He actually wanted to spend the evening out with me. That thought alone made me want to burst out laughing, and every time I opened my mouth was a gamble.

Don't tell him about your family or where you live, and it's all good. And you can just erase his memory if you do let something slip!

"Nope." I smiled, nodding. "Coffee sounds good."

The closest Joe's House was the one inside the Publisher's Ink bookstore around the corner. Jak and I didn't speak for most of the way there as we walked on the sidewalk beside the main road, eventually turning left into the central shopping center.

Maybe he hadn't expected me to actually accept—because *now* he was struggling to fill in the all-too awkward silence.

"Topa, right?" I asked as we passed the store a couple of doors down from Publisher's Ink. "Where do you go to school?"

"Redway. We don't start for another two weeks."

No way. There was only one reason I'd heard of Redway Academy: it was an all-boys boarding school with the same original purpose and cover story as Callistro.

But Jak couldn't know that I knew his cover—then he'd know mine.

"I was actually homeschooled for all of elementary school," Jak added, "and then I went to a different private school until last year. You?"

From the sounds of it, he *already* knew me; how had he managed to recite half of my childhood without knowing a thing about me?

"That's crazy," I said, "I haven't met anyone else who was homeschooled. I was until this year. But I don't meet new people that often in general, I usually stay home or hang out with my friends."

"What about your dad?"

I nearly stopped in my tracks as we walked into Publisher's Ink, hunting for a safe answer. To this day, neither Sarah nor Breanne has ever asked me about my father because Momma told a cover story to their parents, who probably told the girls to never bring the subject up. Jak was officially the first to do so.

"I, um..." I said slowly, "I never got to meet my dad."

Jak paused like I'd set him off course. Regret seemed to settle in him, pulling his eyes down to the dark-blue carpet below us. "Oh. I'm—I'm sorry."

I paid him a weak smile, following his gaze.

Silence lingered between us again all the way until we reached the back of the store and strolled up to the counter at Joe's House to order. Then, Jak slid over to the neighboring pick-up counter, took a magazine, and followed me to a table next to a window.

It wasn't until we sat down that he opened the magazine, and I leaned in for a look at the cover: a slightly blurred photo of a man with brown hair and icy-blue eyes took up the page. His strikingly familiar, rugged face looked off to the side, the motion blur indicating his fast pace. The table hid the headline printed at the bottom, but the top shamelessly boasted the publisher: *Magic.*

"Interesting?" I asked, masking my skepticism.

"Very," Jak replied casually. His eyes moved up to meet mine, and he lowered his voice. "You know about the Ateras, right?"

Seriously? Again?

The pieces connected in my mind, and I realized why the man on the cover looked so familiar, why that familiarity had been blurred; I hadn't seen a photo of him in a long time, and the few that I *had* seen were crystal clear. And he was always smiling.

"Yeah," I said.

"So the world believes that, despite Tristan Atera marrying all those years ago, he and Rebecca were the last of their line. No more Ateras, no more magic. America's finally safe."

Anxiety crept up on me, igniting my skin with a heat that combatted the cold glass of the window. Not even the warm coffee aroma could comfort me as I forced my jaw to remain loose and said, "Yeah... and?"

"Apparently that's not true. He didn't just get married." Jak closed the magazine, dropped it onto the table, and pushed it in my direction. "Less than a year later, Tristan and his wife had a baby."

Chapter

Four

Tristan Atera: Married, in Hiding, and Possibly a Father!

"Possibly" was the operative word. How long until the country found out that "possibly" was actually "definitely"? And what was I going to do right now to avoid verifying that "possibly" really was "definitely"? Shift in my seat? Say something? Take the magazine because I couldn't believe my eyes?

Well, I couldn't believe my eyes; I took the magazine.

Jak chuckled, leaning back in his chair. "Tell me why I'm almost not surprised."

I whipped my head up. "What? Really?"

Translation: *that* was his reaction? This was the most startling breakthrough since the media discovered seventeen years ago that my father was married, and Jak wasn't surprised about the continuance of a bloodthirsty feud that had been waging for centuries?

Okay. Maybe I'm the weird one...

"Come on," Jak deadpanned, letting his hand drop onto the gray surface of the table, "how many people actually believe something like this would never happen again? There'll always be mortals who will never trust anything with a *gram* of magic. Sorcerers and warlocks and mages and all could be a litter of puppies and some people would never trust them. But that could just be me."

I mean, there was truth to that. People will always disagree about everything, some will even find a reason to. But why not Jak? Was he just used to the hierarchy? Or did his inability to do anything stop him from caring?

"So this"—I set down the magazine—"doesn't have any effect on you?"

He looked back down at the table, his light-brown fingers tapping the surface. "No, it does." He tilted his head as he mused. "I guess—I guess I think about his kid, wherever they are right now. How terrified they probably are. They're being hunted just for existing, missing their dad and maybe even their mom, too. Would you wanna live like that?"

I swallowed down the tears desperate to brim on my eyes, pressing my lips together like that would lessen the heat in my nose. Someone who didn't share my secret had broken down feelings that I'd never been able to express. Everything that defined who I was, was locked up with the key thrown into the Black Sea, yet Jak had effortlessly taken every hidden, unspoken component within me and strung it into a few sentences. A mortal had spoken *for* me—not against.

"Sorry," he said, shaking his head and taking the magazine. "That was way too heavy of a subject right now, I shouldn't've picked this up."

"No, it's okay," I said, recovering from my emotions. "It was definitely a brave choice of topic, I'll give you that."

He pressed his lips together before standing to put the magazine back in its rack on the pick-up counter. The barista slid him our drinks. With his back turned to me, my mind succumbed to the battle freely raging inside me: how did I feel about him? How *should* I feel about him? I wasn't even sure it would matter once I got back to Callistro, but he completely intensified my paranoia while tempting me to shove it all away. Or maybe the paranoia was because he was the first stranger I was actually getting to *know* without my mother or Sarah and Breanne next to me.

I licked my lips, eyeing the back of Jak's head as he grabbed our drinks. *Why did he pick* Magic *to talk about? Is he careless or just ignorant?* It was almost like I could tell him I was a magician and he wouldn't bat an eye.

He came back to our table, his stare snagging on something behind me.

"What's wrong?" I asked, turning to face the bookstore over my shoulder: a redhead in the middle of the aisle was searching for her next section to explore, a mother and her two kids were looking through the children's stories on the right side, and a tall man with glasses was reading a book from the computer science shelf on the left.

Jak set my latte onto the table and sat back down across from me. "I thought I saw a guy I used to go to school with—the one I went to before Redway, never mind, I was wrong."

I looked behind me again. The redhead had changed her mind and begun striding toward Joe's, and the man with glasses was picking up a new book. No teenage boys.

I bit the inside of my lip. Jak had said he was wrong, but that wasn't the problem; the problem was that for *once* in my guarded life, I wanted to let my walls fall. I couldn't explain it, but for the first time since meeting Sarah and Breanne, I wanted to let in a stranger beyond "Hi, how are you?"

Because it doesn't matter. This is a first-time experience and probably the only one you're gonna get for a while.

I mentally shook the voice away as easily as it had come. It was a tug-of-war between carelessness and allowing myself something outside the box for once.

I took a few sips of my drink, challenging myself to make this a regular outing. "Thanks for this. It's the first time in a while that I've been truly out. I don't count back-to-school shopping."

"You mentioned your friends earlier, right?"

"Oh, yeah." My gaze jumped from the lid of my latte to the floor to the pastries on display at the counter, once in a blue moon glancing at Jak's warm-brown eyes. I had to stop doing that—but how? "I grew up with these two girls who lived on my street, Sarah and Breanne. We've been best friends since we were, like, eight. You?"

"Oh, nice!" How genuinely kind his smile was. It didn't look like the smiles I'd seen from the grocery store cashiers or the technicians at the nail salon. "My two closest friends and I met in sixth grade. We're rooming together now at Redway."

That was an interesting... coincidence.

My gaze settled on the magazine on display behind Jak, where it finally sank in like a ship to the bottom of the ocean: the man on the cover was my father. That was who he was before I was born. That was the life he had succumbed to all those years ago. It angered me. What kind of a life was that?

"Something wrong?" Jak asked. What I wanted to believe was concern stared back at me.

Great. I was mourning again.

"Sorry, I should start getting home," I replied, standing. "School starts tomorrow for me. This was nice, though, thanks again."

Jak took one last look at me like he was snapping a mental picture. "I'm glad to hear that, thanks. It was nice meeting you."

I turned around before I could give any more of myself away. The conversation somehow felt unfinished, but one of Momma's most valuable lessons is to let sleeping dogs lie. I left with every thought in my head mushed together, but I was perfectly fine with that; it made it all the more difficult for my emotions to surface, so at least I wouldn't be crying on my way home.

But one thing pressed harshly against my mind: the apprehension I *did* have toward Jak had been validated when he never asked for my number. Why the lack of desire to stay in touch after such a strong interest in hanging out? Or was he confident that we'd meet again before he went back?

Capperson is *really small...*

I glanced over my shoulder every other second on the walk home. With each step I took farther away from Jak, it felt like I was stepping further out of a trance and deeper into reality. And the only thing I had to wake up to was my greatest nightmare, because I *had* confided in a stranger about my sympathies toward magic, in a way. I'd broken almost every social rule Momma and I had ever established! For Jak, a stranger? Why had he been the only exception when not even Sarah and Breanne had ever had that privilege? All it had taken was one magazine cover to...

I swallowed hard, kicking a pebble on the sidewalk. My father had been on that magazine cover, on a headline that had said that the country practically knew the truth. How? Momma and Aunt Becca were the only ones who knew about Tristan Atera's daughter. The only way someone could've gathered that intel and tipped off the press was if...

...someone besides Momma knew. A decade and a half going by without any new information about our family surfacing, and *now* my parents' greatest secret rises to the front cover?

Momma had to have confided in someone else.

Nerves popped and burned in my chest as I approached my mother's classroom in the gym that night, like it was wrong to suspect her of confessing the truth after her nearly sixteen-year-long aversion to me even having a friend.

"Hey, Em." A warm smile radiated on her narrow beige face as I walked past her and into the classroom. "How was town?"

Good. Met a boy. Went out for coffee with him. Found out that the country knows about me. Am pretty sure you told someone that you had a kid, and that's the whole reason I'm here.

"Um... good."

She pushed the door shut behind me with one hand on her hip. "Don't tell me we already need to review lying."

Which is definitely not a sentence I think normal mothers say to their daughters.

"No, I mean—" I leaned against one of the front-row desks, trying to get all of my ducks in a row. Lying wasn't the road I was aiming for—it was figuring out the least-upsetting wording. Then I realized that that wasn't possible because this was the worst news we'd ever faced together.

Momma stepped up onto the platform at the front of the fluorescently lit room, mimicking my position and leaning against her desk. I took a deep breath. Despite the hot anxiety swirling throughout my body, I shivered in the air conditioning. She didn't need to know about Jak. He wasn't the reason I was in here, and it wasn't like he'd be showing up again.

"I got coffee at Joe's House," I replied. "And they had *Magic*'s latest issue, with Dad on the cover."

She gave me a nod, nothing more. She was barring me from seeing what was going on in her head. "So Sarah was right about the authorities suspecting that he's in the country?"

"No," I breathed. "They already... They know."

"What do they know?"

Nothing had changed in her stance, her stolid expression, her even cadence. I couldn't pinpoint if she was trying to prevent my panic or cage her true reaction because of the Master Hunter always standing guard in her.

"He had a baby. Or—they suspect that. The headline was 'possibly a father'."

Momma's sharp amber eyes stilled like a deer caught in the headlights, her hand anxiously twisting the golden band on her left ring finger. I knew that the gears in her head were turning just like that ring, but that was it. I really wanted to believe that some-where in that raging sea, her thoughts were aligning with mine: this wasn't supposed to happen yet. Dad was meant to come back before I was found out, we were supposed to face this as a family.

"Does anyone else know?" I forced myself to ask. "Have you ever trusted someone outside of our family?"

"I need to talk to Aunt Becca," Momma said, pulling herself from her desk, "and you need to get ready for bed. You're not sleeping in on the first day of school."

"You didn't answer me," I said, standing straight. Honestly, the temptation to put a truth spell on her burned, and I would have if I weren't so scared of her.

"No. Nobody other than family knows."

My mother is one of the best liars I know, and it has every-thing to do with her celebrity status in her ex-career. She became a Master Hunter less than a year after graduating high school and went on her first real hunt when she was just eighteen. She was good. Like, could-kill-a-crow-with-nothing-but-a-rubber-band-from-three-school-buses-away good. (I neither confirm nor deny that she's actually done that before.) She only quit because of my father, but it was mostly *because* of her skill that Mr. Dawson offered her the self-defense instructor job here—not because he was a good friend. Even now, he didn't know who Momma's late husband was, just that she'd lost him when I was born.

But while the small amount of training she *had* given me while growing up couldn't see if she was lying, it was enough to warn me that argument wasn't an option. She wouldn't give me any answer I wanted whether she was telling the truth or not. With a good-night hug, I left the room, suspicions unchanged.

The second I sat down on my bed with Sarah and Breanne, the story of Jak flooded out. Girl code is different from mother-daughter code; you're legally obligated to tell your best friends about boys even if you're never going to see that boy again.

Sarah pouted on the floor, her elbow resting on the edge of my bed and her chin on her hand. "That's weird he didn't get your number after how he wanted to hang out. I wonder if he plans on seeing you again."

"But how?" I asked, hugging my knees. "I highly doubt he's staying *here* when he's just 'getting something out of his system' before school starts... You don't think it's weird he goes to Redway and is all the way out here?"

If anyone would know if there was cause for concern, it was Breanne Shaw, yet all she said from the foot of my bed was "If he knew you went to Callistro, it would be. I think he really was just curious about another small town."

Both girls had confirmed that Redway was, in fact, dormant like Callistro. As of now, every Hunter school in the country was. Except, that was little relief with the situation being, well, what it was.

I lightly chuckled to myself, as if laughter were strong enough to stop my next sentence. Momma had purposely been no help, and if Sarah was right about the Atera rumor, I wanted to believe she would have more to offer if I gave her more to work with. "So, Jak happened to pick up the latest edition of *Magic* before we sat down. Tristan Atera was on the cover."

"Oh!" Sarah chirped, straightening, her hand falling to my bed. "Did they confirm what Opal Dubois said?"

I licked my lips, loosening my grip on myself. "I don't know about that specifically. But he..."

Stop being an Atera and start being a Marie.

"Okay. Everyone knows he got married a long time ago and then disappeared, but now the authorities think he and his wife *had a baby* less than a year after marrying. 'Possibly'."

Sarah's jaw fell open in my peripheral vision, grabbing my attention first. "No way. You're kidding."

"There's a *possibility* that Tristan's line continued?" Breanne asked in front of me, her small frame as rigid as her voice. Her expression alone threatened my unbiased cover: the share of shock and even panic in her wide blue-hazel eyes, the frown bending her thin lips, her stiffened muscles when the words were still in my mouth. My most defensive instincts wanted to fight for magic's reputation—my *father's* reputation. He wasn't a monster. What did she have to be afraid of?

"You know what that means, right?" Sarah said, glancing between the two of us. "Come on, we know Caldwell isn't gonna let this get past him. They're gonna figure out if it's true, get Tristan's descendant if he has one, and kill them. Money on it."

Not like the girl needed the money with her dad being one of the biggest movie producers on the East Coast.

"Well... I guess we know what a magician's child's life looks like now."

I stopped at Breanne's feeble words. Sarah kept her eyes away from me despite our equal reactions, like locking gazes would expose what was really lying behind them, what we were actually feeling: sympathy for someone who supposedly had no business existing.

But was that actually how she felt about it?

"Yeah, Jak actually..." I began slowly, "brought up something interesting about that. And he said it so casually, like it's common knowledge. He said the war on magic is never gonna end. Magicians could be puppies and nobody would ever trust them."

"I mean," Breanne mused, picking at the light hairs on her arm, "yeah, I guess that's true. I don't think they'll ever live without being hunted."

I still wasn't brave enough to look at Sarah, and she wasn't brave enough to look at me.

What were my friends really feeling right now? Did they have their own façades to protect the truth of their thoughts? More importantly, was I as unreadable to them as they were to me right now?

⚜

It feels pointless writing about the first day of school since it was just introductions, but I had to wonder if the day would've been more interesting if we were still a Hunter school. It probably would have offered a *lot* of different first-day "activities". Classes were shorter this week, which left me more time to find Jak in town if he was still here. Knowing that I didn't have his full story left a gaping hole in my conspiracy, and I wouldn't be satisfied until it was filled.

At least, that *had* been the plan before Momma pulled me from my dorm after school "wanting to see me".

I glimpsed over my shoulder as we walked down the hall toward the staircase. We were alone, which gave me the courage to ask about the suspicion bouncing in my head: "Does this have anything to do with a new schedule for... that *thing*?"

"We do still need to figure that out, but no," she whispered back. "There's someone in my office you need to meet."

Huh. Was it Mr. Dawson? Maybe he wanted to check in on how the first day had gone for me. After all, he and Momma go so far back that they may as well be siblings. Up until this summer, he used to visit us at least once a week at home. The adult talk, if I ever eavesdropped or joined in, was always about my home-schooling system, what my future for college looked like, or even Mr. Dawson's family. (I vaguely remember a conversation about his niece, whom he was forbidden to see because of a family disagreement or something. I was actually pretty interested in that one.) Once I put in my two cents, I'd send myself to my room.

But if he wanted to know how my first day had gone, couldn't Momma have just updated him?

Our footsteps echoed in the gym as we strolled up to her classroom door. She placed her hand on the metal handle.

"Stay calm," she began gently. "No matter what he says, do not panic. And *whatever* you do,"—she leaned in close, tightening her tone—"do not even imply a single word about your magic."

I nodded, heart quickening. Don't panic? What could Mr. Dawson possibly want with me inside *her* classroom that would make me panic, let alone warrant Momma warning me?

I don't like this, I thought as she opened the door.

"Still cold, Merlin?"

I locked my jaw against it dropping, exhaled against my body stiffening, the second I saw Jak standing on the platform at the front of my mother's classroom. His hands rested in his jean pockets with his thumbs sticking out, red hoodie hanging loosely off his frame and complementing the light brown of his skin. That same suave smile that had persuaded me to grab coffee with him last night stared back at me like this was the best game of hide-and-seek he'd ever played.

Momma had said not to panic, but surprise should've been *more* than allowed! I was practically entitled to it given the fact that the one person I'd never been more conflicted about in my life, whom I believed I was never going to meet again, was now standing inside my school and, evidently, knew my mother!

Wait. What had he said? "Merlin"? As in the powerful sorcerer Merlin from the fairy tale? As in... What *did* Jak know?!

"Half an hour ago, Jak took my office number from the

school website and called me," Momma began, coming to stand between me and him with her arms crossed. She turned her head to him. "Go ahead."

So he did stay in town last night if it only took him half an hour to get here. How? Where are his parents?

I looked Jak dead in the eyes, trying to untangle biased from unbiased thoughts. Was I allowed to be mad at him? Had he known my mother this whole time? Had he already known me last night after pretending he hadn't? He couldn't know the truth, not if Momma had told me not to mention a thing about magic. Then what was with the nickname?

"I know it seems like I lied," he said awkwardly, like he was anticipating my objection, "but I was planning on coming here today anyway if I didn't meet you first. I honestly didn't know you last night, not personally, but I saw you and you—looked familiar. It was sheer coincidence we were both there at the same time."

"How?" I asked flatly.

"Because you're the reason I'm here. It's not completely interest. I overheard that someone's... Okay. Hunters—"

He shook his head, scoffing softly to himself and brown eyes dropping to the floor with my heart. I almost glued his mouth shut with my magic when he looked back up, like that would erase the truth when he told me, "A Grand Hunter pack thinks you're Tristan Atera's descendant."

CHAPTER

SIX

I'm dead. The blood in my head drained straight to my feet in a cold rush. *I'm so, so dead.*

It wasn't a regular and it wasn't even a Master after my head: it was an entire *pack* of Hunters who were the best in the industry. Grand Hunters only hunt in packs *because* they're the best of the best, they know how to combine elite skill *and* teamwork! Not even Sarah or Breanne has hope to become one someday; just Master status takes most people a few years to achieve after induction as a regular. There's a reason the family trees in the Hall of Generations only have about three to five Grand Hunters in a tree, and those are just the ones that *do* have any.

Grand Hunters know their targets, and they know how to catch them.

"They think Tristan Atera is my dad?" I forced myself to ask, because my thoughts alone were ready to kill me if I let them spiral any further and expose my panic then and there.

"Well, they're suspecting a few kids," Jak said. "They have a list with an Emmalynn Marie at the top, newly enrolled at the Callistro Academy. And they have access to every student record, so they know the age is right, the last name is close, and the school just seems convenient. You know, with... the history and all."

But Redway's the same way! Was that how he knew? Had Jak been hunted before me? Had someone from his school been?

I chuckled like I wasn't amused, but I was completely amused. I was humored to death. "So federal agents are going off their *best guess?* I have one of the most common last names in America and am the same age Tristan's descendant might be, like every other sophomore in this school, but that makes me the most likely candidate for this guy's daughter?"

Jak stiffly nodded, running a hand down the back of his head of dark-brown hair. "Yeah. That's about it."

Momma's words echoed in my head: *Do not panic. Do not panic. Do not panic.* But how was either Emmalynn Marie *or* Emmalynn Atera supposed to avoid that? How was I supposed to convince my greatest enemy that the truth was a lie?

How did Jak know any of this?

"So you picked up that magazine," I stated slowly, "knowingly. You already knew what that headline meant for me, you just wanted my reaction?"

Even Momma, standing between us, didn't release him from her sharp-eyed stare, but I bet hers was a lot more forgiving than mine in that moment.

"Yes," he said, "I technically already knew—"

"No, not 'technically'," I snapped, crossing my arms. "Why didn't you tell me, why was last night 'let's get to know each other' and not 'I need to tell you something'?"

"I wanted to do this in front of both of you," Jak replied, taking one hand out of his jeans and gesturing loosely between me and Momma. "And see if you were still okay. So when you didn't know anything about it last night, I didn't wanna…"—he dropped his hand with a sigh, innocent eyes stuck on me like I was the only person in the room—"mess that up yet."

"And, Emma," Momma said, turning to me, "you do realize everything Jak is putting on the line by defying the government and their mission, right?" She briefly faced him again. "I do think you should have told her as soon as you found her so she could come to me last night. But you got to her in time, so it wasn't a costly mistake. Right now,"—she stepped back to comfortably glance between us—"that's what matters."

To my anger's dismay, she was right. It wasn't like *I* was perfect at secretly being a sorcerer's daughter yet. Maybe last night, Jak had just been making sure I was really the girl officially being hunted by the U.S. Government and now he was here to warn us.

"But the other reason I came today," he said to her, "is because I wanted to introduce myself to you, Mrs. Marie. I want to help if I can."

I should've been against the offer; it was only valid if he was trying to protect an Atera, not a "mortal". The same especially applied to Momma—but neither she nor I immediately rejected him. Like me, my mother was absorbing everything he said.

A lethal air lingered around this boy. He had the spirit of

someone whose word was impossible to doubt, mostly because he meant it all. I knew that because Momma believed him. But meaning every word made him all the more dangerous—he wasn't protecting what he thought he was.

I shifted my weight. "How about starting by telling us how you even know about all this?"

His mouth opened again, but nothing came out until he glanced sideways. "I was—involved with another case. Everything turned out fine, but when it came to Emma, I... I overheard it. That's all I can say, if that's a good-enough answer for now."

As much as I didn't want it to be, as much as I was silently begging him to give me the answer to every question I had about him, his excuse *had* to be good enough for now. With it, silence swept the air, leaving nothing for my fear to hide behind.

Jak took a few soft steps toward me like I was a stray dog and he didn't want to get bitten. "That's all I came to say. And I've dealt with these guys before, kind of, so if you want my help, you have it."

He turned to my mother and shook her hand. When I didn't offer him any reply, he passed me by and walked out the classroom door. His steps echoed across the gym before the main door eventually clanged shut behind him. He was gone. Momma and I were alone.

I turned to her and thrust myself into her arms, quietly sobbing as if she'd never seen me cry before and I wasn't about to let her now. For the first time in my life, her choice of words for comfort had disappeared. All she did to compensate was smooth my hair and tighten her embrace around me, her familiar floral perfume my best source of comfort right now.

"I'm sorry," she finally whispered. "This is all my fault, I'm so sorry, honey."

Unable to verbally speak, I wished she had magic so I could telepathically tell her that her arms were my one and only panacea. Did she know how often I chose her hugs over venting to my friends? Did she know how many times I'd been left to carry myself through something because she wasn't there to hold me and make my world temporarily right again?

"Em," she whispered, "I'm not mad. But why didn't you tell me you met him last night?"

I sniffed, exhaling a hot breath that suffocated me as much as my thoughts were. "I was dumb enough—to think I'd never see him again."

"You weren't dumb. You made a mistake." She kissed my forehead. "You told me about the magazine, at least. Thank you."

I nodded.

She's always said that my father rubbed off on her with his hugs. Apparently, nobody could hug like he could, and Momma's hugs were how she remembered him; they were one of the few things she had left of him. It was comforting to pretend it *was* my dad's arms around me as she squeezed me and said, "We'll figure it out. Nothing's going to stop us from protecting our family, especially now."

Upon me opening the door to our dorm, Breanne turned around in the white chair at the desk and let her eyes go wide. "What happened?"

I knew I should've given myself more time to look normal after crying.

Lying to my friends is a burden I've never gotten used to, and I almost hope that I never will. Unfortunately, I couldn't keep a pack of Grand Hunters behind the curtain, at least not for long. And if Sarah and Breanne found out about the situation for themselves, how were they supposed to trust me ever again when I was already lying to them about who I was?

I took a few seconds to form the safest sentence, glimpsing Sarah waiting patiently on her bed. The door behind me kept me upright as I steadied my breath. "I'm swearing you both to secrecy right now. Remember Jak?"

"Yeah," Sarah said, pushing her hair behind her ear as if to hear me better.

"He showed up at Mom's classroom to tell us that a pack of Grand Hunters are already trying to find Tristan's descendant. They're not even completely sure he has one, but they're not taking any chances."

"*Grand* Hunters?" Breanne exhaled, round eyes wide. I nodded. "That's like—sending someone to Death Row!"

Sarah's striking features scrunched together with doubt and confusion. "I don't get it, why are you so upset about that?"

The words first came out in a chuckle, and I had to force them to take shape: "They're suspecting *me*."

My roommates stared back at me like victims of Medusa. I finished the story before they could ask: "Jak said my age is right, my last name is close, and the school acts as the perfect cover. I happen to fit the general categories, so I'm first on their list."

Whatever my friends were switching back and forth to believe, I couldn't read it. And if the truth was one of their options, I had to pray that it didn't sound plausible.

"Okay," Sarah said after a nerve-racking silence, "don't freak out. Whatever crazy scheme those people have planned, it doesn't matter, it's so easy to find out you're not his kid. They'll move on before the week is over."

"But *Grand Hunters*!" Breanne whispered-screamed. "Nobody knows what they do to their victims! That's why they call them 'victims'! They could—"

"They have plenty of *harmless* ways to find the truth," Sarah said, shooting her a glare. "I really don't think we have to worry. They're just being thorough..."

With a brief matching of our eyes, I knew exactly what was playing in her mind: the battle between rationality and fear of the unknown, because we simply didn't know what this would entail.

Breanne bit her lip at the desk. "Yeah. That's it. It'll be okay— we'll even vouch for you."

I exhaled and laughed to myself, thinking how fate *must* have been on my side if these girls were. I knew they didn't suspect the truth because of Momma's history, and Hunters and sorcerers just don't mix.

But the truth was just as cruel: they were fighting for my façade, not me. In other words, the thought of another person facing the fate meant for me didn't faze them one bit.

"Em?" Sarah asked, arching a brow. "Did Jak really say they're coming after you purely based on a slightly educated guess?"

"Exactly what he said."

"Where did he hear that from?"

"He said he was involved with a case before this. Then he overheard my name."

Her brows furrowed, like she was slowly putting together pieces even I didn't have. "He was involved? The Redway Boy was involved in a case similar to this?"

Something wanted to click in me, but the circuits weren't connecting. "Yeah..."

Breanne gave Sarah her undivided attention, probably eager to hear whatever theory she had. Sarah tilted her head down at me. "None of this seems off to you?"

"All of it seems off to me," I said, fighting to suppress the bite in my voice. "But if there's even the smallest chance he's telling the truth, *why* would I ignore it? Especially when I have nothing to hide?"

She gave another pause. "Right." She stood up and grabbed her white sweater and handbag on the nightstand. "Then like I said, before the week is over. Let's go out and celebrate."

Knowing what I do now... well, I wish I'd known then what I do now. In that moment, though, "celebrating" was the perfect distraction. I wanted to do anything but think about my upcoming interrogation that those agents were no doubt preparing to put me through. Funny—I'd kind of spent a lifetime preparing for this exact situation, yet it wasn't any less terrifying here on my doorstep.

The three of us put on our casual clothes and then made our way down, soon landing at the top of the Main Staircase. I stopped with my friends, observing a team of classmates crowding around at the bottom like paparazzi. I immediately recognized the girl in the middle from orientation.

"Why's everyone swarming Opal?" I whispered.

"She's probably giving them their daily dose of gossip," Sarah replied, her sweet perfume wafting into my nose as she leaned closer to me. "She was definitely the first to hear about Tristan's maybe-descendant."

We started our descent just as Opal's purple eyes caught us. Nobody knows why she wears those contacts, but the girl makes them work, and they're a striking complement to her black hair. (To this day, not even her roommates have ever seen her take them out, and nobody is brave enough to ask for the story.)

She grinned, worming her way through the crowd of Callistro Girls to the front. "Hi, guys! Have you heard? About"—her voice lowered to a whisper—"Tristan Atera?"

"You mean the unproven rumor?" Sarah asked behind me.

Bless you, Sarah.

Keeping her smile, Opal's dark brows furrowed together. She rested a hand on the banister. "What do you mean?"

Don't get defensive.

"Well, I mean..." I shrugged, focusing on keeping an even tone. "It's a stretch, isn't it? I kind of need more than circumstantial evidence. Tristan's been in hiding for more than a decade, and now all of a sudden, they *think* he *might've* had a baby. How would they even find something like that after, what, two decades?"

"Well, I don't know how they found out yet." Opal traced small circles in the wooden banister with her finger. Her words took on a high lilt as she said, "But it's not a rumor—this is hardcore fact. It's just a matter of figuring out gender and age now."

Against every instinct in my bone, I forced myself to stay relaxed. Emmalynn Marie *needed* to override Emmalynn Atera, especially with the group of girls standing just behind Opal.

"Didn't the magazine say 'possibly'?" I asked.

Opal's thin lips snaked into a grin, her voice unable to shake that high tone. "This is the biggest breakthrough since finding out he was even married. Of course they're gonna find out everything as fast as they can. We just have to wait and see who it is."

A cold chill slithered down my spine; it was like she knew, like she was taunting me and the irony that I was even standing in this school right now. I couldn't help but feel like if the girl had magic, she'd be able to see right through me.

Pick your battles. If I wanted to hold on to this one, I could lose the whole war.

"Okay," I said, nodding. "I can see the possibility. But you can't tell me it's a likely chance they're still alive. I feel like *that* would be the reason we're just now hearing about this: they stayed hidden while they were alive, but what if we're finding clues about them now because they're dead?"

"Maybe. But I don't like giving up that easily." Opal's glittering eyes bored into mine as she stood on the last step of the Main Staircase, like she was giving me one more chance to change my mind. "What if we're finding clues because they're still alive?"

She turned around and walked through her group, parting them like the Red Sea. The short blonde on her left, Ava Baleen, asked what the magazine thought about the whole thing. Teresa Darci, next to her, asked if Opal's mom knew just how close the government was to finding Tristan's descendant. The same questions were rampant in my head, too, but sticking around to hear the answers would dig a deeper hole.

I have to put a forgetting spell on them, I thought before realizing in time that they had a million reminders of Tristan's possible descendant now; they'd remember as fast as they'd forgotten, and them forgetting it at all was *bound* to raise suspicion.

"Nice job," Sarah said behind me. "Can you imagine if that girl found out you're a suspect?"

I watched the group enter the library on the right side of the foyer. "She wouldn't even let 'falsely' slip out before 'suspected'."

We stepped down the rest of the stairs, turned, and went to Mr. Dawson's office behind the Staircase.

Upon opening the door, he glanced between us with deep-set eyes, smiling like he was secretly grateful that we'd interrupted his work. "Hello, ladies."

"Hi, Mr—*Headmaster* Dawson," I said, to which he nodded with approval.

"Good catch, Miss Marie." He moved aside and held the door farther open. The new titles would definitely take more time getting used to. "Come in."

Here's the other thing about Mr. Dawson, and I'm going to be completely honest: he's what every Callistro Girl secretly hopes her future husband will look like. Before I saw his hair, I didn't know that tousled and neat could be friends. The vibrant dark brown highlights the sheer brightness of his blue eyes that match a diamond, so it's pretty fitting that his jawline is sharp enough to *cut* one. (It's also said that he has a mini gym in his dorm, but that's just a rumor.)

"We were wondering if we could step out for a bit to celebrate the first day," I told him as we strolled inside.

He paused, his hands staying in his blazer pockets. A slight frown pulled down his defined lips. "I don't know. I'd like students to stay on campus for the first week to settle in with a more focused mindset."

"Well, what if we said it's also to treat Emma after her first day of real school?" Sarah added sweetly, taking my shoulders and squeezing them. "And we promise to be back in two hours?"

His commanding eyes took a turn with each of us, but they landed on me. It was like a thought had stolen his consciousness and he'd forgotten that he was looking at me.

"Okay. Sure." He ambled to his mahogany desk in the corner of the room and opened a drawer, pulling out a stack of small white slips. Grabbing a pen from his cup of many, he jotted something down and then scribbled his signature. "Two hours."

He tore off the paper and purposely handed it to Breanne (considering Sarah lost four textbooks throughout middle school and excused it by telling the librarian, "The newer editions will be out next year, anyway"). Breanne politely smiled. "Thank you!"

"You're welcome." Mr. Dawson only glimpsed me this time. "Have fun and be safe."

C H A P T E R

SEVEN

Crystal-blue sky blared above us in typical late-summer fashion for Capperson. Sunshine warmed my face the second we stepped outside, a breeze of heat gliding by.

I guess Sarah won't need her sweater, after all.

"Hey, Merlin," a voice chimed when the manor's front doors closed behind us. Jak stood up from leaning against the wall and strolled over, his eyes switching between the girls next to me. "And friends."

"*Hello,*" Sarah sang, pulling her long white purse strap farther up her shoulder. She extended her hand with a dazzling grin. "I'm Sarah."

"Jak," he said, matching her smile and shaking her hand. He turned to the girl beside her. "Breanne?"

"Yeah," she said, unable to muster anything beyond a straight-line smile, but still accepting Jak's hand.

I'm not going to recount what happened to her freshman year with her ex-boyfriend (none of us want to relive it), but it was like Jak already knew. There must have been something in Breanne's touch that made him slow his movements and swap the tease in his smile with sincerity.

"Got it." His voice softened with the rest of his handsome features as he let go. "B for 'blond', easy to remember. Um... do I have to introduce myself?"

His glance at me let me hear the code embedded in the question, and I cursed the words about to leave my mouth. "No. We were actually going out to get our minds off that."

"Stellar job we're doing," Sarah remarked, digging in her purse. "Guess it all worked out, now we can get your number and stay in touch." She looked up at him, pausing her search. "You forgot a step last night. Nice first impression."

He chuckled. For some reason, I had to wonder what went through his head whenever he looked at her. He'd complimented my eyes last night, but what did he think about hers?

"Didn't mean to." As if reading my mind, his gaze shifted to me. "Believe me."

Whoa. That was a weird wave in my stomach.

What does that mean? Is he just talking about his concern with the hunt?

"Ugh," Sarah said, like she'd completely tuned the boy out, letting her purse drop to her side. "I left my phone in our room, I'll be right back. You guys go ahead and start walking."

"I'll go with you," Breanne said, right on her tail as she made for the manor's front doors. "Did you forget yours, too, Em?"

The empty weight in my back jean pocket immediately told me the answer. "Yeah, thanks."

With one hand on the intricate brass handle, Sarah turned her head to look at me. A smirk played on her mauve lips. "We'll try to be long."

The second I opened my mouth, she flung the door open and slipped inside with Breanne. I shut my mouth, burning embarrassment flooding into my cheeks.

I cannot believe her.

Jak snickered beside me. "I like them."

"One of us does." As if walking away would erase the past few seconds, I turned to the stone steps in front of us and continued forward. "That's why Bre's my favorite half the time."

Jak's steps clicked with mine as he followed me down, hands back in his jean pockets with his thumbs sticking out. How was he still wearing his jacket in this heat? "I hope I didn't make her uncomfortable."

"Besides the fact that, believe it or not, they don't completely trust you, it wasn't personal. That's just Breanne when you first meet her."

He nodded, strolling along the gravel of the wide driveway. "I think I did better with Sarah... She did kind of have a point. It honestly completely slipped my mind last night, but I did wanna get your number."

Insatiable curiosity drove the words straight out of my mouth: "Really? How come?"

I really hope that doesn't sound desperate.

"Because you were really cool and easy to hang out with. I

didn't wanna stop talking..." Jak side-eyed me, those lips curved in another soft smile that made my heart beat a little harder. "And I really do like your eyes."

Walking was a fantastic excuse for the deep breath I had to take after that.

"I guess you were right about strangers being friends," I said, keeping my eyes on the gravel because there was no way I was brave enough to give him eye contact now. "That was fast."

"Yeah, nickname basis and everything."

"Good point, what made you pick 'Merlin' of *all* things?"

He held up a hand. "First of all, I'm proud of it. Second, it works as an ironic code name. The ones spies use to emphasize something, like something they hate."

"But Hunters are trying to prove I *am* a Merlin."

Jak shrugged. "So I don't use it when they're around. I think it's *adorable*."

A smile ran across my lips but just as quickly faded. *When they're around.* Right—all I was doing right now was running away from the inevitable. I could forget it for a few seconds, a couple of hours, but I'd always come back to the bounty on my head. It almost made distraction pointless. When was that moment coming for me?

At the black gates, I showed my pass to the security guards and then swiped my ID. The gates swung open in front of us. Stepping outside of our barriers with Jak, it almost felt like a repeat of last night. Now I was grateful I'd changed into a cute blouse and light jeans out of the plaid skirt and crimson blazer—which would've made me feel a lot less cute...

Did I look as good as I felt, or did I look like I was playing an attention game?

The gates clanged shut behind us, locking us from the school. I was free again. I wondered how many more times I'd be able to do this.

"Will I still get to go out like this?" I caught myself asking.

Jak smirked. "I didn't think you'd be anticipating another date so soon."

I internally freaked for a second. *He* thought of last night as a date?!

"You know what I mean," I said, forcing myself to nudge him with my elbow as we approached the entrance of the forest. "As in... am I gonna have this kind of freedom at all for the next few days? Maybe even weeks?"

A few seconds passed with his lips pressed together. "Well, yeah," he eventually said, forestry softly crunching under our feet. "Hunting's confidential. I mean, they can't go after you during school hours because of the exposure, for one, and it's not like they have a lot of opportunities when you're out in public. The entire case is a huge secret meant to be kept *from* the public."

Then how do you know so much about it? I wanted to ask. Jak was right about all of that; if he'd really been involved in a previous case, where else was he getting his information from?

I looked up at the trees we strolled by, gaps in the canopy exposing the warm sunlight amidst the cool, damp shade. "Is Redway hidden like Callistro is?"

"Yep," Jak replied. "It's pretty similar to here, but replace the stone and masonry with concrete. And replace the manor with a renovated prison from 1902."

I laughed, sticking my hands into my back pockets. "A *prison?*

Isn't there a saying about school and—?"

"I've heard every joke already, so *please* don't come up with one right now."

I toned down my laughter. Something seemed different about this Jak, something that left a lot to appreciate. Warmer, friendlier, closer. "I'm surprised you told me you went there at all."

"It felt safe to. Knowing you went here."

All I could offer was a nod—because his affiliation with my background was the one topic he was still avoiding. I knew why he knew, but not how. Honestly, I still wasn't brave enough to press him about it. He'd closed up in Momma's office for a reason. Whatever case he'd been involved in to get my information had to have scarred him somehow.

Birds peeped in the distance, echoing across the realm of the forest. I looked up at Jak's face as he stared ahead. His eyes seemed to trap the sunlight, turning from chocolate to a glistening caramel. No photo could capture how his eyes waltzed in the light right now—but it could definitely capture the soft definition of his jaw.

"They did teach us one useful thing last year," he told me in a lower voice. His stare moved down to mine. "Always look in your peripheral. That's where the most important things happen."

Blood swirled in my cheeks, and I looked away. Maybe it was the way he'd said it, but he had somehow resummoned the butterflies. Who *was* this? *What* was this?

Dangerous, that was what—because this was a new game with different rules, and so far, I was losing because I didn't know the rules.

I forced myself to shake the moment away, focusing on the rhythm of our feet on the dirt and leaves. "Hey, so, since we're alone... can you tell me how you figured out—?"

No sooner than I spoke did my ears perk up. My feet stopped.

"Figured out—?"

I shushed Jak, eyes darting around the forest. We were almost halfway through—far from the sight of the guards at the gate. That definitely didn't ease my rattling nerves.

Five seconds went by. Then ten.

"Sorry." I exhaled. "I thought... Sorry. I wanted to ask how you found out about me. I know you said you were involved in another case before—"

Another twig broke, a few leaves crunched, and more rustling echoed in the woods. I spun in the direction of the school, hoping in vain to see Sarah and Breanne walking up to us. But I already knew that those sounds hadn't come from that direction. My skin tingled, fear infecting every square inch of me.

"Jak?" I whispered.

A second passed.

"We're being followed," he said, answering my unspoken question.

Dead leaves crunched behind us. We whirled around. Six black-uniformed group members stepped out from the side of the path splitting the forest in half. They grouped behind a woman in black jeans and a periwinkle button-up shirt. She was the only one dressed casually, but it was her fierce emerald-green eyes and shoulder-length red hair that pricked something in my mind. Something like—

Recognition. I knew this woman.

"You were at the bookstore last night." My shaky voice betrayed my fear. I wanted to put the pieces together in time, but I was also praying that they wouldn't fit.

"I was," the woman chimed, tilting her head to the side. Her silky voice carried the haunting melody of a ghost's lullaby, maybe even one of a mother. If she was who I refused to believe she was, how was that possible?

"It's nice to meet you, Emmalynn. Emmalynn Marie, right?"

"Yes..."

A sly smile spread across her fair face as she took the walkie-talkie hanging on her belt. "Bring the car over," she said, just as quickly putting the walkie back on her belt and stepping toward me. "Wow, my dear, you have the most striking blue eyes. Just like Tristan's. And your hair,"—she grinned, marveling from the top of my head to the ends of my hair—"red and golden highlights. Defined lips, heart-shaped face. You have so much of him in you."

No. You're not his daughter. You're not supposed to be his daughter. Don't let her trick you.

"Okay," I began, grasping desperately at steadiness, "I know you think I'm his kid—"

"Emma," Jak whispered, pulling my attention. He quickly shook his head no, his fingers grazing my arm like he was trying to pull me behind him without touching me. "Don't engage with her."

The woman straightened, giggling. "I knew it. He likes you, doesn't he? I predicted that would happen—didn't I predict that would happen with this one, Jak?"

Confusion furrowed my brow. "Wait, you—know him? Personally?"

"Emma, don't—"

"I should." The woman nodded to Jak. "He's my stepson."

My jaw fell to the forest floor, breath stolen from me. I jerked my arm away from Jak and whirled on him. "Her stepson? You're a Grand Hunter's *son?*"

Jak held up his hands. "Let me explain first—"

"Hang on, did you *know* she was gonna meet us here? Was anything you said true, about you trying to warn me or prevent this? Is this how you—?"

The words snagged in my throat: *this* was how he'd found out about me. How he knew that my name specifically was on their list, what town I was in, my school.

"Emma, I promise, I didn't know she'd do this!" he exclaimed. "I can help because I know how they work—"

"'They'?"

Jak pressed his lips together like he was caging the words inside. I almost wished the bars had been strong enough when he said, "Alexa and my dad."

Alexa. Stepmom. His dad.

My ears had muted my own breath, in and out. I watched the last piece fall right into place, and it fit whether I wanted it to or not.

I blindly stared at the boy in front of me. He was a stranger all over again. "What's your last name?"

He gazed at me like it was the last time he'd ever see me. The enchantment his eyes had carried just seconds ago was gone. "'Bleu'."

I turned back to the woman and her pack of Grand Hunters, facing her fear-instilling gaze. "You're Alexa Delphine."

EIGHT

"**I want to make this as painless as possible,**" Alexa began gently. "If you admit you're Tristan's descendant, this will be so much easier, I promise."

"I'm not," I said. "I don't know why you think I am!"

Lie. That was a lie. Can she see that?

Alexa cocked her head again. "You know," she replied curiously, "everything else could just be a coincidence. If it weren't for your eyes, I honestly don't know if I would've assumed you were related."

Don't engage with her. That's bait.

I can make people instantly forget their entire lives (with and without magic), set the whole manor on fire in thirty seconds (with and without magic), and stop attempted burglaries by siccing a bunch of wild animals on the perpetrator (unfortunately, only with magic). Yet in that moment, staring back at Alexa with disbelief that this was really happening, I was silent. My greatest weapon had practically been stolen.

"Emmalynn," she said, her expression unexpectedly softening, "I get it, you're afraid. I don't doubt for a minute you've heard nothing but horror stories about suspects like you. I promise, though, that is all you're afraid of: those stories. You never thought that one day, *you'd* be put in the center of them. But if you help us figure out the truth about Tristan Atera, there's a chance you won't have to be put in those stories. You claim you're innocent, so let us verify that."

Jak's glare sent daggers, and I held on to mine for dear life even though I could bet my magic that Alexa could see right through me. I could bet that she knew she was spot on, about everything except me not being afraid of *them*—I was terrified of them. I was terrified of what they'd do after they found out that I was the only liar there. I was also tempted to throw Alexa fifty feet away, but that definitely wouldn't do any good.

This is actually it, this is happening, I realized. *They're gonna make me—*

Wait a minute.

"What're you trying to do right now?" I asked. "Because you can't just take me, that's kidnapping."

"Oh, believe me, we can if we have probable cause," Alexa replied, firming her tone, "which we do. You're one of our most wanted suspects right now. The *very* least we're allowed to do is take you in for questioning. And even a cop would arrest you for evading law enforcement if you tried to run away."

I wanted to throw them all back with telekinesis, knock them out with a sleeping spell, anything—but that was a death sentence in itself.

"*Arrest* her?" Anger bubbled in Jak's chuckle, and he spared himself a glance away to calm down. "The school's right behind us and her friends are about to come back. They'll just tell the headmaster and blow your cover if you take her now. You're not getting anything today."

Alexa sighed, her gaze lingering on the forest around her. Nature's peace seemed to present itself and warn her to obey. A black SUV was now pulling up a few yards behind her.

"Good choice of words," she said. "Not today. Take this as an introduction, then." She took one last look at me before turning around and walking to the car.

One of the men standing behind her stepped into her path, military-grade glasses obstructing half of his face. "Agent—"

"Today's not right," she stated. "We're leaving."

My breath stilled in my lungs. *What?* Had I actually just heard that?

Alexa moved past the agent, whose stare followed her. With one glance at me, an analytical gaze I could feel through those pitch-black lenses, he followed after his leader with the rest of his pack.

"See you later, Emma," Alexa called, shutting the passenger door shut. The SUV turned its tires, performed a U-turn, and drove down the main path.

Did she not come to grab me? I gazed after the car growing smaller and smaller. *Then why did she come at all?* Why would she let her target wander when I was right here for the taking? Sarah and Breanne were on foot while the pack was in a car; Alexa could have easily kidnapped me without blowing her cover.

Something's off, that wasn't supposed to happen. Not like that...

I held my breath until I was comfortable with the distance between us and the SUV. Staring intently at me in the corner of my vision, Jak seemed to be trying to read my mind. I almost wondered if he had the same questions I did until I remembered who he was, and then realized that he probably knew the answers. He most likely knew and he was going to keep them from me again. Apparently that was who he was. Now I knew, I knew I'd been stupid enough to trust him, just like I'd thought.

And yet, some part of me, some unjustified part of me, couldn't help but believe his sincerity. Like he really hadn't known anything about today.

"You..." I began, my breath out shaky. "You need to leave."

"I'm sorry, I am, I didn't—"

"I don't care," I cried, whirling on him. "I said leave! Go!"

I turned away like my looks could kill, which it really felt in that moment like they could. But Jak somehow knew I wasn't done, and he stayed right there while I fought tooth and nail to cage my tears.

"I was nearly kidnapped by top-secret agents a few seconds ago and I can't even tell you why I wasn't! Even worse, they were Grand Hunters. Even worse,"—my eyes stung, but my anger shoved down every emotion associated with weakness—"they were your parents! I don't even wanna know when your dad's gonna show up but I don't have a choice when I'll find out! So excuse me if you're the last person I wanna see right now—"

Padded footsteps turned us around, in the direction of the

school. Almost to my surprise, when I saw Sarah and Breanne approach like they'd just walked in on their parents fighting, I didn't run to them. I didn't run even though they should've been there the first time I'd heard footsteps. Now that they were, now that they'd shattered the nightmare and pulled me back into the real world, I wanted to move on and go back to normal.

"What happened?" Sarah asked hesitantly.

Right. "Normal" had been put to rest the second I'd stepped into the square last night. *This* was normal now. I was already walking in it.

I hugged myself in the forest's shade, refusing to look at the boy next to me. I couldn't bring the story to my lips, but I doubted Jak would sentence himself to another lecture by taking over.

"They found her," he answered.

I looked down at the ground to hide my surprise. *I guess he would.*

"What?" Sarah spat. "The Hunters? The *Grand* Hunters?"

"Yeah."

"Who's 'they'?" Breanne dared to ask.

Jak didn't have the courage for a few seconds, and I almost didn't blame him. "Alexa Delphine and William Bleu."

By how they both jerked into stillness, the words had struck Sarah and Breanne like a bullet. Neither had anything to offer in response, no movement, no reply. But it's easy to read their minds when their thoughts are aligned with mine: the family trees we'd done a cursory study of just the day before were never supposed to go beyond ink on a page. Yet now they were coming to life right in front of us, coming into *our* lives.

I was still too angry to look up at Jak when I told him, "And?"

The weight in his gaze in my peripheral threatened to knock me over. I refused it, making him turn back to my friends. "William's my dad and Alexa's my stepmom."

I waited for the satisfaction of hearing those words from his mouth and his alone. Knowing that he was willing to admit his darkest secret, that he could accept who he was in front of people despite his pre-given reputation, was what I wanted. I waited for the fulfillment, but a gaping hole remained.

Hypocrite.

He has no reason to hide it. I do.

Why did he hide it? Because he didn't want to be judged? Because he was scared of our reaction?

Because he didn't want to be punished for who he was?

"But you're here to *help* Emma?" Sarah asked with her hands on her hips, suspicion laced in her words and striking eyes.

"I promise, I am," Jak replied. He turned to me. "When I said I was involved in another case, I meant it, in a different part of North Carolina. I've been trying to help everyone on their list and make sure they're coming out of it okay."

"Why would you do that," Breanne asked quietly, holding herself, "unless you know who Tristan's descendant actually is?"

He shrugged, letting his hands fall to his sides. "Honestly, I don't even think he has one. I think this whole thing is a desperate plan to lure him out of hiding."

I looked down again to hide my swallow. I hated that. I hated that, according to all the stories Momma had ever told me about Dad, Tristan Atera *was* the kind of man who would turn the world upside down to find his son or daughter if he knew they existed. I hated that Jak was probably spot on.

I kind of hated that that meant I had a reason to believe him, after all.

I thought back on what had unfolded minutes ago, connecting it with Jak's visit in the first place. *Did* I have a reason to not believe him? Something was wrong with how Alexa Delphine had blatantly let her target go, but I couldn't help but feel like Jak was somehow partly responsible. Only he had the answer as to why, and I had to be patient for it. Being angry with him for not telling me the full truth sooner—when I knew what it was like to carry that kind of secret—was pointless.

My anger slowly but surely deteriorated. At least I finally had a better idea of how to feel about him.

"Okay." I shook my head. "This isn't... this isn't his fault. He warned us this would happen, we just weren't prepared."

Sarah and Breanne glimpsed each other, holding back their words like I'd punish them if they didn't agree with me.

"I guess," Sarah said to him, shrugging. "Then—thanks for trying to help."

Help. That word still raised a red flag when it regarded Jak because I still didn't know the why. He didn't think my dad had a descendant, fine, but anyone else would've let the authorities go ahead and prove an innocent suspect as such. What made Jak ambivalent toward what his parents did when an innocent suspect was almost never punished? Why would he go against them just to protect the people on their list?

"Well, now I'm extra sorry we took so long," Sarah said, exhaling and tossing her black hair over her shoulder. "Headmaster Dawson wasn't in his office when we went to get another pass."

I shook my head. "Not your fault. Let's just—"

"Wait," Breanne said, her grip around herself loosening. "If they came for you, how come—you're still here?"

I almost wished I had an answer to that, but maybe I could drag that one out of Jak, too: I turned to him.

"Okay, you have no reason to believe me," he said, holding up his hands, "but I really don't know. I told her to leave but I have no idea why she actually listened."

Why was today not "right"? What was the point of coming at all? Just to taunt me?

"That's comforting," Sarah said, rolling her eyes. "Are we even safe to go out, or do we just go back to the school?"

Silence passed a few rounds between the four of us. Yet again, we were left to look at Jak for the answer.

"She said 'not today'," he said. "I do know that means they won't try anything for the rest of the day."

"But why would Grand Hunters...?" Breanne whispered, narrowed blue-hazel eyes cast to the distance behind me. I almost wanted her to finish that question; out of the four of us, she had the best chance of figuring it out, but that would mean finding out how much time I had left before the pack came back.

"Correct me if I'm wrong to dismiss it," Sarah said, curtly exhaling, "but we only have two hours to pretend this doesn't exist, and we have all night to think about it."

She had a point; I had a feeling that the next two hours would be the only time I'd *be* allowed to forget about the situation. And if we were safe for the rest of the day, I wanted to take advantage of it.

I thought back to the restaurants in town that Momma and I had gone to while I was growing up. I needed something nostalgic, one last visit to my old normal.

"How about Waverly?" I asked.

Sarah scoffed. "The food is great, the play on words isn't."

She and Breanne closed the distance between us, and the four of us continued our walk through the forest. Jak and I made eye contact for a split second as the girls came up to my side. I was never able to figure out what he was really thinking unless he made it possible, which just made him all the more dangerous. Right then, though, he was allowing me to see another apology in his eyes. And sometimes silence is more convincing than words.

I gave him the reassuring look he wanted. Why was he so tempting to trust? Even Sarah and Breanne seemed to be having no trouble in that department.

"So, Jak," Sarah began a few steps into our walk, "you're a Redway Boy. That means you have roommates, too, right?"

"My best friends, actually," he replied. "They even know who my parents are, just not what's going on right now. Top secret, obviously."

"Right. Tell us about them."

Breanne nudged her for me. We knew where this was going.

Jak chuckled, yielding to Sarah's efforts. "Adrien's the oldest out of the three of us. We're just a self-defense school for now, too, but he's still pretty invested in the Hunter game. Blond hair, blue eyes, does water polo—"

Sarah gripped Breanne's arm to keep herself standing, placing a copper hand on her chest. "Oh, I'm sorry," she said breathlessly, "I'm a little dizzy."

In other words, Adrien was Sarah's exact type with an added bonus: he went to a top-secret ex-Hunter school like she did.

Jak went on, testing the waters. "Wyatt's in the middle, he prefers to stay behind the scenes. *Super* dedicated to school. He'll use his free time to work on some Python or study a couple of languages."

Whereas Breanne uses her free time to gather extra credit assignments. (If nothing's available, she gets permission to create them. She's a firm believer in "use it or lose it".)

"Python?" she asked. "I've always wanted to learn it but I've been putting it off until I can find—someone to do it with... Um, if he's interested in a study partner, that'd be nice, since neither of *you* are ever up for it."

Sarah giddily smiled at her from ear to ear. A "study partner" meant study sessions, which were the perfect breeding ground for budding romances—at least, that was where I knew Sarah's head was at.

The fact that that option was even on the table for Breanne now said something. She took a solemn oath freshman year to never let a boy have an effect on her again. To be more precise, to never let a boy escape the friend zone. Maybe she was just being polite, but my mind started wandering. If just the mention of Wyatt's name had poked a hole for Breanne, what had Jak already done to me? *Really* done to me?

NINE

Momma and I had spent a handful of mother-daughter dates at Waverly, and familiarity was exactly what I needed to soothe the remaining adrenaline. One of my favorite things about it is the atmosphere (if you consider painted beach walls, red vinyl booths, and coastal/fishing décor comforting). Here, it was easier to remember those times with Momma, when I could pretend I was just like my friends. When my biggest problem in life was figuring out long division.

And because she'd decided that being subtle was *not* on her agenda for today, Sarah took the spot next to Breanne in the booth before I could even open my mouth to ask who was sitting where. That left me with Jak on the other side. I would've telepathically scolded her for it, because I knew she could do a lot better than that, but mortals can't hear telepathy. At least service was fast and we had our food within the next fifteen minutes.

"Hey."

I looked up, another bite of my shrimp linguini Alfredo halfway to my mouth. The girl at the table next to ours had her arms crossed at her date.

"Theo. Did you hear me?" she asked.

I took my bite before stealing another glance. The boy's attention stayed glued to his phone, his thumbs flying across the screen in every which direction.

"Yeah, hang on, I'm so close to beating this guy."

"You didn't hear anything I just said?"

Sarah, in front of me, followed my gaze, leaning in. "I can't believe some people," she whispered. "You're on a *date*. I'd take that thing out of his hands and drop it into my water."

There's an idea...

"I said—"

"Kim, just wait, I can't pause this," Theo said, resting his elbows on the table.

She leaned back in her chair, silently huffing. "So much for 'never again'."

I looked back at my group. Sarah had gone back to her meal, Breanne's focus hadn't left hers, and Jak couldn't see my eyes with my head turned toward the couple. Nobody in the restaurant was looking my way.

I glimpsed the phone one more time, keeping my head down. *Calfacio.*

"Ow!" Theo yelped, flicking his phone up into the air and shaking his hands.

There was no time to whisper the telekinetic word in my head. I locked my eyes on the phone and dropped it into his glass of water. Overheating probably ruined it enough, but why take chances?

"No!" Theo cried, grabbing my group's attention. Kim covered her mouth, laughter shaking her shoulders, while Theo pulled his phone out of the water and dried it with his shirt.

"Oh, look." Sarah impishly smiled. "He was smart enough to do it himself."

"I'd feel sorry for you," Kim said, shaking her head, "but that was long overdue. We're done, have fun finding a replacement."

She stood, picked up her purse sitting on the floor, and strode out of the restaurant. Theo sat stunned for only a few seconds before running after her.

I mentally smirked, proud of Kim and myself. One of these days, maybe I'll get to thank Sarah for the idea.

Reaching the edge of the Callistro Forest off of Main Street, my stomach turned with my next steps: figuring out when to tell Momma about today. I definitely didn't want it to be as soon as tonight, but she'd probably ground me anyway for not telling her sooner.

There was no winning, and my natural instinct against that was to postpone punishment for as long as possible.

"Well, despite rocky beginnings," Sarah began, facing Jak, "it was nice hanging out and getting to know you."

"Same here." He shared a glance with the three of us before

waving. "I'll see you guys later."

Turning on his heel, he started his walk back in the direction of town. And as much as I wanted to, I couldn't ignore how those last words were true. We just didn't know *when* we'd be seeing Jak again, but right now, our two hours were almost up.

"Why do I feel *sorry* for him?" Breanne mused, pushing a blond lock behind her ear. "He almost felt... too natural."

Sarah furrowed her brows, but Breanne had my attention. "How does someone feel 'too natural'?" Sarah asked.

"Like he's a little too—ready for company, I guess. Because, yeah, he may be living with his parents, but is he living with his *parents*? You know?"

Her words gave me another piece of the puzzle about Jak, why he felt so easy to be around despite his position: he wasn't in a position he'd asked for, and it likely wasn't one he even wanted. If anything, he was trying to earn his place with us since it hadn't been given to him like his title with his parents had been.

"I think you're right," I told Breanne. "That actually makes sense."

"It's not like he's alone, he has Adrien and Wyatt," Sarah said casually, waving it off. "And us now. I think he's fine, he clearly doesn't enjoy being around his parents, so he probably chooses to be with his friends, anyway."

I had a feeling that Jak was the kind of person who only had company around if it approached him first. After all, he'd only come up me last night under pretty specific circumstances, but he seemed like a lone wolf otherwise. Maybe he enjoyed solitude as much as I did—and maybe he needed his friends just as much, too.

We have an uncanny amount in common.

Seconds of outdoor ambiance passed before Breanne turned to me. "Are *you* okay, Emmy?"

It was the first time someone had asked me that since I'd found out I had a Grand Hunter pack after me. I didn't have that answer for myself, let alone her.

"I'm not dead," I said, offering a small smile.

That answer sufficed for now, as my friends gave their agreement and then turned to the forest. As we started our walk back to the school, I allowed the comfort of silence to wrap around me for a few more seconds. All that had happened today had only been a day. It was day one of the school year, and my path had already been set. My fate was locked.

—*Adara.*—

What better cherry on top than hearing voices in your head?

—*Answer if you can hear me.*—

Oh, I could. But everyone can hear their own thoughts.

—*If you can't respond, follow my voice.*—

"Emmy?" Sarah called, breaking my head's trance. I looked up. She and Breanne were a few feet ahead, and I'd drastically slowed. "You good?"

I stepped forward, my senses igniting and setting off a mental alarm: my friends and the voice were taking me to the same destination. A magician was at *the Callistro Academy* trying to contact someone named "Adara"!

I almost dared to consider Momma as the one calling me but had to just as quickly dismiss her. The voice was so low that it... sounded male.

There was only one man I knew who had magic, but there was a 50 percent chance he wasn't even alive.

Why are they contacting me for Adara? How could they misdirect their communication?

I needed to investigate this. I wasn't the only magician at this school anymore, that was painfully obvious.

I pulled out my phone, opening my messages with Momma. "Hey, my mom wants to see you guys."

Sarah looked over her shoulder at me. "Us? Just us?"

I shrugged, hoping she could believe that I wasn't sure what Momma could want. She should believe it, because I really wasn't.

> **E:** We're about to get back to the school from lunch. Sarah and Breanne think you wanna see them, maybe something about an after-school training schedule because of the Hunter thing? I'll explain later, just keep them busy for a while

M: I'll try. Be smart and be safe.

Momma could do anything as long as it was to protect me. I had to believe that to keep my stress levels as low as possible.

She can do this. So can I. This magician was just like me, which meant that for once, I didn't have to be afraid.

I can always just knock them out with magic if things go south.

The rest of the way back was a comfortable blur until the air conditioning in the Grand Foyer struck me like an ice blanket. There was already a chill crawling down my spine from the fact that I was right on top of whoever was still telepathically calling me. I'd never been more anxious to say goodbye to Sarah and Breanne. I watched them walk down the left hall toward the gym before facing the Main Staircase. Except, the telepathic voice was leading me to the office past it.

Stepping across the crimson rug and up to the door, I could almost see the man sitting at his desk through the frosty glass.

—*Go ahead. Open the door.*—

So I did.

My school teaches you what to do when you're grabbed from behind in a dark alley and about to be drugged with a xenon-saturated rag or a syringe loaded with halothane. They don't teach you what to do when your mother has lied to you for your whole life about your godfather. They don't teach you how to stomach the fact that, even when you'd asked your mother directly if anyone else knew your darkest secret, she had answered with a lie. Momma had *lied* to me. About family.

"Shut the door." The headmaster of the Callistro Academy stood from his desk and walked to the center of the bright room. Ink and paper swarmed my nose, making it all the harder to breathe. "I think you know why nobody can hear this conversation."

Oh, right. He had lied to me for my whole life, too.

I closed the door behind me, refusing to take my eyes off him. *He* had been the one speaking to me.

"Thank you for coming so quickly," Mr. Dawson said next. "I know telepathy wasn't the best way to contact you based on how much you know, but it was the most discreet."

"Yeah, you..." I began weakly, afraid to speak, to even let my mind wander. Who *was* the man standing in front of me? "You said—why did you call me 'Adara'?"

"'Adara' is the name you're known by in the magic world.

Kind of like your cover."

My heart was beating too fast. Every breath I took burned my throat.

"Look, Emma," Mr. Dawson told me, gently holding up his hands. I was thankful he kept his distance; this conversation would be all the more intimidating if I had to stand right in front of the six inches he had over me. "I've seen your future. I've dreamed of many different possible futures depending on what path you take, but you have a specific destiny to fulfill, one that only you can accomplish. And I know that today you met one of your greatest enemies who'll stop at nothing to make sure you don't."

He had magic. He'd dreamed of the possible future, and he knew me by a different name—a name not even I knew—one that those of the *magic* world knew me by.

"You..." I said, my mind throbbing with the words. "You're a druid."

TEN

"Yes. I'm a druid."

I wasn't sure if I should lower my head, readdress him with a different title, or even apologize for all the times I didn't. Druids are a highly revered class of magic, wise beyond their years and able to dream of possible futures. They're relatively peaceful people and used to play a large role in problem-solving and decision-making in high courts and governments. They used to be *dominant* in those areas. No wonder everyone around Mr. Dawson seemed to inherently respect him. Those intense eyes and sharp features alone demanded respect.

"Has your mother taught you anything about druids yet?" he asked.

"Yeah," I said, trying to get feeling back in my tongue, "but..."

"I have time to answer all of your questions. Just ask."

Where do I even begin? The second he'd thrown this at me, my life as I knew it officially made zero sense! The pieces weren't fitting—I didn't know what I was supposed to ask or how to ask it.

"Why—I mean, if you know who I am, why did you keep it a secret? Does my mom know?"

I almost didn't want the answer to that; that would set it in stone that Momma *had* lied to me last night.

"Yep. She's known for almost as long as we've known each other—which goes back to high school."

Whoa, whoa, whoa, *high school?* Why, why would she—why would either of them—lie even about that?

"She wanted to raise you in an environment where you had to hide your magic no matter who it was. She figured it'd not only teach you how to keep your identity a secret even around people you thought you could trust, but also show her when you'd be ready for a responsibility like befriending Sarah and Breanne. I agreed and started pretending I was mortal the second you learned how to talk."

"But then how did you ever become friends? How did you know you could trust her?"

He put his hands in the pockets of his suit. "I actually knew your dad first. We were best friends. He introduced me to your mom a little while after I started having dreams about the two of them together."

"How did you meet him?"

"We were roommates at Redway Academy."

No way. Them? At Redway, *Jak's* school?

"I started having dreams of his future," Mr. Dawson said,

keeping my focus out of my mind, "of his future daughter and how he'd eventually go into hiding. Of course, he was under a false name back then so he could enroll in the school, so I didn't even know at first that he was an Atera. Those dreams were what told me who he was and that I could trust him: he was a sorcerer and I was a druid. We were allies with the same idea for a cover."

Did that mean that Mr. Dawson was the entire reason my parents had even gotten together?

He walked back to his desk and leaned on its edge. "We were classmates and friends before, but that secret bound us."

"So you just stayed close to the Ateras after that?"

"Oh, a lot more than that," he replied, smiling. "I married your parents."

My jaw fell slack. "*You*? You're ordained?"

"Yep. We told your mom on their wedding day about the visions I'd had of their future."

Uh oh. Knowing Momma, that couldn't have gone well.

"Wasn't she mad about—her husband going away?"

He rubbed his neck, pressing his lips together like he'd been caught. "I didn't tell her what would happen just before she'd find out she was pregnant. Frankly, I never told your dad he'd have to leave before you were born, either. I figured, what future parents would want to be told something like that?"

So my father had willingly given up all he had and would have for the sake of a family that hadn't even completely formed yet, even though he had no idea when he'd get to have it. Or if.

A new kind of ache pulsed in my heart. Some kind of grief for what he *should* have had.

"After he left," Mr. Dawson said next, "your mom and I stuck together as much as we could. Every time I came over to visit, I was telling her about Callistro, exchanging news regarding new bills and the updated laws, and updating her on what excruciatingly little I could get on Tristan's location. The last thing I ever found out was that he'd successfully fled the country when your mom was around three months pregnant with you. Since then... I've lost all contact."

My heart sank. Those answers were supposed to have been a semblance of closure regarding my dad, considering I didn't even know if he was alive, yet they'd left behind their own gaping hole.

I stepped away from the door, settling into the atmosphere of the room. Now I didn't have anything left in my arsenal except curiosity: "So, do you know for sure what's gonna happen in the future?"

He shook his head. "Druids never do, no. A single person's future has millions of possibilities. I could tell you this will happen if you do this, but you can do something else and it may or may not lead to a different route. That's how I know what you're meant for: you've taken multiple different paths in my visions, yet you end up at the same ultimate destination almost every time."

"Okay..." I said, nodding in understanding. The white sofas against the left and right sides of the room looked more and more tempting the longer I stayed standing, but sitting down during this conversation didn't feel like a respectful option.

"We can't see an entire scenario at one time, either," Mr. Dawson added. "It's all bits and pieces. But the more we learn and practice, the more we're able to see. Now I can see up to four consecutive seconds."

"It must be so comforting," I said, crossing my arms in

thought, "to know what to do to prepare for the future."

He pursed his lips, shaking his head. "That's not often the case. You can prepare all you want for the end of the world, but it doesn't make it any less tragic. Sometimes there's more comfort in what you don't know than there is in what you do."

I thought about it for a second. There were few ways I could've prepared myself for Alexa's visit today, if any at all, and I still would've been *petrified*. Maybe even more so. And in full honesty, I was still scared, but for the first time in my life, I didn't have to hide the real reason as to why.

Wow. I didn't have to hide who I was in front of Mr. Dawson anymore.

I took in a deep breath, trying to pick my next words. Mr. Dawson knowing I was an Atera had unlocked a hundred different conversations, ones that he wouldn't have time for until this weekend. I had to assume that Aunt Becca knew about him, too, then. She despised the idea of me even being a student here, let alone Momma working here, so there wasn't any way she trusted Mr. Dawson like family without knowing what he was.

Aunt Becca... Dad... today...

I lowered my gaze to the wooden floor. Mr. Dawson had said that he'd seen this day in his visions. He'd phrased it like it was the start of some kind of journey. A destiny.

"What am I destined for?"

He stood from his desk, crossed the room to me, and then gently lifted my head. His eyes alone now told a never-ending story of magic, of war, dragons, kingdoms, knights, entirely different worlds. At the same time, the longer he smiled down at me, the more his features softened into warmth and comfort—into the kind of gaze I'd always wanted to see from my father.

"Emmalynn, you were born as Adara, a daughter of magic. You are meant to help unite a place where the mortal and magic worlds become one and prosper in ways never before seen. You will be feared, hunted, betrayed, and adored, but in the very end, you will be recorded as the most powerful sorcerer to ever live."

Every word grew heavier in my ears and rang louder in my head. I could practically *hear* the dust prancing around us, dancing to the silence swallowing me alive. I could barely save myself from my newfound enemies, but now uniting the whole world was on my agenda?

I laughed at myself, shaking my head. "I'm sorry, wait, did you just say I'm the *chosen one?*"

I felt less ridiculous when he laughed with me. "No, you're not *the* chosen one. One person alone can't fix the mess humanity's made."

"But you said *only* I could fulfill that fate."

"Yes. Only you can fulfill your part in it."

"Mr. Dawson..." I began timidly, as if my confusion were my fault. "I don't get it. That doesn't make sense—"

"You don't have to understand right now," he told me. "But today warranted your introduction to this. You *are* growing up."

I scoffed, dramatically shrugging. "That's just it, I'm not even sixteen yet!"

"I'm gonna go out on a limb and guess you have at *least* a week to prepare."

He was joking, but I took every syllable coming out of his mouth to heart. In this conversation, he had the advantage while I was left at the mercy of his word.

I searched his eyes, begging for a different outcome. If he knew I wanted that, he refused to give it to me. Apparently, he really believed that I could handle this. I was growing up and increasing my power every day, now facing powerful enemies that were anything but fantasy because of a reason nobody else could sympathize with except Mr. Dawson. And Aunt Becca. Earlier today, I would've ended the list at just her—and then I realized how much I'd gained in this meeting with the headmaster.

"So what do you say?" he asked. "May I take over for your mom and mentor you?"

I blinked. "You?"

"That was always the plan until we'd tell you about me. She only knows so much. You need to strengthen your magic and know everything there is to know about it if you want even a remote chance at beating Grand Hunters."

"When would we be able to meet? What do I tell Sarah and Breanne?"

"Weekends are best, but I'd like to get in more practice. You should be able to get away with saying you're spending the day with your mother."

"Wait, you want to start *this* weekend?"

"No, I want to start tomorrow. Meet me in your mom's classroom at 3. The gym doors will be locked, so we'll have a warning if anyone tries to come in."

He walked to the door on the right side of the room. Opening it, he went inside and came out with a white clothing box, what Momma always wraps clothes in for Christmas presents.

"Nobody goes in my supply closet, so I knew this would be safe until I could give it to you."

I carefully pulled off the lid and placed it on the arm of the sofa. A black velvet cloak sat in the box, an elegant golden clasp with a small sapphire set in the middle gleaming at me. I gently picked up the cloak by the shoulders and lifted it out of the box.

"Wow," I said, sighing in awe. "This is beautiful, but—I don't know how often I'd need a cloak."

"When you're a magician, you need it a lot more often than you think," Mr. Dawson replied. "This cloak is enchanted. Once you put up the hood, you're completely invisible. I was planning on giving it to you for your birthday and telling you the truth then, but I wasn't expecting today to happen this soon. This'll come in handy, trust me."

The words struck me like a bell as he took the cloak and folded it up. I paused as he put it back into the box and placed the lid on.

"You said you dreamed of me meeting the Hunters today," I mused. "As in, you *knew* when you let me, Sarah, and Breanne go out today?"

He took a slow breath in like he'd been caught again, handing me the box. "I didn't know today was the day until Jak came in a few hours ago for me to approve his meeting with your mother. That moment was part of a vision I'd had where you met Alexa Delphine on the same day. That's why I hesitated when you asked to leave—I knew what you were about to walk into, but I also knew it needed to happen."

I snickered. "Mom would've never let me out if she knew."

"Exactly why I didn't tell her about today. But in most of my visions, you were never taken, so I had a little peace of mind. The only time you had been, you were alone. Sarah and Breanne being with you was why I was able to give you a pass."

Huh... Had Alexa really left just because Jak had told her to?

No. Something's still not right about that by a long shot.

I shifted my weight to one leg, my feet officially sore. "So when Sarah and Breanne came back asking for a second pass..."

"The only reason I didn't drive straight into the forest was because they said you were with Jak."

Things were starting to make a lot more sense. And okay, sure, knowing about Alexa's kidnapping attempt today might not have prepared me for it—but a warning would've been *fantastic.*

But when I looked back up at Mr. Dawson, the cloak box heavy in my hands, I remembered that I was looking at a new man. Better yet, a new ally. *That* present was invaluable.

"Wow," I said, exhaling a hidden sigh of relief. "Thanks, thanks for all of this. I... I needed it."

"I'll see you tomorrow," he told me, briefly squeezing my shoulder. "Don't worry about the future. Just come ready."

After a meeting like that, I was thankful to come back to my room before the girls; that left me a few more necessary moments I needed to finish digesting the last ten minutes. And to hide the invisibility cloak. (Sarah would only be *all* too curious if she ever found it.)

I'd just plopped down onto my bed when the door swayed open. In walked the girls.

"Hey, what did my mom say?" I asked.

"What do you know," Sarah chimed, taking off her sweater

as Breanne shut the door. "She wants to teach us extra self-defense moves and figure out an after-school training schedule for it."

I blinked, furrowing my brows. "Why would she wanna talk to just you guys about that?"

Sarah tossed the sweater onto her bed, then making a beeline for the bathroom dead ahead. Breanne shrugged behind her, wandering to the desk in the corner of the room.

"She wanted to run it by us first," Breanne answered, plopping down into the desk chair. "She didn't know if you were handling the whole... situation as well as you were letting on. But we told her you were doing well and could handle it."

Wow. Momma's good. And I bet the reason the girls hadn't told her that we'd already met said Hunters (evident by how Momma hadn't come bursting through the door with them) was because they wanted me to have the "honor".

I caged my frustrated sigh. *I still have to tell her that it's Alexa Delphine and William Bleu hunting me.* But when? The second she knew that my steps were being tracked every time I stepped outside, it was goodbye to the normal school life I *finally* had with going to an actual school. I'd spent my whole life living at my school until now. The last thing I wanted was to give that up after day one... I at least wanted time to figure out how to convince her that I'd still be okay going out. I just had to figure that out for myself first.

"We said yes, we wanna do it, obviously," Sarah added from the bathroom, pulling a brush through her long waves. "But you still need to tell her about today."

"I know," I breathed. I was pretty sure that the self-defense moves Momma had in mind were only meant to buy us time for escape, which is sometimes all you need to save your life. I was also pretty sure that I already knew them, considering self-defense had been part of Momma's homeschooled-sorceress coursework. But if she knew that not one, but two of the greatest Grand Hunters in the country were hunting her daughter? What if she'd lock me in my dorm for the rest of the semester for the sake of protecting me?

Maybe I could persuade Mr. Dawson to come with me for the conversation; maybe Momma would be so angry at him for keeping his visions about today a secret, she'd forget all about grounding me.

CHAPTER

ELEVEN

"Set!" Momma called the next afternoon, her voice echoing throughout the empty gym. The second day of school had been just as uneventful as the first, except for fifth period when Ms. Durrett took a phone call from her florist and was out in the hall for almost twenty minutes because there was a mix-up with the flowers for her wedding.

I wish that were my biggest problem right now, I thought, taking a deep breath and returning to basic position. Sarah, Breanne, and I stood side by side in the center of the gym, left foot forward, right foot back, fists up, and chins down. Our rubber dummies stood tall in front of us.

"Let's review," Momma announced, standing a few feet behind the dummies. "On my mark, combine all three moves you learned today. I want three reps. Ready...”

In all fairness, I’d been practicing my open hand strikes, jab-hook-uppercut combos, and scissor kicks with Momma in the backyard since I was ten. And yet, it felt like I’d learned them for the first time that afternoon when I practiced them on the dummies next to my best friends, like I had to perform it just as well, if not better, in front of them.

But we all had something to help us: Sarah with an inherent combination of grace yet aggression, Breanne with a physical inability of giving a performance worth less than an A, and me with the fact that (not to sound dramatic or anything) my life depended on me perfecting every move Momma had ever taught me.

“Perfect,” she said when we returned to starting position. “If you wind up face to face with a Hunter, these should at least buy you time to escape. Keep practicing so they get stronger and you don’t forget them if you actually have to use them.”

At least she said “if”—but I didn’t know if that was for my sake or Sarah’s and Breanne’s.

My phone vibrated against the wood on the table in the back. I followed Momma there while Sarah and Breanne took a sip from their water bottles.

Oh?

J: Sarah’s gonna love what I have waiting for
you guys at the park

“Jak texted,” I called, typing my reply. “He wants us to meet him at the park.”

“Do you really think going out alone is the wisest decision

right now?" Momma asked, pulling out her hair tie with ease and letting her chestnut hair fall to her bust. "Considering the whole reason we're doing these private lessons?"

Guilt curdled in my stomach. By the time I'd finished last night's homework, it was too close to bedtime to get Mr. Dawson and have the Delphine-Bleu conversation with her.

"We'll be fine," I assured her before Sarah or Breanne could accidentally expose me. "We'll be in a public area."

Momma took a swig from her own water bottle. "Fine, go. But let's do another lesson tomorrow, same time. And practice those moves when you get back later."

Her permission made me feel all the guiltier.

Upon going to Mr. Dawson's office for a pass, I realized that we'd have to make this a fast trip, anyway: I had lessons with him in an hour. With that now in mind, I started conjuring a list of potential excuses the second Sarah, Breanne, and I left his office.

I want to spend time with Mom? No, I'm gonna be using that one a lot, I should save it for when I really need it.

I want an afternoon to myself in the square—no, even they won't let me out alone after yesterday.

Dawson wants to see me in his office to see how I'm adjusting to real school—or is that more Mom's job to check in on? Never mind, they'll just as quickly find out we're not in his office.

I'm tired and need a nap. Yeah, that's good—except why would I nap somewhere that's not our dorm?

Okay, then maybe Momma would let me use her bedroom because I "don't wanna kick out Sarah and Breanne from our"—

"Is that who I think it is?"

Sarah's question pulled me straight out of my head. Across

the large green field, Jak stood in the white gazebo with his back to us. Two other boys roughly his height, one blond and the other with dark hair, were in front of him.

The blond noticed us first and pointed us out, promptly turning Jak around.

"Hey," he said as we walked up the steps. "This is Adrien and Wyatt."

"Very nice to meet you," Sarah replied with her runway-worthy grin, reaching out a copper hand to shake the dark-haired boy's—Wyatt's—hand. Taking Adrien's, she held on for a second longer.

His ocean-blue eyes *were* charming in color, and their rugged shape further elicited the bump on the bridge of his nose. "Likewise," he said, matching her smirk and rubbing his triangle jaw. "I'm a sucker for green eyes."

Whoa. That was fast.

"I'll let you know if I'll be willing to oblige that," Sarah simpered, releasing his hand and tossing her hair over her shoulder.

I glimpsed Breanne on my other side. Her doe-like eyes flickered between the boys but kept returning to Wyatt. His mono-lid dark-brown eyes stared softly after her as he pushed a hand through his shaggy black hair. He offered his other hand to her.

"It's nice to meet you," he said in a warm, clear voice.

"You, too," she said, giving her straight-line smile and hugging herself as soon as he released her hand.

He gestured loosely to her, tilting his head down. "Jak told me you wanna learn Python and you're kind of tech-savvy."

Sarah scoffed. "If you call shutting down the school's Wi-Fi for two days 'kind of' tech-savvy."

Let's just say, if Breanne hadn't, the three of us wouldn't be roommates. I don't even need to say who'd persuaded her to do it.

Breanne's pale cheeks flushed with pink, her thin lips stretching into a helpless, small smile. "And disabling the outdoor security cameras an hour before orientation last week."

Also true, and the Callistro security staff had only noticed because Amelia Baker asked why the cameras weren't on when we began the outdoor tour.

My gaze switched between the three boys, partial to Jak. "Yep. They had to scan our thumbprints every time we entered a different room."

"You make it sound worse than what it was," Breanne quickly said, dulling her eyes at me. "I didn't *mean* to, it just happened when I tried to sync the camera feed to my laptop."

"Impressive," Wyatt remarked, putting his hands in his back pockets. He arched a brow at Breanne. "Only made that mistake once or five times."

To my surprise, Breanne's smile grew—and so did her blush. "You're into white hat hacking?"

Which, she could only consider it white hat because she'd just wanted to make sure that security had "an extra set of eyes", and she swears that makes it totally ethical.

Wyatt gave a lopsided, shy grin. "Sometimes I dabble in gray, only if the situation calls for it."

"Like tracking down this genius sometimes," Adrien added, elbowing Jak beside him.

"Moving on," he said before Wyatt could open his mouth again. "In case you didn't already figure it out, these two surprised me this morning. They're here to 'visit'. I figured you guys would wanna meet."

"We wanted to go on a trip during the last week of summer." Adrien stuck his hands into his jean pockets with his thumbs out. "But then Headmaster Bleu took off suddenly and Jak left with him. Wasn't hard to piece two and two together."

"I'm sorry," I said, my eyes jumping straight back to Jak. "*Headmaster* Bleu?"

Sarah and Breanne joined me. I wondered how long it'd take to make Jak spill.

"Dude," Adrien said, lightly smacking his arm with the back of his hand, "they didn't know that?"

"No, because I didn't think it mattered." Jak innocently held up his hands again. "Before you hit me, just know I would've told you if I'd known it did."

His round eyes penetrated mine, and then they jumped to his friends before coming back. He either didn't want me saying anything else in front of his friends, or he had something to say that they couldn't hear. Either way, he wanted them gone.

"Okay, well," I began, turning around and taking the first step down the gazebo's stairs, "we have to be back at the school in an hour, so did you guys have any plans for after you found Jak?"

"Nope," Wyatt replied. "Just winging it."

"Do you"—Breanne peered up at him—"want to see more of Capperson?"

"Yeah, if you wanna show us." He smiled at her before gesturing to the steps. I stayed leaning against the banister as Breanne walked past, then Sarah, and then Jak's friends.

Jak stayed just behind me on the top step. "Give us two

minutes," he called out. Adrien and Wyatt gave an acknowledgment, whereas Sarah gave me a smirk that tempted me to run after and shove her for.

"Okay," I said, crossing my arms. "What don't you want them to hear?"

"That you're my dad's current target. It'll just complicate things. They'll wanna 'help out' when the only reason my parents aren't concerned about them is because they stay out of their business."

"And you're 'allowed' to stick your nose in it because you're their son."

"On the nose, Merlin."

I leaned against the support beam of the gazebo. "But they know your parents are Grand Hunters? And your *headmaster?*"

"Nobody else at Redway does because they're under a false name. That's part of the reason I didn't mention the headmaster thing—your only concern is William Bleu, not his cover story."

The main reason Hunter faces stay confidential no matter how big their name gets: they can assume whatever identity they want all the easier.

I stared after Sarah and Breanne, walking farther into the field and toward the sidewalk. "Then I should tell the girls not to say anything."

The longer I stared, the more vivid current affairs swirled in my head, the more theories accompanied the what-ifs and I-wonders. I thought back to another question I was pretty sure I didn't want the answer to, but curiosity has a talent for convincing us that the truth is necessary: "How many other kids have been suspected? Didn't you say you've been involved in a different case?"

"They've been to a lot of counties and checked out a lot of different kids…"

After a few seconds of silence, I looked up at Jak on the top step. He laughed at himself. "I involved myself in every case I could if I managed to find out who they were before my parents went after them. Like I did with you. Sometimes I got there in time, but I never saw them more than three times—they were ruled innocent, so the pack moved on."

"And I'm on the top of their list for here?"

He shrugged. "You'd be first on my list, too, but for different reasons."

I narrowed my eyes at him, the butterflies giving me the courage to lightly shove him. Thank goodness, he laughed.

I crossed my arms again, facing him completely when I saw Sarah and Breanne stop and start to turn around in our direction. "So when this is all over—dare I ask what they do to the kids when they rule them innocent?"

His shoulders rose as he inhaled. "Selective memory wipe."

I furrowed my brows. "That technology exists?"

"No. But the magicians do."

I forced myself to look back at my group so Jak wouldn't see me swallow. I was a Hunter's kid, too, I knew what that meant: extortion. Using a magician against their will for federal purposes, even if that meant that those magicians had to use their magic against their own people. I'd always known that that was a fraction of why the government hunted us down—but now, no matter how this ended, I'd have to face one of my people and witness their punishment firsthand. A punishment I was supposed to be carrying with them because I was one of them. I lost either way.

No—I don't lose like they do. They're *the ones who really lose.*

For the first time in my life, the burden of my people who were struggling felt as heavy as if it were my own. Sure, I *had* struggles, but I wasn't really suffering. Nowhere close in comparison. In that moment, as Jak walked down the gazebo steps with me, I'd lost the freedom of ignorance.

TWELVE

We made it back just before my lessons with Mr. Dawson (and Sarah and Breanne made it back with Adrien's and Wyatt's phone numbers), so I decided to wait in Momma's classroom with her until Mr. Dawson showed up. As much as I hated to admit it, I could see where she was coming from regarding why she'd lied to me about who he was. I mean, I *did* know how to keep a secret now, and a large part of that was because of how Momma had raised me.

Or maybe it was easy to tell myself that I understood because it alleviated the guilt of not telling her about Alexa Delphine and William Bleu.

Well, it didn't matter: when I opened the door, there were already two people waiting for me.

What? I'm not late.

Except, by the way Momma was scowling at me from her desk, her chin resting on her locked-together hands, I was in trouble. Just not for being late. I never earn *those* fiery eyes just because of that.

I looked at Mr. Dawson standing in front of me: arms crossed, sharp features restful like he'd just released every last secret weighing him down—

No. He didn't.

I opened my mouth right as Momma hissed, "Why didn't you tell me you met Alexa Delphine yesterday?"

I can't believe he did it. Without me!

As if Mr. Dawson weren't in the room, I shut the door behind me and faced Momma in full. "I was gonna—"

"Why didn't you?"

"Because I was scared of how you'd react! I was waiting for the right time—"

"When did you ever think there'd be a 'right time' to tell me something like that?"

A bolt of anger made me gesture to Mr. Dawson. "I guess the same 'right time' you were probably thinking to tell me about *him* after my whole life!"

It was the first time that week I'd allowed my anger to engulf my rationality. And I braced myself, because Momma was the *last* person I should've felt safe doing that with.

"You don't get to use that," she stated, straightening in her seat and making me shrink back. "He told you why we *both* chose to hide it. This is about you, *your* safety, it's about my job as your mother to protect you from that kind of threat!"

She side-glared at Mr. Dawson. Good. I wasn't the only one at the mercy of her wrath; I didn't want to be alone in that.

"I ask you again," Momma said, turning her hard amber eyes back to me, "why didn't you tell me?"

I waited until I could trust myself to give an even tone. "Because of that."

"What?"

"Because..."—I glimpsed Mr. Dawson like he would give me the rest—"because it's your job as my mom to protect me from things like that, and I'm not ready to go back to being trapped in my home day in and day out again. Any time you and I went out, it had to be together so you could keep an eye on me. You barely ever let me go out by myself when I was growing up. I know why, but—I didn't wanna have to give that up so soon when I just got here. Once you found out about Alexa, you'd probably never let me leave the manor again. I'm sick of *living* at my school."

"Em..." Now Momma stood from her black chair, stepping around her desk. "Fine, you have all that right, but—I can't..." Her mouth stayed open, but only her breath escaped. Multiple tries to speak eventually led her to look at Mr. Dawson for help, too.

"Another reason I kept Alexa from you," he said, strolling closer to the whiteboard. "You'd just found out that Emma was being hunted at all and told me that you'd try to keep her in the manor. But you know painfully well that hiding a Grand Hunter's prey would do no one except Caldwell any favors."

"It's instinct, Thomas," she said, exhaling. "What do you think will happen when I send my sorceress daughter into the government's open arms?"

"You'd only take the longer route by locking her up here."

"I—"

Another sigh cut Momma off, and she rested her forehead on her hand. Believe it or not, up until that day, I'd never seen *this* from her before: her mother side and Hunter side clash. They usually helped each other out, but if anything, now they seemed to be... suppressing each other.

I wished I knew what to say; there was no winning either way, for either of us.

"We'll set aside a time to plan what to do later," she said lowly, "because that's going to be a long conversation, and Emma needs to strengthen her magic in what excruciatingly little time we have before the pack shows up again." She turned her attention back to me. "I don't want you to miss the point of this conversation: you kept vital, critical information from me. I understand why, but I need *you* to understand how important it is for you to be honest with me about these things. The sooner I know, the sooner we figure things out. Understood?"

It was like she knew the *other* thing I was storing in my back pocket: Jak's last name. And that was completely different from telling her about the specific Grand Hunters. Momma could at least come with me if I picked the right moments to go into town, but she would flat out bar me from even looking at Jak ever again if she knew whose son he was. The worst part was that I under-stood why, but that didn't mean she'd be completely right in her judgment about him.

"Now I'm going to ask you something,"—Momma stepped away from her desk, her heels clicking on the tile with unnerving authority—"and I need your full honesty about it. Did you find out Jak's last name yesterday?"

Seriously?! Mr. Dawson's visions *had* exposed it.

Unfortunately, lying to a Master Hunter is like signing your death warrant, and lying to your ex-Master Hunter mother is like helping her dig out the spot for your casket: "Yes. And I didn't tell you yet because he's a friend and I really feel like I can trust him."

In the corner of my vision, Mr. Dawson observed the two of us like he was taking mental notes for a mission. (I wouldn't have been surprised if he were, considering he'd been a Master Hunter before becoming headmaster.) But I kept my focus on Momma, who slowly shook her head, eyes mindlessly fixed in front of her.

"Em. His entire family is composed of people who want to *kill* you. In fact,"—she scoffed—"they would've already if they had any solid evidence that you're Tristan Atera's daughter. You realize that, don't you?"

"You've seen it yourself," I said, "Jak isn't like them. And Redway's dormant right now, it's not like *he's* being trained to be a Hunter."

"Like how magic is illegal so you're not being trained to strengthen yours?" she shot back. "Nobody knows what you really talk about with me in here or your magic lessons, nobody even knows what you've spent your entire life doing inside the house with me! We never know what Jak is really doing when he's not with us, when he's with his parents. You just *don't know*."

Pressure mounted in the back of my eyes. Maybe it was my pride saying I did know, maybe it was raging teenage hormones telling me I knew better, but all I had on my lips was an argument.

Momma took another step first. "I'm only telling you this because you need to realize that in full before you trust *anyone* and add them to your circle of friends. Before you meet someone who's actually your enemy."

I paused. Who was *actually* my enemy?

Momma nodded, acknowledging my unspoken question. "Mr. Dawson used a truth spell on Jak and verified his sincerity when Jak came by to approve his visit with me."

A weight fell straight off my shoulders and crashed to the floor. I *could* trust Jak. He did want to help.

But why? That vicious question came back for another round of haunting. Why would a mortal help another "mortal" suspected of being a felon? All of these kids he knew nothing about?

Then, I froze—because why hadn't *I* put Jak under a truth spell yesterday? Why hadn't I felt the *need* to? I'd put so much automatic trust in him because of everything, because of how he just had a quality that lulled me into faith, that the thought had never even come to mind...

Okay. Momma and Mr. Dawson had a point. The weight had *partially* fallen off.

"But again, you kept that from me," Momma said next. "We could've figured something out together and fast. And I could've told you this as advice instead of a lecture."

"I just figured," I began, turning to the closest desk and plopping down in it, "he's had *more* than one opportunity to turn me in and hasn't. I didn't want to judge him based on who his parents are. Isn't that the whole narrative magicians are fighting? That we're not evil just because of what everyone assumes about us?"

"I know you're not in training," Mr. Dawson said, leaning against the whiteboard, "but one of the first things you learn as a Hunter is knowing when and where to establish trust. Logical trust like that will get you killed. Until someone has a personal reason to be your ally, there is absolutely no real reason to trust them."

Something didn't sit right with me about that. It touched on Jak, but it didn't align.

"Can't someone have a personal reason and we just don't know what it is?" I asked.

"Sure," Momma replied. "But until we do, in essence, they don't have one. And we need to treat them that way until they do."

"But I'm not the only one," I said, pointing at myself. "All Jak's *been* doing is helping the suspected targets, I'm just next."

"And then there's just the basic principle," Momma said, drawing to a close. "We don't take chances when it's life or death."

Mr. Dawson nodded his agreement. Despite being Momma's boss, it was like he respected this room as her territory, where she ruled and he couldn't overstep.

"So please," she told me, "he may be sincere, but that doesn't make him any less dangerous. He can't control his parents. Be careful."

"Okay," I said simply.

Just as I feared, silence fell over the cold room as quickly as the word had left. I didn't know if Mom or Mr. Dawson felt the awkwardness, but I didn't want to be the one to break it and make it worse.

"Okay," Mr. Dawson echoed, clapping his hands together. "Who's up for lessons?"

I should've been jumping out of my skin to practice my magic, especially at that point. I want to say that I would've been had it not been for our previous conversation: all I could remember now was the main reason I had to do these lessons at all, the reason Mr. Dawson was my mentor now and not Momma anymore. Alexa was intertwined with every aspect of my life now, and I was tangled in a net of paranoia. Mom was right: how were we a match for a federal mission when we couldn't run away from it or run to it? And during the time I wasn't defending myself with it or learning how to strengthen it, magic had to be my enemy from now on. I didn't have it anymore in the way I'd always had.

For the first time in my life, I felt... like I had nothing underneath me anymore.

C H A P T E R

Thirteen

The dim light of the cold alley glared against my vision. I saw myself sprinting to the brick wall at the end that I'd eventually hit, yet it stayed the same distance the farther I ran.

Footsteps behind me slammed against the pavement. They weren't mine, and knowing that pushed me forward.

"Emma! Stop!"

I whirled around. A man ran straight through the darkness and toward me in the lit part of the alley. The terror carved on Mr. Dawson's face spun me back around, warning me that whatever threat that had drove him to me was just behind us.

I forced myself forward despite the strange force against my legs, frightened by his feet banging on the ground. He caught up to me and firmly gripped my shoulders, his fingers tight with fear.

"I know you're scared," he said breathlessly, "but you're fine, I promise. Nobody knows, Emmalynn, do you hear me?"

Another figure appeared from the shadows behind him, her steps desperate: Momma.

"She's behind me!" she exclaimed, glancing over her shoulder and then back at me. "What are you doing, *move!*"

"Get away from her. Now."

The firm yet melodic voice echoed down the alley, carried on the cold, humid draft that blew down with it. It whispered a shiver down my spine, froze the blood in my veins and glued my feet to the concrete.

"I said now."

Alexa stood on the other side of the alley with a group of Hunters behind her. I tried a glare, but my fear resisted the mere attempt to control my own muscles. Alexa stared back, shattering whatever ignorance I had left. That woman knew when she'd won, even in a dream. And right now she knew everything there was to know about me.

"It's either her,"—she dragged another person out from the shadows by his collar—"or him."

I stumbled right into my mother's and Mr. Dawson's arms.

"Amy," my father cried. "Our daughter, don't let them take our daughter!"

I'd seen my father in my dreams before. I'd lived seconds of semblances of an average life with him, as if all were right with our world and magic didn't exist and he had no reason to abandon our family ever again. I'd felt his touch, felt his hugs and warm gazes, even though I'd never been rewarded with any of that in real life. I'd only ever seen him in front of me in a dream.

I think that was what told me it was a dream. That was why I had the courage to scream in my head, *Ite procul!*

The people in front of me flew back, far away, even Momma and Mr. Dawson. Safe from their presence, their touch, I spun around and ran down the alley.

The more desperate I grew, the more it felt like I was running underwater. But I didn't stop. I ran from, in perfect honesty, what my real life had become, things that I prayed would dissipate into thin air: Alexa, the pack, the fact I'd probably never feel the solid touch of my father, everything I hid from the world. The alley never ended.

This is a dream, the real me thought. *It's just a dream*, the dream me thought. *It's not real, stop it!*

"Emma!" another voice called. Familiar. "It's okay, we know now! Wait!"

Only two people followed me now, and their voices were an unnerving familiarity. I'd never pumped my arms and legs faster to escape my best friends.

"Stop! We forgive—!"

Dormio!

At the sleeping spell, Sarah's and Breanne's voices ceased. I kept running. I kept disobeying. I was close enough to reach the end but never close enough to touch it.

You were never supposed to know. You'd turn me straight in—

In a blink, the world around me shut off. My breath echoed in my head and ears, but I never heard them escape. The pressure in my head muffled whatever sound my ears picked up. My heart beat like a rabbit's against my chest.

I wasn't dreaming anymore—but I wasn't awake. I was conscious, but I wasn't back in my room. I wasn't dreaming. This was real. The pitch-black darkness was real. Wasn't it?

A blurry world faded into view, a migraine throbbing in my head. The cold metal of handcuffs rested against my wrists and ankles, clinking with the hard metal of the chair I sat in.

How did I get—?

White walls blinded me as I came to. Even the black carpet below me was so deep that it threatened to swallow me whole.

My view flashed to a different angle. A man now stood in front of me. With my hearing still muffled, every word he said was practically buried under the carpet. A trolley sat beside me, yellow files stuffed with formal documents and printed pictures scattered across the surface. Small jars full of blue fluid accompanied them. Next to those were syringes.

The man's words crescendoed into clarity. "...difficult target," he said, like we'd been talking the entire time. "Do you understand why we had to resort to this?"

I met his familiar brown eyes—why were they so familiar? "'Difficult'?"

The scene flashed again. I was violently shaking my wrists and ankles, somehow knowing what was to come and angry at myself for not knowing how to prevent whatever it was.

"—in that," the man said, an annoyed scowl sitting on his triangle face. "I'll let you go if you tell me the truth—"

My world flashed.

Silent cries shook my body as I watched the man fill a syringe with the blue fluid. I was trapped.

"No," I exclaimed, desperate for him to obey, "no, no, NO—!"

Another flash. The man bent down and grabbed my chin, but I jerked away.

Flash.

"What do you know?!" he shouted, his fingernails digging into my jaw. "I'm not letting you go until you tell me—!"

My world blacked out. I don't remember the rest of his words. I don't remember a prick from the syringe. A faint ringing pierced my head like a needle pulling a thread along. Seconds later, sharp whispers sliced the air.

"Emma!" they snapped as the gift of reality finally and slowly faded back to me. "Wake up!"

Get up, get up, wake up—

"Emmalynn, wake up!"

I shot up, eyes wet and dried tears cracking on my cheeks. Through the dark, my eyes found and focused on the two figures beside my bed.

Sarah and Breanne. I was safe.

Breanne sat beside me, wrapping an arm around my shoulders. Sarah took the spot in front of me with a hand on my knee.

"You were crying!" she whispered-exclaimed. "What happened, what's wrong?"

I opened my mouth, but the words hitched in my throat. I couldn't tell them. They couldn't know that seeing Tristan Atera in my dream was like a truck ramming head on into me because he was actually my dad. They couldn't know that the second dream was only so traumatic because it hadn't been a dream. I'd never dreamt anything like that before, never anything so surreal and awake and... powerful. There was only one thing I knew about it: whatever it had been, it was probably straight up Mr. Dawson's department.

Something else these girls couldn't know.

"I had a nightmare," I whispered, rubbing away the tears under my eyes, "about Alexa finding us and doing all these tests. I was scared—of getting hurt. And never seeing anyone again."

Sarah leaned forward and hugged me. Even hours into the night, her sweet, airy perfume refused to fade, wrapping around me like she was. "We're right here. See? We're still here."

"I know." I exhaled, looking down at my comforter that the darkness painted black. "I'm okay, thanks."

Breanne gave me a consoling shoulder squeeze before following Sarah back to bed. As soon as the squeaking springs and shifting blankets fell quiet from both beds, I jumped into action:

—*Mr. Dawson?*—

I had minimal telepathy experience because Aunt Becca hadn't exactly been an easy option for target practice back when she lived in Charlotte over an hour away, and I never had any other magician to talk to. I could only pray I was doing it right as the seconds ticked by.

—*Are you telepathically communicating with me?*—

That actually worked!

And he's awake? At this hour?

—*I hope I am. I'm so sorry, but this is important.*—

—*Well, congratulations. Okay. I'm guessing you have questions about that dream.*—

He already knew?

—*First of all,*— he said, —*it wasn't a dream. That was my vision.*—

My heart dropped to the center of the earth. That meant there was a decent chance that my nightmare was actually going to happen sometime in the near (hopefully very, very far) future.

I tried to gather my next few thoughts and keep them at the front of my mind, wondering what I could ask that Mr. Dawson could answer. And what I could ask that wouldn't freak me out to the point of never getting back to sleep.

—*That was one of your visions? How was I able to see it?*—

—*Druids can share their visions. I've been having that one since the beginning of August. I just had to wait until you knew about me and had met Alexa so it'd be easier to digest, for lack of better words.*—

I exhaled as quietly as I could even though Breanne was on the other side of the room and a smally snoring Sarah lay between us. This year was already the furthest thing from how I'd imagined it would be (and wanted it to be). If I wanted things to change, it was going to take my blood, sweat, and tears; nothing would change it for me.

—*So there's... a chance that it'll happen?*—

—*Operative word is "chance".*—

—*You realize how that's the furthest thing from comforting, right?*—

After a few moments passed, I almost wondered if I'd accidentally disrespected him somehow. I started thinking of ways to apologize when he said, —*After our lesson today, I want you to meet someone. She lives right here in Capperson and can tell us more. Are you up for it?*—

—*I guess, if we can make it quick.*—

—*We will. Just get some sleep until then.*—

Operative word *there* was "try". Knowing that my first dream hadn't been a vision gave me little relief, but if I'm being honest, a fleck of disappointment barreled in with it. Because, well, I'd seen my dad as my dad. Not as Tristan Atera. Not as a man wanted by the U.S. Government. But as a man who'd been used as bait so his enemies could grab his daughter. And he'd known that I *was* his daughter. I couldn't help but wonder what would have happened next if the vision hadn't interrupted it, if I would've dreamed living with both of my parents, with my family as a whole.

Sinking into my mattress, I realized that I was still telling myself to wake up. Nobody ever tells you that sometimes, only sleep can help you escape some nightmares.

C H A P T E R

FOURTEEN

Her name was "Ingrid", and she lived in the quaint neighborhood on the other side of town. Momma and I drove off campus to meet Mr. Dawson there. She chose to stay in the car for some reason, so it was just me following Mr. Dawson inside the duplex.

He'd already warned me that, despite how she stared at me now with dark-brown eyes, Ingrid was blind. That didn't inhibit her full-lipped smile, accompanied by her perfectly straight spine. Her dusty-rose blouse perfectly complemented her umber skin, and I kind of wished she was able to look at herself in the mirror.

"Emmalynn," she said in a sonorous voice, setting her white cane down next to her against the loveseat, "it's lovely to finally meet you. You'll have to tell me your story sometime."

"Finally" meet me?

"Have you heard about me before?" I asked.

Her gaze slightly shifted to somewhere not quite me and not quite Mr. Dawson. "In a few words."

I glanced at him next to me on the couch, who shrugged like he didn't need to elaborate on that. Sooner or later, I'd have to interrogate him on exactly how much he knew about me and how much of it he'd told other people.

I turned in my spot, better facing Ingrid. "Mr. Dawson said you could tell us more about his vision, like... if it's definitely gonna happen."

"Yes, I can."

"How? Aren't druids' visions just possibilities of the future?"

"Ingrid isn't a druid," Mr. Dawson said, the corner of his mouth lifting. "She's a seer."

I had pretty little prior knowledge of seers. Unlike druids, they could see the *definite* future, and they're all born blind—

Oh. So that's not *a coincidence.*

"Got it," I said.

"Yep." Mr. Dawson nodded. "While I have previews of possibilities, she can tell you inevitable and definite aspects."

"I can tell you bits and pieces," Ingrid added, folding her hands in her lap, "as well as outcomes, but they're vague. It's a tricky puzzle that demands energy and power, and it's not easy. And if you truly want to know..." She shifted her weight, casting her eyes down to the coffee table in front of us. "The price of knowing the future is great. One of you must pay it, and you must do so willingly, or the person who will be most affected by what I tell you will automatically take your place."

"I'll pay it," Mr. Dawson said, almost cutting her off.

"Mr—"

"Go ahead, Ingrid." He went on like I wasn't even in the room. What kind of price was this...?

"You're absolutely sure, Thomas?" Ingrid asked. "There is no turning back, you know this. And there's definitely no refund."

"I'm sure," he said, still refusing to look at me.

Seconds passed before she inhaled and closed her eyes. I stilled, holding my breath so she couldn't hear it. She must have been gathering her energy to enact her seer magic.

I wish sorcerers had a power unique to just them like every other class of magic.

When Ingrid's eyes opened, streams of glowing amber flowed through her irises like a surging river. "Emmalynn, what you witnessed last night will come to pass as punishment for rebellion in a place of freedom and familiarity. This night will permanently alter and shape your course with Alexa Delphine. Your fear will overcome you, and your fate will escape your lips and yours alone. It will be the first step toward your ultimate destination, where your greatest enemy will reveal herself and your full power will manifest. Listen to my warning now: do everything you can to fight the strength of your fear and alleviate your punishment."

She closed her eyes again, exhaling, but her words had my mind in chains. A force field had surrounded it, preventing all thoughts from penetrating, all except one: that nightmare would come true and I had no when. I couldn't stop it! And my fate would escape my lips? Did that mean I'd reveal the truth? To Alexa? How? Why? When?!

Denial was swift to harden my heart, trying to convince me

that somehow and in some way, Ingrid was exaggerating—using big words and eloquent speech to confuse me, something! The chance of me confessing the truth was about the same as my father showing up on our doorstep tomorrow. Alexa couldn't force me to use magic before she ran her tests, anyway. And until I found a way to completely hide my magic, I couldn't let her catch me.

"Emma?" I heard Mr. Dawson say. "Are you okay?"

I shook my head, heat radiating off of my cheeks. A quiet ringing hummed in my ears. I almost wanted to stay right where I sat and lull myself with it.

"Okay…" Mr. Dawson whispered, standing. "Thank you, Ingrid. This was really helpful. We'll get going."

Tiredness and shock pulled down on my body, but I forced myself to stand up with Mr. Dawson. "Thank you," I told Ingrid softly, warily glancing into her eyes that weren't even raised to mine. I turned and followed Mr. Dawson across the living room, into the entry foyer, and out the front door.

"Everything she said," I began after closing the door, stepping down the concrete steps, "is for sure gonna happen?"

"A seer can only prophesy what will," he answered. "She doesn't know *exactly* when events will happen unless it's revealed in her visions, but at least now we know what the future holds. That's all we can really ask for right now."

I stayed silent. Ingrid's words were still ringing. Literally ringing.

"Emma. Your phone's ringing."

"What?"

The vibration in my back pocket finally reached through the fabric of my jeans. At least the cheery, melodic ringtone told me who it was and I could answer with some kind of relief.

"Hi, Emmy," Sarah sang on the other line. "What would you say if I told you that my mom made plans for my family to go out of town this weekend?"

"And if I said my dad wants us to visit my aunt in Charlotte this weekend," Breanne added, "because she's leaving for Hawaii on Monday?"

I wish she could take me with her to Hawaii.

I faced Mom's car parked in front of the house, along the curb. "I'd say I hope you both have a great time, why?"

"We just wanted to make sure," Sarah said. "We didn't really know if it was best, with everything going on…"

The dorm all to myself for the weekend while I was still waiting for Alexa to make her next entrance?

Oh. That makes sense.

"No, it's fine!" I told her. "My mom and Mr. Dawson will be here, I don't mind staying inside the school this weekend."

Mr. Dawson walked a little past me as I slid my phone back into my pocket, then turned around. "Was that a free opportunity I heard?"

"What opportunity?"

"To practice your magic for hours on end without needing to make excuses to anyone—"

"*Hours?*"

"We'll negotiate later," he said, gesturing for me to follow him to Momma's car.

The nerves burned alive in my chest as I obeyed and he opened the passenger door for me. It was time to face the inevitable from my mother: her request for the truth. And, well, I really wished I'd prepared something *before* climbing into the car.

"So? What did Ingrid say?"

I put on my seatbelt to avoid eye contact and took advantage of my rolled-down window: "Mr. Dawson will tell you."

He snickered, leaning against the car. "Nice try."

This was punishment after I'd kept Jak's last name and Alexa from them. It had to be.

"What does that mean?" Momma asked, glancing back and forth between us with a worried pinch in her brow. "What did she say?"

I lightly exhaled and abandoned all optimism, leaning back in the passenger seat. Fine—Mr. Dawson had already paid one price, so this one was mine. I'd already planned on grounding myself to the school for the weekend, anyway.

"The vision's gonna happen and change everything. And that's all she knows."

The glove compartment in front of me kept my gaze, and I cursed the silence swallowing us. Mr. Dawson stayed beside my rolled-down window, waiting for Momma's response. Nothing ever came.

I had to look at her to see why: with red eyes, she gazed at me like it was the last time she would ever see me.

Then, she hugged me.

What is going on?

"I'm so sorry," she whispered. "I'm so sorry."

Okay, something was off. Momma had been apologizing to me ever since Alexa had debuted. Scratch that—ever since she'd found out about the magazine. Did she actually think she was supposed to have control over any of this? Did she really blame herself when she was the entire reason I was even alive?

Why was Momma sorry about this?

"Amy," Mr. Dawson whispered, making a special attempt to focus on her alone, "we should head back."

She let go of me, wiped under her eyes, and then placed her hands on the steering wheel. "Come talk to me when we do."

Maybe he knew what it meant, because he pushed himself off the car, walked to his, and climbed in. Was she angry at him now?

Why couldn't I read my mother anymore?

FIFTEEN

A lot of students were checking out for the weekend, and I wondered what everyone had planned for the next two days. Specifically the Grand Hunters out for my blood.

I wonder what Jak is doing this weekend. Probably hanging out with his friends. I almost considered asking him had it not been for Momma and Mr. Dawson finishing their short, quiet conversation and then taking me to her classroom.

After sitting me in a front-row desk, they stood at the front of the room just like class on a school day.

"All right," Mr. Dawson began, holding up a piece of paper with Latin scribbled from top to bottom, "this is a list of everything you need to learn as soon as you possibly can."

"In *two days?*" I asked flatly. "To defend myself against Alexa?"

"Of course we don't expect you to learn all this by then," Momma said, leaning against the whiteboard. "But as soon as possible, yes. Nothing from here on out is going to be 'easy' like it was for you before. These spells require more of your magic and focus. Understand?"

"Yes, ma'am."

"Good." Mr. Dawson set the list down onto Momma's desk. "Because I also want to get you to start primarily casting in your head so you're not inhibited by speech when you need to use magic."

Oh no. Even Momma had tried to teach me this a few times throughout the years, but I never had the best success rate except with telekinesis, but that's the most basic spell. Casting in your head *sounds* easy—until you realize it's like explaining the taste of water.

"Think about this," Mr. Dawson began. "Why is telekinesis so easy to cast in your head?"

"I've..." I said slowly, like this was a trick question, "always known it. It's just easy to feel, I guess."

Mr. Dawson nodded in satisfaction. "Exactly. You *know* it, and you feel it. The more you practice your magic, the easier it is to cast silently, isn't it?"

"Yeah."

"That's because fully understanding what you're going to do is the foundation of every spell you cast. It's where you're able to feel your power escaping from you onto your target."

I've always found it interesting that spells are called "spells" when they're all just a Latin word empowered by magic. Mages assign their effects, being the only ones who have the power to create and destroy spells, and their power is connected so they know what does and doesn't already exist.

Again, why were sorcerers left out of the "special power" gang?

Mr. Dawson opened one of Momma's desk drawers and took out two Styrofoam cups. "Let's try a few experiments. These are your targets." He walked to my desk and set the cups down next to each other. "With this first cup, cast something that's slightly more advanced than telekinesis."

Fire was probably a safety hazard, but I could do its opposite. Just not in my mind... yet.

I locked my eyes on the cup and repeated Mr. Dawson's words in my head. I knew exactly what I wanted to do, and I knew how to make it happen.

Congelo.

That didn't work.

"Again," Mr. Dawson said when I looked up at him, crossing his arms. "Remember, just telling yourself the word has no power on its own. Don't just *know* what you're casting, but feel it."

This time, I not only focused on what I wanted to do, but also what I needed to make it happen. My magic was there, it was flowing from my very heart, and I commanded it.

With a steady breath in, I released the pressure. *Congelo.*

A thin filigree of ice embarked from the place my eyes were glued on. It spread across the Styrofoam all the way until it reached the inside of the cup, swallowing it in a chamber of ice.

"Great job." Momma nodded and smiled in approval, hands on her hips. Neither of them seemed impressed, but all I cared about was how I'd actually done it.

"That was kind of easy!" I said, straightening in my seat with excitement. "What about the other one?"

"Try something a bit more difficult," Mr. Dawson replied, "and get a more accurate judgment of how 'easy' this really is."

The last new thing Momma had taught me before we moved to Callistro was obliterating an object into a hundred pieces and then putting it back together by reversing the spell. Obliterating it was medium. Reversal of a medium spell was another ballgame.

First, I tried destroying the cup. *Anullo.*

Saying a word in my head was a lot easier than "feeling it".

Anullo.

My confidence just as quickly dissipated; there wasn't enough of it in my ability to cast this one.

Reach toward your target. Establish the connection.

Anullo.

The walls of the cup crumbled apart, startling me. While its walls tumbled down, landing like a feather, the bottom of the cup remained intact.

"Okay," Momma said, "you've definitely done better aloud, but I get that this is more advanced than what we've done before. Can you put it back together?"

I exhaled. Putting myself in the proper mindset took too much time, time I almost wasn't patient enough to give.

Converte, I commanded, my dwindling patience driving the power straight from me. At my strengthened will, each Styrofoam piece flew to its original place and the cracks sewed themselves together.

To be honest, I shocked myself.

Mr. Dawson cocked his brows like he was just as surprised.

"Okay, nice work. Whatever you did just now, that is exactly what you should do every time. How are you feeling with silent casting?"

"Okay," I said, shrugging. "It just takes too long."

"Only because you haven't practiced it. Trust me, as soon as you master it, it'll be the only way you want to cast."

He stepped back up onto the platform at the front of the classroom and clapped his hands together. "Here comes the difficult part: control. Look at the cup you froze. *Slowly* heat it so that the ice melts—without setting anything on fire."

Momma took a napkin from the same desk drawer and then walked down to me. She placed it under the frozen cup, which was already starting to drip despite the ever-frigid air conditioning. I slowly exhaled, freeing myself from the impatience obstructing focus; I knew how to do this one better, but it required very little power right now.

Calfacio.

Control and patience stood alone in my head. I felt the amount of power I'd used before shrink, allowing minimal results.

Clusters of water beads formed around the walls of the cup. They climbed down, racing for the napkin below. In the center of my vision, the layer of ice gave way, exposing the Styrofoam underneath with a gradually growing hole.

This was going a little *too* slowly for me.

I repeated the spell in my head and pressed a little harder into myself. The water and ice evaporated into thin air.

Well, at least I didn't set it on fire.

Momma was not amused. I told her this.

"Control is crucial," she told me. "You don't want to end up setting a fish on fire at a dinner."

"Why not?" I asked. "Wouldn't that cook it?"

She rolled her eyes and looked at Mr. Dawson.

"Try again," he said, ignoring me. "Freeze it with the same thin layer of ice, and then turn it into water. Not steam."

I did as I was told, beginning the heating process. This time, like pressing on the gas pedal of a car, I carefully eased in. Ice melted into water that the napkin absorbed.

I didn't realize I'd been holding my breath the whole time until Mr. Dawson congratulated me. "Great. How did that feel?"

My brow furrowed when the word found me. "Strenuous. It felt like working out a muscle or something."

"Exactly," he said again, smiling. "Because, in a way, you're exercising a muscle of sorts. As long as you keep your focus on your magic and what it's doing, you'll be exercising the right thing. Let's keep going."

I glanced at the clock above his head and mentally strapped in. Considering the main reason I was doing this right now, it made me wonder how many more weekends I had with Alexa in my life. Magic used to be something I could learn without a real motive *forcibly* driving me to learn it. Now I was doing it to save my own life.

I'm almost tempted to tear out this page and submit it to Mr. Broadhurst for history credit, but I want to always be able to remind myself the other reason I have for strengthening my magic: Caralyn Callistro.

Well, okay, more accurately, why she founded the Callistro

Academy at all. The part most people don't know.

In 1819, she discovered that a terrorist was out to kill her father, Henry. After a year of training and tracking the terrorist, Caralyn brought him down with her "unladylike" expertise in archery.

The "terrorist", though, turned out to be a mage—so Caralyn used her father's story to further the hatred of magic. With her family's financial support, she built a school where young girls could train as she did to rid the earth of magicians and "protect their country". Somewhere hidden in the Hunter's Room are the same bow and arrows she used to save her father. With that, she established the first school for Hunters in 1827, and chains of them followed.

While a true story, it's only half of a whole. Few know the mage's side—or, rather, few believe it.

Henry Callistro was a thief of magic. A Hunter himself, he withdrew the magic from his victims before he killed them and pocketed it for himself. The "terrorist" mage was the only person to catch him in the act without being caught, and he found out Henry's true mission: to bring everyone to their knees before him and his unjustly acquired power.

Seeing as Henry had already committed murder tenfold, the mage was determined to create a curse that would quickly kill Henry—but was killed himself before he could create one.

But then Henry was caught in a severe carriage accident off a small cliff, which gave him permanent amnesia. Some of the few others who know this side of the story suspect that Caralyn had had something to do with it—that it hadn't been an accident. After all, nobody but the mage and Caralyn ever knew that Henry had magic. It was as if he'd never had it at all.

I still catch myself wondering sometimes who had been just in that situation: Caralyn or the mage? If the world knew the whole story—even trickier, if it believed it—which side would it be on today? Would there be such a thing as sides? What would have the Callistro Academy become instead of a Hunter school?

Would Adara even exist?

The story looped in my head as the lesson advanced that afternoon. That was probably why I kept messing up with Mr. Dawson's lesson on casting with my *eyes closed* (which I didn't even know was possible until then). Momma and I went out to dinner after that, where she told me to indulge after a hard day's work. On top of the end of the first week of school, my birthday was next week. There was much to celebrate.

"Hey," she said as we walked through the dusk-lit parking lot, toward the car, "how about we visit Auntie?"

I almost stopped walking, like I hadn't heard her properly. "Really? It wouldn't be... dangerous?"

"No," she replied, but like she only half believed it. "I'm sure she's wondering what we've been up to. And we really should update her on... new arrivals."

I kept a keen eye on the backup lights of the cars we passed, thinking on it. If Momma thought it was fine...

"Okay." The trunk of her undecorated white sedan came into view once we got by a red pickup truck. "What does she know?"

"That her family is everywhere else in the world but with her. She'd love the company. You are her favorite niece, after all."

A whole iceberg hid under that sentence. I'd probably be her favorite niece anyway, but I'm Aunt Becca's only niece: Momma had Uncle Brian and Dad had Aunt Becca, but Uncle Brian passed away before he could even marry his fiancée. Aunt Becca, on the other hand, has never risked a relationship, so my parents were the first in their generation to break that ground. Honestly, part of me is sometimes scared that I'll grow up to be like Aunt Becca, not wanting to risk it—but that would mean the end of the Atera line. No Hunters necessary. I kind of had no choice *but* to be brave.

SIXTEEN

Only a week had passed since we'd moved out of my childhood home, but seeing it again was still nostalgic. All Momma and I could hope for was that Aunt Becca was basking in paradise while we were at the school, as best as she could for someone wanted by the government.

Momma had me telepathically warn Auntie that we were coming, and then again when we were walking up. She thought she was going to have to unlock the door with her spare key, but it swung open right as we stepped up. Aunt Becca yanked us inside.

"You guys!" She threw her arms around her and then me. "Finally, what took so long?!"

Aunt Becca had shaven off ten years by pairing platinum-blond hair with her icy-blue eyes—which Momma had even told her not to do because going blond would supposedly age her. It was one of the few things Momma had ever been wrong about, and Aunt Becca had reveled in that. (I think she was just jealous because her beige skin tone doesn't let her wear blond.)

"We just wanted to say hi," Momma said, looking around like she hadn't been here in years. "We missed you and figured you'd like some company."

"You have no idea." Auntie walked past us, eventually turning left into the kitchen. "Can't even talk to the guy who delivers my groceries. The two friends I have are back in Charlotte, and you guys are the only family in town... Thank you."

Momma smiled, taking off her coat and draping it on the head seat of the dining table next to us. "Thanks for taking care of the house while we're gone."

"Not hard to do when you live alone." Pouring coffee into two mugs, she walked out of the kitchen and handed one to Momma. "So, Em, how's the evil school designed to slaughter the remainder of our people working out for you?"

A chuckle sneaked up on me, but Momma rolled her eyes. "Becca," she said as we followed her to the dining table.

"What?" Auntie said, taking the seat across from me, Momma at the head. "I hate that she's going there. Sometimes the best cover stories are the most obvious."

"She's getting older, I can't protect her for the rest of her life. She needs to know how to defend herself. And who would suspect a sorceress attending an ex-Hunter school?"

Oh, the dramatic irony in that sentence was bittersweet.

Neither of them had their attention on me, but I still looked between the two of them as if to gain it as I said, "The first week—"

"Still,"—Aunt Becca scoffed—"you could be teaching her eve-rything that school is right here. Come *on*, Amy, you're the self-defense instructor there! And you know I would've been *more* than happy to mentor her in magic."

"Mr. Dawson's actually—"

"Her friends are there," Momma argued. "Her only friends can't be her mother and aunt throughout high school, that's just sad. She's learning social skills and making new friends—"

"Amassing the mob for when the truth slips out," Aunt Becca muttered, sipping her coffee.

"I'm still in the room, by the way!" I said, turning to Momma. "Shouldn't we just... tell her?"

She tightly pursed her lips like I'd betrayed her. Auntie's fear-less expression of opinion had made telling her about Alexa that much harder, but the entire situation concerned her little brother, whom she hadn't seen in seventeen years. She had every right to know about it, didn't she?

"What happened?" Aunt Becca asked, arching a brow as her eyes dawdled on me.

Momma exhaled, resting her white mug on the mahogany ta-ble. "The authorities suspect that Tristan and I had a baby sixteen years ago. Emma's on their list of suspects as to who that baby is."

Aunt Becca slammed her coffee mug down onto the table, startling me. "Callistro seems like the perfect idea now, doesn't it? You might as well hand her over to the White House personally!"

"I don't need you telling me how to raise my daughter," Momma snapped. "We all knew this was going to happen one day. It's not like nobody was ever gonna find out that Tristan married and had a daughter—they don't even know that his one and only descendant *is* a daughter! And they only suspect her because of her last name and physical similarities. Do you know how many other kids' last names are 'Marie'?"

"I can't believe you just said that." Aunt Becca chuckled in disbelief, shaking her head. "So you're telling me you *didn't* enroll Emma in that school as a cover?"

Honestly, it was more and more tempting to look at things from her point of view—with me continuing to learn from Momma right here at home and then have Auntie mentor me in magic. But Callistro *was* teaching me some needed skills, and where I went to school wouldn't have changed the fact that I was on Alexa's list. If anything, because of that, I was *safer* at Callistro than I would've been here. And that meant so was Aunt Becca.

"It's a self-defense school now, first of all," Momma replied. "There really isn't anything to suspect from the students there, and she *needs* to know advanced self-defense. I've spent her entire life making sure nobody could find anything, do you really think I'd slip up now?"

"Alexa's a *Grand* Hunter who just married William Bleu, another Grand Hunter! Do *you* even understand how bad this is?"

"Do you know who Adara is?" I asked before my hesitation could stop me. Aunt Becca's attention snapped to me. "Mr. Dawson told me the truth about him. He said I'm meant to become Adara and unite the mortal and magic worlds, or—play a part in it. He's had a lot of visions about it with that same outcome."

Aunt Becca rested to silence, her gaze filling with something I couldn't quite name: sorrow? Grief? Remorse? She moved a strand of her unnaturally blond hair away from her face, swallowing.

"So when you said this was bound to happen," she murmured, turning to Momma, "you were being literal? This was all *meant* to happen?"

Momma's tired amber eyes fell back onto the table. "I don't want to think that way. I don't know if our specific situation was meant to happen." She scoffed. "I'm not even sure if I believe anything is 'meant' to happen. But I do think people had to suspect eventually. No matter who they are or when they would."

I watched Aunt Becca for signs of what was going through her head. Her light fingers tapped the ceramic of her mug, a frown pulling on her lips. Then she sighed. "I'm sorry. I'm over here criticizing you for thinking you can protect her from all of this when I'm the one acting like we can."

"Believe me, of all people, I understand where you're coming from," Momma told her. "It's a scary thing, yeah. But we're okay. Plus..."

There was hesitance. I did not like this kind of hesitance.

"Plus, the entire thing's brought Emma a boyfriend."

My posture immediately corrected itself. "Wait a second—"

"Boyfriend?" Aunt Becca sang with a cocked brow. Her grin just as quickly dropped. "Wait, do you really think that's a good idea?"

"He's actually been doing everything he can to protect her," Momma replied. It almost surprised me, considering I still wasn't exactly sure where she stood with Jak. "He genuinely believes she's innocent."

"Why would a random boy—?" Aunt Becca asked with a pinched brow, tilting her head. Then, her features dropped with realization. "He knows she's being hunted?"

I could already smell another cat fight.

"Yep." Momma sighed in defeat. "He's Alexa's stepson."

Aunt Becca choked. Literally choked. "Meaning his parents are Alexa Delphine and William Bleu? Are you kidding me—?"

"I've already talked to Emma about this," Momma stated, holding up her hand. She brought her mug up to her lips as she said, "Em, tell her what you told me."

"Well, first of all, he's not my boyfriend," I said. "Second, Mr. Dawson already used a truth spell on him to make sure he's genuine. And then there's... I can't explain it." I thought about the first impression Jak had left me with, how he'd even persuaded Momma to a small extent to not immediately throw him out of the school when she'd first met him. "If you talked to him, you'd know. He feels so easy to trust because you *can*. He even helped me escape Alexa when she first came for me. We can't judge him based on who his parents are. Look at how the world sees my dad."

Aunt Becca shook her head tiredly. "Do *you* trust any of this, Amy?"

"He was the one who told me about his parents' plans in the first place. Told us everything he possibly could as soon as he got to Capperson and found Emma. And when I first met him... there's just something about him, I don't know. Probably because he *is* sincere. So when it comes to whether or not to label him as an enemy, I'm being patient for now."

"I'm trying to," I added, tracing the veining of the wooden surface with my finger. "The first real 'friend' I meet in almost ten years and it's... him."

Aunt Becca gave me a breathy pity chuckle. Then, she turned back to Mom. "I *am* sorry, Amy. But sometimes I wish you had magic to fully understand what we feel every time the word 'Hunter' is even said around us. I don't think we ever really trust anyone associated with them in the slightest. You were a special case, to say the absolute least."

"Well, I have Emma." Momma's warm gaze reached me, and I smiled. "She's my magic in that sense."

An uncomfortable, foreign silence buzzed around the room. None of us had pictured this visit to turn out *this* way, but I was actually kind of grateful for it. Auntie's perspective definitely wasn't one to be ignored, but I couldn't help but feel a little more secure in my and Momma's choices since the school year began. It doesn't take Hunter training to know that confidence is crucial in any game or battle. Maybe this conversation was meant to happen.

My phone buzzed in my pocket, and I took it out with all eyes on me:

J: Care to meet me at the fountain in fifteen minutes?

Hold the phone. Well, I was, but was Jak trying to ask me out? On an *official* date? Or was he actually trying to turn me in to his parents now?

"Is that the boyfriend?" Aunt Becca asked, sipping from her coffee again.

"No. I mean, it is—I mean, he's not—"

Momma laughed and leaned toward me, looking down at the screen. "What did he say?"

Was I going to tell my mother about the first time a boy was being directly romantic with me (mostly to verify that he was)? Duh.

"I think he's trying to ask me out," I muttered, showing her the text. To my relief, she grinned.

"Honey, he's definitely asking you out. I'll drop you off right now."

"Emma's going on her first date!" Aunt Becca awed. "Can I come?"

"I don't know…" I told Momma. "Well, first, no. I mean—I've never—I've never done this before."

"Okay, if this is what it looks like it is, he's totally crushing on you." Momma paired her puppy eyes with a pout. "In which case, you should go for it."

"My only issue is leaving her alone with him," Aunt Becca remarked.

"And I wouldn't," Momma replied simply. She turned to me. "That's why I'll always have eyes on you."

Oh no, *this* was the burning mortification the teenagers in movies always felt. "Mom—"

She rolled her eyes. "You know even *you* won't see me, Em. If you weren't a target of the U.S. Government right now, you'd be more than welcome to go on your own. I trust you. I don't trust them."

I couldn't argue with that. Frankly, I didn't want to.

I think she read that in my silence, because she rubbed my back, smiling, and then stood from the table. We were ready to leave.

"Okay, fine," Aunt Becca said, standing with us. "Take pictures. Lots of pictures. And update me later tonight!"

I can't believe her, I thought, hiding a chuckle under my breath before following Momma to the door. "I'll try on the update."

Auntie hugged us one more time, her arms tight with affection. "I love you. Visit whenever you can."

"We love you, too," Mom said, "and we'll try. Emma's friends are away for the weekend, so it was the perfect time to do this. We miss you a lot."

"I miss you, too. See you later. And, Emma?"

I turned around and met the comfortingly familiar blue of her eyes.

"I hope you know how proud of you your dad would be."

C H A P T E R

SEVENTEEN

Jak was already waiting for me at one of the benches against the fountain. This was probably about to be my first *real* date, and he did nothing to help the anxiety infecting every part of me by showing up even cuter than usual: he'd put together a button-up shirt with his leather jacket and black jeans. Casual yet... what was the word? Hot.

And even though all I had on were light jeans and an off-the-shoulder shirt, he told me, "Well, you look cute."

"In my defense, I didn't know I'd be going out so late and last minute," I teased, crossing my arms against the subtle cold in the air. "But thanks. What did you wanna talk about?"

"I wanted you"—he slid off his jacket and brought it over my shoulders—"to meet me here because..."

Fifty-foot butterfly waves crashed in my stomach, and I pulled Jak's musk-smelling jacket tighter around me. *I can't believe he just did that. In front of Mom*—wherever she was staking out.

By the pause that had gripped his face, Jak was experiencing something I didn't even know existed in him: trepidation. But I was pretty sure (and hopeful) that that was a good thing in this scenario.

He finally jabbed a thumb behind him, in the direction of the movie theater farther down. "Um, the movie starts in a few minutes."

Maybe it was the heat of the moment. Maybe it was the fact that I'd never experienced anything like this before and had only read about and saw it in books and on TV—but the crashed butterflies had revived and now swarmed inside like bees at the hive.

"Movie? At the theater?"

"That's typically where they play movies, Merlin." His signature million-dollar grin lit up his face. Those stupid, kind brown eyes were all but physically pulling me toward him. "I didn't want one of these tickets going to waste."

"You timed this really well," I noted, pleasantly surprised as he took a white ticket out of his pocket and handed it to me. "And you just knew to buy two?"

He smirked. "Were you gonna say no?"

I laughed—faked or not, Jak's confidence left nothing to be desired. "You're taking advantage of me never experiencing anything like this before."

"That has nothing to do with it. But I do want to make it memorable."

He offered me his arm. I knew Momma was seeing all of this,

but somehow, that gave me all the more courage to accept. I took Jak's arm to prove to myself that this was real. This was the boy Aunt Becca couldn't trust. Then again, she'd never met him; everyone else who knew Jak trusted him. And in that moment, I'd never felt closer to him—literally. We were standing next to each other, arm in arm, walking to the theater. His cologne from his jacket was just strong enough to lend the air a nice whiff here and there. Did I smell as good as he did? Had I showered today? Right, yes, I had showered today. But had I put perfume on after? What if his jacket smelled like me once I gave it back?

Questions like those weren't the only reason it was hard to enjoy the romantic comedy blaring on the theater-width screen in front of me once we got to our seats: I was on a date with the son of Alexa Delphine and William Bleu. He was sitting right next to me, and Momma was watching somewhere in the dark. I probably wasn't allowed to do anything in the same way the pack wasn't allowed to do anything if they really were here.

But a part of me kept reminding me who Jakson Bleu really was—who he was trying to prove to me he was. And I wasn't sure which side of me *I* could really trust. The best part of him told me that he was a good guy; the best part of me told me just the opposite and reiterated every fear and suspicion I had toward him. And yet, right now they somehow felt... irrational. And I couldn't place if that was his fault or my own.

All too disappointingly quickly and agonizingly slowly, the credits began to roll and the dim theater lights faded into existence. *So far, so good,* I thought as Jak and I stood from the padded seats. *I wonder where Mom is.* If only I had something that belonged to her so I could use a locator spell.

Between me and Jak, it was the typical superficial comments about the movie once we arrived back in the lobby. He waited until we were outside in the blue-hazed dusk—letting me wear his jacket all the while—to snap back to normal.

"Definitely wasn't expecting to connect with the main character on such a personal level," he joked. The main character's name had been "Jack", and Jack had pretty much been Jim Carrey in *Liar Liar.* "Sometimes you luck out on your picks."

"Yeah, and sometimes the movie trailer helps you pick," I teased back, pulling out my phone from my back pocket.

"Sorry, there's nothing playing right now with an 'Emma' main character." His gaze shifted, his soft features relaxing and the weight of his eyes increasing. "I looked."

It was the way he simply said my name. Just my name sounded like another world on his lips, one I wanted to visit and see what he thought of it.

"Well, thanks for tonight," I told him. "It was fun. My mom's gonna pick me up at the fountain."

"Then I get to spend the next few minutes walking you there. If I may."

His arm went back up, and my hand went back around it. His touch was different this time; with the end of the date on the horizon, its trance had been broken. Something had been pressing harshly on my mind for the entire evening, brought up again each time I stole a glance in his direction. I was afraid to ask, but I couldn't afford not to know.

"Hey... do you know where Alexa's been?"

As if instinctually, Jak slowed his pace. A moment passed before he settled on his words. "I don't see her much. Around the house, I mean."

"Can she really kidnap me whenever she wants because I'm a suspect?"

He tightly smiled. "You'd have to ask her that yourself, Merlin. I wouldn't know."

Well, that was clearly not the answer I'd been looking for.

"But hey," he said after the first uncomfortable silence of the night, "did you see how they spelled Jack's name wrong?"

I looked up from our feet practically scraping the concrete of the sidewalk. Jak's face was briefly illuminated by the streetlight we walked under. "What? No, they didn't."

"There was a 'c'." Another one of his signature smirks. "There's no 'c'."

"That's how you spell your name?" I asked, tilting my head. "That's really cool, but—where did it come from?"

His lips bent into a gentle, remembering smile as he cast his gaze to our feet. "My mom liked to be a little different."

Whoa. That... This was the first time Jak had ever mentioned anything about his real mom. Did that mean anything? Was he already that comfortable around me?

"Because you were really cool and easy to hang out with." He'd meant that, too.

"I really like that," I said again, softer.

Then, for whatever reason, an impulse of bravery rested my head on his shoulder as we walked. That felt right. Not only was this the first romantic opportunity I'd ever had, but Jak... I trusted him enough with that.

Looking back, I'd completely forgotten that Momma was probably still watching.

Jak didn't say anything, but I'm pretty sure I heard him take a breath like he wanted to: whether it be to ask if I was sure I wanted to walk that way, if I was comfortable, or to just state that he enjoyed us being so close, because he relaxed and exhaled with a smile I could hear. Just anything to check up on me. That's the kind of guy Jakson Bleu is.

Momma was lenient on Jak when we met her at the fountain, only asking about what we'd done, but it all changed after he left: the second I landed in the passenger seat, she ambushed me with her real questions.

"There isn't any way he didn't pick *that* movie on purpose, did he? What did he say about it? And what did he say that made you put your head on his shoulder?"

Wow, it almost felt like I was talking to Sarah and Breanne. Oh, right—I had to repeat tonight to them, too, once they got back.

I clicked my seatbelt into place. "I learned that his name is spelled J-A-K instead of J-A-C-K."

Momma blinked a couple of times. "Oh."

I helplessly grinned and turned to her in my seat. "You *know* he picked it on purpose. He joked about being just like the main character, and—it actually was the spelling of his name that made me do that. It was his mom's choice to spell it that way. I could just tell that... they were close."

Momma's refined features on her narrow face softened, her smile relaxing. "That's really nice... That poor boy. Having to trade that mother for what he has now."

I mean, Alexa hadn't been harsh with me or anything in the forest—but I didn't get the feeling that she was anything like Momma, either.

"I did ask him about Alexa. He says she's basically been MIA. He has no idea what she's doing right now."

Momma rested her hands on the steering wheel, pressing her lips together in an oh-well-what-can-you-do way. "Well, no Grand Hunter wants a teenage boy knowing their top-secret plans."

I expected those words to have an easy landing, but they curdled in my stomach; that was true. Nobody needed Hunter training to put that together, so again, why *did* Jak know the gist of his parents' plans? How did he know who was being targeted?

When Momma started the car after that and drove onto Main Street, I wondered if she was having the same thoughts. She had to have been. Or maybe she just didn't want to share them with me until she found concrete answers. We couldn't really argue about something we hardly knew anything about.

Night had descended in full by the time we pulled into the school's parking lot, but interestingly enough, a gentle comfort settled over me as we stepped inside the Grand Foyer. The manor is inexplicably comforting at night. The crimson-red carpet runners in the corridors blend in a little more with the dark-oak floorboards underneath, and the floor-to-ceiling windows on the top floor draw in a stream of soothing moonlight. You even have a view of the forest and a bit of Capperson if you're on the top floor. It's beautiful.

For some reason, though, I slid into my bed with an odd, nameless weight pressing down on me. When I looked over, I was able to name it: neither of my roommates were here. I was alone.

Maybe the school's nightly comfort depended on who was with me, because unsteadiness lurked in my chest that knowledge of my safety couldn't suppress.

Jak might not have been on his parents' side that night, but a date still would've made the perfect plan if he had been; the exhaustion and fading adrenaline lulled me into a dangerously heavy sleep. So heavy that I thought the glimpse of someone carrying me out of bed with a rag over my mouth was a dream.

CHAPTER

EIGHTEEN

I woke up disoriented like I was thousands of miles underwater. All sense of time, location, and reality had been submerged with me.

Blinking my vision clear despite the blinding white light, I forced my awareness to manifest. Just about the smallest room I'd ever seen, crème bricks on all sides, surrounded me. Maybe nine people could be seated, twelve standing—

This isn't my dorm. This isn't my dorm, this isn't my dorm!

The second I tried to stand, I was shoved straight back down with a bunch of clinks. Something cold and metal pressed harshly into my wrists and ankles. I looked down at the handcuffs chaining me to the chair I sat in.

She got me. She got me, I'm dead, I'm so dead.

No, please, I'm sorry! I'm sorry! Someone help! Anyone help me, please!

If not for the fact that I couldn't show weakness in front of the pack—if not for the fact that I couldn't use my magic to escape without incriminating myself—I would've let the hot tears fall. A bitterly humid cold swept around me thanks to the polished-concrete floors and brick walls. But this was not my dorm. That was why I couldn't cry.

Did they already figure everything out? Why did they wait a couple days to do this? Would they kill me here? Do they have a process like Death Row?

Was I already sitting there?

The large door in front of me groaned open. With my heart banging against me like a hammer, my chest tightened with fear. Shoulder-length red hair, emerald-green eyes, and an all-black suit starkly contrasted the walls as Alexa stepped inside.

"Hello, Emmalynn." She smiled at me like she was picking me up from school. "Did you have fun last night?"

"Please, please, don't do this!" I cried. I tried gripping the armrests of the metal chair, but the nervous sweat already pooling in my palms made my hands slip straight off. "I wanna go home, please don't—"

Alexa held up a fair hand. "We just want to ask you a few questions, okay? You're free to go once you answer them. We'll even escort you back to the school."

The serenity in her tone left behind a loud silence—one that emphasized my every frantic breath to my ears. I had to calm down. I had to think clearly. Nobody was holding a gun to my head yet, and if Alexa saw how terrified I was now when I supposedly had nothing to hide, it'd be game over. Only my rationality would get me out of this.

I calmed my breath, something even Alexa seemed to wait for. "H—how—" I began in a whisper, building trust in myself to increase my volume, "how did you break into the school?"

"I know a few things about the Callistro Academy," she replied simply. She walked to the doorway behind her and nodded in my direction to someone in the hall. Then, she came to unlock the cuffs on one side while a different Hunter worked on my other.

"So," Alexa sang, "is that a no to last night?"

"Did you send him?" I asked, preparing to close off my ears to the answer. "Was he part of this?"

"No, not at all." She shrugged, her short waves bouncing with every minor head movement. "He's just fond of you. It's cute."

"Were you following us?" I dared to ask, my voice trapped in a whisper.

She looked up after unlocking my ankle, gazing happily into my eyes as if to say, *What do you think?*

They couldn't've gotten past Momma. She would've seen them, there's no way she—

"No," Alexa chirped, standing. Her delicate hand rested on my shoulder like we were friends—but it was probably to hold me down. Like I was dumb enough to try escaping. "But he left the house all dressed up and wearing his most expensive cologne. We didn't need to guess."

Jak had accidentally tipped them off that last night was the perfect night to act. After a couple of days, after a night out, when I was calmest and most tired, preparing for the weekend.

I didn't know where to place my furious regret.

The second Hunter grabbed my arm, and Alexa led us out of the room. Fluorescent lights beamed above us, the scent of (weirdly enough) sticky notes and tape swirling in the large, office-like room we stepped into. A hallway lay to my left and another straight ahead, dark carpet cushioning our steps. A long, square counter sat in the middle of the room, complete with empty chairs and asleep computers. Normalcy was the *last* thing I expected a Grand Hunter lair to resemble.

Okay. Don't freak out. Don't freak out and expose everything.

I'm sorry, Momma, I'm so sorry, I should've slept in your room with you.

Alexa continued until we reached a door far down the corridor in front of us. "Before we go in," she said, placing her hand on the scanner, "you have my word that we won't hurt you. You're just here for questioning, so stay calm for us, okay?"

What, does she feel bad that they're doing this? Why was my emotional comfort at the front of her mind?

She opened the door, revealing a conference room. (Why the entire place resembled an office, I didn't want to know.) A long table in the center, black desk chairs (of which I had to assume weren't the fun spinning kind) encompassing it. A flat-screen TV was mounted on the back wall. I didn't want to know what that was for, either.

The Hunter who held my arm walked me inside and sat me at the head of the table, close to the door.

"We're ready in here," Alexa said, pressing a Bluetooth in her ear and strolling to the front of the room to turn the TV on. We were definitely going to use it. That wasn't a good sign.

Another Hunter accompanied the one who'd walked me in

here as they came out from behind me. One rolled a familiar device to the chair on my left side: a metal box with wires stretching out from it, a sensor attached to each ends. A screen stared back at me with a computer cable in the side, attached to a laptop one of the Hunters was setting onto the table. An image from the night before school started flashed in my memory: a cerebral polygraph.

I'm dead.

Anxiety swirled in my head, but passing out right now was going to send all the wrong messages. I forced deep, quiet breaths, reminding myself that despite the truth, I had to fight it. I had to embody a different "truth".

The two Hunters attached wires to my head, neck, and hands. I kept my stare on the machine as the second Hunter sat in the chair next to me, behind the laptop. He synced the computer's screen to the TV's, displaying my pulse, respiratory rates, blood pressure, skin conductivity, and brain activity. The first thing I—and everyone else—noticed was the rapid oscillation reflecting my heartbeat. Well, yelling at it in my head to slow down clearly wasn't working—it was actually making it a lot worse.

"Your heart rate is pretty high," Alexa noted, facing me. "Again: try to relax. Take a few deep breaths. You'll be free once you're done here if you're not the Atera descendant. There's nothing to be afraid of."

That's not true. That's not true, that's not true, I am.

I'm not making it out of here.

Hang on—Alexa assuming that my heart was palpitating because of excessive nerves and not because these people were on top of the truth? How? This woman was a greater mystery than her stepson.

There had to be a way to force my body to relax. Could I use telekinesis on my heart and brain? Or would that kill me?

"Here's how this is going to work," Alexa began, pressing the tips of her slender fingers together. "First step is a few baseline questions to verify everything is working properly. Then we'll formally begin with a few background questions to make sure our intel on you is accurate, and in case we find any leads in your knowledge. After that, we'll go from there."

Translation: after that, they would ask me if I was my father's descendant, and then detain me without ever escorting me back to the school.

Sorry, Momma. When we get to that point, magic is gonna be necessary. After that... maybe we could move again. Maybe I'd even get to say goodbye to Sarah and Breanne.

"We'll start with the baseline questions," the Hunter sitting beside me said. I jumped out of my thoughts. "State your legal name."

Thank God it actually *was* my legal name thanks to Momma: "'Emmalynn Marie'."

It wasn't a lie.

"State your current age."

"Fifteen years old."

It wasn't a lie.

"State the full name of your current place of residence."

"The Callistro Academy of Self-Defense and Advanced Academics."

It wasn't a lie.

"We're ready," the Hunter said, nodding at Alexa and then looking back at me. I could still feel the first Hunter who'd walked me in here standing right behind me at the door. "Are you aware of the Callistro Academy's primary purpose of establishment, Miss Marie?"

"Yes."

"Please state that purpose."

"To train its students as Hunters the same way Caralyn Callistro did to save her father."

"Why did you enroll?"

"My mom wanted me to be able to protect and defend myself if I'm ever alone or if we're separated."

That *clearly worked out.*

Still, it wasn't a lie.

"Being aware of the Callistro Academy's original purpose, are you aware of the family records the school maintains in its sublevel?"

The Hall of Generations. "Yes."

"Have you seen the Atera family tree down there?"

I didn't like where this was going. "Yes."

"When did you see it?"

"Tuesday night." I looked down at the surface of the table, hardening my grip on the padded armrest of my chair. "My friends and I went down into the Hunter's Room to look at the family trees."

"Why did you want to see the Atera family tree?"

Here we go...

"It wasn't just that one," I answered, silently thanking Sarah and Breanne for their never-ending curiosity. "We wanted to look at the Hunters and the magicians. My friend heard a rumor about the Ateras, and we looked at the Delphine and Bleu family trees because of them... getting married." For some reason, I couldn't bring my gaze up to Alexa while those words left my mouth. "We got to the Atera tree and then started wondering about where these families were and... about their kids, if any of them even had any. My other friend wondered what their lives would look like." I dared myself to glimpse the polygraph. The stickiness of the sensors tugged at my skin just a little more. "Now I know."

It wasn't a lie. The Hunter turned his head to Alexa at the front—who tilted hers with a confused scrunch in her brow.

"I'm sorry?" she asked. "*Now* you know what their life would look like?"

The quiet in the room rooted itself into the very ground. Caution took control at the front of my mind, because whatever I'd just said had either set me free or sentenced me to death. Until I knew which one, I wouldn't speak.

Alexa met me with narrowed eyes, like she sensed this. "Emmalynn, do you know why we suspect Tristan Atera has a descendant?"

HA—that's literally the whole problem!

"I wish I *did*," I replied, matching the confusion carved in her features.

And it wasn't a lie, because if I did know what had sentenced my fate to catch up with me, I probably wouldn't have done whatever had tipped them off!

Alexa blindly gazed at me, the gears in her head turning. With a curt breath and a shake of her head, she eventually let her hands fall to her sides. "Okay. You're free to go."

Wait. *What?*

The two other agents in the room repeated that exactly.

"I said she's free to go," Alexa said simply. "Escort her back to the school."

"Agent—"

"Escort her back to the school," she stated. "We're done for now. I just found a lead."

Oh no. What did I say? What did I just say?

Something wasn't right. She couldn't have just set me free—and claiming she had found a lead on top of that? By me telling the *truth?* It was... it wasn't right!

It's just like when we first met in the forest. If anything, they should've asked me then and there if I was Tristan's descendant after saying that. They should've taken me from the forest that very day when their target was in reach. Why hadn't they taken me, why weren't they asking—?

"Wait," Alexa said when the Hunter behind me reached to unhook me. "Emmalynn, one more thing."

The gears were still turning, but she definitely already knew her question. What she would do with my answer was the terrifying mystery.

"Do you know anything about Tristan's descendant?"

So *that* was why she'd made it seem like she was setting me free. She was setting up the perfect moment for her to corner me and then carry on with the next phase of my interrogation/execution!

Looking back, I can think of a dozen different responses—something else; something that avoided the question altogether; even maybe, just *maybe*, a promise for an answer for next time (not that I wanted there to be a next time). Now it's all obvious, everything in hindsight is. But in that moment, fear and anxiety blocked any other option from my brain. Only one answer presented itself:

"Yes."

And it wasn't a lie.

NINETEEN

Alexa said nothing after my confession. She just instructed the two Hunters to unhook me, knowing I'd be entertained by that as she injected me with a sleeping drug.

Comfortingly (or terrifyingly) enough, I woke up in my own bed. As if my worst nightmare coming to life had been just that: a nightmare. The clock on my bedside table read just past 8. Saturday. Was it really only Saturday?

I wanted to stay in bed for the day—because *clearly* it was safest for me. I wasn't even safe at my school, where I lived, not even in my own dorm! If not here, where? Did I have *any* control over my own safety anymore? Could I have somehow prevented last night?

How was I supposed to sleep here tonight?

One thought leaped into my head as I threw my comforter off me: I officially had a nonofficial appointment with Momma and Mr. Dawson.

After getting dressed, I slowly made my way down to the first floor. Slowly because a handful of other Callistro Girls were walking around despite the early hour (early for Saturday, at least) and it was a great chance for small talk and getting to better know them outside of the classroom. Also because I needed to prepare myself for the whole honesty thing despite my fears—if Momma had been ready to ground me from leaving the manor *before* Alexa had kidnapped me from it, what lengths would she go to now?

"Morning, Emmalynn!" someone chirped as they passed me in the Grand Foyer.

I turned around. Oh boy. If there was anyone I needed to keep quiet around regarding my life right now, it was Opal Dubois.

"Good morning!" I said back. "Any plans for today?"

With her purple contacts glimmering, Opal walked back in my direction, surprised that I'd actually started a conversation. In full honesty, I was, too.

She shrugged, pushing a straight lock of black hair behind her ear. "Amelia and Caroline are gone for the weekend. But it's kind of nice to be almost alone when you live with so many people. I'm an only child, so I had my own room back home, and I kind of miss it."

Funnily enough, I didn't share that sentiment; maybe it had something to do with how Sarah, Breanne, and I had spent the last couple of years only *dreaming* about what it would be like to live together.

"What about you?" Opal asked. "Where are Sarah and

Breanne?"

"Out of town, too, so I'm just wandering for now. I'd visit my mom, but I think she's working."

And I'm about to interrupt her to tell her that her daughter was kidnapped last night. All morning, it had been weird talking to my classmates as if nothing had happened last night. I had to grin and bear the burden of its existence, unknowing of what to do with the fact, unknowing of how to move past it as fast as possible. And as terrifying as it sounded, with my existence having been introduced to Hunters at all, I realized that this probably wasn't going to be the last time I'd be in this situation. I guess that was why I kept talking: practice.

"I wish my mom could be an elective teacher here," Opal mused, looking around the Foyer as she thought. "Like for journalism or creative writing, that'd be so cool if we had, like, a school newspaper or something. We need a more than a couple electives and sports."

We definitely *had* a lot more a century ago.

"I don't know," Opal said, sucking on her teeth. "I think I'm just craving some excitement."

I'd experienced "excitement" on more than one occasion by then, and Momma's definition back when she was a Hunter typically involved a life-or-death version of hide-and-seek; one or two weapons only legal in South America; and a few nameless, poisonous concoctions the United States Drug Enforcement Administration wanted her to "test out on the next hunt". I wasn't too sure that that was the excitement Opal wanted to experience.

"Oh, hey." She perked up, her dark brows bent in confusion. "Did I tell you what's been going on with *Magic*, the magazine?"

Here we go. I braced myself to play the role of another Callistro Girl hungry for the latest gossip in magic.

"No, what's up?" I asked, crossing my arms.

"It's so weird, it's like the company's taken a break. Either them or Tristan. They made the biggest breakthrough in decades and now they haven't found anything new since. Like, they *can't* find anything new."

I furrowed my brow. "Who're their usual sources?"

"They do a little undercover work here and there," she said, tilting her head. "That's all my mom's ever been allowed to tell me about it."

Before I could reply, her eyes widened with curiosity, a sly grin spreading across her pale face. "*We* should do something fun, me and you."

The girl was the standing definition of "unsettling" right now. "What do you mean?"

"I don't know, maybe—do our own detective work. Find our way down to the *Hunter's Room* and explore a little bit."

Nope, I'd already gone down that path, instantly regretted it, and promised Momma (and myself) that I'd never go down it again.

"Why would you wanna explore the Hunter's Room? It's just a museum right now."

"Not true." Opal's voice shot into a high, airy lilt, like she couldn't contain her excitement. "I snuck in a couple of days before school started, the entire main room is set up like a training gym. They're preparing for something."

What? That wasn't true—the entire main room *was* a Hunter museum. What was she talking about?

"So that means we should prepare for next semester." Her grin grew, and she bit her lip with excitement. "They're one hundred percent reopening the Hunter's Room, which means we're gonna start training to become *Hunters*."

I narrowed my eyes, smiling to maintain the lighthearted atmosphere. "I can't believe you went down there."

She politely rolled her eyes. "Why not? I was just getting a head start." Her voice finally dropped back into her regular register. "And especially with the rumor of Tristan's descendant, they could even reopen it within the next couple of months."

I knew she liked gossip, but that was a valid point I didn't want to hear or accept.

"Or we can try the *secret passageways*," she told me. "I heard from Teresa and Sloane that there's—"

"Good morning, Emma," a voice behind Opal chimed.

Although Opal had my curiosity with the secret passageways, I internally sighed with relief. *Thank you, Mother.*

"Hi, Mom." I smiled as she approached and came to stand in front of us. "I thought you were working today."

"I have a bit of free time right now," she said, looking at the girl beside me. "Good morning, Opal. Do you have any plans for the day?"

"Good morning, Mrs. Marie. I think I'm just gonna change and head into town." She glanced at me in a maybe-next-time kind of way. "It was nice talking to you, Em, let's hang out soon!"

"Em"? Nobody called me that unless they were close to me.

"Sure!" I said anyway, but the chances of that happening relied solely on her. "See you."

She strode by Momma and turned to the Main Staircase,

practically hopping up the steps. Momma and I improvised conversation until she was past the Second Staircase and out of earshot. And every second Opal was gone, the clammier my hands got, the harder my heart beat.

I exhaled shakily, anxiety brewing in me as my and Momma's casual conversation faded. It was *much* different from the kind I'd felt last night when I was with Jak, and I didn't enjoy the nausea or mild spinning of the room one bit.

"I need to tell you something," I said. "You and Mr. Dawson."

Apparently honesty *is* the best policy, because that was all it took for her to follow me to his office.

At least he seemed to be in a good mood when Momma opened his door, smiling from his desk and tilting down the lid of his laptop. "Good morning, ladies. What can I do for you?"

"Emma says she has something to tell us," Momma said curiously, concern trailing the words. Mr. Dawson closed his laptop all the way.

I sat myself on the white sofa on the right side of the room, Momma placing herself next to me. Locking my eyes on the rug under the glass coffee table in front of me, I tried a dozen different introductions in my head. How was I supposed to start a story like this?

"Alexa—kidnapped me last night." I decided to rip off the Band-Aid, denying myself their reactions to force myself to keep going. "And she took me to some kind of... I guess it was their lair. They put me under a cerebral polygraph to question me."

One instance and one instance alone isolated itself in my memory: the last word I'd spoken to Alexa and her team. One syllable, three letters, resounded in my head. I swallowed, because crying felt like breaking some kind of code. I was supposed to be stronger than that. Under no circumstances could I allow myself to be anything weaker after what I'd confessed last night.

No words could find Momma and she them. Whom she was angry with, though, I couldn't pin down. I dared to look up at her sitting next to me: her nose flared with every heavy breath out, furious eyes on the table.

"I don't care what it takes," she uttered. "I don't care where I end up because of it, I'm gonna kill her."

"Amy–"

"She KIDNAPPED my daughter in the middle of the night! Thomas, can you even *begin* to understand–can–do you know how–?"

"You're speaking out of anger," he said, leaning forward on his desk. The tightness in his sharp jaw told me that he was trying to tame his own rage right now. "You know every reason you can't actually kill her, and it has nothing to do with morality."

Momma sprang from her seat, meeting his eyes with amber fire. "What parent wouldn't kill their child's kidnapper? If you expect me to tolerate what she's doing while Caldwell gets closer to eliminating magic in America, shredding every last atom of humanity and morality, then you take me for a fool, Thomas. I am no fool, I am one of the last vessels used to carry the next generation, our whole future, forward, and it's my job to keep it alive. If you think I'm gonna sit back and offer mercy in a world with falsely sovereign laws of 'goodness', then you're the fool."

I didn't know whose side to take: my morals' or Momma's. I couldn't find the lie in her speech, but *killing* Alexa...? I wasn't even sure I wanted to know if Momma was being dead serious or just speaking out of motherly instinct.

Mr. Dawson passed a hand over his face. "Nobody called you a fool," he said, leaning back in his desk chair.

Momma curtly exhaled and sat back down next to me. I couldn't tell her the rest now! She'd just released the anger accumulating since Wednesday afternoon, and the truth would just restore it!

"Emma," Mr. Dawson said, practically reading my mind again. His deep-set eyes had an authoritative hold on me as he asked, "What did you tell Alexa?"

I realized then that a right time to confess this simply didn't exist. I prepared to rip off the next Band-Aid.

"I said I didn't know why they thought my dad has a descendant in the first place. Everyone acted like I'd just asked what my own name was. They thought I already knew. Alexa let me go after that. But..."

The truth was on a roll; who was I to stop it?

"Before they unhooked me, Alexa asked me if... if I knew anything about Tristan's descendant."

"Emmalynn." Momma sighed in defeat, closing her eyes. "You didn't."

"I couldn't think of anything else," I murmured, too timidly. "If I lied, it would've told them anyway."

Regret wrenched my stomach. I hadn't thought of anything else in time, and even as I sat on that sofa, I still didn't know what I could've answered with.

"I'm sorry," I whispered.

"But she still let you go?" Mr. Dawson asked.

I'm here, aren't I?

"She didn't even say anything. They just gave me a sleeping drug, and I woke up back in bed."

"Hang on," Momma said, fully turning to me. "You're telling me that Jak asked you out on the same night the pack kidnapped you? Did he have anything to do with last night?"

"No," I said "Alexa said he had nothing to do with the entire thing."

She scoffed, twisting the golden band on her left ring finger. "Right, and she's so trustworthy."

"I don't think he even knows about it..." I mused. "And I don't think he should."

"Good point," Mr. Dawson said. "Are we keeping this whole thing from Sarah and Breanne?"

At Momma's sigh, I looked at her. Her gaze remained stuck on a mindless point in front of her, meaning she was still thinking. For once, I had an answer to a question like that (which was "yes"), but I definitely trusted hers more.

"For now," she said, nodding lightly. "Until we have all our answers, we can't frivolously give away what we do have. We don't know how the rest of this is going to play out. We don't even know how long we'll be dealing with it." Her honey-like eyes fell onto me. "You need to know how much to hide from them before you can know how much to tell them."

Thank goodness. We were on the same page.

"That makes sense," I said.

Momma nodded. "Good. Then last night never happened. It was just another night. As long as we're the only people who know the truth, this doesn't have to blow up into anything bigger."

Wait, just like that? "But we—"

"What's done is done," she told me. "And whenever Sarah and Breanne are gone, you're sleeping with me in my room. For now, though, you're here with us, back at the school, unharmed. That's what matters."

It wouldn't last, though, I knew. How much time I had before something like last night happened again, I didn't know. How much time I needed, I didn't know, which meant I didn't know how much I needed to buy myself. There was nothing to do except wait. Wait for Alexa to come back. Wait for the truth to manifest. Wait for Ingrid's prophecy to pass. Wait to see where I'd be spending my sixteenth birthday and whom with: at the Callistro Academy with my family and friends, or in another one of Alexa's lairs with a pack of Grand Hunters.

TWENTY

r. Dawson held our lessons that day in his office. As I grew in my ability to cast in my head, it became slightly easier to do with my eyes closed. It still wasn't mastered, but it was coming along at a comfortable pace. Momma sparred with me in the gym to practice the self-defense side of things. Extra credit wasn't possible for her class (much to Breanne's disappointment), but I was readying myself as much as I could for an unfair fight.

The scariest thing that came from the past week was actually, of all things, the transformation slowly happening within my mother. I wanted to blame it on the fact that I was growing up and already taking on what we thought we wouldn't have to worry about for at least a couple more years, but that week, she gradually became less of my best friend and more of a, well, mother. A mother who had to fend for herself and what was left of her family at all costs because she was all that her family had in this world.

Because of that, it was like every ounce of trouble that followed us, she immediately deemed as her own fault. And nobody could convince her otherwise, not even me as her daughter. I couldn't do anything to change or help it, only watch it.

Back in my dorm, I thought about my roommates to keep myself calm, wondering how their weekends were going. Wondering how normal theirs probably were. Realizing that a "normal" weekend was no longer part of my life, and hating myself for never fully appreciating all the normal weekends I'd had before this school year.

Wondering if any of us were actually safe in here.

How *had* Alexa managed to get all the way to my room without security catching her? Did she have that much power to force them all silent as she simply walked into the school? What had been her excuse?

"I know a few things about the Callistro Academy."

What did that mean? Did Callistro have other secrets besides the Hunter's Room?

It's a Hunter school. That actually didn't sound implausible.

Think like a Hunter. Think like Caralyn. What could Caralyn have built into the school that would allow people to sneak in? And why would she have built it?

There would have to be some kind of shortcut in, something granting passage into and throughout the school. Something hidden, something secret...

The secret passageways Opal had mentioned!

I stood at my dorm door with my hand on the knob, trying to work out the best place to start. According to books and movies, libraries usually hid secret passageways behind a bookshelf or fireplace. Unfortunately, our library was pretty sizeable; we had the bookshelves and fireplace, but time and patience were scarce—if Alexa planned on making another round tonight.

Maybe I was overthinking this. Caralyn's biggest secret in this school was the Hunter's Room. But that was underground. I couldn't access a secret passageway underground from here, but one could *lead* underground. And where would it start from? Outside. It had to for Alexa to make her way in.

That was it. I turned the doorknob and left my room; I knew I was going to need some help, especially since Callistro and I were more or less acquaintances now. Who better to ask about the architecture of an ex-Hunter school than the headmaster, who was actually a druid?

"Weekends don't exist for headmasters, Emma," Mr. Dawson said from his desk when I walked into his office for the third time that morning. "I need to work."

"It'll be quick," I said, shutting the door behind me. I took my spot on the white sofa against the right wall of the room. "Do you know everything about the manor? Like, do you know it inside and out?"

"What are you trying to ask?" he said flatly, perfectly aware of my intentions.

I made the mistake of glimpsing to the side. "I wanna explore the school. And maybe a bit of the forest."

"It's insulting you don't remember how easy it is for a magician, let alone ex-Master, to figure out if you're lying," he said, unamused. "Second of all, you know you're not going anywhere outside the manor alone after last night. Third, your mom wouldn't appreciate me feeding your curiosity."

I heavily leaned against the armrest of the sofa, dropping my hands into my lap. "I can't just be some overly preserved artifact until this whole thing blows over. Please? It's not like I'm involving myself with anyone, I'm staying inside the school."

"You didn't intend to involve yourself with anyone the night you met Jak."

I lightly rolled my eyes. "You sound like my mom... Fine. What do you know about the secret passageways?"

He laughed, going back to typing like the conversation was already finished. "No. The last thing you're doing is exploring those."

"How come? The other girls already know about them—"

"Yes, and they're also not on the federal government's wanted list right now. That means they can explore the passageways without the risk of being kidnapped."

My shoulders sank as I tried to find the right excuse. "What if I need them one day? What if they become the safest place in the manor for me to hide in?"

Which I prayed he wouldn't use a truth spell for, considering the reason I was trying to find the secret passageway system in the first place.

He looked up from his laptop, holding my gaze for a few seconds that felt loud with his thoughts. Then, he sat back in his seat with another tired exhale.

"Okay. I'll make you a deal." He closed his laptop, warning me to brace myself. "There's a rumor about a passageway that leads underground, and most think its entrance is in this room. Well—it's not really a rumor more so much as it is a riddle. Caralyn wrote a lot of riddles about the school's secrets, only a few of which still haven't been cracked yet. Including this one."

Huh? Why would Caralyn build a separate system of passageways *underneath* the school?

"If you can figure it out," Mr. Dawson said next, lifting his index finger, "I'll give you one entrance to a secret passageway. Okay?"

"Okay," I replied with an excitement that would've made even me second-guess the wisdom of proposing that deal.

Still, Mr. Dawson began his speech slowly: "'To the likely, who will be blind, the soul of unity is sure to find. The center of the quarters they'll see the right place for the given key. Our level precedes that which is sought, but the world below can be bought with a single breath of the soul, who shall discover the truth that will unfold.'"

Something poignant lay in that riddle—no, in its answer, like Caralyn had somehow known two centuries ago every question I'd have in this moment.

"When did you memorize that?" I asked.

"When I took office a few years ago. People have been trying to solve it since Caralyn wrote it. They finally came to the conclusion that she was referring to the head's office, which made the most sense, considering she was headmistress. I'm a believer that it's the entrance of the passageway that leads underground—which means it probably leads to the Hunter's Room."

Then this was my new mission: I was going to decipher that riddle if it was the last thing I'd do... today. Aunt Becca always says that the best way to tackle any problem is in parts.

To the likely, who will be blind, / The soul of unity is sure to find.

Was the "soul of unity" a person or a metaphor? It was time to take any possible chance.

"The soul of unity," I began, resting my elbow on the armrest of the sofa and fiddling with my fingers, "do you know what that *could* mean?"

"No idea." Mr. Dawson lightly rocked in his chair. Then, he paused, a subtle furrow denting his brow. "Actually, knowing what I do today about you… if I heard that riddle for the very first time, I'd think of you."

My head jerked back with skepticism. "Me?"

"Sure." He shrugged. "Or, I guess, Adara, seeing as she's destined to *unite* our two worlds."

I mentally gasped. It suddenly made a hundred times more sense.

"What if… Adara is the 'soul of unity'?" I said, chuckling at how ridiculous it sounded coming out of my mouth. "If that's what she's meant to do, maybe Caralyn wanted her—me—to find this passageway."

"The only way that would be the case," Mr. Dawson said dully, folding his hands on his desk, "is if she somehow knew about your destiny. And if that were true, she would've done everything in her power to make sure you'd never accomplish it."

"I'm not saying it's the answer, but can we just pretend it is and see how far we get?"

He sighed again. I imagined that he was surrendering to the fact that this was how he was going to spend the rest of his Saturday morning.

"So who would be the 'likely'?" I asked.

"Well, those who've taught and trained at the school have been trying to piece this together for two hundred years. The 'likely' could be the people here since they've been blind to the answer but they're... common, or likely."

That sparked the perfect idea. "Or the world," I said, sitting up straighter. "The 'likely', those who are *like* everyone else. Mortals. They're likely in terms of regularity and numbers, statistically speaking."

Mr. Dawson shrugged, pressing his lips together.

In the center of the quarters, they'll see / The right place for the given key.

According to the second part of that line, the key to unlocking the passageway had already been given to me. Or it came with me. Or vice versa. If the world was blind to it, that meant they couldn't have it—at least, they couldn't see what the key truly was.

It was the only thing I could think of that would piece together my interpretation of the puzzle: magic.

But "quarters"? The head's office was rumored to be the location of this secret passageway's entrance. Why would Caralyn refer to it as "quarters"?

Main office. Head. Quarters.

Headquarters.

"I think 'quarters' is an abbreviation for 'headquarters'," I said, speeding my words, "so the entrance is in the center of your office, and I'm supposed to unlock it with magic!"

"A logical conclusion," Mr. Dawson said, nodding slowly, "except you're in a school that was built with the sole purpose of *destroying* magic."

"Which is also a school that has a lot more secrets than we think," I argued. "The Hunter's Room and secret passageways can't be the only thing Caralyn and her family were hiding. Look at Henry Callistro."

Mr. Dawson's diamond-blue eyes glazed over with a daze, lost in either thought or revelation. I continued anyway; half of the riddle was solved if we had it right.

Our level precedes that which is sought, / But the world below can be bought...

You can't have a secret passageway just appear in the middle of a room. "Precedes" and "below" were too specific to not give it away: that was how everyone knew this passageway was underground. What came before and was above underground? The ground we walked on. "Our level" was the surface.

...with a single breath of the soul, / Who shall discover the truth that will unfold.

I wasn't sure if I could interpret the last part, but "a breath", if I had the beginning right, must have meant magic. A spell. That was the key.

"I think I have it," I said, holding my gaze with the glass coffee table in front of me to steady my concentration. "If I do, the rest of the world couldn't figure it out because of Caralyn's background, they'd never think of the answer, and they'd have to know about Adara. The entrance to the passageway is in the middle of your office, where I, the soul of unity, have to use magic to unlock it. And Caralyn directly states that it's underground and can be found with my magic, if I have that part right."

Mr. Dawson's head dropped in astonishment. I was ready for all objection, for something about how Caralyn had been against magic, until he said, "Then what are we waiting for?"

I froze on the sofa. Good question—what was next? What was I supposed to say that would make the passageway reveal itself?

Underneath...

I stood up and gestured to the coffee table. "Can we move this? And the rug?"

Suspiciously wordlessly, Mr. Dawson stood from his desk and helped me push away the furniture. Caralyn hadn't wanted anyone to find this passageway, or, more accurately, she hadn't wanted *just* anyone—but how could she have known about me? How could she have known two centuries into the future? The Callistro family definitely hadn't been seers or druids... Besides, why would a family of magicians start a legacy of destroying their own people?

And why had Caralyn Callistro, founder of the Callistro Academy for Hunters, created a secret passageway underground that could only be unlocked with magic?

Mr. Dawson folded back the dark-blue rug, exposing the dark oak wood underneath. We'd cracked Caralyn's code, and now we were about to verify it.

Something to open the passageway...

I decided on an opening spell first: "*Aperta.*"

The floorboard in the center of the room slid into the ground, the five next to it on both sides following suit. It was a pattern of that until an opening in the ground formed, unveiling a long cobblestone staircase that had been lying underneath us the entire time.

"You solved it."

I looked at Mr. Dawson, suppressing a triumphant laugh at

the bewilderment that had widened his eyes and opened his jaw.

"I—I mean, I didn't exactly doubt you would, but..."

I freed a smile before placing my foot onto the first concrete step. The dark corridor blew up a cold draft, ensnaring me as I took another step down. Only a couple of feet of the walls were exposed under the fluorescent lights of Mr. Dawson's office, revealing cracked cobblestone. Caralyn never needed to worry about other people finding this place as far as I was concerned; the entrance was enough to scare them away. Or were all secret passageway entrances this creepy?

"Emma," Mr. Dawson said behind me, finally shaking himself out of his surprise, "let me go first. Just in case."

He stepped in front of me, and I followed his slow crawl down the long staircase. His gaze inspected every inch of the hallway until we reached the bottom. The vintage glass lanterns dangling above us flickered to life, and I jumped.

"That was me," Mr. Dawson whispered, looking all around him. "I wonder when they were last on. If they ever were."

Considering the fact that there was still oil or fat to burn, I couldn't answer that; anything from 1827 would have degraded or at least gone rancid by now.

A chill ran down my back, and it wasn't because of the draft. *Who was last in these passageways?*

Mr. Dawson continued ahead while I looked behind me, his door slightly visible over the edge of the top of the staircase. I focused on it and silently used a locking spell.

I followed Mr. Dawson wherever he went. We might've been underground and in an area practically no one had ever set foot in, but it was still easier to rely on him to make sure we didn't get lost.

Our steps echoed down the corridors on the stone floor. Mr. Dawson was the only thing pulling me along those hallways. I could almost hear water dripping from the ceiling though nothing was there, but the air was damp with the chill. Now I had to find out what Caralyn was keeping down here; why else would these passageways exist?

"This is insane." I sighed in awe. "Did Caralyn hide something in here and that's why she made it underground?"

"I still can't pin down why she would incorporate magic like this, being who she was..." he whispered back, approaching a four-way intersection. His words softly reverberated through the air. "But there's a reason she wanted only you down here. Even if she didn't know that you were the one she wanted."

I stayed close behind him when he turned left. "I wonder if there's another way to get back up."

"There'll probably be another staircase if we find one," he answered. "We just have to know where we're ending up. It's obvious nobody can know about this, especially if Caralyn did hide something down here. But we need to make this trip quick—someone could show up at my door."

"I locked it." I proudly smiled. "Don't worry."

He came to a stop, eyes on me as I approached his side. With a light nod of his head, he cocked his brows. "Good thinking. But I still have a lot of work to do, so we're making this quick anyway."

Turning his gaze ahead, his irises flashed a glowing amber. Just as the light faded, he jolted, straightening. "There's a document down here," he said. "At a dead end, framed on the wall."

"What? How do you know? What did you cast?"

"Lookout spell. I'll teach it to you someday." He patted my back to signal me forward with him again. "It's almost like echolocation. It lets you look throughout a building or general area you're in. Pretty helpful if you're in a maze or a new place."

I almost wanted to regret that I hadn't known that spell last night to help me escape, but it wasn't like I'd had many opportunities to use it, anyway.

"Can we find the document with that?" I asked. "Do you just feel if you're close to it?"

"The lookout spell shows you where you are, so you'll see the path once you cast it."

Wow. *That* was a spell I wanted to use, and not just for the passageways and escaping Alexa. (I'd never have to worry about quietly sneaking snacks at night ever again.)

A vibration emanated across the halls. Mr. Dawson stopped walking again and took his phone out of his blazer pocket, sighing at the screen. "There it is. One of the board members is calling, and I doubt I get enough signal down here for a clear phone call."

I'm surprised he got the call at all, I thought as I followed him back the way we'd come. His phone vibrated the entire way, and by the time we got back up, it had begun another cycle.

"Hello, Mrs. Gonzales," Mr. Dawson answered, glancing at me. "I'm sorry to have missed your first call... Monday's perfect... You, too."

He hung up, sliding the phone back into his pocket. "Well, I have a meeting with some of the board members on Monday, which means even more prep work today and tomorrow. Please try not to get into any trouble for the rest of the weekend."

"I have no idea what you're talking about," I teased, looking down at the gaping hole in the floor. "How do we close this?"

It only took him a few seconds to decide on "*Converte.*"

The opening pattern we'd witnessed a few minutes ago reversed itself, the floorboards covering the entrance back up. Got it: a reversal spell.

He helped me move the rug and table back into place, my mind heavy with everything that had gathered in it. Each thought demanded my attention, and I had no idea how to tackle any of them. I was obviously going back, right? I had to figure out that lookout spell if I was going to find that document; I could bet my magic that Caralyn's reason for needing magic to open the passageway was on it.

Speaking of, since I'd solved the riddle...

"So which passageway are you gonna tell me about?" I chimed as Mr. Dawson strolled back to his desk. "Because I'm pretty sure Alexa used one to get in last night. She probably used one that leads outside and somehow found my room once she got into the school."

Mr. Dawson plopped down into his chair. "I don't want to say you're wrong, but I won't say you're right. How would she have found *your* dorm specifically?"

I scoffed. "*Someone* came into my dorm to grab me, that's for sure. I wouldn't put hacking into the school's student records past her for a second. She said she knows a few things about Callistro. So I'm assuming she knows more than we think."

He pursed his lips, silence overcoming him for a few seconds. By the daze falling over his eyes, the presence of his thoughts was palpable—but I knew asking about them was pointless if it'd taken him an entire negotiation just to tell me about one passageway entrance.

"Okay," he finally said, folding his hands on his desk. "In the hall that leads to the gym, with the candle sconces on the walls, one of them has a plastic candle painted to look like wax. Pull the candle sconce toward you, and you'll open a secret passageway in the wall."

I smirked with excitement. "Good to know. Thanks."

"I have to get back to work, so I mean it: *try* not to get into any trouble for the rest of the weekend."

I rolled my eyes. "Because I *choose* when Alexa kidnaps me?"

"You know what I mean."

I did. But all I could think about in that moment was how Alexa probably didn't know about the underground passageways, let alone how to get to them. I'd gained a *real* safe place today, and that was enough.

"I promise," I told him, turning to his door and unlocking it.

Twenty-One

You'd think Jak would've come bursting through the school's front doors by Sunday afternoon, but I was constantly having to remind myself that he probably didn't know about Friday night. I was pretty confident that his stepmother wouldn't tell him about the successful kidnapping attempt she'd set out on. She *would* tell him about my answer, though, wouldn't she? To turn him against me? To make him realize he was wrong to protect me?

Sitting at the desk in my dorm after lunch, I realized that Jak *was* going to have to turn against me eventually. Either automatically because of what I was, or because I'd unnecessarily endangered him because I'd lied to him. And it was impossible to imagine a world where he simply forgave me for that. After he'd already tried being open with me.

The door behind me banged open. "SURPRISE!"

I yelped, whirling around in the chair. Sarah and Breanne ran across the room and up to me, throwing their arms around me.

"Why would you do that?!" I exclaimed, a firm hand resting on my heaving chest. "With everything going on right now?"

"Oh, you're right." Breanne pouted, her light fingers picking at her nails. "Sorry. But surprise."

"What're you doing here? I thought you weren't gonna be back until tonight."

"It's your *birth-week!*" Sarah smiled with mischievous bright-green eyes, pulling me up from the chair. "And we have plans. Invite your boyfriend and his friends, it'll be more fun."

I rolled my eyes. "Shut up. What're we doing?"

"Tonight's the first night of the carnival," Breanne said, blue-hazel eyes scanning me like I might've had a concussion. "Did you actually forget?"

Now that look made sense: five or six years ago, the three of us went to the annual Capperson Fall Carnival for the first time together, and we decided to make it a best friend tradition to go every year. This year was meant to be extra special, though, because we were going to go alone for the first time without our parents to chaperone. But after this weekend...

I suppressed a deep sigh, and it tightened my chest. My best friends in the entire world not only couldn't know who I really was, but also couldn't know what had happened this weekend with Alexa. If it'd been either of them, I would want to know. It'd kill me not to know. I guess ignorance really is bliss, because they didn't even know there was something to know.

"If you can convince my mom to let me go, fine," I said, walking across the room and to my bed. "Otherwise, we're probably staying here tonight."

"Why?" Sarah whined.

"She's a lot more paranoid," I said, which wasn't a lie, at least. "A crowded place is a pretty great place to get kidnapped."

"But you'll have *Jak* to protect you," Breanne sang, twirling the ends of her blond hair. "And us. And we're doing those extra self-defense classes for a reason. Even if you don't execute the moves successfully, someone's bound to notice you're trying to escape someone."

"I know," I muttered. "But Alexa's still…"

"Emmy," Sarah cooed, meandering toward my bed. "Not that I believe she's gonna try something there, but the street will be so full of people, it'll be hard to *not* notice someone throwing a teenage girl into the back of a van."

The words, however silly she'd intended them to be, sent a chill down my back.

"Thanks—I think."

"Let's go talk to your mom," she said, gesturing for me to follow her. "She knows how much we look forward to this every year. And she has to make an exception for your birthday."

To avoid an interrogation for not wanting to go, I didn't argue. Besides, I trusted Momma's judgment on what to do a lot more than I trusted my own.

"Fine."

I blinked, straightening in my spot next to Sarah and Breanne in front of Momma's desk. *Fine?* The same woman who once debated making *me* wear colored contacts when I was little because she was scared people would "recognize the Atera blue"—now she was letting me out on a crowded street with Grand Hunters on the prowl?

She set down the stack of highlighted papers in front of her. "But I'm coming with you."

There it is. "Mom—"

"Great idea!" Sarah chimed, tossing her black waves over her shoulder. "Smart, wise, let's do it. Thanks, Mrs. Marie!"

"Nobody's happier than when Mom says yes." Momma pressed her lips into a tight, thin smile, tossing her highlighter into her pencil cup. "Be ready to leave at 6."

Okay, I *did* want to go; it might've been the only way I could celebrate my birthday this year. I kind of figured I'd be fine as long as someone I knew was watching me—at least, I wanted to justify going with that. But Momma had to have some kind of reason for actually allowing it. If she'd told Sarah and Breanne it wasn't a good idea with the pack lurking around, they wouldn't have questioned her...

I guess that means she thinks I'll be safe. Or she has a plan for it.

I softly smiled as Sarah, Breanne, and I walked down the hall toward the Grand Foyer. Maybe I could enjoy tonight, after all.

I took out my phone to fulfill my end of the bargain.

E: Hey, the Capperson Fall Carnival starts to-
night if you guys wanna come

J: Sure :) When and where?

E: Meet us at the fountain in the square at 6:10,

This was going to be like every other night we'd spent there, I told myself. This was going to be an evening full of fun, laughter, freedom, and familiarity, one that promised we could explore this night like it was the first time. Why not bring three new people into the mix?

Twenty-Two

My mother once had to convince the head of her agency that writing a mission report in crayon was a suitable encryption method when a magician had trapped her in a day care during a hunt. That was when she'd first started helping magicians escape, so the fact that Momma had pulled that lie off at all tells you that she's a lot more qualified to be a runaway magician than I am.

But it really comes in handy for situations like that night, when she shook Adrien's and Wyatt's hands at the fountain and said with a welcoming grin, "I'm glad you could join us tonight! How long will you be in Capperson?"

Because there was no way she automatically trusted the two of them, and part of her was definitely going to stay in Master

Hunter mode tonight just in case they found out anything they weren't supposed to.

"Until Jak says we're leaving," Adrien joked, running a hand through his loose blond hair. "Thanks for letting us tag along."

"The more, the merrier," she chimed. Translation: *The more watching over my daughter, the better.* "Don't worry, I'm not here to hover, but make sure you stay roughly within my vicinity. And have fun."

Yes, my cheeks were bright red. Yes, my chest was burning with embarrassment. Yes, I tried forcing the group away from my mother as soon as possible.

We weaseled our way through the crowd on the sidewalk and to the black asphalt of Main Street. The road stayed clear and open for carnival goers, food stands and games overwhelming the sidewalks in condensed booths. Popcorn mingled with corn dogs and funnel cakes in the warm air, more potently the farther down the street we walked—or, rather, squeezed through. I looked over at every child's holler of joy, every oversized stuffed animal that flashed past my peripheral. All of it almost nostalgic, but something in the air crackled like a new force had erased the familiarity for new experiences.

—*Already desperate to get away from your mom?*—

I almost stopped walking and barely suppressed the drop of my jaw in time. Thankfully, my group's eyes were focused on not slamming into anyone, anyway.

That was why Momma had let us come tonight: she had planned on grabbing Mr. Dawson for an extra set of eyes.

—*Where are you?*— I asked.

—*Close enough. I have one half of the carnival, she has the other.*

Do your best to stay visible tonight. You deserve to have this for your birthday, especially amidst everything.—

Two ex-Masters had their eyes on me. Now I could smile wide; I was safe.

It was in front of a milk bottle game that Sarah turned to face the five of us with a sly grin, placing her hands on her hips. "Let's make this more interesting," she called over the winning dings, clapping, and children's laughter. "How about a game?"

"Depends," Breanne said for me, raising her usually small voice to be heard. I noticed Wyatt keeping his distance beside her. "What game?"

Sarah dug out three popsicle sticks and three markers from her small black purse. Had she really packed those just for tonight? Where had she gotten popsicle sticks?

"Each pair will have one stick and one marker," she began. "If another pair catches you, they give your stick one tally. Whoever has the most tallies by the time we leave gets to treat everyone to dinner tomorrow, and they have to sing Emma an original birthday song on her birthday."

A warm flush flooded my cheeks as I shook my head, hiding my face in my hand. "No song," I shouted.

"That's the main incentive to win!" she argued.

"Wait," Breanne called, her arms tight around her. "So we enjoy the carnival with just our... partners... and try to avoid the others?"

"Yep! But each pair gets a timeout to hang out with another." Sarah scurried to Adrien, next to Jak, grabbing his arm and then gesturing between us. "Go ahead, pick your partner!"

Just as Breanne started to turn toward me, Wyatt held out a

cautious hand. He arched a brow above his narrow dark-brown eyes, gently smiling. Breanne hesitantly took it, never sparing me even the start of a glance back.

I wonder if they've been texting since last week. That was fairly suggested by how Breanne had released herself at all and was now pushing a lock behind her ear. A vibrant red swarmed her pale cheeks instead, a soft smile touching her pink-glossed lips.

Jak's brown eyes met mine, their playfulness all too knowing. A light breeze ruffled the tips of his brown hair that curled slightly upward at his ears. He offered me his hand. "Hi, I'm Jak."

I acted on every teenage girl instinct in me: smiled like an idiot and accepted.

"Thirty-second head start!" Sarah announced, pulling Adrien with her back in the direction we'd come from. Jak just as quickly dragged me in the opposite direction like a dog on a leash, almost as if he knew the carnival better than I did. Then again, experiencing it with him erased everything I used to know about it; I didn't know anything about what the carnival would look like with him. As far as I was pleasantly concerned, we were evenly matched.

"What about the photo booth?" I called.

"Not a good idea," he replied, the warmth of his hand impossible to ignore as we weaved between the crowd. My stomach growled for a hot dog. "Someone can catch you as soon as you leave. Wyatt and Breanne are heading there, anyway."

"Then let's—"—I apologized to a middle-aged couple I'd swayed into—"let's catch them."

"Not yet, Merlin." Jak smiled, darting around a group of young adults. I followed his lead. "First, we need to find a place nobody can follow *us* to."

I quickly found out that that meant the short line for the Ferris wheel. When our thirty seconds were up, Jak and I were at the front. Brilliant: I'd technically be out of sight from Momma and Mr. Dawson, but not even Alexa and William could grab me from up there.

Jak looked up at the cabin arriving at the top as we reached the entry gate. "Nobody can reach us if we're up there," he said. My stomach swirled at how we were thinking the same thing.

"I see," I teased. "You just wanted us to be alone *and* somewhere nobody can get us. My mom isn't gonna like that."

"I think you hate it because you love how smart it is," he said with that stupid smirk that did stupid things to my nerves. "And Mrs. Marie can see us perfectly fine way up there. Unless you're scared of heights. Or me."

A little bit of both.

"Of course not," I said as he took out his leather wallet.

"Well,"—he handed the operator six dollars—"too late to back out now."

He let me step ahead of him and inside the metal cabin first. I noticed the gap he kept between us as the operator closed the door. Pastel-yellow paint chipped off the seat and walls, exposing rust underneath. I kept my eyes far from Jak's, scanning the street crowd and wondering where my friends were among it.

Our cabin moved two slots back to allow newcomers on before we slowly started making our way to the top. The closer we drew, I was finally brave enough to look at Jak. His light-brown skin was as smooth as our gym floors, soft lips just below a straight button nose. He must have had plastic surgery or something to be this naturally attractive! Did he know how handsome he was?

Did I have that kind of natural beauty?

The only makeup I'd put on tonight were lip gloss and mascara on curled lashes. Sitting next to Jak, though, I started comparing my "makeup job" to Sarah's everyday looks... and then how naturally sweet and cute Breanne looked... and I had to wonder, what did my friends think? What did everyone else who met me or sees me every day think?

"Peripheral vision." Jak's gentle eyes shifted from the scenery in front of us to me. "Or do you wanna take a picture? Because I have a few in my phone already I could send you."

"Shut up," I teased back, chuckling and looking back out over the town. Thinking of what to say next felt calm, relaxed, like I had all the time in the world to find it because Jak would give it to me. Searching wasn't a frantic test anymore; it was just a matter of choosing what I wanted to tell him. And that was when I realized exactly what he had meant when he'd said I was easy to talk to. I felt like I could tell him anything and he'd always have a reply, he'd *want* to reply. It was almost like I could trust him with any thought I had.

We now overlooked the entire street, fairground, and even the highways traveling to and from Capperson. Cars drove in slow motion in and out of town. I'd ridden the Ferris wheel with Sarah and Breanne countless times before, but this was new. This was something I didn't want to forget.

I picked the first complete thought that came to mind, the easiest: "I never thought I'd be here one day with someone other than Sarah and Breanne. I always thought it was gonna be just the three of us every year."

"Really? Even after high school?"

"I haven't really thought past that point," I mused. Another breeze fluttered by, threatening me with a shiver, as we reached halfway back down to the ground. "Considering where we are today, I've honestly let the years fly. I think I was nine when we first came to the carnival together."

"I wish I couldn't say the same," Jak said. "Letting time zoom by isn't the smartest thing when I'm not sure what I wanna do after school."

"Aren't you planning on following your family's footsteps even if Redway doesn't open back up as a Hunter school?"

He shrugged. "Our schools let us choose whatever career we want, Merlin. Hunting's just the most encouraged."

Another breeze blew past us, and my body succumbed to the shiver. Apparently a long-sleeved blouse with a cardigan on top really *weren't* enough to keep me warm, but I wasn't about to let Breanne know that she was right. (She hears that enough every day.)

"Do you want my jacket?" Jak asked.

Nope. I'm not letting him see what that does to me while we're in a confined space.

"I'm fine," I said, setting my gaze ahead again.

"Are you sure?"

Without a second thought, my gaze caught his eyes for a second too long and then stole itself away. But he read me like a book and slid off his jacket. He draped it around my shoulders like he was waiting for my objection—which never came. I smiled a thank-you at him. His soft eyes seemed to dare me to look away, knowing too well that I wouldn't.

Something flickered in my teenage mind. It craved more of the new experiences I'd missed out on throughout middle and freshman year of high school, and impulse was breaking down the wall inside: I leaned into Jak and laid my head on his chest, crossing my arms to preserve heat. A whiff of his cologne—his most expensive, according to Alexa herself—wafted into my nose, all while Jak tried a quiet, undetectable sigh of contentment. My heart skipped a hard beat at the combination, especially with my ear pressed close to his heart and lungs. You always manage to hear those kinds of things, especially if the other person doesn't want you to.

The sun gradually set over the hills in the distance, casting shadows below and painting the sky with streaks of orange, pink, and cotton-candy blue. Peace. Serene.

Safe, even.

The hair on my arms stood on end, every muscle in my body straining to relax as I shifted slightly against Jak. This was *too* peaceful. Goosebumps prickled on my arms, not because of the chill, but because of that small voice in the back of my head trying to psych me out and tell me that I *wasn't* safe. And that no backup could change that.

"We're fine, Merlin," Jak whispered just above my head. "Don't worry."

"I don't... wanna go back down." I swallowed the saliva pooling in my mouth, hoping he couldn't feel it.

"She wouldn't try anything here." He rested his hand securely on my shoulder. I knew that kind of touch: a friend's. "Some other bad guy, yeah, but not someone who's never allowed to show her face while working. She can't pull off anything without drawing attention. And security is everywhere."

It would've relaxed me some. It *should* have; I even had two personal bodyguards. But Alexa was a hunter and I had her prey: information about my father's descendant. If weekends didn't exist for headmasters, they definitely didn't exist for Hunters with their target in sight.

"You were able to protect all those other kids, right?" I asked.

"Yeah."

"How? How did you figure out who was being targeted?"

Jak chuckled, his chest moving under me—warming his laugh all the more to my ears. "I kid you not—my parents. Parents who are desperate enough for me to follow in their footsteps that they include me in the hunts a lot more than they should. Don't tell anyone."

I couldn't help but give him a chuckle. "Sorry to hear."

When his chest inflated with a deep breath, I followed suit. I wanted to sink into him, to forget every flaw of my reality. We were here to celebrate the start of my birth-week. I only had tonight. If nothing else, just for the next one or two hours, I had to give myself this. I couldn't have come just to be afraid.

We went three more cycles around before coming back down to Earth. Walking down the steps from the wheel, I glanced up from the sidewalk, pausing.

Before I could take another breath, Jak came to my side, his hand resting on my shoulder again and taking my attention. I realized I was blocking traffic, and I stepped onto the street with him.

"You okay?" he asked above the carnival noise, a sizeable contrast to the quieter space of the Ferris wheel cabin. "See someone?"

Behind a line of trash cans where a booth could have been, in front of the mechanic's, three people in worn, raggedy clothes stood huddled together. The big, gruff man was attempting to set fire to a pile of sticks and crumbled-up papers sitting on top of the garbage in a trash can. Holes had been eaten into his gloves. His lighter refused to spark.

"All good," I told Jak, turning to him and pointing in the direction we'd come from. "Check that way."

His gaze obeyed, scanning the carnival down the other side of the street. I looked straight ahead at the mechanic's and group of three.

The small, stout woman sitting next to the large man visibly sighed, then muttered something to him. The man gave a seemingly curt reply, shaking his head and then banging the lighter against his palm as if to make it work.

Mr. Dawson's lessons came back to me: I channeled my focus onto the pile of sticks and balled-up paper, allowing myself to feel my power and understand my will. I needed control.

Keep the power steady and understand that you're the one who wields it.

Uro.

It felt like a whisper, a heavy whisper, traveling from my mind to the small pile in the trash can just as the gruff man flicked the lighter again. A small fire waved to life, eating at the paper and sticks and just big enough for the three of them.

The large man laughed in triumph, his friends grinning with comfort. They each reached out their hands over the flames.

—I saw that.—

I bluntly sighed with relief. *—You were already watching me. It's* *fine as long as you're the only one who did.—*

—You're asking to get caught. Anyone could've seen your eyes. You need to be more careful.—

I crossed my arms and gazed out at the other end of the carnival and sea of people. *—What else are we supposed to use magic for?—*

It took Mr. Dawson a couple of seconds to tell me, *—You did a good thing, I'm proud of you for that. Next time, though, don't just jump into it. Preparing protects you and those around you.—*

"Hey," Jak said, tapping my shoulder. His other hand pointed at his targets sharing a bag of caramel corn farther down the street. "Wyatt and—"

I followed his finger just as Breanne looked over and exclaimed next to the caramel corn cart, "Emma and Jak!"

Uh oh. It was probably the first time in my life that I'd thought those words with a smile.

Jak and I sprinted down the street, back in the direction we'd come from, my chest pulsing with the adrenaline of playing tag in a maze. With Breanne's and Wyatt's footsteps lost in the clamor of the carnival, I glanced behind us: they were somehow catching all the clearings in the crowd to gain on us.

I ran up beside Jak, took his hand, waited for the mob to gather in front of us, and then darted across the street. There was one place nearby that I was all too familiar with and would hide us. Squeezing between a slushy cart and deep-fried dessert booth, Jak and I ran all the way down the alley between two buildings. I turned us left at the end, into the back alley running behind. Our breaths caught up with us in fast pants as we grinned at each other, peering our heads around the corner. Wyatt and Breanne walked straight past the entry to our hiding spot.

"We lost them." Jak laughed breathlessly behind me as I panted, like he was surprised. "Nice hiding spot, Merlin."

"I've been here a few times," I said matter-of-factly, straightening and leaning against the brick wall to calm my deep breaths. The alleys used to be the place Sarah, Breanne, and I would explore when we wanted to do something extra "rebellious" when we were younger.

I poked my head around the corner again, smiling again. "You know what?" I said, my breaths slowing. I stared after the people strolling by in opposite directions on Main Street, envying the cotton candy and nachos in their hands. "Sarah was right, this is kind of fun."

"Well, I'm glad you're having fun, my dear."

That sweet tone—that hauntingly soothing voice turned my blood to jelly, freezing me in my spot against the building's corner. I knew that voice. Her presence filled the damp alley like ice, but I refused to face her. To cement the fact that she was here.

Wait. That meant Jak wasn't behind me anymore.

I spun around. Two tall, broad Hunters gripped an unconscious Jak by the arms.

"Jak!" I stepped toward him like I could save him, but two agents grabbed my arms and pulled me back.

"Believe it or not," Alexa began, black boots thumping against the concrete as she strolled toward me, "he has nothing to do with this. It's all just procedure. He's due for questioning."

"What?" I snapped, jerking in the frustrating, stone-like grips of the man and woman who held me in place. "Why would you need to question *him*? I haven't told him anything I didn't tell you! What else do you want?"

Alexa traced my body with her venomous green eyes. "It's just procedure."

I was ready to scream for help until I remembered that nobody would hear me. My voice would be drowned out by the music, joyful cheers and laughter, games—

My *verbal* voice would be. Mr. Dawson.

—Mr—!

My thoughts stumbled when a third hand from behind me slid a rag over my mouth and nose. A nauseatingly sweet, chemical odor inflamed my airways, traveling straight to my brain and blaring an alarm in my head. Sedative. Sedative, I needed help *now*.

—Mr. Dawson...—

His name echoed like a distance voice across a chasm as the world faded into black.

C H A P T E R

Twenty-Three

I wanted to scream for help as my consciousness faded into reality. By the time I completely came to, I knew that my best option was silence and to pretend that I *hadn't* just been kidnapped again. No one on my side would hear me, let alone know where I'd been taken to.

Did they find out? I groggily thought, squinting my eyes open against what looked like a hundred white suns. *Are they gonna kill me...?*

It took longer than I wanted it to for my eyes to fully adjust and focus on the black-and-white room. The only thing I was sure of was that Alexa had taken me to her lair. One of them, at least. And it turns out that metal chairs are a Grand-Hunter favorite, because that was what I'd been handcuffed to yet again. This time, though, unlike the last room, a camera sat in the two corners of the ceiling and faced me. Magic was even less of an option. Escape wasn't an option at all.

The white walls glared harshly under the fluorescent lights installed above, even brightening the black carpet under my feet. A fully stocked bookshelf sat against the wall on my left and next to a doorway far down, while another bookshelf stood against the wall in front of me. Mere feet away sat a white leather couch—like this place was a living room. Which I honestly think would've made me all the more terrified.

At the doorway, a man I'd never seen before—never in my conscious life, at least—walked straight through, adjusting his suit jacket.

No—no, wait, that was just it, I *had* seen him before. I'd seen all this before. The last time I'd been in this situation, I'd been in a nightmare, Mr. Dawson's vision...

The nightmare. This *was* my nightmare.

My shaking fingers gripped the metal armrests of the chair, panic gripping my chest and cutting off my breaths. This couldn't be happening now! I needed more time! I needed help!

—*Mr. Dawson, please, can you hear me?!*—

Why wasn't he answering?!

"I'm sorry you had to wake up like this, Emmalynn."

I looked up, freezing. The man's suit couldn't hide his muscular build underneath, almost threatening to break the stitching. With a roman nose and square jaw, his dark-brown hair reminded me of Jak's, and his brown eyes were almost an exact replica—save for the callousness and sheer insanity in place of the tender loving care. I was pretty sure this wasn't sane in any world no matter the laws.

A trolley stood next to me. Files, pictures, books, and a couple of small jars with blue fluid inside lay scattered across it. And... the syringes.

"You're safe," the man said next as I fought a tremble in my jaw. "I promise."

Are you kidding me?

No—I wasn't going to let this happen without getting as many answers as I deserved. But that meant I had to rip off a Band-Aid, and I couldn't afford to care about the sting. Despite the contrast between Jak's brown skin and this man's white, I asked, "You're William Bleu?"

"Good observation skills."

So *this* was Jak's father.

"And I really do hope you can believe me," he added, strolling toward the couch in front of me. "You don't have to be scared. Actually, I have to say, you've been a rather difficult target. Do you understand why we had to resort to this?"

"'Difficult'?" I repeated, wondering if he actually meant it. "No, I don't! There's no excuse for any of this! I answered everything honestly, Alexa let me *go!*"

Everything was coming true. Mr. Dawson's vision, my nightmare, they were coming true.

Ingrid had warned me about this. I had to do everything I could to fight it; Mr. Dawson couldn't have paid the price, whatever it was, in vain.

"You were honest, yes," William replied, turning back to me and pressing his fingertips together, "but you understand why we'd take you in again after that answer, right?"

"Yeah—"

"Then we have our right."

I knew I'd regret saying that.

"We *need* to know everything we can about Tristan Atera's lost descendant, Emmalynn. Every lead we get is one small step closer to finding out who they are and where Tristan is hiding—but we have a giant leap in you. Please don't let all this be for nothing."

He stepped toward me. If my heart pumped any faster, I was pretty sure I'd be on the verge of cardiac arrest.

"Do you see where we're coming from?"

"What about where I am?" I stated, using my anger to cover my fear. "Did you ever think there's a reason I've kept quiet for so long, why I never told the authorities that I knew something? Accomplices are *killed* for helping magicians escape, I didn't know if anyone would actually let me give my side of things before they shot me dead! What if it wasn't my choice to know, what do *you* define as an accomplice? Would you actually believe that I didn't want to get involved, or would Caldwell kill me anyway?"

"That's all understandable," William said gently and slowly. Like he did understand, like he'd been in my shoes before. "But we're giving you a chance to tell us all of that now."

He's not promising my freedom. Because even if I hadn't "chosen to be an accomplice", even if my story were true, I'd still withheld information. My fate was sealed either way, and William knew it.

He ambled over to the trolley, his eyes glazing over the yellow file and sheets of paper scattered about the surface. "You can tell me, Emmalynn. That's why we're both here. And I really want it to be your choice."

He unscrewed the cap to one of the bottles of fluid. The idea in his head was as plain as if it were being projected onto the wall.

Hard, round eyes fell onto me. "What do you know about Tristan's descendant?"

I wanted to tell him, I realized. At his question I wanted to throw up the truth like my brain was swirling it around and pouring the words down into my mouth. I wanted to release them and make them someone else's burden.

It was almost the same force of a truth spell. But this wasn't magic. This was a chemical reaction. A serum.

Truth serum.

I can't. I can't! Where's Jak, Mr. Dawson, Mom?

Reading all this back, my first instinct should have been some kind of distraction I could cause with magic that was natural enough to happen on its own. But I couldn't think—the adrenaline from the carnival was gone, infected by the terror possessing my body now. I finally let go and jerked my wrists and ankles, hoping to prevent the inevitable.

"I already told you," William said, "I'll let you go if you tell me the truth."

I fought harder, demanding unnatural strength to come into my arms and legs, driven by fight-or-flight and I was in flight. My survival instincts were on fire, and I'd fight until I freed myself from the prison I'd landed myself in.

You can go if you tell him, just say it!

Don't—no, don't!

"Emmalynn, stop," William stated, his tone lowering into an octave that could shake the entire room if he tried.

I hated my body for letting the cuffs restrain it. I hated my body for the dull pain of my ankles and wrists digging into the cold metal, hated my hands for being too big to pull themselves out. I shook harder as if to compensate for the fact that I couldn't use magic.

"*Emmalynn*," William growled, taking a firm step toward me to scare me into obedience.

Don't tell him anything!

I just want it to stop!

"Fine," he said, picking up an empty syringe. He dipped it into the blue jar. "But I did want it to be your choice."

"No," I cried, because I already knew that another dose would be all it would take. "No, please, don't!"

"You know something about Tristan's descendant," William snapped, his frustration manifesting. "We can't let you get away knowing that!"

"You're gonna kill me if I say something!" I cried, my wrists and ankles throbbing with soreness. "I didn't want any of this, let me go!"

William bent down and grabbed my chin. "You have one more chance to tell me out of free will," he hissed, the needle taunting me in his hand, "or you can tell me fully under the influence."

I jerked out of his hold, my body temperature and breaths suffocating me.

"*Your fear will overcome you, and your fate will escape your lips and yours alone.*"

I understood now. And I didn't want to have to fight it. I just wanted my nightmare to end.

No, I'm not caving! I can fight it!

William gripped my chin harder, his fingers cold against my hot skin. I threw my head to the side, reaching as far as I could away from him. I squeezed my eyes shut and prayed this wasn't real, that I'd wake up somewhere else—as someone else. Where was Momma? Why wasn't she here to save me?

William's fingers pulled my head to face him again. I was too exhausted, too breathless, to shake away this time. The very thought of escape was pointless. It was over. This was the moment I'd spent the weekend preparing for.

Tell him, make it end!

Don't, don't, don't—!

"What do you know?" he snarled. "I'm not letting you go until you tell me—"

"I know where Tristan's daughter is hiding!"

The silence pierced straight through my head. Despite the cold clamminess in my face, like the blood had drained from it, the heat radiating off of me was stultifying all the same. And by William's dropped jaw and frozen eyes, I knew we shared the same blank mind. All thoughts had dispersed, but for completely separate reasons.

Then, one burst through the front doors of my head: *I couldn't fight it.*

Each time it repeated took me a step closer to breaking. Like I could've stopped William from injecting me any other way.

He gawked, his eyes narrowing. "You..." he said under his breath. "You *know—*?"

His body crashed to the floor, severing his words. We'd been so deep in our tug-of-war that we hadn't noticed the teenage boy who'd snuck into the room and up behind his father.

I sucked in a breath of relief. *He made it, he made it!*

Jak grabbed the back of William's collar and brought him up, both of his hands behind his back. William thrashed in an attempt to twist out, but Jak kicked him forward first, sending him onto the couch. He darted to me with something clenched in his hand.

"Let's make this quick, Merlin," he said, unlocking my right hand and then putting the key in it. Without another breath, he turned back to William.

"*Exsolvo*," I whispered, bending down to pretend to unlock my left ankle and then doing the same for the other cuffs.

Thank God.

"Jak!"

He looked up at me from beneath William and threw another kick at his chest. I lunged forward and pulled William off, sweeping a kick under him while he stumbled. Jak grabbed my wrist and dragged me out of the lair before William could stand.

"Just follow me!" was all Jak said before he led us upstairs and into a narrow hallway with an ornately patterned carpet runner.

Is this... a house?

Jak dragged me left, to the wooden door at the end. Just before he pulled me out of the house, a living area flashed in the left corner of my vision, a lounge on my right.

Where did they take us to?

A sharp cold front blew around me as Jak tugged me through the front door and then slammed it shut behind us. Relief. I couldn't tell if the oxygen had been scarce down there or if it was the mountain of terror suffocating me, but outside was offering me a redo and I wasn't going to waste it.

Wait. Houses, almost mini mansions. They lined both sides of the wide street, left and right, all along a nearly white sidewalk.

Jak anxiously looked around. "Where's—?"

Cutting himself off, he grabbed my hand and took me down the street. I dared a glance behind us: a two-story crème-and-brown house glared back at me with windows for eyes and a door for a maw. Hidden in plain sight. And yet, nobody else burst through that front door as Jak ran down the street with me before stopping at joyfully familiar sedan.

Before I could catch up with reality in front of me, I was being shoved into the backseat. Jak took the spot next to me and yanked the car door shut.

"Is she okay?" Momma cried, stepping on the gas pedal and executing the most violent U-turn she's ever done with me in the car. "Emmalynn, are you okay? What happened? How could I let this happen?"

"I..." I breathlessly stammered, resisting the forceful urge to sob amidst my panting. "It's not—I don't..."

How am I supposed to tell her?

"It's not your fault," Jak told her for me, clicking his seatbelt into place. Oh, right, I had to do that, too.

"No," Momma stated, "it is. I let you out of sight. My sight. That is my fault. I can't believe I thought I could keep an eye on you in a place that crowded."

But she hadn't been alone in that. What about Mr. Dawson? What had happened to him, did she know? Why wasn't he here?

"Even I said Alexa wouldn't try anything," Jak replied, the blur of the street way too fast for my comfort in a residential zone. "They weren't supposed to do that, they could've exposed their faces."

Which is why they waited until we were alone and segregated.

"Then why did they?" Momma demanded, only slowing at the stop sign that would take us onto the main road.

Jak glimpsed me in my peripheral, but my eyes were stuck on Momma's headrest. I silently begged Jak to say something, even if it was the truth.

"We went into a back alley for a shortcut," he said. Shame quieted his words. "They caught us there."

It's terrifying enough when I can't read my mother; when I can't even *see* her and the seconds are ticking by in silence, sometimes I start wondering what kind of coffin she'll get me.

"This..." she finally began, turning off her blinker as we drove on the nearly empty road, "this is on me. I shouldn't have let you guys go out tonight."

The words were too close to what I had a fear of her deciding. "Mom—"

"No, Emma."

So her anger was split: she was a little bit mad at me, a little mad at Sarah and Breanne for convincing her about tonight, possibly even mad at Jak—and she was no doubt infuriated with Alexa. "Special permission" from Caldwell or not, Alexa had to have been abusing her power somewhere, this wasn't fair. It wasn't fair, but we couldn't change it. I know my mother: impotence is a cage. And all she could do now was restlessly pace it.

Speaking of, the only reason I'd escaped at all tonight was

because of... Jak.

He definitely heard me say it, I thought, wringing out my hands. *William and I didn't see him, but he definitely heard me.*

Jak wasn't showing any signs of rage as a result of betrayal yet, but I didn't know him well enough to determine if he was saving that for when we got back to the school. I braced myself either way.

My thoughts soon overtook the sound of the car driving through Capperson, if we were even still in Capperson. There was so much I had to say to and ask Jak. I had to tell Momma and Mr. Dawson what had happened before Jak had appeared out of nowhere. He'd been kidnapped, too (if you even can kidnap your son when you're his legal guardian), yet he'd known exactly where we were. And he'd somehow been able to get Momma there just in time. It almost seemed planned or, at the very least, expected.

Momma eventually pulled into the school's parking lot on the side of the manor. When Jak stayed next to me, I knew he wasn't finished with me yet—but Momma made us walk to the front doors of the school to talk (since I definitely wasn't ready for other Callistro Girls to ask about the boy showing up at an all-girls school). I hated that it made sense for us to talk there so that we could easily dart inside in case Alexa and William came back for us.

Jak's head hung low, his hands in his jacket pockets. Oh, right—I'd been wearing it when they'd taken us. They'd given it back to him.

All too quickly, he raised his eyes to mine. I couldn't translate his lack of expression, yet for whatever reason, it twinged a heartstring.

"You know where Tristan's daughter is hiding?" he asked.

"You know Tristan's descendant is… a daughter?"

Can I make him forget with a spell? Should I?

"I'm sorry," I whispered too timidly. "He got too close, I said it before I could think, I didn't…"

The time I'd had on the Ferris wheel to speak had dissipated; it was back to frantic searching in case Jak was ready to chew me out. "I get why you're mad. I lied, I get why."

He stared for a few seconds like he was trying to read every thought going through my head, every fear I was confronting. Then, he scoffed, a light smile playing at his lips. "That's great, but—I'm not."

Wait. What?

"You're just like everyone else, you're innocent. I just didn't know you were protecting their real target… I'm…" He had to look away to concentrate on his next sentence. "I don't think I know how to feel about that yet."

I wondered if even Ingrid would've been able to predict a response like that. Was I really off the hook with him? Did he believe me that easily? Could he believe me that easily?

"Do you know," I dared to ask, "what it means? For us?"

"I didn't know you thought of us as an 'us', Merlin," Jak simpered.

I tightly pursed my lips to subdue the smile.

He exhaled, his shoulders finally relaxing. "Were you mad at me for not telling you who my parents were sooner?"

"I was, but that was before I knew you were genuine and had good intentions."

"Well, there you go."

The thing was, I already knew it wasn't that simple. Jak's side of the story was *supposed* to be and it wasn't! He wanted to protect the innocent; I wasn't innocent. It was our side of the story that was much more complicated, having to send away Grand Hunters who already had their target, all without confirming that. Jak's protection only made sense to me if he was part of *our* side of the story, because I was pretty sure that none of the other kids he'd helped had known the location of Tristan's daughter. How far could I go in asking him for the answer?

"I have to know," I began, dropping my hands to my sides. I almost wanted to lean against the front doors, but Momma could come grab me any minute and accidentally knock me straight to the ground. "You're protecting all their targets. Why are you doing all of this even after what I said tonight? You said you wanted to help the innocent kids." I shrugged smally, my mouth going dry with the words: "I'm not innocent."

Jak kicked at a pebble, sending it tumbling down the cobblestone steps. I was starting to envy the warm leather around his shoulders. "Okay. You all have the same reason I'm doing this." He deprived me of eye contact. "And I wanna protect the kids falsely suspected of being Tristan's kid. So maybe you're not innocent to the government. But you are to me."

Those words shouldn't have plucked the heartstrings they did, shouldn't have wrenched a knife of guilt in my gut and twisted it with every syllable.

I forced myself to shake it away. For once, I was in the clear, but I still needed more answers before I went inside and asked about Mr. Dawson. "How did my mom know where to find us?"

"I know what I said about Alexa not being desperate enough to try something tonight, but that doesn't mean I trusted her not to anyway." Jak shrugged like he was apologizing for his mistake. "I texted your mom the street to come to if nobody had heard from you in fifteen minutes. So she was waiting for us by the time we got out.

"*I* have to know, though..."—he stepped toward me, almost pushing me against the door anyway—"how do you know where Tristan's daughter is hiding? Or that she's even a daughter?"

I didn't have a lie for "accidentally knowing", like I'd told William. I only knew a version of the truth: "My mom is close friends with her mom. They've been that way since... I guess forever. They're both in hiding while they look for Tristan."

"Were you sent to take their place or something?"

"No, just—cover for them. They're really good friends, Jak. They don't deserve what I've already gone through, nobody does."

He nodded. "Trust me. I know. So, being an accomplice is why you've been so resistant to Alexa taking you in for questioning."

"Yeah. Can you tell me why I woke up at your house, of all places?"

He shook his head, chuckling. "That was one of their 'headquarters', believe it or not," he said, digging his hands farther into his pockets. "Who's gonna suspect Grand Hunters are stationed out in a town as small as this?"

Kind of what I thought. I mean, it was a beautiful and convincing cover—one that made me seriously start to question who my neighbors on my street really were.

"Have you ever been down there before?" I hesitantly asked.

"More or less. They've done everything they can to keep me out until tonight, when they debriefed me."

"So then how did you get the key?"

"It sounds crazy,"—he chuckled, running a hand through his dark-brown hair—"but I've managed to smuggle a couple. You learn to keep whatever you find over the years when you live with them."

"So you somehow managed to escape them, attack your own dad, *and* get us out without being caught?"

"More or less," he repeated. "I have secrets to keep, too, Merlin. You're forgetting who my parents are."

I nodded, pressing my lips together. I dared to consider the possibility that Jak had been *allowed* to leave the room and find me, as if Alexa had actually made a bet with him and said, "We'll let you go if you can find her." Jak could've had a reason like mine to not say; I kept secrets to save my life, and he kept his to... well, I didn't know yet. But I had a feeling that they were kept for the better. Or his reason to keep them was just as great.

"Regardless," I said. "Thanks for tonight. Every part of it."

I wondered if it was the memory of the Ferris wheel causing that warm tint in his cheeks.

"See you later," I said. With a quick wave, I turned and opened one of the heavy front doors.

Twenty-Four

I didn't want to believe it when I went to Mr. Dawson's office and he was already there talking to Momma. It turned out, he'd heard my call right before Alexa had drugged me. When I didn't answer his call back, he immediately grabbed Momma. That was when she gathered Sarah and Breanne, found an excuse to ditch Jak's friends, and dropped the girls off at the school. (It wasn't like they could know that Mr. Dawson was there without exposing how he'd even known that I'd been kidnapped. And, as much as Momma despised it, a magician rescuing me from a Grand Hunter lair wasn't the wisest idea.)

But Mr. Dawson was safe. We all were. Jak didn't know it, but Mr. Dawson was the reason Momma had saved us as fast as she had.

Sarah and Breanne held me the longest they'd ever had when I came into our dorm a few minutes later. If Momma felt guilty about tonight, I couldn't imagine what was going through their heads.

"Just so you know," Sarah said, pulling away and sniffing, "Adrien and I won."

"Are you guys okay?" I asked, wringing my hands. "Was I gone long?"

"Just an hour and a half," Breanne spat, but her concern shone more than her regret. "What happened?"

"What do you think?" I stared down the carpet below our feet, shaking my head. "It was... She just took me in for questioning, it... it wasn't that bad."

It was one of the biggest lies I'd ever told them. And they saw right through it.

"Emma." Sarah sighed. She placed firm hands on her hips, shaking her head. "I was so stupid tonight."

"Why is everyone deciding this is their fault?" I walked past her and Breanne to the center of the room. "Is everyone forgetting the person who kidnapped me in the first place? Have you just chosen to forget who's caused this entire thing? Does any of that mean something to you?"

"It's hard to blame someone we've never met," Breanne murmured.

I opened my mouth to argue, but truth immediately silenced me. My best friends had never met Alexa Delphine. Ha, they didn't even know that this hadn't been my first time being kidnapped.

"We *don't* want you thinking it's your fault, though," Sarah told me. "You're right on whose fault it is, but—we're easiest to accuse, I guess."

I'd never thought of it that way before. Had my best friends taken up some sort of maternal responsibility over me since Wednesday afternoon happened? I saw what it was doing to my mother. That was the last thing I wanted for them.

Sarah stepped forward, fiddling with her manicured nails. That single gesture screamed her guilt. "I'm sorry. I just wanted to make tonight as fun as possible without having to worry about any of that. We should've listened to your mom, I'm sorry."

No. Alexa had said that Jak was due for questioning. A kidnapping tonight had always been planned, she'd just changed her pick-up location.

"We all played a role in going, believe it or not." I smiled softly at them both. "Trust me."

By the lack of relief on their faces, they didn't—and that meant that there was nothing I could say to convince them.

We seemed to tacitly agree to drop the conversation. Sarah sat on her bed in the middle of the room, Breanne at the desk in the corner. For the first time in years, I didn't know how to fill the silence between us.

"Other than tonight," I hesitantly began, strolling to Sarah's bed to join her, "did you guys have a good weekend?"

"Honestly, we were worried about you the entire time." She ran a hand through her hair as I plopped down next to her. "It was nice seeing family, but Alexa was in the back of my mind all day Saturday and today."

I know the feeling.

"I thought..." Breanne said timidly, picking at the hairs on her wrist. "I couldn't stop thinking that she'd kidnap us because we're your friends and might know something."

I wanted to laugh at that, to at least force it; I wanted to tell her that that wouldn't happen, that Alexa probably didn't even know about her or Sarah or that they'd been my best friends since third grade. But I couldn't say that with one hundred percent certainty, and Breanne would be able to see that a mile away.

"I'm the only one she has to make sure has nothing to do with the Ateras," I assured her. Sarah tiredly leaned her head on my shoulder, sending another waft of her sweet perfume up my nose. Was this just the girl's natural scent? "She's never brought you guys up before. I don't think you're on her radar."

A smile tightened Breanne's thin lips, her lip gloss worn off. "Well, other than that, it was good. Did you enjoy your time alone with Jak?"

Now the girl could give me a smile.

"Ooh, yes!" Sarah beamed, straightening and grabbing my arm. "What happened, was he romantic, did he try to kiss you?"

"Sarah!"

"She's blushing!" she squealed, pointing at my cheeks and grinning at Breanne. Wide pear-green eyes landed on me again. "Do like him back? *Would* you have let him kiss you?"

So even they thought that Jak liked me that way. I was pretty sure I only needed the date Friday night to confirm it, but now that I had witnesses, there was no denying it.

Oh, right. The date.

I laughed, fiddling with my fingers as Sarah nudged me. "Wanna hear what I did Friday night?"

The story hypnotized them so deeply that Sarah never picked

up her phone and Breanne never turned on her laptop at the desk once. For just those thirty minutes, it felt like we were the same girls who grew up braiding each other's hair at sleepovers, planning mall days to the minute, and fantasizing about high school graduation together. We felt like three girls who had nothing to do with the Hunter world—honestly, the girls we should've stayed as.

Breakfast the next morning consisted of wondering whether or not Alexa would leak to the press that Tristan had a daughter specifically—especially when Teresa Darci asked Opal Dubois for updates on the situation. Opal said the press was stuck, like she'd told me Saturday morning. I obviously knew *why* the press was stuck, but that was little comfort compared to how life was going at the time.

Breanne sat next to me and silently ate her eggs while Sarah, on my other side, was sneaking texts to Adrien under the table. The girl's more cut out for the Hunter game than any of us if I'm being honest; she needs no training when it comes to sneaking around. (Her selfies on the catwalk above the middle school auditorium stage with Breanne behind her on her laptop, secretly controlling the music at the school dance, prove it.)

I glanced at the teachers' tables at the back of the Dining Hall for my mother. There she sat conversing with Ms. Perketti and Mr. Dale, gracefully taking a bite of her food every few seconds. I almost smiled from the brief relief of seeing her have a couple of normal moments... until I saw the empty headmaster's seat.

Wait. What?

I glanced all around the room, hoping he was fashionably late or talking to the Callistro Girls around the Dining Hall. Breakfast had started half an hour ago. Mr. Dawson was nowhere to be seen.

"What's wrong?" Breanne whispered to me.

"Headmaster Dawson." I kept eye contact as her gaze moved to the table in the back.

Her round brows furrowed together. "Is he sick?" she asked, but shrugging was my only option for a response.

It was a great question, though. *—Mr. Dawson? Are you okay?—*

I tried to expect the worst-case scenario: that he was out of range for telepathy and wouldn't even hear me. My fork swirled around my scrambled eggs for as long as the quiet in my head lasted.

—Do you trust me?—

I swallowed my sigh of relief, a bite of toast following it to keep me quiet. That meant he was at least still in Capperson. *—Of course.—*

—Then everything's fine. Don't worry. Just wait for me after school in your mom's classroom.—

I reminded myself to keep chewing, that asking him what on Earth he was doing was not, in fact, trusting him. He'd never asked that of me before, but I had a feeling that those words, from him, were meant to be as solid as steel.

Twenty-Five

Despite the table of pastries sitting just outside the Dining Hall, the only thing Sarah, Breanne, and I were ready for after the final bell was a nap. But that would have to wait until after my appointment in Momma's classroom, which had been taunting me all day.

Sarah and Breanne took my backpack for me when I said that needed to talk to Momma. Dropping twenty-five pounds definitely made the journey faster, and it served my anxious impatience well. I would've gone upstairs to change out of my uniform, too, if it weren't for said impatience.

Momma answered her door like all was right with the world, and gestured me inside. Mr. Dawson stood leaning against the whiteboard, in a polyester vest and slacks instead of his typical blazer suits. For him, that was casualwear. Where had he gone today?

"So?" Momma asked him, shutting the door behind me.

Interesting—he had been waiting for both of us so he could start this conversation.

"I owe you the full context of our current situation," he replied, crossing his arms. "Part of the reason I was able to leave today was because of my history—with Alexa."

My head jerked back. *I'm sorry, what?*

"You knew her before all this?" I asked, hesitant to move.

"A *lot* more than that." Mr. Dawson exhaled, rubbing his neck. "I was about to propose to her."

Momma had to catch me when I tripped over my own feet, but she was gawking all the same. When did this man ever know the Grand Hunter we did today to the intimate extent that he was going to *propose?*

"You were about to marry her?" Momma repeated, helping me steady myself. "Meaning you dated? Alexa Delphine, a Hunter, with you, a *druid?*"

Mr. Dawson shrugged. "You married Tristan Atera, didn't you?"

The man was *asking* for her infamous guillotine choke (which once helped her escape the owner of a coffee factory during a hunt in New York—she's not proud of it... anymore).

"Alexa never knew about me, and frankly, I'm mostly convinced she still doesn't. We broke it off a little before we graduated."

"When you graduated from Redway?" I asked.

"Yes," he answered slowly, "and she from Callistro."

No way.

He was telling me that not only was I attending a school built to train the hunters of my people, but I was also attending the same school that had turned my greatest enemy into a Grand Hunter? I was standing in Alexa Delphine's school?

When I told him how Alexa said that she knew a few things about Callistro... He'd known. That was why he'd stayed silent. Had *that* been the main reason he'd decided to help me with the passageways, after all? Because he already knew that she had an advantage?

"Hang on," Momma said, holding up a hand. "You're saying that you were gone today to see her?"

He nodded, his lips tight together. "Yep. She called my office last night, and we agreed that we needed to talk." The tile floor stole his gaze, as if he couldn't look at us as long as he was telling the story. "I notified the school secretary and told her a family emergency had come up. Then we had coffee."

I would've laughed at the mundaneness of it, but the night I'd met Jak flashed in my memory. We'd grabbed coffee and discussed magic, too. Alexa had been there, too, toward the very end. It was like the woman had planned out the entire week and we were falling right into it.

"And coffee made everything all better?" Momma asked flatly, hands on her hips.

"I told her she knows me," he replied, standing from the whiteboard and gesturing to himself. "And she even knows your background, Amy. The chances of us being the guardians of Tristan Atera's descendant are embarrassingly low, especially *because* of the school."

"She's a high-up federal agent," I said, my patience thinning, "what could you've done to get her to actually leave us alone?"

His diamond-blue eyes dulled at me, almost turning gray, like I'd ruined his big reveal or something. When he exhaled, I realized that I'd either made the mistake of asking, or giving us less time to prepare for the answer. "I didn't get to tell her anything I had planned after that. She rebutted everything with your outburst last night, where you admitted that you know where Tristan's *daughter* is hiding."

"*What?*" my mother shouted, whirling on me. "You said what?! Emmalynn Marie—!"

"Don't, Amy," Mr. Dawson stated, holding up his hand. "Emma may have said the best thing she could've."

I snapped my head up to him. Did he even hear what he was saying?

"What, did your old flame cast another love spell on you?" Momma snapped with narrowed eyes, holding out her hands in bafflement. "How is Emma exposing—?"

"Because Alexa concluded with the fact that the pack is now after his *real* descendant, who they suspect may not be in Capperson, after all, possibly even North Carolina. But they also now have their strongest lead since whenever they decided that Tristan has a descendant." His attention fell back onto me. "You were under a truth serum when you confessed that, so they know you weren't lying. They're going to do everything in their power to get his daughter's location out of you."

I tried not to ask myself why I'd let William win last night. It had been a knee-jerk reaction where fight-or-flight had amplified the effects of the truth serum and both had worked against me. I wanted to believe that I hadn't been in complete control of myself, it wasn't completely my fault.

But I could've been stronger. I *should've* been stronger. At least strong enough to fight back my fear.

To my disappointment, Momma turned to face me, crossing her arms in her teacher pose. I was anything but off the hook with her. "Let me guess. Jak heard you say that and that's what you talked about last night."

"Yeah," I muttered, my breath tired as I brought myself to the closest front desk and sat on it. "Now he thinks we're here to protect Tristan's daughter and *her* mom instead of ourselves. And he said he just wants to protect the kids who aren't his descendant, so he's still on our side. I told him Tristan's daughter and I are close friends, so... maybe Alexa thinks that now, too. That's better than knowing the truth, isn't it?"

Momma heavily sighed, her breath hitching as she buried her face into her hands. Training even teaches you how to master silent crying, and yet hers were the loudest thing in the room then. She turned to her desk, refusing to expose what lay behind those hands.

"I can't..." she whispered.

What's going on? I thought, straightening in my spot on the desk. *If this is good news, why is she—?*

At her sniff, I realized, I'd seen this before. Three times, actually. *Her* fault, she'd always said. It finally clicked into place why, what was behind Momma's transformation the past week. If I was right, if I could read my mother as well as I thought I could, then she had reached her breaking point. If I was right, she was cracking under the weight she'd been carrying for almost a week—the weight of her own secret. And if I was right, she'd *had* her own secret since coming to the Callistro Academy, she'd known something about this hunt the rest of us didn't. The school really had been a cover, but not just mine.

That deer-in-the-headlights look in her eyes last Tuesday night. Her avoidance of any elaborative questions I'd asked. Her feeling responsible at every little development despite all the things we didn't know yet.

"Why do you keep saying it's your fault?" I finally asked, standing from the desk, anger seeping into chest. Because if I actually was right, my mother had every reason to apologize to me. "*What's* your fault? Why have you been blaming yourself for all this? Why've you been apologizing to me since—?"

She pointed at herself with desperation. "Because I'm the one who told them Tristan has a descendant!"

Twenty-Six

Oxygen had been sucked out of the room. Every time I took a breath in, an invisible rock in my throat stopped it. I couldn't believe it. I didn't want to believe it because it just wasn't plausible. And yet my stomach was churning. Rage was gripping my mind with a violent shake.

"You *what?*" Mr. Dawson hissed, something I'd never seen in him before engulfing him. His once gentle eyes were aflame, their deep-set shape intensifying them. It's always the calm ones with the scariest angry side, but I was ready to back him up in full and join him.

Avoiding both of our eyes, my mother stepped up the platform and to her desk. She used her hands to lean against its surface, keeping her head down. "When I found out I was pregnant...

all I could do was sit down on the couch and just stare at the test. It felt like someone had hit me with a baseball bat and I'd stepped into a dream. An impossible, unbelievable dream. I could barely process my own thoughts, I was in shock.

"And then a young agent showed up at the door. Probably the same age I was at the time." She exhaled as if regretting that she couldn't change the truth of what she was saying. "He knew exactly who I was. Not just Tristan Atera's wife, but Amy Dalbert, who used to be a Master Hunter."

"How?" Mr. Dawson demanded to know.

"He was in the room when they debriefed me the night before I became a Master, which let him catch a few glimpses of me throughout my career afterward. I think he always suspected something wasn't right... He had no reason to keep any tabs on me. When I suddenly quit and disappeared, he went out looking for me. But when a Hunter doesn't want to be found, we don't let ourselves be."

Mr. Dawson looked to the back of the room. I couldn't help but wonder if he had a few of his own secrets from that time, secrets neither of my parents knew. Ha, maybe he'd even gotten back together with Alexa during that time.

"But he did find me," Momma said next. "That day I found out about Emma. And it wasn't like I had magic to make him forget what he'd just seen, so he knew I was expecting Tristan Atera's son or daughter." She finally looked up at us, shrugging as if to say, *What do you want from me?* "He had all the power, I was at his mercy.

"Emma," she said, facing me, "he threatened to expose me and kill our family if I didn't tell him where your dad was."

Tears brimmed my eyes, and I mentally kicked myself for it—because I was starting to see Momma's exact thought process that day, but that meant admitting that there was a valid reason I was going through all of this today.

"But I didn't know where he was by that time, nobody did. So that agent demanded for a lead, any lead, and he'd let me go."

"Why would he let you go?" I asked. Was this just a bad habit among all Hunters?

"I honestly think he was a little afraid of me. My name intimidated him, because I was more than able to kill him on the spot, but so could he with me. But maybe he also wanted to believe I'd grown rusty so he could come up to me at all."

"What lead did you give him?" I dared to ask.

Momma mindlessly twisted the golden band around her finger. "I told him about the Atera family beach house, gave him the name of the beach, and then slammed the door in his face."

We have a beach house? How could a random Hunter who'd *blackmailed* my mother know that about my family, and not me?

"Mom, why didn't you just lie? Literally *anything* else—"

"It was Hunter against Hunter, Emma," she snapped, amber eyes hardening with her narrow jaw. "We're trained to be human lie detectors, lying was useless. You wanna hear it, fine, I was *weak*. I was still trying to digest the fact I was pregnant and had no way of contacting my husband, barely able to process that he wouldn't be there for our baby, and I still don't know if he ever will be! I could ask you the same thing about what you admitted last night!"

You were still mad at me for saying it! was ready to fly out of my mouth, but I glued my lips shut.

Momma's red eyes were swollen with tears, yet not one fell as we stared back at each other. Probably both regretting parts of our lives that not even magic could take back.

"I told him what I did because I had a plan," she stated. "I knew I could afford to. Right after he left,"—she looked at Mr. Dawson—"I called you."

My gaze followed suit. His sharp features fell in realization, his arms slowly unfolding. "*That's* how he was a 'threat to the Ateras'."

"You made him forget us, and that's all that matters," Momma said, her glances taking turns between us. "I moved because I knew something like that was bound to happen again, but with my background, the last place they'd think to look for me was the same town they'd found me in. Well, it took them almost seventeen years to find me again, so mission mostly accomplished."

"Then how do Alexa and William know about me today?"

"I don't know." With an exhale, she rested one hand on her hip. She'd managed to physically calm herself, which was more than what I could say about myself. "I know memory spells don't last forever, but it takes a decent trigger to undo them. God only knows when he got his memories back and how."

"But..." I said, angry at my words for not accumulating faster, "but—why is this whole thing public today? After almost two decades?"

"Hunters only make their missions public if it's a significant case *and* they know they're not wasting their time," Mr. Dawson answered. "It's their way of warning the people. Something must've happened recently that brought the topic back up for investigation. But after last night, they know for a fact that Tristan has a daughter."

So last night was my fault. Today was my fault.

But both had only happened because of Mom.

"So it is your fault," I muttered to her, staring daggers into the tile floor. "You *are* the reason we're in this."

Her features dropped with discipline. "Excuse you?"

My anger was finally having its turn and I was ready to indulge. "You are *literally* the reason I'm being hunted at all! You couldn't think of one stupid lie to make him forget instead, and *I'm* being punished for that!"

"You have *no* right to speak to me that way," she growled, pointing an authoritative finger at me. "I made a mistake, I admit that, but I did everything I could to fix it. I'm *human*, Emmalynn! Every single thing I've done since the day I found out about you has been to protect you. It's not like I narrowed down Alexa's search for Tristan's *daughter!*"

My eyes swelled with tears, heart throbbing with fury and humiliation. "No, you were just the reason I ever had to go down there in the first place, you have yourself to thank!"

"Emmalynn—" Mr. Dawson said, but Momma cut him off.

"Talk to me like that one more time and see if I let you out of this school ever again," she spat, pushing past every one of our old limits. "You know what, no, see whether or not I pull you straight out—"

"You're the biggest hypocrite I've ever known." It was my turn. I was ready to push us straight off the edge. "You made me afraid of everyone I've ever met, even *Mr. Dawson*, to keep me safe, when you're the one who made me a target in the first place! Fantastic job 'protecting' me, I'm glad Dad and I could distract the hunt while you went and hid."

I remember storming out of the room. I remember slamming the door shut behind me. I remember Mom shouting after me but nobody coming after me. I remember thinking about how that was only because neither of them knew what I was about to do. I remember running across the Grand Foyer and unlocking Mr. Dawson's office door with magic. And I remember going inside and unlocking the secret passageway underground.

The fading of adrenaline left a ringing in my ears as I closed the entrance above me. I had to stand there on the staircase for a few seconds to adapt to the sudden stillness, for my mind to catch up. The cobblestone beneath my feet held my attention captive as I tried to organize my next steps. I was untouchable down here for now—especially if I moved now and managed to get outside. But first I had to figure out how to get outside. I needed answers, and my family clearly wouldn't give them to me. I did know someone who could, though.

Finishing the long descent from the stairs, I noted how cleanly the ground met the cobblestone walls. Even down here, the architecture felt intentional, like Caralyn had individually measured each passageway and counted every step per tunnel. My eyes traced the length of the left wall, stopping short at something just before the corner.

Was that... writing?

No, not writing, I realized as I approached the first intersection. I bent down at the corner. *Inscribing.* A small "H.R." with an arrow pointing left had been carved into the ground.

I crossed over to the right wall: "SURFACE" with an arrow pointing forward. Caralyn hadn't just built secret underground passageways for me; she'd given me directions, too.

Outside was easy to find: all the way straight down the tunnel. I kept my chest tight, prepared for anything to jump out, as each step softly echoed against the concrete. At the end, an identical staircase to the one I'd walked down faced me, leading into the darkness above.

"*Aperta*," I whispered.

A large, circular opening appeared above. Sunlight blinded me for a split second, flooding down the stairs before I could process the glimpse I'd caught from the world above: *trees*.

I crept up the stairs, keeping my eyes peeled for my new surroundings. Halfway up, I realized that I wasn't even on campus anymore. Eventually, I stepped onto the forest floor, a warm breeze flying past me. I walked around the opening of the passageway: a tree stump on a hinge, like a compact mirror. The back of the school now faced me dead ahead. No security guards to spot me.

Smart, Caralyn.

I manually closed the entrance and dashed into the forest. Finally—I was on my way to freedom, to truth, to real answers.

Despite how I'd run almost all the way to Ingrid's house, I still prayed that I'd have enough time to catch my breath after ringing the doorbell. Only a few seconds passed before the mahogany door creaked open. Ingrid's dark-brown eyes fell just above my head.

"Hi, Ingrid," I breathed, wiping my sweat on my crimson blazer. "It's—it's Emma."

Her full lips parted, a white cane in one hand and her other resting on the golden doorknob. "Emma? Where's Thomas? Or your mother? What are you doing here?"

I looked behind me as if they were right on my tail. Being that Mr. Dawson could easily use a locator spell on me, I didn't doubt it. "May I come in, I don't have a lot of time."

She quickly moved aside and allowed me into the entry foyer. Closing the door behind me, she faced me, pushing her black hair behind her ear. "Is everything all right?"

"If you can help me, it will be," I said, then silently locking the front door with my magic. It'd buy at least a few seconds against Mom and Mr. Dawson. "I'm begging you, I need to know my future."

Ingrid's jaw dropped, her hand flying to her chest. "I can't do that. You know I can't do that, the price is too great. Knowing the future has consequences you are yet able to face. I'm sorry, but if that's what you came here for, you need to leave."

"Please," I cried, "I have to know. I—I can't get answers anywhere, all my family does is hide everything from me, and I'm scared. I'm so scared, please, I need something."

My words faded into a silence I could only assume she was reading.

"Coming here was an impulsive act out of anger and betrayal. Your mind is clouded. I won't let you pay a price you wouldn't pay out of free will."

"I'm willing to—"

"No," her smooth voice said gently. "Right now, you're at the mercy of your anger. It's controlling your tongue and actions. You wouldn't be here for any other reason otherwise."

I let out a shaky breath. Wisdom was the last thing I needed to hear.

"You've been hurt by the people you love and trust most, I can tell," she told me. "I can only imagine what happened. But I can't do this for you under these circumstances. Please understand that."

"*Please*," I cried, a quiver affecting my words. My tears started stealing my breaths more than the workout. "I need to know. Whether it's something that happens now or years later, just *something* to pacify my nerves, anything that'll tell me what to expect. Not knowing is eating me alive, I can't live like this anymore."

Her soft jaw tightened, my plea now weighing down her dark irises. If she made the wrong choice, I would have to face the consequences—but I was okay with that. I had to be.

Swinging her cane back and forth, Ingrid walked past me and into the bright living area. When she stopped at the loveseat, her head turned toward the window—behind the couch Mr. Dawson and I had sat in last time. "Have a seat."

I mentally beamed, dashing to take my original spot. Ingrid settled into hers. My breathing started to slow, but my body was still radiating the heat of exhaustion and anxiety. I now had an entire world of questions able to meet their answers.

"I'll only answer one question about your future," Ingrid said with perfect posture. "What would you like to know?"

Too easy.

"My dad," I said, trying to exhale the rest of my nerves. "Is he...? Do you know if he's alive? Or where he is?"

"I'm afraid I can't tell you present circumstances unless they're told through future ones."

Well, this wasn't going to be easy. I had a hundred questions that could figure out if my dad was alive based on the future, but I needed a question that would also give me answers regarding the hunt—regarding my future as an Atera...

I demanded my head to clear up, to think quickly before my mother actually came busting down Ingrid's door. Security had never been so close, and the only thing keeping me from it now was my endlessly buffering mind. Why couldn't I have had a vision about the possible future like Mr. Dawson had and get a question that way—?

Wait. That's it!

I leaned forward. "I had a dream the night Mr. Dawson shared his vision with me. Right before he shared it with me. It was night, and I was running as fast as I could away from something in an alley. Mr. Dawson caught up to me, and then my mom came, saying Alexa Delphine was behind us. Then Alexa appeared at the end of the alley and... she brought out my dad. She threatened my family to trade me for him. Everything felt almost as real as Mr. Dawson's vision, I even woke up crying and... I wanna know if that dream will come true."

Ingrid's head softly jolted back in surprise. "Emma—you're a sorceress, not a druid. Your dreams can't predict the future."

"I know, but... will anything like that happen in my future at all?"

I wasn't asking if my dream would come true; I just wanted to know if my future held any of those events in store because it involved my dad anyway, and more importantly, it contained Alexa's involvement with us.

Ingrid quietly exhaled, closing her eyes. When she opened

them, a glowing amber now swirled in her irises. "While this dream specifically won't come to pass, you will find yourself in an identical situation, but not with an identical group of people. Your sacrifices on this imminent morning will permanently lock the course of your fate, saving you from your enemy. But be warned, Emmalynn: your future will arrive when you least expect it. When it does, don't allow your pride to precede your judgment."

The second Ingrid closed her eyes, breaking her trance, a small wave pushed me back in my seat. I leaned against the couch, shutting my eyes against the nausea sweeping over my stomach. It felt like the earth had somehow stopped orbiting the sun and I couldn't keep up.

"Emma?" Ingrid asked.

"I'm here, um..." I said, trying to blink the nausea away. "Do you know exactly when that's gonna happen?"

"I only feel the strength of its imminence the closer it is. This one is powerful, but that's all I can tell you."

"Then..."—I leaned to one side on the couch, resting a hand on my stomach—"what about the price?"

She swallowed. That couldn't be good. "As you know, all seers are born without their sight. It's one of the things humans—"

Furious pounding on the front door cut her straight off. Ingrid's name was scarcely audible through the wood, but I already knew who was on the other side. I almost ran into Ingrid's bedroom, wherever it was, for safety, but that was just prolonging the inevitable. I had two prices to pay for knowing my future.

Ingrid sprang from her spot on the loveseat, using her white cane to rush to the door. When she opened it, Momma and Mr. Dawson almost bulldozed over her—crying my name.

"Emmalynn Marie!" Mom exclaimed, dashing into the living area and kneeling down in front of me with a grip on my shoulders. Her honey-colored eyes dripped with angry worry. "I can't believe you did that, what were you thinking?"

Even in that moment, I knew I hadn't been thinking—I only knew how to react.

Ingrid shut the door, grabbing Mom's and Mr. Dawson's attention. Reality set in for all of us.

"Ingrid," Momma said, her voice hollow. "Don't, don't tell me."

Ingrid's grip on her white cane only tightened in response.

Momma sharply exhaled, shut her eyes, and turned her head away from me. When I looked up, Mr. Dawson was rubbing his face with both hands in defeat.

The nausea came back twofold, but for a reason that set my nerves on fire. "What?" I dared to ask. "What's the price?"

"Emma," Mr. Dawson said, "all seers are born blind. They're deprived of one of the things humans depend on most. So the price for knowing your future is losing what you depend on most until that event comes to pass."

My stare jumped from him to Ingrid and then to my mother, tacitly begging for clarification.

"Em," Momma whispered, taking my hands, "think about it. What is the one thing you depend on most in this world?"

Revelation paralyzed my being like a scorpion's sting. My magic. I needed my magic more than anything, and it was gone.

TWENTY-SEVEN

I laughed. I kind of hated myself for it, but it was all my body was letting me do. The fact was slamming into a brick wall in my head, preventing it from reaching my rationality. "That's not—it can't just—no, it's a physical part of me, how can it…?"

As Momma kept her gaze down on the wooden floor, I could almost feel the intensity of her breath, like a dragon's, as she heaved another hard, heavy sigh. "Why," she growled, raising her head at Ingrid standing behind her, "would you let my daughter pay that price?"

"No," I quickly said, "don't blame her, I begged her to. I just— I had to know."

Someday I'd find out why Ingrid told me. Why she'd actually obeyed me. As of now, though, I couldn't find a single reason, and that made me feel worse.

"This whole thing is completely out of hand…" Mr. Dawson muttered. "Part of me gets closer to convincing myself it'd be easier to confess at this point."

Despite all that had happened in the past thirty minutes, I wanted to yell more than anything. Whose fault was this? Who *was* to blame for our situation? Where could I take out my rage?

"I'm sorry, Em." Momma rose from the ground and sat on the wooden coffee table in front of me. "I am. There hasn't been one day that I haven't regretted my choice from that day. I need you to know that. I need you to know that I love your father so much, and it's still not as much as I love you. Every single thing I've done since I found out about you *has* been to protect you. His safety was out of my control, but when you came along, there was suddenly a life I *could* protect. It is my inherent duty to protect you, and until I die, I'm going to do everything in my power to do so. Does that make sense?"

I nodded, drying my eye before my tear could fall. "I'm sorry," I whispered. My words echoed back at me in a clear mind, bouncing off the walls. "I didn't mean what I said. And I'm sorry for running, I shouldn't have—"

"You're right, you shouldn't have."

Wow, Mother, you really know how to encourage a teenager to take responsibility.

"What if Alexa happened to have followed you here? What if you'd never made it here at all? And even then, because you did, you lost—"

"I'm sorry," I said again, fighting to sound polite. Above all else, the last thing I was able to hear right now were the words she was no doubt about to end that sentence with.

I looked up at Mr. Dawson standing with Ingrid by the door. I remember how he'd heard my telepathic calls at the carnival last night, which meant he was still a magician...

"You paid the price, too," I mused, "but you still have your magic."

"My magic isn't what I depend on most," he said simply, rubbing his neck. He hesitated to add, "It's my visions."

No... He'd lost the very attribute that made him a druid just to help *me*. Now he was just another magician.

And I was just another mortal.

"But," he said hopefully, stealing a glimpse in Ingrid's direction, "now that the last dream happened, I have them back."

"What?" Ingrid asked, her black brows furrowing and gaze lost in the direction of the window in front of her. "The first half of my prophecy came true. But the second, we have long to go before then."

"You said I'd reveal the truth," I said, "and I did, the last time Alexa kidnapped me."

"No,"—Ingrid shook her head—"that's not where the second half is to take place. The next part of my prophecy is still waiting on its time. Until then... I'm sorry, Thomas."

In other words, I was going to reveal the *whole* truth?

No. Never. Not even a truth serum could get that out of me. We had to be misinterpreting something, because... I'd just never give up the whole truth!

Another wave of nausea crashed in my stomach. *Like how you'd never give away that you know where Tristan's daughter's hiding?*

"Well," Momma said, sighing and standing from the coffee

table, "we have to get back. I'm sorry for speaking harshly to you, Ingrid. I shouldn't have shot the messenger."

"Thank you." Ingrid's full lips turned upward in a smile. "I don't know if this helps, Amy, but with a matter as delicate as this, every event in Emma's path plays its own part. They all work together to eventually fulfill her fate one day. She'll be fine."

Momma hummed a quick acknowledgment, but I could hear the doubt behind the curtain. She turned back to me, reaching out her hand. "Come on, Em."

In full honesty, with that eerily calm tone, I was worried that she was preparing for a *full* lecture in the car. Strangely enough, though, she and Mr. Dawson left it quiet between us the entire way back to the school. I wouldn't complain, though—my furious regret gave me all the remorse I needed.

And thankfully, when I got back to my dorm, Sarah kept her question at a simple "Have fun with your mom?"

I closed the door behind me, glancing at her texting away on her bed. Breanne was silently working away at the desk. "I wish. We got into a stupid argument about Alexa." I moved to my bed and fell onto it. "She's doing dirty work even when she's not here."

Sarah looked up from her phone and Breanne set her pencil down onto the desk. Their eyes met each other, exchanging a language that I—somehow—wasn't fluent in. Whatever they were saying, though, it was undeniably about me.

"Emmy?" Breanne began slowly, picking at the hairs on her arms. "Have you ever realized that this whole time, we've been aimlessly wondering *why* you're Alexa's target? I mean, I guess, why you're even a suspect? Like, did you—did you do something in the past, something we somehow don't know about?"

I couldn't help but smile at how earnestly she was trying to avoid offending me. "You're fine," I assured her. "Jak actually asked the same thing. Believe me, so am I."

The serenity in my voice fooled them, but anxiety had crashed into me like a plane on fire. I'd known this question was inevitable, but I never wanted to prepare for it. I wanted to believe that maybe, just maybe, it would never be asked. What was there to say that wouldn't lead to another why?

"Basically," Sarah said, dropping her hands into her lap, "why hasn't she let you go yet after questioning you twice?"

"I'm trying to figure out the same thing," I said, unsure of where to take my answer. "They know I'm not the descendant."

No, what I was really trying to figure out was why Alexa *had* let me go—*twice*—why she hadn't blatantly asked me if I was my father's daughter. Any Grand Hunter with that level of stupidity would've never made it to Grand Hunter status at all, which meant Alexa wasn't being stupid; she was being intentional. She had some kind of plan, something that must have been gathering the most intel as thoroughly as possible. Had she done this with all the other suspects?

My gaze blindly traced the floral patterns in my comforter, lost deep in the maze I called my mind. I fought back tears of fire. There was a bittersweet comfort talking to my best friends now about this; I was exactly like them now. And every time I said something of the sort, it was no longer a lie. A bitter reality with sweet relief. How was that even possible?

"Emma," Sarah said, "did you hear me?"

I looked up. "No, sorry."

"I said the guys wanna see us tomorrow. Are you gonna be

okay here by yourself?"

Ha, no. "Just you two?"

"Yeah," she said hesitantly, growing a sly smirk and tossing her hair over her shoulder. "We can sacrifice Jak and send him over if you want."

I rolled my eyes. "Thanks. I'll be fine—"

A knock cut me off. I pushed myself off my bed and stood, walking to the door and then swinging it open.

My jaw fall slack. *Speak of the devil.*

"How did *you* get in here?" I asked, stepping aside for Jak to come in. "And—why?"

"I wanted to talk," he replied casually, turning on his heel as I shut the door. Before he could elaborate, his gaze started wandering around our room.

It was then I fully realized that Jakson Bleu was in our room. A boy. In our dorm room. Looking at our things.

"Nice place." He nodded with approval, sticking his hands into the pockets of his black leather jacket.

"What's it like at Redway?" Sarah asked, standing from her bed.

"Pretty basic," Jak said, shrugging. "Or, actually, I think the guys and I are just minimalists."

"So," I drawled, "you're here because...?"

"The headmaster let me in," he replied simply, like he was that innocently ignorant. "Okay, fine. I wanted to visit without repeating what happened at the carnival. Alexa can't follow me and kidnap you here."

I pressed my lips together. *Wanna make a bet?*

"She already *is* following us everywhere," Breanne said on the other side of the room, mindlessly twisting in the desk chair. "We were just talking about her, and now you're here—no offense."

Jak dismissed it with a wave. Then he turned back to me. "I wanted to make sure you were still okay."

I shrugged lightly. I didn't know exactly what he wanted from me with that, because I could've given him the easy answer, or I could've given him the truth.

"Hey, Em," Breanne said, standing, "has Alexa never asked you directly whether or not you're Tristan's descendant?"

I took a deep breath in and opened my mouth, but then hesitated. Even this answer had to be safe. "No. I actually ended up telling them I didn't know why they think Tristan even has a descendant. After that, she let me go."

Sarah tilted her head down with her hands on her hips, raising an arched brow. "Just because you don't know why they think he had a baby?"

"They were *surprised*," I said. "I mean, everyone knows why they're after his kid, but does anyone know *how* this kid was even found out about?"

Breanne's thin brows furrowed tightly in their traditional analysis manner. "Good question... Why *do* they think there's another generation—?"

Sarah groaned, throwing a pillow at her for me. "You ask too many questions. Go do your homework or something."

I silently thanked her as Jak tapped my shoulder, turning me to him.

"Can I talk to you for a bit?"

At this point, that could've meant anything plus my social security number. I didn't bother asking questions (or punishing

Sarah for the smirk she was giving us). I walked out the door with him and stepped onto the crimson carpet runner in the hallway.

He closed the door behind him, and I braced myself for the worst. "Catch me up here," he began. "They don't know you know something?"

I sighed, grateful for the easy question for once. "No, and life's a lot easier that way. You weren't supposed to know, either. Nobody was, you know why."

"I'm not sure how long you'll be able to get away with that, Merlin," he said. "But if you've managed a few years, what's a lifetime more?"

"Jak," I whispered, crossing my arms, "seriously, please don't even imply you know something. It would *kill* them if they found out that someone I've barely known for a week knows my darkest secret and they still don't."

"I know. Your secret's safe with me."

Really? I thought. *Is it really?*

I couldn't help but stare, ruminating on the boy in front of me. Although I knew a handful more about him than I did six days ago, I still didn't know the one piece of information that I *needed* to.

"Do you realize what you're doing?" I whispered, leaning in. "My mom and I are accomplices in a crime punishable by death. You keeping this a secret adds you to that list. Why would you do that for people you barely even know? Have you spent any time thinking about the risks you're putting yourself at?"

A weak smile bent his lips. "More than you think."

I'm seriously about to put him under a truth—

The cold truth barreled into me as I remembered. A hollow

cavity burned in my chest.

Jak strolled backwards toward the stairs, oblivious, before turning around.

"Jak," I called.

He turned back to face me. "There's a time and place for everything, Merlin," he said. Then, he trotted down the stairs with his hands in his pockets.

It's like he doesn't even have to try *to be cryptic.* Left in the hall, I started thinking about how he'd actually make for a fantastic Hunter. After all, he was the son of one of the greatest, the stepson of possibly the greatest, and attending an elite boarding school originally built to train him to be just that. What was stopping him?

Opal Dubois made dinner especially memorable—or maybe I was way too invested in anything that had remotely to do with Jak, because that was the topic she'd chosen for the night.

Sitting across from me, she spoke like she was more enthralled than anyone. "Did you guys see the guy walking around campus?" she asked, unable to pick one girl to focus on. Her purple contacts seemed even brighter with her excitement. "I talked to him before dinner. His name is 'Jak', but he spells it without a 'c'. How *cute* is that?"

The emotion that burst in my chest at those words was greener than the sautéed asparagus sitting on my plate. I'd never felt it before—at least, not this level of it. After all, Jak and I had had to go on an official-ish date for me to discover that about him, but Opal had gotten it in the first conversation?

"Do you know why he's here?" Ava asked next to her.

"Oh, that's the best part," Opal replied. "He's visiting on behalf of *Redway Academy*."

Teresa gasped on her other side, pushing her brown bangs behind her ear. "Isn't that school just like us? Meaning *he's* like—?"

"Em," Breanne whispered, pointing to our right at the Dining Hall entrance.

I followed her eyes—and the rest of the sophomore table followed suit. Had he been given stage directions or something?

"Look who it is," Elizabeth Moody simpered next to Ava.

Soon every Callistro Girl in the room had her head turned in his direction, but Jak remained unfazed by the attention. He left each girl with a million-dollar smile accompanied by the kindest eyes I'd ever seen on him. He was heading for the buffet in the back of the room. Where he'd go afterward was the question.

"He's *way* too cute to be single." Jackie Cortez's brown eyes gazed deep into his soul, resting her chin on her hand.

Caroline Walker scoffed next to her. "I definitely wouldn't want *my* boyfriend surrounding himself with this many girls in one place—wait!" Her blond waves flew over her shoulders as she turned to Opal. "You said he's here on *behalf* of Redway?"

Opal smirked back, setting down her fork on her plate. "How does a *joint semester* sound?"

"You're kidding," Sarah said, jaw falling agape. "No, there's no way. Why would we do that?"

"To compare schools," Opal replied effortlessly, shrugging. "To see how the other side trains. I think it'd be awesome."

"That'd only work if we were still a Hunter school," I argued, picking up a stalk of asparagus.

"Well, the school hasn't exactly said they *aren't* reopening the Hunter's Room," Teresa remarked, leaning in. "And Tristan's possible descendant is *bound* to give the board the final push—"

"Where's he going?" Sarah mused, her eyes following Jak.

Our gazes fell onto the teachers' tables near the buffet. Jak walked straight to them.

"You might be right about a joint semester," Elizabeth said, glancing at Opal. But why would Jak persuade the Callistro Academy to join semesters with another ex-Hunter school an hour away? What would that do for Alexa and her team? Make it even harder for her to grab me?

I was ready to walk over there and present the idea myself.

"Nothing left to do but wait." Caroline moved her blond waves to the side. "But on the topic of second semester..."

That was my cue to tune out. My brain capacity couldn't afford anything beyond priorities at this point.

Jak didn't come up to us after dinner. In fact, I want to say that I saw him leave with Mr. Dawson. Easier said than done to maintain eyes on your target when he leaves with the headmaster ten minutes before you and your roommates do.

What is *he doing here if not just to check on me like he said?*

All Sarah, Breanne, and I had left to do after getting back to our room was homework (only able to finish the front side of our algebra assignment; half of our history essay on the significance of the underground tunnels the Patriots built during the American Revolution; and reading a 2008 article about the Great Recession in English and Spanish and then summarize it in both languages— which was, apparently, considered *light* work compared to the rest of the year). Then we enjoyed a few pieces of candy from our secret stash in the closet before saying good night. After the past week-end, going to bed with my best friends again was as comforting as sleeping in Momma's room with her.

I think my mind had temporarily erased my visit to Ingrid's. Today had been a day I would've never dared to even speak into existence. Sleep would be my best distraction—so go figure, that was the night I discovered that you can be too tired to sleep. (I'll never ask Momma again why she didn't just "nap more" when I was a newborn.) Your mind hovers above your body, desperate for anything to put it down—anything that isn't sleep. Every time I glimpsed my bedside clock, another fifteen minutes had gone by. And that only increased the anxiety of how much less sleep I'd get if I didn't fall asleep right now.

Oh. This is *insomnia.*

After an hour and a half, I would've taken a walk through the school to help lull me if not for the Alexa anxiety. Any night was now fair kidnapping game, which meant...

I'd almost finished that thought when my phone vibrated on my bedside table. I grabbed it with a desperation for relief.

J: By any slight chance that you're up... are you
up?

Just like that, Jak had saved me again.

C H A P T E R

Twenty-Eight

"**Couldn't sleep?**" **I whispered at the top of the stairs.** Jak let his hands fall loosely to his sides as he started his climb. "Wow. They'll make a Hunter out of you yet."

He was too far away to smack, so I settled on an eye roll. "Shut up. And since when are you allowed to spend the night here?"

He finished his ascent and met me at the top with that cocky smirk. "Callistro's really accommodating."

Geez, even in a long-sleeved shirt and sweatpants, he was cute. And then I had to pause, because I'd never seen a boy in his pajamas before, and a boy had *definitely* never seen me in mine. I prayed that the moonlight wasn't enough to expose the warm blush swarming my cheeks.

"And you just happened to know to text me at the right time?" I asked to take my mind off the fact.

"It actually would've been my last guess, but"—he glanced at the floor-to-ceiling windows overlooking Capperson—"maybe it's a sign. That this is the right place and time."

I instantly recognized the words: he'd said them right here earlier today, about... why he was okay with being an accomplice.

"You mean...?"

"Yeah," he whispered with a light nod. "I was actually gonna tell you this tomorrow, but—but then I was thinking about a few things from earlier today, and I started thinking that I wouldn't get a moment to tell you anything, and I just—enter insomnia."

"Yeah," I said. "I was in the same boat before your text."

He went quiet, fiddling with his fingers. But this was Jak, the guy who always had something to say to make you feel what he wanted you to, the guy who always knew how to fill the silence. Now he couldn't even look at me. What was going on?

"Jak?"

"Okay, I admit it." He finally met our eyes. "I'm on your side for a few reasons. To be honest, there are even fewer why I'm keeping your secret—because..." He took in a deep breath, moving his hands to his back pockets before remembering that he didn't have any. "It's my mom."

I exhaled with strain to keep quiet. This was the one topic Jak had never explored with me. And as a daughter who also had only one parent, I read every line in the eyes of a son who'd lost a parent against his will. Even then, I had to consider who his one parent was. And then compare him to mine.

"She was a Hunter, too," Jak began, back to fiddling with his fingers, "but only because it was the family business. She was against it from the start. She believed in... a world that was mortal *and* magic. And a long time ago, my dad got that. I really wanna believe he even agreed with her. She's why he worked off field, because he felt like it was the perfect compromise to make his wife happy while supporting his family."

Jak paused and looked at the carpet runner below us, like his thoughts were gathering. "He was their greatest Hunter, though," he said even quieter. "So changing fields brought up suspicion. They knew he didn't have magic. Mom, though... She made it a little too obvious she didn't agree with what they did. And being so talented while wanting to quit, I guess, raised a lot of red flags. So to find out what was going on, they started hunting her."

I almost wanted to tell him to stop when my nose started stinging. He didn't have to say another word, why he was on my side: both his mom's and my hunts had begun at the fault of suspicion. And in full honesty, Jak's mom's background was too similar to Momma's—I didn't want to hear the end of this story. I was pretty sure that I knew where it was going.

The rhythm of Jak's words broke, ebbing and flowing like trying to find signal on a radio. "Hunters are way too thorough. There's no room for belief. They hunt until they *know* a target doesn't have magic—magicians have been able to trick the machines, dodge the weapons, and get away. But a Hunter-versus-Hunter mission can quickly turn into a stalemate—so the agency decided to bring my mom out by kidnapping me. They told her where to find me the next morning.

"I wish—I wish I could remember more, but I woke up in the backseat of her car. I think they drugged me in the in-between parts. My mom said we were on our way home after a drive. Look-ing back, she seemed…" He shook his head and looked behind me, down the hall. His throat bobbed. "She was terrified. Con-stantly looking in her rearview mirror until we took a sharp turn into the woods. She had to stop the car because the forest was too thick. She tried running while carrying me, but I was—too big for her by that point." He exhaled. The kind of exhale meant to push tears back down. "I slowed her down. The Hunters caught up to us. Shot her. With—a bullet coated with something that changes blood color if there's magic."

Jak looked out over the quiet town of Capperson beside us, the moonlight betraying the glisten in his eyes. Then he looked at the ceiling, breathing out again, and then back at the ground. This was a whole war against his trapped tears.

"Jak?" I whispered.

He finally matched my eyes, his voice cracking despite his vol-ume matching mine. "She didn't have magic."

My heart throbbed in my throat, trying to beat properly. The silence was growing louder and louder to the point where I just wanted to cut straight through it to stop it no matter what it took—anything but live in the hushed echoes of Jak's story.

"She used," he added, "her last breaths to tell me—to protect the Atera descendant."

I stepped back. Jak's mom had *known*? How had she known? Who'd told her about me, had she known either of my parents? Wouldn't Momma have mentioned her? Or—had she been a friend of my father's?

Wait. Wait, if she'd known that my parents had had me… didn't that mean that she'd known my name?

"I didn't get a name before she died," Jak whispered, like the boy really was a mind reader. I almost felt guilty for the sheer relief that fell over me like a tidal wave. "And now you're the only one who knows anything about her. "If I protect you, I protect her. I *have* to protect her, Emma. If she stays safe..."—another hard lump passed in his throat—"that night wasn't for nothing."

That was why she ran even though she was mortal, I realized. She hadn't been carrying magic—but she'd been carrying something just as lethal.

"How old were you?" I dared to ask.

"Seven." he said. He nodded lightly. "I was seven."

It was Jak's composure throughout his story—throughout reliving the trauma he'd endured as an innocent boy who shouldn't have been exposed to the horrors of this industry yet—that ripped me apart shred by shred. He was strong, stronger than I was. He was so strong because that was how he'd grown up the last nine years, too experienced in practicing that kind of fortitude. That same boy stood in front of me now: a boy who was too strong.

"My dad found out his wife was dead," he said, giving a long exhale, "and blamed magic. Magic was why she was hunted in the first place. But I blamed the people who let their fear turn into the destructive judgment she spent my whole childhood warning me about."

He paused again, taking another deep breath in. I didn't have the right words, so I didn't bother opening my mouth.

"So,"—Jak exhaled again—"there. My side of things. I don't want history to repeat. Yeah, you know something, you're a target for a reason, but knowing the truth, I can't... I can't let you suffer for protecting someone whose only crime right now is existing. It's not right, it's never felt right, mindlessly calling these people enemies. What if"—he stepped closer to me—"they've been turned *into* enemies?"

The gap between us was gradually closing. Maybe it had something to do with the proximity of the stairs, but my legs started wobbling.

That's the thing about Jakson Bleu: he's a little too observant, a little too considerate, because he gently took my hand and pulled me to the protection of the banister away from the staircase.

"Thanks," I whispered.

"Can I say something crazy and you won't think I'm crazy for saying it?"

I didn't know if it was out of pity or because I was sleep deprived, but I chuckled. "Go ahead."

"Okay. Because the night we met, I found myself... easily able to talk to you, like just being around you was enough to pull everything in my mind out of my mouth. I can trust you with who I am, you're someone I can find good moments in this messed-up world with. That means a lot to me. And there's something—just *something* about you that I still can't name. Like, a person never knows what kind of memories they'll make with you or—" He laughed at himself. "Never mind. You can call me crazy."

"No, no," I rushed to say, relieved that I might not have been insane, after all. "You felt it, too? Like the trust was just there even though we'd just met?"

"*Yes*," he said, like I'd stolen the words straight out of his mind, "and maybe it's because of that something I can't pin down. Maybe it makes you trustworthy, I don't know. I'm..." His gaze down at me softened with his words. "I'm hoping someday I'll figure it out so I can say this right."

There was only one thing blaring inside my head regarding what "this" meant, warning me about what was about to happen. Nothing like what I was imagining had ever happened to me before—it had never had the opportunity to—so I didn't know what to expect. But if this was truly it, it was one of the best feelings in the world.

"Look." Jak took my hand again. He didn't have to this time, but he did, and t he sheer warmth of his skin was enough to melt me. "I wasn't planning on ever doing this, forget tonight. The timing is awful, believe me, I get it, but it's been driving me crazy. I wanna get it out."

This kind of courage, I'd seen from Jak before, but what he couldn't hide this time was what he was really feeling behind those brown eyes: fear yet excitement. Doubt yet certainty. Impulse yet readiness.

"Why has it been driving you crazy?" I asked.

"Because I haven't told you, and I won't know anything until I do. I'm sorry, part of me is grateful my parents found you just because we met. It's been less than a week, but it feels like so much longer. Hunt or no hunt, it doesn't change the fact that—I like you, Emma. I like you a lot."

The tectonic plates of my mind shifted the second those words crashed down. I'd wanted to hear them from Jak's lips more than anything in that moment—but then I looked at the boy in front of me. Really looked at him, and not just as the son of the Hunters who were after me—but a boy who had fallen too hard and too fast.

I cleared my throat and stepped back. I wanted to indulge

more than anything. But the reality, *our* reality, was heavier, meant more.

"I'm sorry. I can't... That's it, I just can't."

"What do you mean?"

"I'm not—I don't know." I scoffed, breaking my own heart. "Jak, don't do this to yourself, don't get yourself trapped deeper—"

"'Trapped'?" he said, locking our eyes. Whether my words had offended him or he was ready to defend my honor, his confidence was back and he didn't need to fake an ounce of it anymore.

"I can't put you in even more danger with the whole hunt—"

"You're not." He pushed a couple of stray strands away from my forehead. This boy was too good, he knew me too well. "I'm not asking for anything, Emma, I just—I needed it out. I needed you to know how I feel. If that makes this *any* easier, even believing me about everything, it's worth it."

His eyes distracted me long enough so that I didn't notice him taking my hand. By the time he pulled me closer to him, it was too late: our chests were almost meeting.

He was too close. He could hear my heart thumping, couldn't he? He could feel my hot breath, see the slightest tremble in my jaw that his proximity was inciting. He could see exactly what being this close did to me.

Maybe it was the midnight hour, maybe it was the faint traces of his cologne, or maybe it was a combination of it all that inhibited my judgement—because the last thing I wanted to do, despite the last few shreds of my rationality screaming at me otherwise, was pull away.

"I guess it's just stupid insecurity after the past few days," I whispered.

"Okay." He looked down at me, pushing my hair behind my ear and igniting my skin with goosebumps. "Then let's take care of that."

That hand fell to my jaw, steadying it like he was trying to fix what he was doing to me. Both hands cupped my face, warming me in a way that sent electricity down my back. When he leaned down toward me, he closed his eyes as I closed mine. My heart was sprinting a marathon, palpitating so hard that I was terrified he could feel it through my shirt. This moment was it, and all I could think about was how my ignorance could possibly mess it up.

But then, largely because of him, no part of me had to worry. Jak's soft lips met mine in a kiss I'd only ever squealed at in movies and kicked my feet at in books. A tender peck, nothing more, nothing else needed. He lightly brushed his right thumb down my cheek and held it for a second longer before releasing. I opened my eyes, which refused to leave my feet.

"Em," Jak whispered, his nose brushing against mine. "I'm up here."

There was no controlling the quivering exhale that left my mouth then. "You don't get to call me that."

His thumbs brushed my cheeks. "Why not?"

Because it makes me want to kiss you again. But there was no way I was inflating this boy's ego with that. The ball was already in his court, and I still wasn't sure if I wanted a turn or if he was playing the game too well.

"Because I said so."

"Yes, ma'am."

He was definitely playing the game too well.

His forehead rested on mine. Smirking, he brought his hands

a little farther down to my neck. "I don't see what you're insecure about. You're pretty good for a first-timer."

"I never said it was my first," I said too defensively. That was a pretty difficult lie when I was jumping up and down on the inside with the fact that I'd just had my first kiss.

"Neither did I." That knowing smirk grew. "I meant your first with me. But it's an honor to be your first ever."

I caught his smile, finally getting to smack his arm. He'd caught me on that one.

"Good night, Jak," I said, letting the night settle around me. "Thanks for... trusting me."

"Thanks for being safe to trust, Merlin."

It was definitely the midnight hour, or the teenage hormones—anything but rationality acting on my mind when I wanted to return it and say, "You, too." But I turned around before I could open my mouth, and walked back down the hall to my dorm.

I was tempted to skip the whole way there—I couldn't wait to tell Sarah and Breanne! Sarah had had her very first kiss in eighth grade, and even Breanne had had hers last year. Yet another club I'd officially gained access to.

I almost forgot to keep quiet as I sneaked back into the room and dove under my covers. My trust in Jak had finally been affirmed, he'd opened up to me on two new levels, and I'd had my first kiss! For the first time in a long time, the issues of the real world no longer existed. They'd simply melted away and evaporated into thin air.

I knew getting up was a good idea.

CHAPTER

Twenty-Nine

"The first step of rhetorically analyzing any piece of prose is knowing what the author's purpose is," Ms. Durrett said the next afternoon, strolling down the middle of the bright classroom and clicking to the next slide. "Some of you were confused about Hazlitt's purpose for this passage and said he wrote it because he wanted to show what a real desire for money is. I think not. That said, what is Hazlitt really saying?"

As usual, the girl next to me raised her hand.

"Miss Shaw, go ahead."

"Instead, Hazlitt was saying that it's not fair that people can't live nicely without money," Breanne answered in her sturdy academic tone in front of me. "He believes that it shouldn't be a rule of society that if you don't have it, you can't have a good life."

"Exactly." Ms. Durrett nodded, pressing her clicker. Breanne's answer slid onto the presentation. "As he says, 'one cannot get on well in the world without money.' He's insisting that this system shouldn't be. He then goes on to say that, eventually, once you die, striving to become wealthy only…"

As great a writer as William Hazlitt had been and how much I liked Ms. Durrett, I was too rooted in my own struggles that were preventing *me* from having a good life. Except, replace the poverty with Alexa Delphine and keep the endless struggle to climb out.

And every coin just jumps down a well.

"Hey," Sarah whispered on my left, gaining my attention. "What're you doing after school while we're gone?"

I continued with my notes, glancing back and forth between the board and my paper. "Probably visiting my aunt and uncle with my mom."

For obvious reasons, Sarah and Breanne have never met Aunt Becca, nor do they know that her name is "Rebecca" or that she isn't married. At that point, they did know that my "aunt and uncle" had moved into our house once Momma and I moved out and stayed in touch with us.

"Ooh, good idea," Sarah replied, tapping the tip of her pencil on her binder. "Wanted to make sure you'd be okay without us. We won't be gone long. Maybe we can head to the mall after or something. How about 4?"

Visiting Aunt Becca after school was as great a distraction as any; Jak had left the school this morning and was meeting with the girls later, but I wasn't about to even imply my slight disappointment about that—not with Sarah able to pick up any scent of romance like a bloodhound. And even then, I didn't know if I actually was fully interested in Jak like *that* or if he was just able to effortlessly provide perfect moments... Sitting at my desk now, away from him, I was too afraid to jump down that rabbit hole; feeling anything like that toward him meant surrendering the same amount of trust I had in Sarah and Breanne to him.

Why am I still so conflicted about him? My rationality and emotions were constantly at war fighting over him, just like they had been the night we met. I knew *something* was there—I just wasn't ready to know exactly what it was. And I couldn't even secretly put him under a truth spell anymore.

After school, Sarah, Breanne, and I dropped off our things in our room, got changed, and then said goodbye in the Grand Foyer. There wasn't a single doubt in my mind that this meeting between my friends tied into my birthday tomorrow. Still, I pretended my ignorance and left first, starting down the hall toward the gym; it was more exciting that way.

Just as I pushed open the gym door, Momma was coming out of her classroom and stuffing her keys into her purse.

She was leaving?

"Hey," I said, the acoustics carrying my voice across. She looked up, stopping short when she realized it was me. "Where are you going?"

She sighed, closing the distance between us. Her wedges provided an eerie reverb across the gym. "Don't freak out," she said—in the same gentle tone she used whenever she had bad news with only a plan, no solution, in sight. "I'm going out to look for Mr. Dawson."

What? What was that supposed to mean? Sarah and Breanne

were on their way to his office now for a pass, why would Momma need to go out looking for him?

"What're you talking about?"

"He disappeared after lunch. I called him during my free period with no answer, went to his office with him gone, called him on my personal phone—"

"It's fine," I said, pushing down my panic, "I can just use—"

—*a locator spell.* No, I couldn't.

Telepathy—was also magic. Come on!

Momma pressed her lips amidst the tension that had descended like a dark cloud. "I found his phone in his room."

He left it behind.

I tried to swallow past the constriction in my throat. Anger and frustration burned a hole in my stomach that panic just as quickly filled.

"I don't know why Alexa would want to talk to him again and vice versa," Momma said, adjusting her purse strap on her shoulder. "But this isn't like him, leaving with *no* method of contact. Last time, he was able to telepathically communicate with you, so there are too many red flags for me to ignore. Make sure you have your phone on you at *all* times so I can contact you in case I find anything or he comes back."

"Okay," I said, forcing my voice into its normal register. If Momma could be brave about this, so could I. "But Sarah and Breanne need a pass to go out."

"They can still leave. They just need to formally sign out with security at the front gates." She gestured to my normal-clothes outfit. "You're not going with them?"

All I could do was shake my head. After that, it only took a few seconds of my silence for Momma to wrap her arms around me. Right—I still had her. She'd be fine. She wasn't a magician, and getting rusty didn't seem realistic for my mother. She had a motive to constantly stay in shape.

"Stay with someone at all times, okay?" she said, breaking away. "I mean it."

There was a nagging voice in the back of my mind telling me something that I couldn't translate yet. I nodded anyway, and she kissed me on my forehead and escorted me out of the gym.

When Momma walked through those front doors in the Grand Foyer, I was officially home alone (with almost two hundred other girls).

I know—I *know* I should've listened and stayed among the wandering Callistro Girls all over the school. But I still had a couple of secrets to explore, all of which I was fairly confident would help me like the underground passageways already had. I needed to plan another escape route for when Alexa came back.

My top priority was figuring out the entire underground system. Caralyn had inscribed directions on how to get to the Hunter's Room, and underground was also where Mr. Dawson had found that document. Whatever was on it *had* to have been written for my eyes and my eyes only if Caralyn hadn't wanted the rest of the world looking at it.

If mortals can access the Hunter's Room without magic and the underground passageways lead there, maybe I don't have to use magic to get down there.

The elevator was technically available, and I was pretty sure nobody else (except, apparently, Opal) knew the code to get down into the Hunter's Room. My only problem now was avoiding the cameras... and the ever-present fear of setting off an alarm. Security would be at the cameras in a heartbeat, and I wanted to be safe than sorry. Was my only option to wear a hoodie and change into sweatpants or something concealing to make myself unrecognizable on film? There had to be a way to turn myself—

—invisible!

Thank you, Mr. Dawson.

I darted back up to my room and dug out the invisibility cloak in my dresser. I could hang it over my arm like a coat and put it on in the elevator—and hope the cameras didn't catch the doors opening when "nobody" was there.

For once, my plan went off without a hitch.

The elevator doors closed behind me, leaving me invisible inside a vault of weapons aimed directly at me. Any idea that wouldn't result in immediate exposure or death, I had to try without a second thought.

There could be a passageway in any of these classrooms. But I was pretty sure the doors were locked—and I couldn't use my magic to unlock them. That meant my only hope was the Hall of Generations. If I found nothing, I'd have to give up here for now; if I tripped a silent alarm, that would be enough for security to look at the film. But which side of the Hall to begin with? Hunter or Magician?

Despite Caralyn Callistro's reputation as a nationally famous Hunter, newly accumulated evidence accused her of an alliance with magic. I would've assumed the Hunter side because it made the most sense. But if she was trying to help a magician...

I stepped into the beginning of the hall where my family tree hung, the very first one displayed. My eyes dragged themselves over every name again, all the way until I came to the bottom of the frame. I looked along the wall where the other trees hung, and then back at my own. Something was off, some kind of difference was dangling in front of me. Some kind of...

As if my family from the dead was guiding me themselves, I hesitantly took the sides of my family tree's ornate golden frame.

This is crazy.

So is Caralyn building these underground passageways at all.

With a single jolt, I had it: the wall was loose. I jumped back, covering my gasp with my hand like the cameras could hear it. I didn't know if they could, but I wasn't risking it.

I looked up at the corner of the ceiling. A camera prowled just above me. If security never checked unless a crime—a crime they knew about—had been committed, maybe I *could* get away with moving the tree...

I gripped the frame again and lifted up. It pushed against me like it was glued in place. I lifted again as if I'd made a mistake the first time, and then tried sliding left. Then right. The wall budged. I startled, releasing the frame. The Atera family tree was a sliding door to a passageway!

I slid it as far to the right as it would go. I'd assumed that the three-foot margin between the wall and the edge of the frame was for aesthetic! No—it was meant to *look* like it was for aesthetic when, really, it was giving room for the person who would discover another one of Caralyn's secrets.

A cold, damp draft blew into the room. Straight ahead, all the way down at the end of the passageway, was a framed document mounted on the wall. It had to be the one Mr. Dawson had seen down here. One light hung above it, still under the light spell he'd cast.

I looked behind me as if someone would be there and then walked in, my invisible footsteps echoing on the hard concrete. I passed one passageway on my right that led back into the underground system. This hallway was segregated...

I approached the end as if one footstep would shatter the glass protecting the aging handwritten letter framed on the wall. My eyes dashed to the first word on the parchment:

These words are reserved for the eyes of the one capable of finding them at all. Unfathomable consequences, chains of suffering, lie in wait for my family, should the truth be encountered.

The world knows my father's hero. The world knows who sought his life. May the world even regard his profession, but not a soul knows what lies behind our walls, or what transpires between my father and his prey. None know what lies behind.

Henry Callistro consumes the despicable plague of our enemies and allocates it for himself. Power has corrupted the blood in his veins and disrupted his senses. In his all-consuming madness, he has disclosed unto me his objective: to empower his family as the greatest symbols of magic on this earth—to succeed the Ateras—to dominate our globe. This day, we fulfill our roles as Hunters. The next, we take our place as the most powerful sorcerers the world has come to know.

Countless lives have been lost at my father's hand, at that of this organization we call Hunters, and all for an abominable reward! Here lies my mission to end this; alongside the rightful reign of the nation's Hunters, we shall continue our profession with honor, dignity, and indomitable strength—the righteous manner our legacy has always demanded. Severing ourselves and the world from magic's, we shall destroy every last conceivable atom of the enemy. So now is the purpose and foundation that I, Caralyn Callistro, hereby institute for the Callistro Academy of Self-Defense and Advanced Academics.

The words read like a dream. *That* was why this document was almost impossible to find for mortals: this had to be where it was discovered that Henry Callistro abused his power to take it from magicians! And it was also why not many knew the other side of the story: should anyone discover that a great Hunter, a Callistro, used his power to gain what he did, anarchy would break out. Especially with today's technology, more mortals would gain the confidence to follow in his footsteps.

These words... Anyone "capable of finding them at all" would know that about them and keep quiet. At least, I had to hope they would.

I guess Caralyn wasn't an ally of magic...

But if I was supposedly the first to discover this, *was* this how the story came to be known? Why would Caralyn put it in the magician's side of the hall? Behind the *Atera* family tree? And why would she require magic to open the secret underground passageways? And how had she known about my destiny?

No, there was much more to this letter than what she had made visible to the naked eye. This very paper had to have its own secret, like everything else in this school seemed to. There was a small margin under the last line, but it wasn't enough for anything more than "By the way, I secretly don't hate magic."

Well, I was satisfied for now. Sneaking around had paid off, and I couldn't be greedy with that. I dashed down the passageway, closed the entrance, and made it out of the Hunter's Room and back to my dorm.

For once, my first instinct was actually to tell Mr. Dawson what I'd found—but my magic couldn't help me with that. At this point in the game, knowing that not even Momma was omnipotent when it came to a hunt, I just had to pray that I'd get to tell him at all.

THIRTY

The invisibility cloak had given me the perfect idea to distract myself for the rest of the time Momma and my friends would be gone: what better place to pre-birthday shop *and* always be around someone than the mall? With the invisibility cloak, I could walk through the forest and town without being grabbed. I just didn't want to stay inside the school, not with every direction I looked reminding me of present circumstances.

On my way through town, it was all the easier to tune out the faces of everyone around me. I had the best night of my life—last night—to play and replay in my head for entertainment. I didn't even have to hide the stupid, giddy smile with the cloak concealing me. I had to tell the girls about it as soon as they got back tonight!

And then Sarah will relentlessly tease me, want to plan our dates, never stop asking when we'll become an official...

...couple. She would never leave it alone until we became a couple. But I was still an Atera. Jak was still the son of the Hunters after my family. He still wasn't a magician.

And just because he doesn't condone what your enemies are doing doesn't mean he'll forgive you, let alone accept you, for lying to him and being—

I cut myself off before I could really start spiraling. This was the last thing I should be thinking about before my birthday.

I pulled open one of the glass doors of the mall, welcomed back into a place I hadn't been to in, surprisingly, a few weeks. It used to be my favorite spot growing up because, as I'd told Momma, I "liked the variety". Actual words from Emmalynn Marie, age six. Momma had thought it was hilarious.

My first stop was the bathroom to take off the cloak and stuff it into the purse I'd "borrowed" from Sarah. After that, I wasn't expecting the chill down my back as I walked back onto the white tile cutting the mall in half. My skin prickled the entire way to the elevator like someone was lightly poking me with their fingernails. Sure, I was in public—but you never realize how exposed you are until you've been invisible. I just had to stick to Momma's word: stay close with someone, anyone, and I'd be safe. Too many good people here would notice if I was being kidnapped. I had my phone. People had their phones. I was safe.

Just keep saying it. That should work.

Apparently there's a thing about elevators being the most awkward place on the planet, but for me, they're a breeding ground for anxiety that I'll somehow expose myself by standing in one place and magic will just burst out. It's impossible, but I don't trust myself to not somehow accidentally find a way—similar to how it's always the most difficult not to laugh as soon as you're not allowed to laugh.

Oh no.

A boy, a *cute* boy, with hickory-brown hair under a blue beanie followed me inside the elevator just as I reached to press the button.

"Going up to second?" he asked with a lopsided smile on a pale face. I'm not sure if you can call a voice cute, and maybe it was that boyish smile, but his voice was... well, *very* cute.

Still, I held on tighter to the strap of Sarah's purse over my shoulder. I only had so much allowance saved up, and I was pretty sure half of it would cover a quarter of the purse cost if it were stolen. "Yeah," I said, "thanks."

I then saw exactly why people fear the elevator. I also understood the whole concept of social anxiety.

If the boy had the same thoughts, he didn't show it; he instantly broke the ice barely a second after the doors closed. "I'm guessing you don't go out much on your own, do you?"

I laughed. *Not anymore, but close enough.* "How'd you know?"

"You're totally tense and darting your eyes every which way like I'm gonna jump out at you."

"Sorry," I said, a nervous smile bending my lips.

"And you apologize for things that don't need an apology." He found it amusing, one corner of his mouth turning upward. "So who're you trying to avoid?"

A list of people, actually.

"Mom always told me to avoid strangers," I said as the doors slid open.

He threw me a chuckle, one that I almost hoped was out of pity—because then that would mean that he'd end the conversation after we walked out of the elevator, whereas I already knew I was too nervous to continue this conversation. Why was I so nervous?

"Well, I'm Nolan," he said, holding out his hand once we did step out. "Now we're not strangers."

I paused. *He didn't.* What was it with boys and their insistence to be friends?

I prayed that my hands weren't as clammy as I was scared they were, and accepted his. "Emma."

"Pretty," Nolan said, brushing a dark-brown bang out of his green eyes. "It's fitting."

I stopped (as much as I could for standing in place). That was a flirt. That was him flirting, wasn't it?

Was I even allowed to smile at it like I was right now, to accept it in any way? I'd just kissed Jak last night! Weren't there rules about this? How was I supposed to react when Nolan said things like that?

"So what about you?" I said, taking my first step forward and daring to see where he'd go. "Who're you avoiding?"

"Parents and little brother," he replied—walking with me toward the food court in front of us. "He's only two years younger but acts like he's the boss of me, so sometimes I need to get away from how much of a control freak he is. I'm just here to get as much fun out of the week as I can before school starts tomorrow."

I tilted my head. "Huh, we started school last Wednesday."

"Really?" he said with furrowed brows, reaching the edge of

the food court with me. "So you don't go to Capperson?"

I opened my mouth to answer, instinctually stopping in my tracks (because I didn't even know if I could afford a snack this close to dinner). It was obvious why Nolan had assumed that I went to the normal high school, but would he think I was pretentious or snobby if I told him that I went to the private school in the forest?

"No—I'm at Callistro," I said, fiddling with my fingernails.

"Oh, that self-defense boarding school? Nice. Must be cool to get to go there."

I internally sighed with relief, following him as he resumed our stroll into the food court. "Yeah, everyone's really nice. Teachers are great, I'm rooming with my best friends, and the classes are actually pretty fun if you look past the mountains of homework every night."

Before I knew it, we were at the smoothie booth on the right side of the court, the first store available. I no longer knew who was following whom. Or if we were following each other at all.

"Can I buy you something?" Nolan asked, like he'd practiced that question a hundred times in front of the mirror to one day ask a girl.

The twenty dollars I had in Sarah's purse started to burn a hole. I'd grabbed it from the wooden jewelry box that once belonged to my great grandmother on my father's side. My father gave it to Momma as a wedding gift, and then she gave it to me for my tenth birthday. I keep everything special to me in that box, so I wasn't sure if I even *could* use the twenty—it was like everything turned sacred once I put it in the box. And this was the *last* context I'd expected to use the money in.

But what was politest: accepting, declining, or insisting to pay for myself?

"You don't mind?" I finally asked.

"Not at all," Nolan replied. Those straight lips lent him a unique smile that I honestly couldn't stop looking at.

After ordering, he leaned against the pick-up counter, which I wasn't sure was the most sanitary. My nerves came straight out of hiding again (as if they'd ever gone away) as we waited: what now? What were we supposed to talk about?

"Well," Nolan said, pushing up the blue beanie on his head and saving me from the anxiety again, "Callistro sounds a lot better than Capperson. Well, I guess it depends on what classes you take, but junior year's already run me over a few times with the summer homework. I took way too many APs."

So he was an *older* boy. "You're a junior?"

"Yeah, I—"

The obnoxious grind of the blender ignited, startling Nolan right off the counter. At least it gave something for me to laugh about, something to fill the moments he'd stopped talking.

Thankfully, he laughed, too. "Forgot about that," he called, leaning in so as to not shout across the whole food court. "I turn seventeen next year in March, what about you?"

"Sophomore," I said, no room for shyness in my louder volume. "Would you believe me if I told you my sixteenth birthday is tomorrow?"

"Wow!" He grinned, nodding and gesturing loosely to me. "So we met just in time, happy birthday."

Oh, this felt wrong. Why did this feel wrong? He was just keeping things lighthearted, right? What if I sent him the wrong message? What would be *not* flirting with him?

"Did Callistro bring you to Capperson," he asked, stuffing his hands into his denim jacket pockets, "or did you live around here already?"

"Grew up here."

"Same."

The blender turned off, fading into the mall ambiance at his last word. I prepared myself for the next round.

"I'm kind of surprised I haven't seen you before," he said. "Or that I don't recognize you at least a bit."

I'm not *surprised*, I almost said. Not when I spent a decent chunk of my childhood in my and my best friends' houses and was focused on Momma every time we *did* go out.

"I was homeschooled until this year," I said, shrugging it off, just as the cashier slid Nolan his smoothie across the counter.

"Oh, so Callistro's gotta be even more exciting, huh?"

I opened my mouth just as the next blender whirred to mechanical life. Nolan shared a chuckle with me, and I shook my head, dismissing my answer.

He hadn't sipped from his smoothie yet. Was he waiting for me to get mine?

"What're your plans for tomorrow?" he asked, raising his voice and leaning in again. Geez, every time he did, my heart lost control of its rhythm.

"I honestly don't know. My friends went off to do something today, and knowing them, it probably has to do with that. My mom hasn't said anything yet, but she's been really..."—I tried not to let the reality of my words leave me stagnant for too long, tried to hold on the surface-level cover story they had—"busy with other things. I don't know... I haven't really had time to think about tomorrow."

His brows furrowed. "Callistro keeps you *that* busy?"

"Oh, no, that's not what I meant," I said quickly, plunged deeper into the pit when the blender shut off. I tried thinking of a lie to justify my answer with, just as quickly saved by the buzz.

I slid my phone out of my back pocket. Upon processing the ringtone and name on screen, my gaze widened: it was already that late?

I sighed, declining Sarah's call. "I'm so sorry, my friends are here so we can do some birthday shopping. I have to go."

"Oh, sure, no problem," Nolan said, like he really meant the words, like we were old friends. He took my smoothie off the counter. "But I have to take this as compensation."

"That's fair—"

"I'm kidding!" He burst into laughter, handing me my smoothie. "Hey, think of it as a birthday present. Have fun with your friends."

There it was, my heart losing its rhythm again. My lips melted into a smile. "Thanks."

"Oh, wait, one more thing." Nolan dug out his phone from his pocket, promptly unlocking the screen and tapping a few buttons. His contacts.

No, no, no, don't, please *don't ask—*

"Would it be okay if—I got your number and sent a 'happy birthday' text tomorrow?"

No, I couldn't take it! What if *he* somehow became involved in the entire mess with Alexa? What if he even happened to be the first one to unravel the truth about me? What if he met Jak one day and there was high tension between them and I ended up losing both?

Jak. I couldn't even think about him right now.

Okay. Nolan was just like my classmates: a new friend. We could be friends, even distant friends, without it endangering either of us, couldn't we?

"Sure, if you want," I said, only filling out the blank space for my number. "Thanks again. This was nice."

I held up my hand as a goodbye and sped past him, leaving him with another smile. That was it: our paths were officially running together, and I had to pray that I hadn't just made a mistake on both of our behalves.

Thirty-One

I came home that night with two new tops and a cute sundress—in case there really was a secret celebration planned for tomorrow. After Sarah forgave me for borrowing her purse, the girls' cover story for the afternoon was a double date, which failed to explain why Jak had gone with them. I pretended to believe it anyway, just like they pretended that they weren't planning a birthday surprise.

Getting back to the room, though, Sarah locked us in and arranged me and Breanne on her bed. Which was a warning in itself for us to brace ourselves. (The last time the girl had called an impromptu meeting, I ended up spending a week washing glow-in-the-dark paint out of my hair.)

"Okay, before dinner," she began, "yesterday I heard from

Amelia, who heard from Kimia after Teresa told her, about something we *have* to explore—"

"No," Breanne jumped to say, shoving a finger at her. "The last time you wanted to 'explore', we were almost expelled!"

"We were not almost expelled," Sarah deadpanned, rolling her eyes and putting her hands on her hips. "This time's safer, I wanna find the secret passageways!"

Breanne's blue-hazel eyes lit up, her lips spreading into a child-like grin. "Oh! Yeah, I wanted to do that, too!"

"See?" Sarah chirped. "I have good ideas! Em, are you in?"

I glanced between the two of them. After the mall, the *last* thing I wanted to do before dinner was play detective—but if I wanted to learn the passageway system better, I did have to familiarize myself with it more.

I shrugged. "You're dragging me along either way."

"Correct," Sarah chimed.

I guess it was as good a time as any *because* I didn't have my magic; I could actually have fun with my friends here for the first time without worrying about whether or not we were doing something illegal, and I wouldn't need magic to access it or correct our mistakes.

I *really* hoped I wouldn't have to correct any mistakes.

"There are supposed to be a ton of entrances in the subject wings," Sarah added, holding out her hands as if to request ideas. "So?"

"Right, Caralyn Callistro wrote riddles about them for her students to solve," Breanne said, joining her in the enthusiasm. "In her autobiography. There's a copy in the library."

We left without another word. Now I had something to be

excited about, too, because I've always thought of the Callistro library as more of a cozy ballroom. The crème fleur-de-lis wallpaper was a nice break from the school's otherwise dark color palette, for one. My favorite part, though, is the large brick fireplace in the back with two big armchairs, where I can get lost in a good book—which is easy to find in a room with bookshelves that stand seven feet tall, stocked with books of *every* kind (including the first editions of *Combining the Arts of Knitting and Arson* and *Foreign Language Codes—What Your Pack Really Means*).

Sarah, Breanne, and I scurried to the nonfiction section, glancing at each spine along the shelves. Finally: *White Lies for Sacred Ties*.

I slid Caralyn's autobiography off the shelf and led my friends to the tables by the windows. Sitting down, I flipped to the table of contents, skimming until my eyes snagged on the seventh chapter: "Behind Them Lie".

I have a gut feeling about this one. I turned to the page and started reading:

> *It's risen to my attention that the Academy, while soon to be the home of many young girls following in their founder's footsteps, lacks a sanctuary of its own though its greatest secret remains safely hidden in its own. The grant for safety, that for protection against the great evil of magic, is significant, and nonetheless grows in the name of shelter within the Callistro Academy, within its very walls.*

I turned the page, my eyes widening: a riddle was neatly printed below the next, perfectly aligned in the center of the pages. I only had to turn one page to find the one that Mr. Dawson had told me—the one taking the world two centuries to solve.

I flipped the page back. "Each one of these must be the key for different entrances."

Breanne, huddled beside me, reserved a few seconds of thinking before pointing at the very first riddle. "Look at the first letter of each line in this one. They spell out 'English'."

I leaned in, jumping to the one directly across from it on the next page. "This one spells 'math'."

"As in," Sarah said, "the English and math wings?"

Breanne grinned, her small finger sliding to the second riddle. "This one spells 'history'! 'Sciences', 'language', 'gymnasium'... Wow, who knew this many passageways were in this school?"

Caralyn had said herself that these passageways were meant to be a "sanctuary" for the school. Almost like she had expected intruders or breaches in security. I'd probably have to wait until the school's history unit in Mr. Broadhurst's class later this month to learn more, but did this have anything to do with the underground system, too? Because why would the main entrance to it need magic, whereas her letter had exposed a distinct disdain for it?

It felt like nothing short of my mission to find the truth about Caralyn; she hadn't been the Callistro Girl the world knew her as, and there was a lot more to that document I hadn't uncovered yet.

"I'm going to check this out," Breanne said, shutting the book. "You guys get to the English wing since it's closest, hurry."

Dinner was in ten minutes, so Sarah and I rushed out of the library and crept into the left hallway we'd left hours ago. At the end and around the corner lay Ms. Durrett's door, sandwiched between two paintings. Now its seclusion stuck out to me; I had a good feeling that our answer was right here.

Breanne met us a minute later with Caralyn's autobiography in hand. "Okay, let's try to interpret this." She flipped to the riddle, reading aloud:

> *Entering through the painted door*
> *Navigates the one looking for more.*
> *Gliding left shall it be revealed,*
> *Leaving behind my hidden shield.*
> *If you fear, you must know this:*
> *Safety lies here, as does its bliss.*
> *Have faith in yourself, as well as your wits.*

I cocked my head. My first instinct was to divide it into parts, but something was tugging at me, telling me that it was much simpler than I wanted to believe. This time, I could make out one thought explicitly: *Don't overthink it.*

I don't even know *how* magic could help me with this one. "Entering through the painted door"... Painted? Was the door literally painted onto the—no, then it wouldn't be a real door at all...

Paint. I looked behind Breanne. We stood between two paintings right now.

It clicked: the Atera family tree was one of the entrances to the underground passageways. "Painted" had to refer to one of these paintings. It made "gliding left shall it be revealed" make perfect sense, too. The tree had slid right, so this was Caralyn's most blatant hint for how to open the door.

"What're you thinking?" Sarah asked, reading me too well.

I explained to them my thought process (leaving out the Atera part) and then turned back to the paintings: daisies in a lavender vase on the left wall and a painting of the school on the right. Sarah and Breanne followed suit.

"Wait," Sarah mused, "I think you're right. We know Ms. Durrett's classroom is behind the school painting, so the daisies have to be the 'painted door'."

My fingertips wrapped around the golden frame, my thumbs on the textured canvas. I gently tried to slide the painting over. After three nudges, the door budged. I jumped back as the girls gasped, gawking at the narrow opening in the wall.

"We found one!" Breanne squealed.

The dinner bell rang as if to spite her.

"No!" Sarah sighed. "Ugh, I knew we shouldn't've spent so much time at the mall. Fine, next time, we can come back with... proper equipment."

"Yeah, *that* doesn't sound sketchy." After sliding the passageway entrance closed, the three of us started our walk back down the corridor and into the Foyer. "You promised Bre you wouldn't get us suspended."

"Simple Emmy," Sarah teased, patting my head. "Secret passageways equal escape routes."

Breanne walked faster as if to disassociate herself from the crime completely, and it was no wonder. There wasn't technically anything wrong in what Sarah had said, especially in a school like ours—and for people like me. And I couldn't help but wonder the secrets lying within the regular passageways, too.

CHAPTER

Thirty-Two

Mr. Dawson wasn't back by dinner, but at least—at the very least—Momma was. So Alexa didn't *seem* to be on the hunt for the adults in my life. There were, however, other terrifying possibilities: Alexa could've been busy torturing Mr. Dawson, he could've been lying in a hospital bed with fatal injuries, or Momma had just happened to *scarcely* avoid Alexa—

I tried to slow my thoughts at the dinner table and breathe. I refused to panic here, especially with Teresa Darci angrily rambling about her older brother studying abroad with a girl he'd just met two weeks ago.

With how many secrets Caralyn had, my feet were itching to explore more of the passageways; there had to be something useful, not just up here, but underground, too. Caralyn had clearly been an intentional woman; my mission wasn't complete until I knew what her true intentions had been.

If I got security's approval to go off campus, I could go to the tree stump behind the school and try again with the document. But when would I get to do that without raising suspicion? I wasn't sure I had the patience to wait until the next time my friends went out without me; not only was that rare, but it had only happened tonight because of the birthday planning. If I *asked* them to leave, suspicion was inevitable.

Unless I catch another case of insomnia tonight.

Wait a minute. At night, when everyone else was asleep...

Don't do it. Don't.

If I took the invisibility cloak...

The idea pressed heavily against my mind as I said good night to Momma in the Dining Hall, and during the whole time Sarah, Breanne, and I worked on homework. I wouldn't have to worry about Alexa if I took my cloak. I wouldn't have to worry about *anything* as long as I took the cloak. And I was already someone who woke up constantly throughout the night. The plan was falling right into my lap.

"Good night," Sarah said sweetly in bed, one hand holding the lamp's dangling chain. She looked at Breanne behind her, then at me in front of her with a smile. "Happy birthday, Emmy."

"Thanks," I told her with a smile. She pulled on the chain and sent us into a comforting and quiet darkness.

I already knew how this was going to go: my anticipation for my upcoming mission would be the very thing to tire me out before I'd be able to detect it. It was just before 11 when my eyes became too heavy to check again. What felt like shortly after, my mind slipped into a dream.

Fictional journeys through the passageways played like a movie: ten-year-old me walked through the tunnels from earlier that day, looking for adventure, some special secret. Instead of lanterns, torches sat on both sides of the walls. A crimson carpet runner blanketed the solid-concrete ground. Navigating the passageways was a blur until I found Caralyn's framed document mounted on the wall. I stepped up to it. Caralyn's riddles and poems about the passageways were now scribbled across it.

Dust caked the bottom margin. Dream Emmalynn somehow knew to blow it away. The dirt wafted into the air like magic, a new page fading into existence under it:

Now that the world knows of Emmalynn's power, her greatest enemy has finally found her and begun her family's end.

The air shifted around me, ice prickling my skin. I spun around, now my fifteen-year-old self. Mere feet away, Alexa's cold stare stunned my heartbeat, two Hunters grabbing my arms from behind.

Alexa strode up to me and grabbed my chin, bending down to my level. "You're *mine*, Atera."

Darkness engulfed me on all sides. My eyes shot open as my body sprang up.

The reality of my dream dissipated, my sense of touch fading back into my fingers. It was only the cushioning of my mattress and blankets preventing full-on panic. I curtly exhaled, pressing my hand to my chest. My heart sent a reverberating thump all across it.

Just a dream. Not real. Not real. Not this time.

Wait, time—what time is it?

I looked at the digital clock beside me: almost 1 in the morning.

Now was as good a time as ever. I was pretty sure sleep would avoid me at all costs after that dream, anyway.

I threw the covers off me and swung my legs over the bed. Letting the rods in my eyes adjust to the darkness, my best friends in their beds came into view. *Dormio—*

I clenched my teeth in frustrating disappointment: no magic. Right. I had to do this the old-fashioned way.

Breanne's small snoring and Sarah's shallow breathing verified that they were, in fact, sound asleep. I crept away from my bed, put on some black flats and a cardigan, and paused. Knowing that I wouldn't change my mind, I still gave myself the time to. But I was already in the leggings, T-shirt, and cardigan, which was the perfect outfit for an expedition.

I grabbed my cloak from the bottom drawer of my dresser. My hands tightened around the velvet, my shoulders sagging. Could I risk the elevator this late? That mechanical grinding sounded like a purr during the day, but at night, it might as well have been a foghorn. If *anyone* heard or even suspected the elevator was going, security would be sprinting to check the cameras— and they'd see the elevator door opening with nobody walking inside.

Okay. Caralyn wasn't a magician but still had another entrance to the underground system built. She had to have built an entrance to it from the first floor. Maybe even a first-floor passageway led to one.

I had all the time in the world to test it.

I closed my drawer and took another thirty seconds to quietly leave my dorm.

Reaching the Grand Foyer, I went for the English wing; finding the right candle sconce to open the passageway that Mr. Dawson had told me about required too much time because of the dark. At Ms. Durrett's door, I trudged past the fear of being too loud and slowly slid the daisy painting aside. Thank goodness these passageways were well-known and maintained: the lights above were already on, making it infinitely easier to tell my feet to move.

The second I turned around and slid the door shut, regret inflated like a balloon in my chest. I was alone in a system of passageways I wasn't familiar with and no magic to defend myself with. The lights soothed some nerves, but how was I supposed to know if I'd be followed or snuck up on?

It's okay. It's too late for anyone to be in here right now.

Except Alexa. Like in my dream—

No! Don't you dare. I was invisible; she couldn't grab me even if she were here. I was safe.

I forced my steps forward through the narrow tunnel, repeating those words in my head. Keeping my eyes on the stone floor, I stopped at the first intersection mere paces from the entrance. Something was carved into the ground along the wall just before the corner. There were directions in these passageways, too!

If I could make my way to Mr. Dawson's office, there had to be an entrance to underground there.

I followed the inscription no matter what turns it took me around, checking behind my shoulder after each one. Thankfully, my footsteps were the only ones echoing throughout the stone. Eventually, I arrived at a wall—the wall behind Mr. Dawson's office. Sure enough, a square was cut out in it *and* in the floor. It was so easy—and, hopefully, quiet.

I pushed against the left edge of the wall, gently and then by engaging my entire arm (which is a pretty trippy sight when you're invisible). With a jolt, it creaked in large, ancient protest, and I jumped back.

Should've gone with the elevator! I also made a mental note to propose extra arm exercises to Momma tomorrow.

I slowly tried again, needing just as much muscle. The antiquity of the first creak had faded, leaving behind one that mimicked a grand door whose hinges needed oil. I pushed the wall forward just enough for me to slip through a crack. It shut behind me, facing me with the front door of Mr. Dawson's office on the other end of the room. Stepping deeper into the pitch-dark room, I glanced behind me: his bookshelf was an entrance to a passageway. His two white sofas sat against the left and right side of the room, the glass coffee in the middle. His desk sat next to me in the corner—with his chair that had been empty for twelve hours now.

I really hope you're okay. Please be okay.

Hang on. If I was in his office, that meant the underground passageway was directly underneath me.

Why would there be a square cut out in the floor if the floor didn't turn with the...?

I spun around, barreling back into the passageways. So Caralyn *had* had the idea to build her own way down into them, and I was right on top of it!

I looked all around to find something that would open the

ground. Maybe something to do with the wall, with its cutout...

Or the brick next to it.

Maybe it didn't look like it completely filled its place, maybe it was a slightly different color, a combination of the two—it was too late in the night for me to figure out exactly why it stuck out. But you don't typically notice something like that unless you're looking for it. This was my brick.

Remembering that I hadn't seen another staircase so close to the one that Mr. Dawson and I had walked down, I stepped out of the cutout part of the ground and used both hands to push the brick in. Lo and behold, the concrete slowly opened on a hinge with another ancient groan—one that inspired enough anxiety for me to cover my ears. Too many seconds later, a long ramp led down into the floor below.

I shuffled my way down before I could convince myself that someone actually had heard and woken up.

Finally, I was where I needed to be. Refusing to spare myself a second thought, I followed the directions to the Hunter's Room, already thinking about how I was going to have to drag Ingrid over here later to close the gaping hole that any Callistro Girl could find, should they explore the passageways.

I found the corridor that intersected the one in the Hunter's Room and turned right. The document faced me again at the end, and I was determined to dissect it. My steps scraped against the stone with an unnerving reverb as I approached Caralyn's letter. I reread it just in case because, by that point, I was pretty sure I knew her well enough to believe that she had left a clue of some kind somewhere in this document alone.

This time, my eyes practically snagged on the code:

The repetition of "behind", especially with "None know what
lies behind" being on its own line, was enough for me to start
asking questions. My memory traced back to the title of the chapter in Caralyn's autobiography about the secret passageways: "Behind Them Lie".

What had I thought when Sarah, Breanne, and I were in the
library? That there was more behind this document I hadn't uncovered? And in my dream, when I blew away the dust, there'd
been something under the first page... like my brain was proposing
every possibility.

Could it really be that simple?

I had to see exactly where I was aiming when I broke the glass,
so I threw off the hood of my invisibility cloak to reappear. I took
off one of my flats, steeled myself, and jammed my shoe through
the thin glass barrier. Carefully removing the bigger shards and
letting them drop to the floor, I pushed down the parchment. Another paper lay behind it.

No way. No way.

I gently pushed the first page all the way down. The paper fell
to my feet, unveiling a completely new letter:

*According to Samuel, these words shall only befall the eyes meant to
alter the course of the war between mortal and magic—a war of
which I've committed myself to the latter side. And I shall be killed
for it should my loyalties precede me.*

Should this document be prematurely uncovered, the truth—that regarding myself, my father, and the development of this school—is vaguely and, to an extent, falsely printed on the former page, for only someone worthy to find it. I place my faith in this.

Until the soul of unity sees the beginning of her days, may those most trusted bequeath this truth from generation to generation: Samuel has discovered that my father, Henry Callistro, seeks the magic of his victims. I've allied with Samuel as a means to end this war, for I live day by day haunted by its binding, inevitable repercussions. How many more lives are needed to end what should have never begun?

Samuel has disclosed unto me secrets that bear the power to sentence one to their grave. It is he who so zealously shared with me the future of our world, one where a risen power unites us so that we may live as one. However, this generation, part of which the soul of unity shall be, resides lifetimes away; until such a day, in the establishment of the Callistro Academy, may the soul unveil the precarious truth here.

And therefore, I implore you: Protect the Atera family disregarding the costs, for in them resides the ultimate connection to our hope. Their enemy, though against them, will in fact be one of them: The Delphines, I've been a victim to know, have worn their title as masterful Hunters for centuries—but be wary, Soul of Unity, for my father follows in your enemies' footsteps. The Delphines wield that which they claim to despise and destroy. They carry significant power as Hunters and magicians. Do not allow them to fool you, or, forbid it, allow yourself to fall as their prey. Let it never be known their plans for you and then your power, should such tragedy erupt.

A suffocating, muffled fuzz had overcome my hearing, left behind by the truth. If I didn't know any better, I would've believed that the passageways had flooded and I was underwater. Every image, every thought, blurred with one another. One foot took a step back, the only part of me I could feel. Some faraway shred of my rationality screamed at me to move, to wake up, but the truth had buried the rest of me alive.

The Delphines are...

A boot scraped the stone behind me. I whirled around.

Alexa Delphine's emerald-green eyes flashed with a magician's amber.

At her will, I fell where I stood back to sleep.

Thirty-Three

What felt like hours later—not that I was able to tell—Alexa stood in front of me in the small, cold room I'd found myself in when she'd first questioned me. Except, this time, the headmaster of the Callistro Academy was handcuffed in the chair next to me.

He was *taken*. Why? What did Alexa want with him? Why him and not my mother?

Alexa stood in front of us with her arms crossed. "Thanks for joining us, Emmalynn. If only I could've gotten to you in time."

That was right. The Delphines—the nationally renowned Delphine family, known for their brutality as Hunters and record-high mission successes—were magicians.

I dared to look at Mr. Dawson. He kept his head and eyes low.

I wanted to telepathically say something to him, but Ingrid's price shushed me before I could try.

I'd never seen the man so defeated. His wit was as sharp as his features. He was always the one sitting up straight or standing with his shoulders back, masking his plans and emotions behind his face like it was second nature.

Why did I feel like this was it? Like we'd lost?

"Did you know?" I whispered to him instead. "About her?"

"Not until yesterday," Alexa replied in the same even tone, never letting her eyes leave me. I could only stare back at her soft chin. "I went to privately interrogate him and figured a truth spell was the fastest route. Mortals aren't familiar with the weight of a truth spell. So I guess it makes sense that Thomas immediately felt it—considering, I found out, he's not a mortal."

It *was* over. Even if we somehow managed to convince the pack that we had nothing to do with the Ateras—which was now, in every single sense possible, impossible—Alexa had a magician in her hold.

"But—" I stammered, "but why did you come for *him?* What does he—?"

Alexa sneered, shaking her head at me. "There's the real irony: he came to me and said he was the reason you knew about Tristan's daughter. He offered to tell us everything if we just left you alone."

What? Mr. Dawson was ready to trade places with me?

"You broke your side of the deal," he spat, like a child complaining about a cheater on the playground.

"After I realized what you were," Alexa said. "Which gave me reason to believe that Emma has a little more than I originally thought. And I have one more question I want to ask before I uphold our 'deal'."

The word was nothing more than mockery. She still had all the power, and she knew it.

"Who do you think you are," Mr. Dawson hissed, anger simmering in his voice, "to do this to us when you're out there slaughtering your own people with the same thing they're being punished for?"

"Is that how you see it?" Alexa tilted her head like a curious puppy, her tone matching it. "I wouldn't judge a situation you only have one angle of. Everything has a story behind it."

"Oh, really? What's your story?" He scoffed, my throat tightening the longer their glares lasered each other. "What could *possibly* be driving you to participate in generational genocide, let's hear it."

Alexa gave a toneless laugh. "You won't get it until you realize that that's not what it is." She looked back at me, her refined eyes glinting. "Look, Emmalynn. We're just about ready to pack up and pursue Tristan's daughter depending on your lead. As soon as we go through this last debriefing, as long as we gain sufficient direction, we'll be done here. What do you say?"

I was so deep in the web of lies and stories I'd made that I knew my wisest option was silence. Silence meant a number of different things that Alexa could interpret for herself.

Wait. What did she mean by they'd be done here?

"You're letting us go?" Mr. Dawson asked for me.

"We'll be done," she repeated. She was deflecting. That meant we only had two outcomes for this situation. "May we continue?"

She didn't give us a moment to reply before she and a few other Hunters moved us into the conference room. I absolutely hate to admit it, but I was definitely grateful that Mr. Dawson was here with me this time, sitting across from me at the end of the table. I kept my gaze away from the Hunter who operated both cerebral polygraphs at my old spot at the head of the table. Sometimes there's more comfort in what you don't know than there is in what you do, and if I didn't look at that Hunter... maybe he wouldn't be as real. Our thoughts were the only things we could keep to ourselves as the flat-screen TV on the other end of the room turned on.

"Let's start with you, Thomas." Alexa kept her arms crossed, her stance firm beside the TV. "State your name, place of residence, and occupation."

"Thomas Dawson. The Callistro Academy. Headmaster."

They weren't lies.

Alexa's eyes landed on me, a burst of nerves exploding in my stomach. The Hunter at the polygraph was the only other one in the room, but I still felt like I had an audience to impress with the right voice. In a way, that was exactly what I had to do.

"Emmalynn Marie," I said, adjusting as I went. "The Callistro Academy. Student."

They weren't lies.

"It's come to my attention that Emmalynn may not be Tristan Atera's descendant, after all," Alexa said thoughtfully, strolling down one side of the cold room. My side. "According to Jak, you've been telling the truth."

I defiantly met her eyes. "What?"

"When he told me you weren't Tristan's daughter, he wasn't

lying." She rounded the table, coming up behind Mr. Dawson. "He was pretty persistent about it, and truthful. So either you've trusted him with information about her, or he was simply lied to. That with everything else we've accumulated, give me one more answer, Emmalynn."

She stopped when she reached the TV, her posture impeccable as she folded her hands together. Her emerald-green gaze sliced through me as my heart took off, the evidence blaring on the screen.

"Do you have magic?"

Like breaking through the surface of a raging sea, the realization burst through my head: *that* was why Ingrid had told me my future! That moment in my future, she must have seen a fragment where I didn't have my magic. Every moment leading up to it, knowing who my enemies were—she was *preparing* me for it all.

I used my rapid heartbeat to my advantage, leaning into the word. "No."

It wasn't a lie.

The Hunter at the polygraph shattered Alexa's smirk: "She's not lying."

She shot him a glare of death. "What?"

"She's not lying," he repeated, only his tone admitting his defeat. I still refused to look at him.

Alexa spun to look at the TV behind her, verifying the results for herself. Mr. Dawson and I watched her, anticipating the next few seconds that would make or break our entire fates.

She recollected herself, slowly exhaling and turning back around. "Emmalynn," she began, "you mean to tell me that you do *not* possess any magical abilities? You can't ignite a fire, force someone's mouth shut, or even move this TV"—she pointed at it—"off its mount with nothing but your mind?"

"No," I told her. "I don't have magic."

She turned around, thinking, and I spared a look at Mr. Dawson. I think that one glance helped us suppress our gratitude; we were each other's reminder about present circumstances and why we couldn't afford even an implication of truth.

Alexa turned back around. "Got it. Then here's my offer: I'm going to take you somewhere that will prove your innocence, if you are. Just me and you. Your final test that will tell me who you really are: a Marie, or an Atera. Sound fair?"

She was offering an end to this cat-and-mouse game once and for all—but it meant leaping into an unknown I wasn't sure I could afford. The unknown was going to either lead me to my demise or save me from it. I had a 50 percent chance of making it out. A 50 percent chance of getting Mr. Dawson out. I couldn't go any further unless I said yes, neither of us could.

I swallowed down my hesitance, the word heavy in my mouth. "Fine."

"I'm glad you agree, my dear." The excitement gleaming in Alexa's irises warned me that I'd just declared my own sentence. Walking past me, she closed the polygraph laptop in front of the other Hunter. "We leave in ten minutes."

It was 2 in the morning when I was escorted to a silver SUV. Next to me sat Alexa Delphine, Grand Hunter and powerful magician, now driving us to an unknown destination that would seal my fate.

The best part? I was blindfolded until she drove out of town.

As angry and terrified as I was, there had never been a moment in my life more awkward than the ones spent in that car that morning. I think Alexa enjoyed every second of it, because I was being tormented in more ways than one.

"I've always liked road trips," she said, gazing out at the dark, empty highway that stretched out in front of us. "Especially across the country. American scenery is beautiful."

"I've never been out of town," I replied, sounding deceptively brave. "Until now."

"You've spent your whole life in Capperson?" She glanced at me. For a second, I could believe that her surprise was genuine. "Huh. You should visit us in Topa someday."

"Is that where you're taking me?"

"No. But you should." She smirked, side-eyeing me. "Jak would love it. You've gotten pretty cozy with each other, haven't you?"

Nausea swirled in my stomach. What could she know about that beyond us hanging out at the carnival? I highly doubted Jak was opening up to her about his feelings.

I was thankful that I could scarcely make out her face in the night as I asked, "What do you mean?"

"You trust him, don't you?" It wasn't a question. It was a statement, like she knew everything about the war that had been waging in my head since last week. "Ever since the moment you met, you've trusted him no matter what your instincts told you."

It wasn't possible. "How did you know that?"

"You've never wondered why? Haven't there been moments when you knew your faith in him should've wavered, when you've been tempted to tell him all your secrets, yet you went on trusting him anyway? You're welcome."

No. There's no way she...

"*You* did that?"

She'd been toying with me—*manipulating* me—on more than one level this whole time!

"Trust spell," she said, far too casually for my anger to be justified. Especially since, despite the empty highway, she refused to look at me as she confessed her sins. "It makes your target trustworthy to anyone around them. I was honestly hoping you'd admit something to him before today besides just knowing something... You're pretty headstrong, I can't help but admire that. Well, either that, or you really do have nothing to hide, but I need a lot of help believing that."

She'd been playing me like a violin since day one.

I finally knew why trusting Jak had felt so safe yet so wrong. My instincts had been right all along. Had he been part of this since the beginning despite what Mr. Dawson's truth spell had told us?

"Am I under one, too?" I dared to ask, because Jak had confessed to immediately trusting me, too.

"No," Alexa said simply. Then, a smile lifted the corner of her lips. "I told you: he's just fond of you. He obviously doesn't know about it, either. Not all of your feelings are artificial."

Rage blocked my sense and rationality. "Anything else? Like how you found me in the passageway? How did you even know about the underground system?"

"It took me until my senior year at Callistro to find the Hunter's Room entrance to those passageways, and that was thanks to a lookout spell. I didn't have a lot of time to explore them, but I did find Caralyn's document. The one on top, at least. I kept her secret, but only because I thought she was on the mortal side."

It clicked in me. "So when you took me—every time you found me, that was because of magic?"

"Locator spell, but the carnival was because of Jak."

I took a nervous breath in. "And you got past security—"

"Sleeping spell. Then a forgetting spell to make them forget falling asleep." She shook her head with a chuckle, sighing contently. "Magic definitely makes a lot of things easier. When you can hide it, at least."

Was she the only magician in her pack? It'd make sense if the Delphines were in separate packs for the sake of identity, but why had I always had it in mind that they were a family pack? Was it because she hunted with her husband?

"But then why did you let me go when I said I knew something?"

Finally, she glanced at me, like it was okay again. Thankfully, I still couldn't see her eyes well. "You weren't lying when you said the life of a magician's kid was new to you, and you didn't even know why we believe he has a descendant. And yet, you were under a truth serum when you said you knew where she's hiding. Keeping you around was pointless until we figured out the best plan to move forward."

My blood boiled under my skin, almost hot enough to burn me, but I was still too afraid to anger her. "You won't get far if you take me somewhere hours away and my friends notice I'm gone, you know."

Alexa merely laughed, driving with one hand now as the other fell to the gear shift. "That's the best part: if I take you somewhere far *enough* away, they can't reach you before I've determined your innocence."

"That's a joke," I spat. "*I'm* supposedly guilty while you use what you're supposed to be getting rid of? I don't get it, were you born with it, or is your family like Henry Callistro?"

The hills passed peacefully behind her, almost inviting me to jump out of the car and roll down them. Honestly, if the car had been traveling any slower than eighty, I would have.

"We were born with it," Alexa answered with reassurance.

I scoffed. "How did you *possibly* land this job?"

"Easy to when your family's the one that founded the field."

I gawked, almost wishing I *could* see what was running behind those eyes as she said these things to me. "*Your* family? The Delphines started all of this?"

"We chose not to be on the persecuted side, simple as that. Funny how that works, isn't it: it was supposedly *not* having magic that told the world we weren't weak or powerless."

My stomach tossed and turned, and I had to put my eyes dead ahead on the road to ease it. It felt like we were the only two people in the world. Like I really had used up my last chance.

It's the ultimate cover—but why Hunters? Why not anything else? Why not just simply hide their magic like the rest of us do?

I still didn't understand. I *couldn't* understand. I knew why the Delphines were who they were, but not the justification. Not how they were so unfazed by slaughtering their own people, let alone why they couldn't do what Momma or Mr. Dawson did when they were Hunters and helped their targets escape... What did the Delphines gain from killing—?

Gain. From magicians.

…my father follows in your enemies' footsteps…

Henry Callistro stole his victims' magic and used it to empower himself, and he'd been about to do the same for his family. He wanted them to be known as the most powerful magicians and Hunters to exist, and he was going to bring the world to its knees before them. If he was following in the Delphines' footsteps, Alexa was following in his. And if Alexa was following in Henry's footsteps…

I drew in a breath of revelation. It was too late to pray that it had been quieter than what it was.

"Connected the dots?" Alexa said. "Smart girl. That brain of yours should really get some rest before we get there."

I turned my head to her just before the amber flashed in her irises. My body slumped against the passenger seat.

THIRTY-FOUR

A whishing sound echoed softly in the distance as my eyes pried open. Midnight blue still saturated the atmosphere, the rods in my eyes taking longer than I wanted to adjust to the dark. I groggily looked around me as something clicked beside me: Alexa had taken off her seatbelt and was opening her door.

"Ready?"

We were here.

Forcing some more alertness into my body, I undid my seatbelt and climbed out of the car. I almost startled when my feet sank into the plush piles of sand.

With one breeze, I shivered, rubbing my arms. Moisture—*salt*—clung to the air.

Walking around the SUV, an ocean lay less than half a mile away. We were on a *beach*. I'd never been to one before.

Seriously? This is my first experience at the beach?

Moonlight glimmered on the water calmly folding over itself in gentle, foamy waves. No pictures or videos I'd ever seen could do the sight justice. Save for the seaweed trailing the air, this was... paradise. I couldn't understand why Momma had never taken me here before—

Wait. If we were on the North Carolina coast, we were *at least* two hours away from home.

I turned to Alexa as she rounded the hood of the car. *That was what she'd meant when she'd said "far enough away".* Nobody was getting here in time to save me—whatever time it was.

"Here's your first Hunter lesson, Emmalynn," Alexa said, scanning the coastline. "Always take note of your surroundings first. Never react until you've observed and analyzed." Her eyes fell to me. "What do you see?"

I slowly turned to face the seemingly white sand on the coast, a tiny hill in front of us with grass attempting to grow through the sand, and...

My body stiffened. A beach house ahead.

"Do you recognize that?"

"No," I said. At least it was the truth.

"That house is the other reason I let you go the first time we questioned you. This house is how we know Tristan has a descendant. Do you know why?"

The beach house Mom told them about.

But I'd found that out *after* the pack had questioned me. It all finally made sense; if I were Tristan's daughter, I should have already known about this. Momma *had* done the right thing in never telling me about it…

My silence gave Alexa my now false answer. "The mother of Tristan's daughter told an agent years ago about this house. We never got her name because that agent 'forgot' his whole encounter with her. He was demoted to fieldwork, and then I realized months later that he'd been put under a forgetting spell. I managed to reverse it, and we had who Mama Bear was: none other than Amy Dalbert."

My stomach twisted with a protective instinct at my mother's name on Alexa Delphine's lips; Alexa was too close to her just by saying it.

"She was a natural-born Hunter," Alexa said, "and we even wanted to recruit her to our pack. Then, out of the blue, she dropped out of the business without warning. Nobody heard from her again. Your mother's name is, coincidentally enough, 'Amy'. And I do find it pretty convenient that we've never met."

My mother working alongside Alexa Delphine and William Bleu. The nausea returned, and I shuddered as the wind blew harder.

I wasn't sure if I should ask the question, but I had little to lose at this point. "Who was the agent that confronted Amy?"

"Greenwell. Turns out, he's pretty good at fieldwork."

Without another word, Alexa trudged up the small sand hill. What could possibly be here? An old family artifact I'd recognize? Forgotten memories? A secret about my family that only Momma and I knew? Maybe even something here to remind me of my childhood with Momma?

My heart rattled my ribcage as we stepped across the wooden

porch and up to the front door. Alexa looked up at the house, studying it as though she was coming home after she hadn't been here in years. She dug out a pair of keys from her pocket and unlocked the door. It opened with a creak that warned me to run back home.

Where did she get those keys?

I followed her inside, shadows preceding and following us. I wondered if someone had been here recently, a Hunter other than Alexa. Each step I took on the wooden floor boasted its presence with another creak, another burst of nerves popping in my chest. I was finally the closest to my family heritage that I'd ever been, but as part of a Grand Hunter's mission to find them. And then capture them. And then probably kill them.

Probably kill *me* just as quickly. I swallowed my throbbing heart back down.

A stone fireplace sat against the left side with a full seating set in front of it. On our other side lay an outdated kitchen with tiled counters and wooden cupboards that had probably collected plates of dust by now, yet I still wanted to look through them like this was a normal middle-of-the-night snacking adventure. The open blinds on the two windows in front of us cascaded moonlight onto a buffet, and I realized it then—what gave this house its uncanny atmosphere on the inside. Clear plastic tarps covered every piece of furniture in sight.

"Always protect your evidence," Alexa said, answering my unspoken question. "You never know if the most innocent-looking thing in the room is actually your criminal."

She stepped to what looked like a closet door in the far right corner of the main area. I forced myself to follow her. Opening the door, it took my eyes a few seconds to make out the staircase that stretched far down into the darkness. A basement. Part of me hoped that this one would resemble an office like her lair did.

With no other choice, I took my place in front of her. She flicked on a switch next to me, lighting up the stairs and the hallway in a flash. I shut my strained eyes against the glaring brightness, gripping the wooden rail for balance. Alexa must have needed time to adjust, too, because she only spoke when my vision was ready.

"Watch your step," she warned. "They're steep."

I slowly took my first step down, needing to reach out my foot farther than I'd thought. Cold, humid air squeezed me tighter the deeper I descended thanks to the concrete all around me: the stairs, the floor, the white walls. I succumbed to a shiver every few seconds. Alexa was probably cozy in her black jacket, but I was still in my cardigan, leggings, and flats. Despite my heart sprinting a hundred miles an hour in my chest, it did nothing to warm me up. I couldn't tell if it was paranoia, fear, or reality telling me that Alexa could hear ever pound.

I tightly hugged myself as we reached the bottom of the stairs. The hallway reached out in front of us, the fluorescent lights above running down with it.

"Go ahead," Alexa said when I stopped—like that kind tone meant that I had a choice.

Her steps stayed consistently, uncomfortably close behind me until we reached the end, where we eventually broke into a small, empty room. A large metal door stood in front of us. Next to it was a keypad.

"There it is." Alexa stopped in the middle of the room with

me. "Imagine our disappointment when we bypassed the code and there was just a panic room behind this door, nothing else. Understandable, but we'd been hoping for something of more value."

You mean "incriminating".

Alexa walked to the keypad and brushed her fingers along the numbers. That day in the elevator, trying to find the Hunter's Room's button, haunted my memory. "Once we cleaned it out, though, we found the value. We realized that this place would really come in handy..." She turned back to me. "Welcome to your final test, Emmalynn."

She pushed in a four-digit code, and the small light next to the zero flashed green. This was it. As soon as she opened the door, she would know the truth. Ingrid's words burst through my head as if I'd just heard them the day before:

"Your fear will overcome you, and your fate will escape your lips and yours alone. It will be the first step toward your ultimate destination, where your greatest enemy will reveal herself and your full power will manifest."

Here was my greatest enemy. The sleeping spell in the passageway had unveiled her darkest secret, the same as my own, meaning Alexa had already exposed herself. I swallowed. My fate was next.

All I could do now was cling to my cover for dear life while knowing how useless it was. A triumphant grin spread across Alexa's fair face as she took the handle and turned it. She pulled open the door.

My body froze.

My mind shut down.

My heart finally broke free.

"Dad?"

Thirty-Five

his isn't real.

This wasn't real, this couldn't be real. My father was sitting in a chair in the center of the room with his arms stuck behind his back. Tristan Atera was alive and in America, at the mercy of his enemies. And in the space of a breath, a man I'd never met before in my life had become all that mattered in it.

There was suddenly no wall in front of my tears, like it had never existed at all, as my legs shook under me and I practically limped into the room. The man whose death had been my greatest fear for the last sixteen years was sitting in front of me. His icy-blue eyes, his chestnut hair, and his dimples that appeared even when he wasn't smiling stared right back at me—like a mirror.

I had all that. I looked like him.

I was his.

And what united all of my mixed emotions together was when Tristan Atera looked me dead in the eyes and asked, "Who are you?"

A gentle and sonorous voice, deep with a kind lilt, and it reminded me to breathe.

"Your daughter," I whispered, sobs jerking my body. It was impossible to believe that I was saying these words to him. It was impossible to believe that I was saying them because he didn't already know. I was the one who got to tell him, "Your daughter, Emmalynn! I'm your—"

—*daughter.*

Every piece clicked together in my head. My rationality had finally broken free from the cage my desires and impulse had trapped it in. The words I'd dreaded for so long, the words I'd vowed to never let sneak by me, I had dropped my defenses for a split second and given them enough time to run past me.

I spun around. Triumph and satisfaction beamed on Alexa's lips.

"You knew," I hissed, my blood so hot that it nearly burned my skin from the inside out. "Showing him to me—"

"—and your initial reaction would give me my final answer," she said, nodding. "Admit it, it was clever. I don't see why you're upset. I just gave you the best birthday present ever."

My birthday. I'd completely forgotten about my birthday.

My father stayed silent, watching us. I couldn't imagine what was running through his head. I wasn't sure if I wanted to know. His enemy returns after who knows how long in the middle of the night with a sixteen-year-old girl claiming to be his daughter?

I would've clung to silence for the sake of my sanity, too.

"But what I can't figure out," Alexa mused, tilting her head, "is how you don't have magic."

It was a reflex to look at my father: that question was radiating off his refined features.

"I just don't," I stated. "What do you want me to say?"

Alexa straightened. "Fair point."

Amber flashed in her irises, my instincts telling me to take action, but I had no idea what she'd just cast. I tried to step out of the room, honestly ready to strangle the woman, but was immediately knocked back once I reached the doorway.

A force field? Are you kidding me?

Alexa grinned, pulling out a pair of gloves and sliding them onto her hands. "I obviously can't have you two running around! An unlocking spell is a lot easier than one to take a force field down. Just in case."

Wait. My dad is supposed to be a powerful sorcerer, but she doesn't think he can take down a force field?

She turned around and began her walk back down the hallway. "Thanks for everything I needed to know. And, Emmalynn?"

She paused, turning her head of red hair to look at me. Rage swarmed my cheeks in a hot flash as she stood in all her pride, accomplishment, and freedom.

"Happy birthday."

Her black boots thudded on the concrete until she began her ascent up the basement stairs. Eventually, the door above shut with a disheartening click.

I was alone—with my father.

Suddenly, I couldn't think about the Grand Hunter aspect of the situation as I tried to turn around—"tried" because I wasn't sure if he'd still be there. If I'd just hallucinated him in my sleep-deprived delirium. And if I hadn't, what was I supposed to say to him now?

"Sorry," he began, as if this whole situation were his fault. I dragged my eyes to his feet, still half turned. "Um, who did you say you were?"

Despite the thick fear in the air, honestly keeping me warm in the cold, a smile twitched on my lips as I slowly faced him. I glimpsed his eyes before falling to the stubble on his square chin. He was here. My dad was in front of me.

"Emmalynn. I'm Amy's—Amy Dalbert's daughter."

His lips parted like something was falling into place for him. "Amy had a...? She had—?"

His gaze bored into mine, exposing the gears spinning in his head as the pieces connected. I waited and waited for my mother's name in that sentence to become "we".

His throat bobbed. My heart tightened with that hope. "I've seen you before."

I clenched my jaw.

"I saw you in Thomas Dawson's visions. When he shared his visions about my future daughter. That was you. I know you."

I know you.

There wasn't anything else to say. I'd seen my father when Alexa had opened that door, but now I'd gained him.

I stepped toward him slowly like I needed his permission just to approach—or like he'd disintegrate in front of me. I still wasn't ready to let myself believe that this was real.

The glisten in my father's reddening eyes jolted me out of my head. "Did you say 'Emmalynn'?"

I nodded, too afraid of my voice.

"'Emma' for my mom, 'Lynn' for hers." He exhaled with a hard stop in his throat, shaking his head. I've always loved how Momma came up with my name. "I can't—how did you end up all the way here? How did Alexa ever find you and... your mom?"

Speak. Anything!

"I—" I began, all but burning a hole into his chin with my stare. "It... I was..."

"Okay," he said with a slight quiver in his voice, like he was just as full to the brim with emotions as I was, "I don't need the entire story right now. I'll just ask you whatever comes to mind, and you answer the best you can."

"Okay," I whispered, nodding. Even the air felt dangerous to breathe; one breath and this would all disintegrate into ash.

"Today's your birthday?"

I nodded.

The first crack of a smile bent his defined lips. "Happy birthday, kiddo."

You always laugh when you're not supposed to; it's a law of human biology, and that was why a breathless laugh burst from me right then. A tear I hadn't known was building in my eye raced down my cheek with it. "Kiddo". My father had just called me "kiddo" like I was really his daughter. Adrenaline and emotion were so high that I'd practically become a space heater amidst the cold, yet I couldn't stop shaking on the inside.

"Sorry, sorry," he said, chuckling with me. "I know, we have a lot of ground to cover and I gotta fit it all in somehow. What's today's date, then?"

"September 5."

"Wow." He exhaled, the strength of his smile fading. I thought about the possibility that something had happened in this month seventeen years ago—maybe him enjoying his life and having no clue what was to come within the next two to three months—that made today significant to him beyond my birthday. "How did Amy keep you a secret? When did she find out she was pregnant?"

"A month after you left. She changed her last name to 'Marie' and moved to a new house in Capperson to raise me there. And she had help from—Thomas. She homeschooled me and he helped her mentor me in magic."

He turned his head slightly, a divot forming between his strong brows. "You *do* have magic?"

I glanced behind me to make sure that Alexa wasn't right there—like it even mattered at this point. "I *did.* Do you know the seer Ingrid?"

He thought on the name for a few seconds, then nodded. "Met her once *years* ago."

"I asked her to tell me my future. Turns out, magic is what I depend on most. But Alexa only took me here when I said I didn't have magic, so I guess losing it... brought me to you."

"I just—I can't believe I missed that. I missed you. I missed being there for the biggest moment of..."

Oh no. I'd said the wrong thing. I'd made him feel guilty when the situation had been out of his hands, out of *all* of our hands.

I opened my mouth to reassure him, but he beat me to it. "Okay, you're gonna have to tell me the entire story soon." His throat bobbed with a swallow, setting his gaze ahead on the empty hallway. "We need to get out of here."

I walked behind him. Three black zip ties bound his wrists, three more for each ankle. It was one of the cruelest things I'd ever seen a Hunter do to their victims (but that's not saying a lot).

Why hadn't he tried to escape on his own?

"You wanna know a secret?" he said, turning his head to look at me. "I don't exactly have magic, either."

I'm sorry—*what*? I was meant to become the most powerful sorcerer to ever live because I was the daughter of one of the most powerful men in history, and he didn't even have magic?

"What do you mean?"

"Long story short, I asked Thomas to take it before I left. In case I was caught. I figured I'd pose less of a threat—turns out, that's the entire reason Alexa's spared me at all. I have no idea what she wants to do with us, but until I have my magic, I don't think she can do it."

That was why Alexa hadn't killed us yet despite having us: she wouldn't unless we had our magic. That was her mission, her real target, and we were her only leads to it.

"Have you really been tied up like this all these years?" I asked, kneeling down. When I remembered with frustration that an unlocking spell wasn't an option, my hands got to work. His were rough and cold, but at the front of my mind was the disbelief that mine were actually touching them for the first time in my life.

"No, actually," he replied. "Someone came a while ago to do this."

"And you didn't try to... kill them or something?"

He laughed. The words had surprised me, too, but that really would've been the only way for him to escape. "Never. They're just blindly following orders. They think what they're doing is the right thing to do. And we never know what would happen to them if they *didn't* do this. Maybe one day they'll see that... none of this was ever right. And their punishment will be a lifetime of regret."

How could he be so sympathetic to the people who'd stolen his entire life from him? Who had done who knew what to him down here? Who had taken him from his best friend, his wife, his sister, his family?

"You gave up your magic?" I asked, accidentally bending a fingernail backwards as I tried to undo the top tie. "All of it?"

"Well—not all of it. You can't extract someone's magic completely. I mean, you can, but it's a dangerous process. In your case, your magic is still there. It's just been... momentarily nullified by a greater power."

I stood up. "Maybe you have enough left to break these ties. I'm not getting anywhere."

"Neither did I with magic when they were first put on..." He sighed, hanging his head of chestnut hair. Evidently, I'd gotten my hair color from *both* parents. "Bummer yours is gone. But I'll try again."

"Yours is only temporarily gone, too," I said, walking around to stand in front of him. "As soon as we get home, you'll get it back. You'll have what makes you, you again."

Finally, I earned a full smile from him—the tender smile I'd spent my entire life wanting to see from my father. "Magic doesn't make us who we are. Sure, it helps characterize us, but what we do with it is a lot more important. *That's* what separates us from everyone else. We're labeled as evil because of what some of us have done with our magic. It's our mistaken identity, but it's not who we are."

This man is my *father.* Good things really do come to those who wait.

"Let me see if I remember this," he said, licking his lips. "I haven't practiced in a while. A bit of telekinesis here and there, but I only ever got in a few successful attempts."

"Destroy the ties?"

He pursed his lips. "Too much."

"Unlock them?"

An unlocking spell is simple, almost as easy as telekinesis. He could do it. I hoped and prayed that he could do it.

He exhaled in concentration and looked down at his feet. Silence only lasted for a few seconds.

"*Exsolvo,*" he said.

Nothing.

I kneeled down next to him, tentatively resting my hands on his knee. "I don't know if pressure helps in this case, but you're kind of our only hope of getting home. My mom is waiting for us right now. She's been waiting all these years, she doesn't even know you're alive. And it'd be the best Sweet Sixteen ever if my family was united for the first time. I'll never ask you for anything for Christmas or any other birthday."

He breathily laughed. "I'll get us out, kiddo. Don't worry."

That word again. I wondered how many years would pass before I'd get tired of hearing him say it. (It took me eleven with Momma.)

"If this helps," I began carefully, "when my mom and Mr. Dawson were teaching me how to cast in my head, they first helped me realize why I can do telekinesis so easily: it's easy to feel. They said... don't just say the words in your mind. Don't just know what you're casting, but understand what you're doing and the power you have."

My father gazed at me like he was searching for a little bit of Momma and a little bit of himself in me. "Solid advice."

He looked down at the ties around his ankle and closed his eyes. I imagined he was thinking about all that he'd been able to do in his life, all the events that had led him—led us—to this moment.

He opened his eyes again. "*Exsolvo*," he said with a flash of amber.

The top tie on his left ankle snapped undone and fell off.

My heart skipped a beat in shocked relief because, if I'm being completely honest, I was afraid that he didn't have enough magic. And I'd experienced firsthand how much self-doubt removed on top of it.

"I know I can do better than that," my father said before I could say a word, shaking his head. His confidence had been fully restored. "*Exsolvo*."

The remaining ties broke clean off his ankle.

I gasped as he sighed in relief, shaking out his foot and looking at his other side. It was all I could do to watch silently, to let him concentrate, as he released his other ankle. Before I could let my joy overcome me, the ultimate challenge loomed: undoing the three behind him, the ones he couldn't see.

I kept quiet again, staring down the hallway Alexa and I had come from like she'd reappear. My father's silence lasted much longer this time, and I realized what was happening in his head:

he had to believe in his own power and who he was again. Maybe, just maybe, he'd stopped once realizing that he couldn't escape. He'd temporarily lost faith.

I faced him again. The word never came, but all three ties behind him fell to the ground.

I stepped back. "You did it!"

"Told you I could do better than that." He grinned, rubbing his wrists and standing. That was my runner's bell to leap into his arms for the first time, for the very first time. They wrapped all the way around my back, the top of my head meeting his stubbled chin. Despite our location, I was home. I was in the arms of comfort itself. This, this was it. The hugs I chose over venting to Sarah and Breanne, the hugs I sometimes had to go without and, instead, carry myself through. The ones always there to hold me and make my world right again. This was it.

My father embraced me like he'd known me all my life, or known that I existed during the time he was gone and had finally found me. The sixteen years I'd spent waiting for this melted into seconds as he held me close, as I heard his heart beat strongly in my ear. I buried my face into his chest, desperately trying, in vain, to suppress the tight breaths and gasps from my uncontrollable sobs. Hot tears poured down my face like my body was trying to warm me up with them.

I don't need it. Not when he's hugging me.

"My daughter," he whispered, squeezing me tighter. "Wow, my daughter."

Hearing those words—his own affirmation that I was his—was the rock that shattered the constriction of the four walls around us. It wasn't about magic or Hunters during those few seconds. It was just about us.

"Mom always said," I began, wiping my face dry as we let go, "that you gave the best hugs."

He gently grazed my cheek with his finger. "Then let's get home to her."

No sooner than he spoke did shouting and banging ensue from upstairs: a man and a woman. Had Alexa called for backup and now they were arguing?

Dad approached the doorway, staring down the hall. The basement door banged open, and I ran up next to him.

"Emma!"

My stomach dropped. Following that familiar voice, footsteps echoed down the concrete stairs.

"Emma, are you down here?"

I glanced up at my father's stunned features as he whispered, "Thomas?"

Thirty-Six

Mr. Dawson stumbled over himself halfway down the hall like someone had just shot him. His body stiffened, as solid as the concrete encasing us. "Tristan?" he whispered, face as pale as the walls. "*Tristan—?*"

Alexa was just behind him. When I called out to him, she was already putting him in a chokehold. He turned away from her body, elbowing her in the stomach. The hallway was too narrow for a fight, but neither of them cared; this was now life-or-death.

"Don't be an idiot, Thomas!" Alexa growled, keeping her distance as they slowly revolved. "You *know* better than to test the Hunter in me, let alone the magician."

"She put a force field up in the doorway!" I called. "You have to break it!"

Alexa's eyes shot to me with flaring hatred just as Mr. Dawson threw a right hook. Expecting her dodge, he spun around, gave her a roundhouse kick, and then tripped her. On the floor, one hand wrapped around her neck and the other stopped her from pushing him off. He turned his head in our direction and cast something I'd never heard before. Dad and I ran through the doorway.

Alexa pulled Mr. Dawson to the ground and rolled out from underneath him, now above him. She yanked him up with his arm behind his back. He winced with a harsh grunt that kicked me square in the chest.

They were closest to the basement door. One wrong move meant Alexa could push us all right back into the room we'd just escaped. Dad stayed in front of me as we faced Alexa tightly holding Mr. Dawson as her prisoner.

A cruel smile contorted her lips, her laugh coming between breaths. "Well," she said, panting, "who would've thought we'd end up here after high school?"

"Let him go," my father demanded, one arm stretched out in front of me. "Come on, Alexa, we're all the same. We all come from the same roots, we can all do—"

"As far as I'm concerned, the Ateras are powerless right now," she spat, her delicate yet sharp features hardening to stone. "But— I'm prepared to make you a deal."

"So am I," Dad said, the slightest quiver infecting his arm. "Let Thomas and Emmalynn go, and I'll stay with you."

"No!" I exclaimed, furious he'd even suggested it.

Alexa cackled. "Are you kidding? I've never had a greater prize than you *and* your daughter! You're both capable of extraordinary power, I'm not letting that go. In fact..."—she eyed Mr. Dawson like he was prey, her breakfast for the morning—"I'll bet there's a way to get her magic back. I really thought yours would've returned by now, Tristan—but I think I lost hope after the fourth year. You know what, I may just let the two of you go and keep Emmalynn instead."

I'll take it. I'll make that deal—

"No," my father stated, gravely shaking his head. "No. I won't let you."

"Well, it's either her,"—Alexa jerked Mr. Dawson and shoved his arm farther up his back—"or him."

Those words. I'd heard those words before, I knew those words.

"Alexa, please," Dad said, a beg weighing down his tone. "Not my daughter. I can't let you take her, please."

A small wave softly push me back where I stood. I shut my eyes again, lightly stumbling, unable to grasp the world in front of me for more than one reason. Something deep inside me billowed into fulfillment, nausea bubbling in my stomach. As if the earth had suddenly stopped orbiting the sun.

Knowing what it meant gave me all the more power.

Caution steeled Alexa's eyes, pulling my father's attention to me. "Emmalynn?" he asked. "What's wrong?"

"Nothing," I whispered, gathering the last of my thoughts. I looked up at Alexa. "I'm great."

The telekinesis spell was absent from my head, but power took its place. Alexa flew to the end of the hallway like a dummy, all the way to the bottom of the stairs.

I'd been wanting to do that since the day we formally met.

"Your magic's back!" Mr. Dawson exclaimed, holding his shoulder.

Alexa propped herself up behind him with a grunt. "That's convenient," she said, a foreign strain in her voice. Her eyes rose up to me. I'd never felt so exposed under her gaze. "Knowing it is one thing, but seeing you use it... Ha. Wow."

It was me and Mr. Dawson against her. We had the upper hand in terms of magic—but she had that *and* the training.

"What do we do?" I whispered.

Mr. Dawson's sharp features stiffened, his demeanor slowing. I didn't like the caution on his face: whatever idea he had, it was dangerous. Based on our current situation, I had to assume that it was lethal.

—Tristan, Emma,— he said, eyes on Alexa, *—go.—*

—What?— Dad said for me. *—What do you mean?—*

Alexa grunted again, slowly standing.

—Tristan,— Mr. Dawson replied, closing his eyes, *—take Emma and get as far away from here as you can, as fast as you can.—*

"You're crazy!" Dad whispered—what I had to assume was accidentally out loud.

"What is?" Alexa leaned against the concrete wall, grinning like a psychopath. I wanted to slap it off her face. "*Oh. Telepathy. Ha, you look insane, Tristan.*"

Mr. Dawson was the only person in that hallway who knew exactly what he was about to do. Now I know why he wanted it that way: then nobody could stop him.

—Run straight past Alexa and out of the house,— he said. *—Trust me, I'll keep her distracted while you run, but you need to do it now. Do not look back.—*

"Mr—"

"Go," he whispered, daring to meet our eyes. "Trust me."

I had faith in both of them; I had to.

Dad and I faced Alexa again. Running straight into her wouldn't do anything; we needed her as far away from the stairs as possible. Mr. Dawson was about to throw himself into another fight, we knew that much, but what scared me was his plan afterward. He *had* said to trust him—and I knew that those words were as hard as steel.

Alexa straightened, stepping toward us. "What's the plan? Are we all gonna stand here and wait for someone to attack?"

"Sure," Mr. Dawson said. "Let's do it."

He lunged forward and threw a right-hand jab. Alexa swiftly dodged, but he grabbed her waist as a counter and knocked her down. Her only choice was to fight back.

"You *really* need to learn when to stop!" she snarled, hooking her foot around his ankle and tripping him.

Dad grabbed my hand and dragged me down the hallway, straight past them, until we reached the bottom of the stairs. Sprinting up the steep steps, I almost tripped. Alexa growled behind us as she tried to escape Mr. Dawson. I had to—I had to look behind me, and I almost did. I almost did until Dad and I found ourselves on the first floor and a hot orange glow blared in our faces.

Those few seconds when Mr. Dawson had shut his eyes—he'd been casting. With the flames engulfing the walls and furniture of the beach house, it had been a fire spell. And it was *spreading*.

"Hurry up and go!" Mr. Dawson shouted from below, pushing against Alexa at the bottom of the stairs.

"Mr. Dawson!" I yelled. How were we supposed to leave him behind in a burning building?

"Just *go!*" he shouted, pulling Alexa's ankle when she tried to run up the stairs. "I said to trust me! Do NOT look back!"

"I know that tone," my father muttered, squeezing my hand. "We have to trust him, come on."

We turned left from the basement door. Dad pulled me through the house, running across the flaming living room. Two wooden bookshelves beside the fireplace splintered apart and crashed to the floor. Dad dragged me out the front door before I could look back.

The salty, cold air soared past us as we ran across the porch and then down steps. My knees wobbled under me, my hand shaking in my father's, the longer we stood in the sand. Why were we standing in the sand?

"I haven't been outside in over a decade..." Dad whispered. "Not without being blindfolded, at least."

That's *what's on his mind right now?!* "Mr. Dawson is still—"

"Get to that car," he told me, running to the silver SUV Alexa and I had taken to get here. The keys were in the driver's door; Mr. Dawson must have arrived at the same moment Alexa was about to drive off. I guess she really had planned on leaving me and my father down there.

"Say a prayer," Dad said in the car as I shut my door, sticking the key into the ignition. "I haven't driven in a *long* time."

The car reversed with a jerk before it turned around and sped forward. Dad drove onto the hill, on a path that led to the main road, and then stopped. I gawked at him just as the beach house began to bleed smoke in the distance.

"Okay," he said before I could get a word out. He put the car in park and pulled up the emergency break. He gazed out at the house through his window before turning to me.

I tightened at the love and hope in his eyes, the moonlight lending them their shine even amidst the vibrant navy blue of the sky. Waves whished behind us on the coast, warning us of the raging sea we were already caught in—and how we only had one chance to escape.

"Emma—Emmalynn... I know this isn't what you want to hear, but it's what I have to do. I need you to stay in this car no matter what."

"What do you mean?" I forced myself to ask.

"I came out here with you so Thomas could focus on whatever insane plan he has, but I need to go back in there and get him out."

"No!" I cried. "No, I'm not—you can't—!"

I hated that there was no right way to respond to that; it was either let my father run into a burning and collapsing house to *possibly* save my godfather, or leave my godfather behind to escape with my father. There was no response to that.

"I have to, sweetheart." Dad cupped my face with his cold, rough hands. "Listen. I need you to be brave. Do exactly as I say, okay? You have to trust us."

"But Alexa—!"

"Thomas and I will be right back, I promise," he said, one of his thumbs gently wiping away a runaway tear on my cheek. "Trust me."

"Dad..." I quietly cried, the word poignant on my lips.

"You were my last dream in life, Emma." He leaned in, kissed my forehead. "So it'll be okay. I'll be back. We both will."

He jumped out of the car before I could say anything else—which was just as well, because I didn't have anything else. I watched my father sprint down the hill and back toward the house. Its red-and-orange glow glared harshly against the early-morning sky. I squeezed my eyes shut, trying to keep the fact that I was alone at bay.

The most difficult thing I did that entire week was decide if I should have ever left my bed that night. Regret made countless attempts on my mind, but the conflict alone was enough to push it back. I didn't even know if I had the capacity to reason through it. But I couldn't regret it. I couldn't. I couldn't.

Not if I didn't lose anyone.

I waited with nothing but the crackling of the bonfire off in the distance. That was good. That stopped the quiet from driving me insane. My stomach churned with each second that passed, each second I didn't have my father or Mr. Dawson with me. Sitting in that car with nothing but my thoughts, my paranoid and ruthless thoughts, to take my mind off of where I was forced me to face the reality of the last week. It had only been one week. Why did that night in the Hunter's Room feel so far away?

Because the girl I'd been then was stuck there, and I only had the girl Alexa had formed moving forward. And she was stuck in the Hunter world.

It struck me then: if Dad and I *did* get out of here, how was I supposed to explain coming home with the nation's most famous wanted man to my mother? To my aunt? Without telling them about tonight in its entirety? How was I supposed to justify any of this to my friends when they'd undoubtedly ask why Alexa was no longer in my life?

How was I supposed to convince Alexa not to expose me now that she knew who I was?

A belligerent crash ruptured from the beach house. I snapped my head to it: the roof had collapsed. The silhouette of a shattered house frame weakly stood amidst the dark. The house had collapsed.

I swallowed as a breath hitched in my throat. I searched for a thought, anything to hold on to, but a muddled blankness stared back at me in my head. Stun had shut it off. I knew what was in front of me but couldn't *see* it. My heart felt like it was only beating because it knew that it needed to—but my senses had shut down. My thoughts had shut down. And all I really had to hold on to now was the unstable, violent storm of my emotions—the only thing I could still feel was *real*.

Guilt and fear curdled in my veins. What if they were both dead?

We should've stayed in there with him, I thought. We should've escaped with him. We should have done anything else but what we had done—

"Emmalynn!"

The voice echoed too dreamily to be anything else than a thought. It wasn't real. I refused to let myself believe—

"*Emma!*"

I jolted upright and swung my head to look behind me. It was him. There was my dad!

I flung open the car door, leaped out, and sprinted around the car and straight into his arms. He almost tumbled backwards, having to lean against the back of the SUV as I locked myself in his embrace again. Everything revived in me: my thoughts, my emotions, the sense of feeling, all as he held me again.

Wait. It was different this time. His body was too tense, too slow, to be the same comforting hug from my father.

My arms loosened around him, but I didn't dare look up. "What happened?" I whispered.

"I waited for him." His voice vibrated across his chest. I heard a lump pass in his throat. "I looked for him. He never came. Neither of them…"

I let go. I couldn't look him in the eye. I couldn't look at the family member I'd gained without remembering the one I'd lost. He plodded to the driver's door, and I forced myself to follow. He was the only one I had to follow now.

As I trudged through the sand to the passenger door, the fire still roaring in the distance, memories of Mr. Dawson from my childhood to Callistro sped in one short movie in my head. The clearest ones—when he'd first told me of my destiny, when he'd introduced me to Ingrid, and when we'd discovered the underground passageways together—asserted themselves to the front. They were the most important, after all. They were the ones that had prepared me for the day I'd find Dad, when I'd lock my fate in place. For the day I would realize exactly what it means to be Emmalynn Melicent-Marie Atera.

Thirty-Seven

Dad drove us back to Capperson using the SUV's built-in GPS. The only problem now was sneaking him into town; my invisibility cloak was probably back in Alexa's lair.

The highways were empty thanks to the early hour. It was mostly daylight when we reached the county line. At least the silence that lasted the entire drive was never awkward; awkwardness is shoved far down below grief—which we were drowning in.

Finally, we were stopping at the light that Main Street began at. Then Dad finally spoke. "For obvious reasons," he began hoarsely, "she moved. But she stayed in the same town."

"She said it would throw them off. Looking in the same town would fly right over them."

Half a smile appeared on his face. It was the first sign of relief shed in that car that morning.

He cleared his throat, keeping his eyes on the road as the light turned green. "Do you know anything about Becca?"

I gasped. "Aunt Becca—I can't believe I forgot about her. She's been living at our house for the past week, but she made it living in Charlotte for a few years."

"Thank God." He exhaled, slouching in his seat. "Well... maybe you should go in first and put—tape over her mouth or something so she doesn't wake up the whole neighborhood."

I gave myself that chuckle; I needed it. And at least I didn't have to worry about Aunt Becca being mad for waking her up so early: for her brother, whom she hadn't seen in more than a decade, never knowing whether he was even alive, I was pretty sure that she'd *gladly* thank me for interrupting her sleep.

With Dad close behind me, my heart leaped straight into my throat as we approached the front door of my childhood home. My magic unlocked it, and I gently pushed it open.

Stay calm. It's okay.

I'm so glad I can use magic again.

As we tiptoed inside, I couldn't help but glance at my father. He looked around the living room, and I realized in full that this was his first time inside my home—what was supposed to be *our* home, and finally could be.

He closed the door. I left him in the entry foyer, walking down the hallway ahead. At the end and on the left side was Aunt Becca's (or, I guess, Momma's) bedroom.

In the bed in the middle of the room, Auntie lay in a deep sleep under her comforter. Besides the whole never-being-able-to-go-out-without-being-discovered-and-turned-in-to-the-government part, she had a fairly peaceful life here.

I crept to her side of bed—like accidentally waking her up would matter in a few seconds. "Auntie," I whispered, adjusting myself to sound in the deafening quiet. "Auntie," I said a little louder, placing my hand on her shoulder. I gently shook her until she groggily groaned. "Aunt Becca."

"Huh?" She sucked in a tired breath, eyes squinting in the dim daylight. "Wh...? Emma?" Eyes now wide, she shot up, ready to throw the blankets off. "*Emma? Are you okay? Is your mom okay?*"

"We're fine, I just—I need to show you something. But you have to promise you're not gonna scream."

Skepticism contorted her soft features. "What's wrong?"

"Nothing," I said. "Please."

It only took a five-second staring contest for her to climb out of bed.

Walking down the hallway, I heard her take a breath in to say something. Then, we stopped in the entryway.

I turned: Aunt Becca had frozen as if a bullet had struck her square in the chest. Her icy eyes stayed on her brother standing in the middle of the living room, and his on her. Neither said a word. In that moment, words felt destructive enough to shatter the scene, a house of cards.

In a blink, Aunt Becca bulldozed that fear aside and sprinted into her brother's open arms.

I watched her body shake with silent cries, and then I realized that Dad wasn't any different. This was it: my aunt in her brother's arms and my father in his sister's. It took too long for it to sink in that this was real, that for once, I wasn't dreaming this. For lack of better words, they looked right. They looked like family. And somehow, it took me until that moment to realize that I had a real family, after all.

"I thought you left!" Aunt Becca cried, breaking away. "I thought you made it out of the country!"

"I did," Dad replied, taking a sob-choked breath in, "and I was just as quickly caught."

"Where is that woman?" Aunt Becca demanded, whirling around to me. "She needs a high five. In the face. With an axe."

Dad and I traded glances of hesitance.

"Later," he said, taking her hands into his. Although he was her younger brother, he still slightly looked down at her. "I need to know how you managed to stay alive this whole time. I mean— you're blond! When did that happen?"

She laughed, throwing her arms around him again. I owed Aunt Becca a story, too, but like Dad had said, it was for later. We should probably wait to include Momma.

Momma.

"Auntie," I said, excitement shaking my voice, "can I use your phone?"

She snapped, then pointed at me. "Yes, go get it, it's on my nightstand."

I looked up at the clock that hung on the wall behind the dining table: it was almost 6:30. The school would be waking up in half an hour. I had to make that call *now*.

I grabbed Aunt Becca's phone in her bedroom and called Momma while coming back down the hallway. It was one of those phone calls where each dial tone rushes your heart just a little more and multiplies your nerves each time it rings. Then I heard her familiar hello and almost forgot how to speak.

"M—Momma?" I whispered.

"*Emma?*" Angry fear swept away all grogginess from her tone. "What're you doing there?! How did you leave campus?"

Great question. Never mind the security guards were already awake and had forgotten ever being asleep, according to she-who-wouldn't-be-mentioned.

"I need you to get here as soon as you can."

"Do you think this is funny? What are you doing there?"

Well, that meant no telling her that Dad was here; she'd *definitely* think that that was an unfunny "joke".

"Mom, please, *please*, get here as soon as possible."

I've heard of liquid courage, but apparently family reunions have the same effect: I hung up on my mother before she could say another word. And when she called back, I declined. She'd thank me later.

Auntie's phone buzzed in my hand.

M: I'm on my way, but don't you dare think for a
second you're not in trouble.

"Wow," Dad whispered before I could let that text scare me, ambling to the couch. "My daughter just spoke to my wife."

He locked his hands on the back of his neck, plopping down. I wasn't even sure I'd tried to wrap my own head around things yet, but all this would probably take more than a few hours to completely grasp, anyway.

"Yeah, 'crazy' is one word for it." Aunt Becca fiddled with her fingers before running a hand through her short hair. "But when I met Emma for the first time, that was it for me. Only an Atera is born with eyes that bright when they're a day old. And it just hit that..."—she shrugged, dropping her hands to her sides—"she was real. I saw so much of you in her while she was growing up." Her smiling eyes landed on me. "She's headstrong and brave and always ready to do the right thing. She never lets anything scare her away or stop her from getting herself through it. She's... everything you could ever want in your daughter, Tristan."

Dad leaned back in the couch like he already felt right at home. "I know."

Ten minutes later, Momma knocked on the door. Each one shot a torpedo of anxiety straight through my being. Aunt Becca was the one to get up from her spot next to her brother on the couch, and took a deep breath that I needed. Dad and I stood with her, my hand in his. We glued our eyes to the door.

"I'm about to meet my wife I haven't seen in almost seventeen years," he muttered. I tightly hugged his arm, holding his hand, as Aunt Becca cracked the door open.

"Amy," she whispered, "I need you to completely calm down before I let you in. We're fine, but you *need* to calm down first."

"Do not test me, Becca," Momma hissed, breathless. Dad squeezed my hand at her voice. "I didn't break every traffic law in North Carolina for nothing!"

"Calm down," Auntie said with soothing emphasis. "Please."

Seconds passed. I was surprised that Momma listened to her

at all, but Auntie only ever uses that tone when it matters, and my mother knows it.

She took in a few deep breaths. I let go of Dad and stepped aside. Aunt Becca pulled open the door, letting Momma walk in with a messy bun and clothes she'd no doubt thrown on after our call. Without any help, her honey-like eyes were pulled straight to us like we were a magnet. Her purse dropped to the floor from her rigid fingers.

With her chest heaving with breaths too big for her, her lips tried to form what had to be the beginning of "Tristan". The second she stepped forward, she crumpled to the floor.

Dad ran to her, kneeling down and holding her up by the shoulders. "Amy," he whispered with a sob choking him, the name ancient on his lips. He probably hadn't said it in years. "Amy, thank God, Amy—"

Momma threw her arms around his neck with a heart-lifting cry, and Dad wrapped his arms around her waist. Tears had no place to hide that morning, not for Aunt Becca and not for me, who was giving myself wrinkles wiping away the relentless tears with my cardigan. The relief was enough to knock me over like a bowling pin: we were a family that unity had finally found.

Momma grabbed Dad's face and gave him a kiss seventeen years in the making. The air itself seemed to hold its breath with them, Momma's fingers shaking as she held Dad's face like he'd dissipate if she didn't. And Dad held her as if they'd lost no time at all, kissing her with a tenderness that just *felt* familiar, even to me. Familiar for them. The kiss softened just before they broke away, another sob hiccupping in my throat.

Momma looked up at me over Dad's shoulder. He turned,

following her gaze. And when he reached out his arm to me, I ran home. Sandwiching myself between my parents, both of my parents, they tucked me safely in their arms. This was it. I'd waited my entire life, sixteen long years, for this. Now that I know exactly what's been missing, now that the last empty space inside has been filled, I'll never let a single power on this earth tear us apart again. And I will protect that promise with my life.

Thirty-Eight

omma and I were due back at the school soon, and everyone there was already waking up; there wasn't nearly enough time to explain to Dad what we'd been doing since he left, which was just as well because we couldn't give Momma and Auntie our story, either. Leaving that morning and facing seven hours away from him was, to say the least, a sweet sorrow. After what he'd been through already and then what we'd endured together, leaving felt like leaving him out as bait for the wolves. But if Momma, Aunt Becca, and I had been safe here, he would be, too. I hoped.

Momma didn't say a word to me as we walked out of the house and to her car parked in the driveway. It was when we put on our seatbelts and she placed her hand on the steering wheel that she finally exposed exactly what had been running through her head this whole time:

"Where on God's earth did you go last night?" Her sharp amber eyes sliced straight through the windshield. "How did you find him?"

I bit the inside of my lip. "You don't sound happy—"

"Of course not, Emmalynn!" she snapped, her hands flying off the steering wheel in exasperation. "I'm not stupid! There's only *one* possible scenario that led you to finding America's most wanted man, whose status top secret agents can't even agree on! And in that scenario, where you are *once again* kidnapped, your godfather still isn't anywhere to be seen! You think I'm happy about this entire thing?"

My lips were zipped as tightly as the zip ties that had bound my father's wrists. I controlled my every breath, quiet and slow to prevent my sniffs should I breathe normally. It wasn't time to tell her. Not yet.

"Not to mention that you somehow escaped the woman who caused all of this in the first place!" Momma added. "Where is she, huh?"

"I can't tell you," I said with a crack that I cursed. "Not yet."

"No, you're going to tell me right now, or..." She glanced all around the car like she needed a lifeline. "Or—!"

With my next breath, Momma gave up. Her head fell forward onto her steering wheel. Evidently, her well of tears was still full as her body shook again. And every second that I waited for her to say something made me remember that I still wasn't in school, where my roommates were probably driving themselves into hysteria wondering where I was.

But Momma was a sleeping dragon right now—any small action could result in fire. I waited for her body to still and her breathing to regulate again. After a minute, she finally looked back up at the windshield.

"Maybe it is, maybe it isn't," she rasped, exhaling, "but I feel like this is *all* my fault. Like we're all where we are now because of me. Maybe it's a mixture of different things. But I've been blaming myself for the last week—" She pressed her lips together, then shook her head. "No. Since the day I found out about you."

Her eyes fell onto me, where I saw just how drained and deprived she was of life. The gray bags under her eyes boasted of how much of it had been sucked out of her the last week.

"I'm sure this isn't how you wanted to spend your birthday," she said, her hand ruffling my hair and then coming down to cup my face. "I wish things weren't such a mess right now, and I'm sorry they are, but... happy birthday, Emma. I love you."

Those h-b-words had been permanently ruined for me, but the ones at the end lifted my head above the water. It felt like months had passed since I'd last spoken those words to someone else. Especially my mother.

"I love you, too," I said, clinging to them in case this was the last time I'd get to tell her.

With my next deep breath, it felt like I was releasing the rest of the world's weight. Only then did Momma start the car and reverse into the street.

The entire way back to the school, we prepared our act and cover story. We'd have to pretend that all was normal with the world for the next seven hours straight. After the rough and practically sleepless night I'd had, that was the challenge of the decade.

Because I hadn't once stopped to let myself think about how I hadn't just left my godfather behind—I'd lost him. Maybe that had been some kind of brain defense mechanism: the second I let myself think about that, I'd stop. And no acting, no cover story, would've been able to save me. Looking back, I felt myself building that wall, even leaning against it, the wall separating fantasy from reality. But I couldn't stop. I had to keep going. I had to keep going no matter what dismal hope was nagging at me to still trust him. Sometimes denial is suffocating, and other times, it's the only thing that lets you breathe.

I opened the door to my dorm, startling the girls laying out their crimson uniforms on their beds.

"Emma!" Sarah and Breanne cried, running to hug me. "Happy birthday!"

"Thank you!" I grinned, internally wincing. "Sorry, I woke up early and wanted to visit my mom before the day started."

"I told you," Sarah muttered, lightly nudging Breanne. "We saw you weren't in bed and... yeah."

"I'm fine," I said. To this day, I still don't know if I meant it. "But thanks for worrying."

"Do you think... *she'll...?*" Breanne asked, furiously picking at the hairs on her arms with wide, doe-like eyes.

In other words, did I think Alexa was going to try something today? It stung most of all that my best friend couldn't know that she already had. But bringing up that woman, the pack in general, on today of all days was like putting vinegar in chocolate milk (which Breanne actually made us do for a science experiment in sixth grade).

"I don't wanna talk about her," I said. "Today's my day, I'm the only one allowed to ruin it."

"I'm so proud of you," Sarah squealed, hugging me again. "Also, we're reserving you after school. No questions asked."

I took in a deep breath before I had the words prepared. "I'm sorry," I began slowly, almost guiltily. "My—"

"No!" Sarah cried. "We already reserved you, and I said no questions asked."

"My mom had something special planned!" I told her—understatement of the century. "She wants to have her daughter on her birthday."

Sarah rolled her eyes, landing on Breanne, who shrugged.

"Fine," Sarah said. "But tell her to drive you to the park *right* after. And wear your new dress. How long will you be?"

"I'm not sure. It just depends."

"*Fine*," she said again. Only for my sake did she turn away without argument. Just as quickly, I found my phone charging on the nightstand.

The first thing I saw in my notifications when I tapped the screen was a photo from Auntie. Her message had come through roughly when Momma and I were walking into the school.

I opened the photo: a selfie of my aunt and my dad, who was holding up the TV remote.

A: Teaching him how modern technology works!

I stifled my laughter, but Sarah didn't let it slip by.

"What did he say?" she sang, sliding on her blazer.

"Who?"

She scoffed, tossing out her long waves from underneath her uniform. "Don't even try it. What did Jak say?"

I smiled just to humor her. "Nothing that concerns you." Tossing my phone onto my bed, I grabbed my own uniform from the closet and prepared for the day.

C H A P T E R

Thirty-Nine

Not that I don't love going over exponential and logarithmic functions, but Mr. Dale's class dragged on for hours that day—especially since he was my last class. On the bright side, my classmates spent the entire day sending me birthday wishes. (Monsieur Goubeaux even had everyone sing "Happy Birthday" in Spanish.) That was definitely something I never got while being homeschooled.

When that 2:30 bell finally rang, I was the first person out the door. I paid no mind to how fast my feet moved on the rug across the Grand Foyer on my way to meet Momma, or how I barely acknowledged the girls I strode past. My only concern was getting home, where my dad and aunt were waiting. Apparently, Momma felt the same way: she was already halfway down the hall leading to the gym just as I stepped into it.

"Calm down," she whispered, approaching me. "Anticipation won't bring us there faster."

I was too excited to argue. Afraid, actually. Afraid that we'd walk into the house and Dad, or Dad *and* Aunt Becca, wouldn't be there. Or, worst of all, that they'd be there, but they wouldn't be... *breathing.*

In the passenger seat of Momma's car, I thought about Dad sitting on our couch with Aunt Becca and becoming familiar with today's world, being welcomed back into it... yet being banished to that house at the same time. Was it really that different from where he'd just escaped? Nothing would change just because Tristan Atera was home, now that one of the best Grand Hunters in the country was gone. The world wasn't going to suddenly change its views.

He has us. He's loved and protected here. That was the difference. I prayed that it would be different enough for him.

The second Momma and I walked through the front door, Dad looked up from the coffee table. The hundreds of photos Auntie had taken over the years sat scattered in front of him. He sprang up from the couch and strode to me and Momma, pulling us in for a hug.

"You're still here," Momma whispered, speaking my mind exactly. "I kind of thought you would've..."

"I almost did, too." Dad breathily chuckled, pulling away. "But no, we made it. We're safe." His kind eyes fell onto me. "How was school, kiddo?"

I'd left my blazer in the car for this reason. We could tell him about Callistro later.

"I don't remember," I told him, lips stuck in a grin. "I couldn't pay attention."

"Well, we've been occupied all day," Aunt Becca remarked, walking to the kitchen and grabbing the coffee pot. "We were just time traveling through the past decade. I've been tutoring him in the modern ways."

"They stole all those years from you," Mom murmured, resting a hesitant hand on Dad's chest. "Where were you all that time? What did you do?"

"I owe you a story," he said, glancing at me, "and you me."

The three of us took a seat on the couch, where Momma cuddled up next to Dad and commented on how he smelled like her favorite shampoo and body wash. He confessed to using both in his shower this morning, and Aunt Becca grew defensive, asking how she could've possibly known to buy men's hair care for her long-lost brother, who'd show up on her doorstep today.

"I love it." Momma smiled, lost in his eyes. They shared another kiss, and it reminded me of how I'd had my first kiss this week and *still* hadn't told a soul.

Later. After we get past...

...this morning.

I was starting to remember. He was starting to come back to mind. I tightened, unsure of where to put my stare that wouldn't expose who was—

"Hey, Em," Aunt Becca called, coming back from the kitchen. She sat down in the recliner next to the couch. "Where's Mr. Dawson? Why hasn't he come by yet?"

One glance at Dad was all it took to thrust me back into the darkest moment of my life: right before I saw the beach house in its shadows and ashes. The moment I was alone as darkness surrounded me and borrowed a new and nameless emotion, one I hadn't come to know yet. If I could, in any way, avoid revisiting it, I'd try. But now I had to trudge through it all over again. I had to stop. I had to remember him.

"It's..." Dad said quickly, coming to my rescue. "It's, um..."

"It's what?" Momma asked, her tone sharpening. "What happened? Where's Thomas, what about the woman that dragged us into all this, where are either of them?"

"Dead."

The word flew out of my mouth like it was the easiest answer in the world. But I had to give up the hope that if I said it, it'd be false, it would change reality according to how I wanted it to. Because while half of that statement was too good to be true, the other half was the price for it.

Mom gaped at me with the precision of a cat. "Excuse me?"

"He helped us escape." My throat ached like a fist was pressing against it. "He told us to trust him. I see why now. To get us to leave so we couldn't stop him."

"What *happened?*" Momma demanded to know, grief's rage carving her narrow features.

"I'm—" Aunt Becca began, gawking at the living room window that overlooked the street. She slowly stood and crept toward it. "I'm asking the same thing."

I followed her gaze to the black SUV that had parked along the curb. An SUV that matched the silver one Dad and I had taken to get here.

I know that SUV.

The driver's door opened and shut. One person came out

from behind the car.

I sprang from my seat and bolted out the front door.

Mr. Dawson had barely stepped onto the sidewalk before I threw my arms around him, nearly knocking him over. He had no time to react and didn't need it, because he'd missed me just as much and reciprocated even tighter.

"I knew I'd see you again," he whispered, one hand on the back of my head. The pungent stench of smoke burned my throat every time I inhaled, and ash caked his T-shirt—but he was here in one piece, right in front of me. "I told you to trust me."

It's pretty hard to believe that a man can escape death when you've all but seen his charred body. All the more so when his only survival partner was a fatal secret agent whose very assignment by the government was to sentence him to death if he was caught. But Dad had told me to trust him—trust Mr. Dawson, both of them.

In that moment, I'd never felt safer, more protected.

Almost as quickly as he'd climbed out of the car, Mr. Dawson ushered me toward the front door of the house. The atmosphere was frozen as we walked in, stunned by the reality of a man who'd risen from a fiery grave.

"He's not dead," I chirped.

"Thankfully." Mr. Dawson took his eyes to Dad on the couch, like he wasn't able to believe *his* existence. "I wanted to know what you've been up to all these years."

Dad stood, rugged features stiffening. "We thought you died in the fire."

"I gave you your best shot," Mr. Dawson said. "You took it and escaped. You're welcome."

"We thought—"

"You took it and escaped," he repeated, emphasizing each word. "We're alive, aren't we?"

Seconds passed before Dad marched out from behind the coffee table and pulled his best friend in for a hug. The relief was palpable and yet didn't feel real. I kept blinking, anticipating a blank scene every time. When it never came, I finally let myself believe that we really were together. *Together.* For the first time. Everything that had been slipping through my fingers for the last week had suddenly gathered straight into my palms. All of the holes in my family had finally been filled.

Aunt Becca rose from the recliner—even setting down her mug on the table—and was next to wrap her arms around Mr. Dawson. Coughing, she stepped back. "Wow, first time I see you in over a week and now you're taking my breath away."

"I'm gonna fix that right now," Mr. Dawson said, wandering toward the hallway. "And then we can exchange stories."

Mr. Dawson was locked back in the small room I'd woken up in when Alexa and I left the lair, where he unlocked the door with magic. (Being an ex-Master, he had a *lot* more plausible excuses for being able to escape without magic than I did.) His setting-the-house-on-fire idea made sense after he explained that he set three computers on fire for distraction and used his magic to navigate his way out, where he was able to hijack an SUV.

While Dad and I were making our own escape, Mr. Dawson wasn't far behind. He drove back to Capperson in the SUV, but the battery died and he had to pull over on the side of the freeway. With no phone to call for help, he waited until someone was kind enough to pull over and jumpstart the car.

Momma was furious that I'd left my room in the middle of the night, found the underground passageways and never told her (so I tattled on Mr. Dawson for helping me find them at all—he did not appreciate that), and hit every other point on the list I knew she would. Then I told them how Alexa knew about the underground system—and that it was safe to assume she'd read the rest of Caralyn's letter.

After Dad was captured on an island in Bermuda, Alexa and William dragged him wherever they went as their prisoner. They locked him in the beach house basement once the hunt for his descendant began. He didn't know the Delphines were magicians. It was likely that Jak and his family didn't know, either. Alexa's family had deceived the world just as mine had.

Dad never knew why they *kept* him instead of turning him in to President Caldwell. Alexa and William were on a hunt, but apparently Alexa had had her own plan since the beginning. Based on what she'd told us after I'd confessed who I was, she didn't care what her plan with William was as long as she had us in one place. She must've assumed that she'd figure out how to extract our magic once we were together. And then... we had to assume the rest.

Mr. Dawson stopped me there, leaning against Auntie's recliner. "So she wanted to extract your magic?"

"That was her plan," I said on the couch, "based on Caralyn's letter. But Dad doesn't have his magic, and neither did I at the time."

"Speaking of," Dad said, turning in his spot next to me to face Mr. Dawson, "do you remember where you put mine?"

Auntie peered up at Mr. Dawson from her spot, sipping on her coffee. He bit back a smile as he looked from Dad to me. "In Emma."

"What?" we—except Momma—asked.

"Tristan asked me to extract *most* of his magic. I kept it safe until Emma came along. Then I figured it'd be safest with her."

I turned my head to Momma, on Dad's other side. "Did you know?"

She did. But apparently it had never been relevant enough to bring up.

"Hey, maybe that's part of the reason she's destined to become so powerful," Mr. Dawson added. "Why she's known telekinesis since she could talk."

"What?" Dad asked me. "Were you born knowing magic?"

"It kind of feels like that," I answered. "I remember it that way, at least. Sometimes I've just... done it."

"Tristan," Aunt Becca said in realization, straightening in the recliner, "remember what Mom and Dad told us when they were mentoring us? About our generation? Why they were so excited for us to have kids?"

Dad thought about it for a second. With the widening of his bright eyes, their minds were in sync: "Emma's the next hundredth."

"What?" I asked.

"Okay, say the Ateras have only been around for ninety-nine generations," Auntie began, the gears in her head turning faster. "That ninety-ninth would be me and your dad, and you'd be the one hundredth. You're *a* hundredth, just not the *one* hundredth."

"Again—what?" Momma asked, like she was mistrustful of any and all prophecies at this point.

"There's an Atera family legend," Dad replied. "Every one hundredth generation is born with the potential of magic equivalent to the past ninety-nine generations *combined*—as long as they can unlock it."

Momma looked from me to Aunt Becca to Dad and then back to me. Her warm-beige skin paled, and the blood draining from my head told me that I was no different. "She's known magic since she was two because of *that?*"

All eyes were now on me like I knew exactly what to do with that information.

"So if she figures out how to 'unlock it'," Mr. Dawson said, "she might know how to do other things. She's just never had to use them before, or she hasn't been introduced to them yet."

Wait, wait a second. When I threw Theo's phone into his water at Waverly, and then at the beach house when I threw Alexa down the hall—I'd done both of those things without the telekinesis spell.

"I..." I said, forcing more volume into my tentative voice. "Lately I've been using telekinesis without—having to use the spell. I just felt it, like I was using my magic itself instead of a word."

The room paused, telling me that I didn't understand the gravity of what I'd just said. Too many seconds of silence went by where my family spared each other a glance but completely avoided me, leaving me out of the family meeting.

"Are you saying," Mr. Dawson finally said, "you don't need a spell to cast telekinesis?"

"No—I don't know," I replied hesitantly. "Maybe the word is being subconsciously said and I just don't realize it."

"Well," he said, "considering what happened in the last week, I think it's in everyone's best interest to give your dad's magic back, don't you?"

I couldn't fault him for saying that; I'd been used as a vessel to keep another Atera's magic, and I'd lost it because of my recklessness and impulse. I'd never even known exactly what I'd lost until now! Knowing who my enemies were and what they were after, though—I couldn't even trust myself to protect it.

That was the plan we made for Saturday; it was a weekend matter. For the rest of this afternoon, though, we didn't want to waste it with business. Time felt so fragile that we needed to absorb every second together we had. None of them were guaranteed and never would be.

Saying goodbye later tonight would be impossible, but saying "see you later" after a couple of hours came a close second.

"I'll be here when you get back," Dad assured me, "and when you do, you'll never stop hearing me say thank you. You led me to everything I never thought I'd have again, even things I never thought I'd have at all." His thumb lightly rubbed my cheek. "I couldn't be happier you're my daughter, Emma."

He wrapped his arms around me, and I let myself sink into him, to trust that this was real and wouldn't disappear. Tightly pressing my lips together, I strained not to squeeze him; Alexa and William had kept Dad alive, sure, but that didn't mean they'd fed him well.

After he let me go, my parents shared a kiss before Momma brought her arm around my shoulders. "Are you staying here,

Thomas?" she asked.

"For now," he replied. "But meet us back here later to celebrate. We'll have something special for Emma."

School had released over two hours ago, and Sarah and Breanne were spamming me with calls and texts. All of which I ignored as I faced my complete family in the doorway.

Aunt Becca beamed at me. "Happy birthday, Emmy. You're my favorite niece, and I love you."

I smiled. "You're my favorite aunt, and I love you, too."

With that, Momma opened the door. We walked out of the house and hopped into the car in the driveway for whatever birthday surprise Sarah and Breanne had planned. Both girls were reminding me in multiple texts to wear the sundress I'd gotten last night.

C H A P T E R

FORTY

From the curb we pulled up along, the gazebo sat far away in the park, twinkling with white fairy lights. Momma dropped me off, and I walked across the grass in the tepid air that seemed to have cooled just for my birthday.

The outdoor couch inside the gazebo stared back at me as I approached, littered with presents right and left. Cupcakes and a pitcher of iced coffee sat on the table; "healthy" was clearly not on my best friends' radars this evening, and I loved them for it.

The fairy lights had been strung around the gazebo with baby-pink streamers wrapped around the posts. A large golden "1" and "6" balloon were tied around the two front ones.

I can't believe them, I thought with a helpless grin. *This is—!*

Sarah and Breanne ran out from behind the gazebo and to

me, squealing, "Happy birthday!" and tightly hugging me. Three Redway Boys came out after them.

"You guys!" I sighed in awe. "When did you do this? Is this what you were planning yesterday?"

Breanne pouted, fiddling with her fingers under her sweater. "You knew?"

I laughed, nudging her. "Well, duh, but—this is above and beyond what I could've imagined. I love it, thank you."

With another hug, the girls led Adrien and Wyatt into the gazebo to start serving "dinner". Which left me and Jak alone.

Seeing him after last night felt like toppling over a Jenga tower. I still trusted him—but he didn't know the real reason why, and he never could. There was so much to say to him, most of it things I *couldn't* say to him—things he couldn't know without me implying that something had happened last night at all. If I wanted to convince him that the last time I'd thought about him was Monday night, I had to pretend that last night never happened.

"Happy birthday, Merlin," he said with a smile I found too familiar by now. The trust in him was buried too deep; I wanted to indulge and spill every last secret like he'd earned his right to know. Hadn't he? After everything he'd done and I knew his feelings weren't false? Or was that just the spell whispering to me?

I smiled shyly. "Thanks. How much of this was your idea?"

"It was all Sarah and Breanne," he said, turning his head to look at them behind him. They were already sipping on iced coffee with Adrien and Wyatt. "We just helped set everything up."

"You guys are amazing," I said, daring myself to be brave. "But are you sure you can... be here right now?"

"Alexa's gone again." He shrugged, and I barely managed to

suppress my shock in time. She was gone? She still hadn't come back even though Mr. Dawson had? "And my dad's trying to figure out their next step—we're probably leaving Capperson within the next few days. But I don't think you wanna talk about them, so close your eyes."

"What?"

"Close your eyes," he repeated, "or I'll start calling you 'Antoinette'."

"Marie".

I laughed, obeying. "Now you're *way* stretching it."

"I have more ideas," he told me, now behind me and moving my hair out of the way. His warm fingers brushed against my neck, inviting the butterflies into my stomach. "You and I just adapted to 'Merlin'"—he moved to stand in front of me again—"faster. Open."

My first instinct was to look down: a locket now hung from my neck. "Emma" was engraved in the middle of the silver heart, a vibrant sapphire set in the top of the charm.

"Jak..." I awed, gently picking up the heart like it was made of wet sand. "I love it, where did you get this?"

"Right here in town. I was walking by and the jewelry store was advertising their personalized birthstone lockets in the window."

"And you thought of me?"

"I don't think I've stopped since we met." He smiled softly at me. "Happy birthday."

I hesitantly hugged him, but it wasn't until he reciprocated that I realized it was a mistake: he rested his head against mine, embracing me like he hadn't seen me in days. My heart raced straight through my dress, and I was pretty sure he could feel it.

This hug was different; in fact, it was new. It was warm and sweet, but it was also dangerous because I still wasn't supposed to feel this way toward him. Knowing why I did didn't excuse it. And Jak was now a reminder of everything I'd escaped last night. He might not have lost any *biological* family members, but was it because of my family that his father had just lost another wife?

And would William use that as an excuse for vengeance?

I forced that out of my head. What mattered right now was that I was with my friends, and we were going to celebrate with no magic, no Hunters, and no secrets to ruin it.

For my last present of the night with my family, Momma placed a beautiful crimson-red journal in my lap. She said that life had grown pretty hectic the last week and would only continue to change, so journaling would help slow things down. This thing has actually been pretty useful—I mean, I'm writing this on the second-to-last page, which I've never accomplished before with any kind of notebook.

What terrifies me, though, is that *Caralyn's* documents are gone. I don't know where Alexa put them, if her pack has them and is ready to unleash chaos, or even if the pack is smart enough to keep the secret—but I don't have them anymore. Yet another thing I'd lost to my impulsivity, and now I could only pray. For what, I didn't even know, but I had to.

Looking back through these pages, I still have to remind myself that everything in here happened in a week. A *week*. Wanting nothing more than to leave it all in the past, I was excited for the rest of September. I had to be ready for the future, I told myself, whether it was five years from now or one.

Or even if it was one month later, when Momma guided our third-period class down into the forbidden level below the Callistro Academy. Even if Momma was no longer just a self-defense instructor and was now walking out of the elevator with her class, facing the opulent crimson room in front of us.

"Ladies," she said, turning around and meeting my eyes. "Welcome to the Hunter's Room."

ACKNOWLEDGEMENTS

This book set me on the most incredible journey I've ever been privileged enough to call mine, and it began my author journey. I wouldn't have any of the blessings I do today in the publishing or even social media world without it, so it thrills me that I was able to breathe life into it.

That brings me to you, the wonderful reader holding this book. Whether you're someone who was kind enough to give it a chance or you're one of my Instagram readers who wanted the new (and final, I *promise*) edition of the *Emmalynn Atera* Series, my heart beats with thrilled gratitude. The fulfillment that you reading Emma's story gives me exceeds my greatest ability to communicate, but nonetheless, thank you.

And, of course, thank you to every single person who played a part in this book's publication and release into the world—whether it was encouragement, beta reading, or even designing merch for me to bring the uniform to life (and get some stickers):

Mom, Signe Wikström, Brianna Smith, McKenna Rowell, Jimmy Gonzales, MiblArt (for designing four covers in two months for me), every one of my Instagram readers, and more. You made this possible. I could not have asked for a better community to foster and publish the EA Series in.

Words will never do my gratitude justice.

ABOUT THE AUTHOR

Ariana Tosado is a 22-year-old author, musician, university student, book editor, and content creator for teen and young-adult audiences. She started pursuing her passion of writing novels in middle school. Today, she's homed her focus on the *Emmalynn Atera* Series, marketing *Thy Kingdom Come*, and producing music. She aims to create relatable and encouraging content through her platforms, all with her cat, Sophie, in one hand and an iced vanilla latte in the other.

You can find out more about what she's up to on her website (www.arianatosado.com) or on Instagram (@thearianatosado).